WHAT I'D DO FOR LOVE

What I'd Do For Love

K.F. Johnson

One Ironwoman Publishing

Contents

One Ironwoman Publishing
Grayson, GA 30017

ISBN : 978-1-954469-04-4

Cover Design by Christine N. Davis

What I'd Do For Love

The deepest of depths, the length of infinity,
None could compare to the horizons of my love for you.
The purest of its kind since the day we said I do,
None could compare to the horizons of my love for you.
For all the sunshine's we've shared together,
All the sundown's we spent embraced in each other's trust,
Nothing could ever change my feelings for you…
EXCEPT betrayal.
I've been holding a premonition at arm's length for fear it is
too close to home.
But dangerous liaisons could only justify the beginning of
YOUR end.
The noose you wear on your finger would hang you beyond
reach of any chair.
It was your choice "So long as we both shall live."
Lies penetrating my soul until I must slit the cord that spews
them.
Each breathless plea for forgiveness
Slowly…slowly…passing into eternal sleep.
I would mourn each day without you,
but praise the day you left
Cleansed of the wrongs committed to me,
Knowing WHAT I'D DO FOR LOVE
By K.F. Johnson 1995

1

Greer

May 2014

I ran my tongue across my teeth and let the anger marinate while watching the couple performing on my cellphone screen. It wasn't the first time I'd seen video of my husband and his side-bitch Marlene screwing in my bed, but it was the first time I watched it live stream... and it would be my last. Sitting on the bottom step of my basement staircase, I took a swig of water and tossed the empty bottle in the trash.

The basement was unfinished, so we rarely spent any time in it other than to use the laundry room. It was cluttered with stacked boxes against the walls holding nick knacks from our past, unused electronics, fall and winter clothes awaiting their season, old furniture and shelves housing books and old boxed photos. The corner of my wedding album seemed to be beckoning me from the top of one box and I glared at it like it had spit on me.

I'd experienced enough heartache and treachery by the time I met Michael 9 years ago that he had to jump through a number of hoops to break through my ironclad heart. Once he did; however, it was full speed ahead and we were married 2 years later. I took my vows seriously when I committed to forever. Obviously, he had not.

I was the first one supporting his choice to change careers from a Football Coach at the local High School to a Sleep Technician. I didn't complain when he took a year off to go to school for it and I had to support us by myself. *Noooo.* Sweet, understanding Greer was happy to take one for the team to help her man do better. And look what it got me.

He got a job right out of the program and has been working Tuesday through Saturday from 7:00pm to 7:00am for the past 10 months. That conflicted with my weekday hours of 7:00am to 4:00pm as an OM for a family medical practice, but did I bitch and moan? No. I grinned and bared it while bringing him dinner at his job and cheerleading for him every chance I got.

Sometimes, we *literally,* saw each other a few hours a day except on Sunday's, but I would've stuck it out with a smile on my face for as long as it took... before I found out he was cheating. This mofo sacrificed 9 years together and 7 years of marriage for some new pussy as though I wasn't already giving him whatever he wanted at home. And that would not go unpunished.

The man I would've done almost anything for. The man I shared my love, secrets and *bed* with, was willing to trade me in for frequent sex with a random bitch at work, who hadn't sacrificed or suffered through *anything* with him before. What hurt the most, is that despite knowing about the hellish treatment I suffered from being the product of my father's infidelity, he'd risked our marriage. I made it very clear that cheating is the only infraction I'd find unforgivable. I guess he didn't give a shit, because here he was betraying me... in my own bed.

Plastic stuck to my naked flesh and crinkled beneath my feet as I wiped sweat from my brow. I'd fully encased myself in black garbage bags from the neck down with oversized trashcan rubber bands securing them in place around my ankles, thighs, wrists, waist and biceps as soon as the action began.

Besides my head, only my hands were exposed, and I wore 2 coats of surgical gloves on each as a precaution. I'd been swaddled in plastic for nearly 40 minutes while they fornicated in my marital bed and I prepared to make them pay for it. I was hot as hell physically and mentally!

They finally finished and lay sprawled out beside each other breathing heavily and caressing each other's moist skin. He stroked a strand of hair away from her face and said something that made her laugh and made me fume even more.

The video stream transmitted via the camera inside of the alarm clock on my bedside table didn't transmit sound, but I didn't really need it anyway. I was breathing so heavily through my nostrils in anticipation that I probably wouldn't have heard anything they said. Besides, I already knew everything that I needed to know from watching videos of their prior rendezvous to ensure my plan would work.

"Go on bitch," I coached her image through clenched teeth.

As if on cue, she pecked him on the lips and got up from the bed disappearing from the camera's view. The sound of water running through the basement pipes indicated the start of the bathroom shower. Michael remained on the bed stretching out his pecan toned limbs and rolled over, looking up at the ceiling as though he was reminiscing on their bad acts.

Watching him marinating on the sex-soaked sheets that he wouldn't have had the decency to change before I got home, coupled with his blissful expression just added to my rage. I rubbed the fingers on my free hand against each other in frustration and exhaled deeply. They needed to hurry up so I could do what I came to do.

He reached near the clock and grabbed the bottle of Ambien CR he kept there shortly before the home-wrecking wench came back into view. He suffered from insomnia and sleep deprivation himself due to his odd work hours, so he customarily took Ambien to help him sleep during the day.

He must've expected ol' girl to leave in the next 15 minutes or so because he was rarely able to function coherently after that with the dosage he took. Good. It would happen sooner than I anticipated. I could see her dressing as he tossed two 10 mg pills into his mouth and washed them down with a mouthful of juice on the bedside table on his side.

"Sweet dreams mother fucker," I said lowly getting up and standing in front of the full-length mirror beside the stairs to scrutinize myself.

I again wiped sweat from my forehead and smoothed escaped hairs back into the bun tightly wound at the back of my head. I hated my complexion. My wide nose, plump lips and brown kinky hair indicated to white people that I was black, but my green eyes, light complexion and petite frame screamed to black people that I wasn't fully bred.

I was always trying to prove myself to be authentic for the sins of my black father and white mother giving me such an ambiguous look. I grew up in a black household in a predominantly black neighborhood and that's how I was socialized. Regardless, a lot of black girls including my half-siblings teased, fought and harassed me; calling me "white girl" at every opportunity and claiming I thought I was better than them.

Most black boys in my neighborhood assumed I was stuck up, fake or fast for reasons I didn't understand since I kept to myself and had few friends. Still, my attraction to black boys had never wavered; even after I was eternally scarred by one of them.

Once Michael and I got together though, I thought I'd found my chocolate Prince Charming. I thought we were going to spend the rest of our lives in holy, happy matrimony. How wrong I was.

The squeaking of the floorboards overhead signaled a descent to the first floor and the cellphone screen was now blank which meant that both of them were coming downstairs. They had a brief muffled exchange in the foyer that I couldn't decipher from my position in the basement until the digitized voice of our alarm system announced an opened front door.

Shortly afterwards, his slow foot falls headed back to the second floor. I let out a nervous breath and ran over the details of my plans execution in my head one more time. The time on the cellphone was 8:41am when I powered it off and dropped it into a box in the corner that was filled with other old phones, clocks, and random cords to things we no longer used.

The sweat suit and underwear I wore was neatly folded on top of a box by the basement door with my sneakers backpack and keys beside them. I waited 10 more minutes and grabbed both the black 60-gallon garbage bag atop my clothes and the smaller garbage bag beside it. Placing the smaller bag over my head, I positioned the holes I made earlier over my eyes and took a few deep breaths.

My skin was so hot that it almost felt like the bags were melting against it. I ascended the steps in twos without worrying about the noise because Michael was way upstairs and plus, he slept like the dead once he was medicated. I emerged from the basement into my modestly decorated kitchen and seized a 4" butcher knife from a drawer in the island. Looking at my reflection in it, I smirked and strolled towards the stairs and the sounds of his lawnmower like snoring.

I lingered in the doorway a few minutes to soak in his toned naked body and reminisce over the love we'd made. Michael was a 6'1" linebacker in college and although he never went pro, he still maintained a similarly fit and toned physique now at 31. His close-cut fade was starting to grow out and his full sexy lips were slightly parted as he snored up the sleep gods.

It was a shame we would never be able to do the things we dreamed of doing together now. I really wasn't looking forward to being single and lonely again... but oh well. Once his 500-thousand-dollar life insurance policy paid out I'm sure I would get over it. We both took policies out on each other the first year we were married at his mom's suggestion. My mother in-law was a retired accountant, and she was always meddling in our finances. For once, I was glad she had though.

The plan was to ensure the survivor could pay off the house, our car notes, student loans and any other debts with ease. Welp... he was the one who violated our "Till death do us part" clause. Not me. Not only did I deserve to be avenged, but I deserved to be rewarded too.

I spread the mouth of the 60-gallon bag out over the threshold between our bedroom and the master bathroom. The bags I wore crinkled and clung to me with every move as I approached him lying on his back with his head near the end of the bed and his feet propped up on the pillows at the head. I couldn't have asked for a more perfect position. I stood by his head, gazing down at his handsome face and cocked my head, squatting and angling my knife at his jugular.

My hand was as steady as a surgeon's though adrenaline was racing through my veins like a Tasmanian devil. An eerie calm engulfed me as I watched the hypnotic rise and fall of his Adam's apple. He made a loud snort and brought one hand up to rub his nose, never even touching the knife. I almost laughed. One thing I wouldn't miss was his loud ass snoring even though I rarely had a chance to sleep when he did anymore this past year.

I wanted to stab him mercilessly. Cut his dick off and shove it down his throat. But I couldn't. Not at the risk of him overpowering me or accidentally cutting myself in the frenzy and leaving DNA that couldn't be explained. No. As much as I wanted him to suffer. I had to be methodical and clean.

"I hope it was worth it."

He shifted his head toward my voice then. There was movement under his lids, but he didn't open his eyes.

"Wha... what?" he garbled.

"Open your eyes baby. I want to see those pretty lying eyes," I spoke into his ear sinisterly.

His lids struggled to open, and he shifted slightly left causing me to re-position the knife I held in my right hand. The pressure of the metal against his flesh must've alarmed him even in his sleep because his eyes began to flutter open at the same time he was raising a hand to investigate.

"I loved you," I told him ripping the blade deeply and sleekly across his throat causing it to unzip his neck into a V shaped window of his esophagus. His eyes bucked open in confusion as blood gushed thickly in spurts onto my plastic covered face, his chest and everything else in range.

He wrenched forward into a sitting position with his hands clasping his throat and gurgled indistinguishable words while gasping for oxygen. My heartbeat with excitement as I stood to my full height, dropping the knife and watching in awe as his rubbery legs betrayed his attempt to stand sending him to the floor. I leaned forward on my tippy toes since the bed now obstructed my view of him, then maneuvered around it instead.

"Damn baby, you are strong. I thought you would go down like a sack of potatoes once I cut your air off," I teased shaking my head. Miraculously, I wasn't angry anymore. In fact, I was damn close to feeling jovial. "I couldn't Google search what *exactly* to expect before I did it and chance that being in my searches history." I chuckled.

He labored towards the door crawling on his elbows and knees while blood oozed between his fingers and gurgled from his throat like a babbling brook. The sight gave me... butterflies. Something about watching him suffer relieved a lot of anger I always felt balling up in the pit of my stomach that yoga had never been able to relieve.

The macabre look on his blood covered face made me think of the creepy thing that crawled out of the well in that horror movie *The Ring*. His head bobbed so much I thought it might actually rip off of his neck had his hands not been the glue to keep it attached.

He feebly fell forward onto his face, slowly writhing on the carpet and turning blue as his eyes rolled wildly around in their sockets. I've never seen anyone die before in person, but this was rather exhilarating. Who knew?

Abruptly, his flailing stopped, and his body lay still with both hands still grasping the wound as blood dribbled in a pool beneath him. I sighed, happy he hadn't made much headway toward the door. I didn't want to have to play hopscotch around any more blood spots than I absolutely had to. His eyes were fascinatingly lodged upwards into a dead man's stare that was fixated on nothingness.

A smile played on my lips beneath the blood-soaked garbage bag, satisfied with his ending. The more I looked, the more I wanted to keep looking. Sadly, I had to get my ass in gear because time was of the essence.

Hustling, I turned on the shower in the master bathroom and sat on the edge of the tub rinsing blood from my hands and leaning in to allow water to wash the rest from me. I used the same towel Marlene used to dry off and rested it on the sink as I stood in the bag across the entry.

Quickly, I removed everything I wore except one layer of gloves and let them fall inside the bag, then stepped outside of it. Naked, I knotted the bag and scooped it and the towel up in one hand and stepped around my handy work in the room.

Resting my sack on a clear area of the bed, I carefully picked up the knife holding the blade with one end of the towel and rubbed the handle clean with the other end. Lifting clothes from the hamper by the door, I placed the towel and the knife inside and then buried them with the same clothes I'd pulled out.

Slinging the bag over my shoulder like Santa Claus, I paused to study my husband's corpse a final time. His gaping neck had finally stopped flowing by then and his body lay stiff in a darkening mass of blood. Stepping over his corpse I exited the room humming the words to Pharell's song *Happy*. It was time to head back to Daddy's.

2

Greer

My heart thumped a mile a minute with anxiety and excitement as I glanced repeatedly into my rear-view mirror, carefully obeying traffic signals and speed limits of the rural streets on the way to Daddy's house. Visions of the sheer terror and confused regret in Michael's eyes looped blissfully in my mind as I rode the tree lined back roads avoiding traffic cameras the same way I came.

I never expected it to feel so... so... invigorating. I volleyed between anger and sorrow so many nights while plotting his demise that I sort of expected to feel remorse when it was all said and done.

I mean, after 9 years of being with the same man, marrying him and mapping out our future together, I never expected it to end like this. I never expected it to end at all. I envisioned myself driving back to Daddy's with my face drenched in tears and my heart heavy with regret; but it wasn't like that at all. In fact, I felt like I'd just had a B-12 shot and could run a 3-minute mile.

I took a bite of my Hershey almond chocolate bar and dabbed the light perspiration from my face with the back of my hand. Glancing at the clock, I was making good time and wouldn't need gas since I filled the tank from a canister Friday night. Nobody's driven my stepmother's car since her passing, so that made it the perfect vehicle to use without anyone keeping track of it.

When I finished eating my candy, I drove inside a random apartment complex and disposed of the wrapping and all of the garbage bags I'd used earlier. An uncontrollable giggle rose to my throat at the thought of how Michael's THOT would look being arrested for his murder. She truly was the one responsible for his death if you looked at it technically. Had it not been for her whoring ways with my otherwise faithful husband, none of us would be in the position we were in right now.

"I hope that last fuck was worth it," I said aloud to her even though she wasn't around to hear it.

The funny thing is, I knew that heifer was no good the first time Michael introduced her to me at his job. My hoe-dar went off like a tornado warning on sight, but I still maintained my poise.

"Greer, this is Marlene. Marlene Braxton. She's our newest Sleep Tech," Michael introduced with a hand gesture and a smile as we stood outside of the entrance to SLEEP ONE one evening.

I handed him the plastic bag with the dinner I'd prepared in Tupperware and greeted her with a smile that matched his. I was casually dressed in jeans and a tank top with sandals on and my curly brown hair in a ponytail. Had I known I was going to be meeting a new female that night, I would've worn make up and something more intimidating.

"Nice to meet you Marlene. When did you start?" I asked extending my hand while noticing the tight fit of her scrubs and the absence of an engagement ring or wedding band from her finger.

"I started last week Monday. It's so nice to meet you. You have beautiful eyes," she answered barely grasping my fingers while sizing me up with her shiny red lips in a smirk.

"Thank you. So... almost 2 whole weeks now. Is Arty on vacation?" I inquired maintaining my plastered smile and turning to Michael to explain why I wasn't notified previously of this tramp's arrival.

His thick lips parted beneath his neatly trimmed mustache to answer me, but she answered for him.

"No. I think he left for another job. I'm his permanent replacement. Michael has been showing me the ropes around here and preparing me for the nights when I'll be working alone or with the other tech Felix. I've been shadowing him like white on rice since I started," she said lightly tapping him on the shoulder with a chuckle I wished she'd choke on while Michael's doofy expression grated at my nerves.

I nodded pleasantly cutting my eyes between the 2 of them and clasping my hands in front of me instead of wrapping them around her neck. I'd addressed the question to my husband, not her. Clearly, she was unclear what her place was here.

"Arty got a new job at Sleep Med Atlanta remember? I thought I told you that," Michael said nonchalantly placing his hand on the small of my back and kissing me on my cheek. "Anyway, that's why I've been getting home later than usual on some days while I'm training her and she's getting acclimated to things. Not that it would matter to you since you're usually at work when I get home. But, just so you know why."

I frowned confusedly at that but quickly fixed my face so's not to show this trick that I was in any way becoming unraveled by these new revelations.

"Everything that concerns you matters to me," I told him grabbing one arm and pulling him down to plant a kiss on his cheek.

"Awww, y'all are so cuuuuute. Mike talks about you all the time. I need a good man like your husband in my life," she complimented crossing her arms. "You're a lucky woman," she continued with a wink and a Cheshire cat's grin.

That, 'You're a lucky woman' mess didn't go over my head. Believe me. It's just a subtle code for 'I wish your man was mine' and I could feel my chest tightening with the need to throat chop her for even making the statement. Anyone could see that my husband was fine, and the salt sprinkled throughout his low fade since his last birthday gave his sexy a distinguished kind of flare. But he was mine. And I don't share.

I looked at Michael curiously, waiting for him to correct her calling him Mike since he hated the nickname, but he didn't. Everybody called him Michael. He insisted on it since he was a junior and his father, who was M.I.A. most of his childhood and abusive when he wasn't, was called Mike. Somehow, this new trick had garnered the ability to use it freely and he was unfazed.

No way did I want this hoe spending time with my man in close quarters 12 hours at a time, 5 days a week. My eyes narrowed and I forced a broader smile as I leaned into Michael's broad chest, wrapping my arms around his waist and snuggling into him possessively.

"You're single? A pretty woman like yourself shouldn't have any problems getting a man of her own. All I know is that this one right here... is mine," I snickered with a feigned playfulness.

Michael stiffened and simultaneously coughed into one hand while removing himself from my hold with the other. Marlene appeared amused but didn't answer my question as she shifted her weight to one leg and eyed me.

She stood 5'4", with a full figure and a black Chinese bob stopping at the nape of her neck. Her eyes were dark brown and lustful, and her skin was a pretty dark chocolate that I envied above my own tortilla complexion. Mine had earned me a lot of taunting growing up and I assumed hers gave her the confidence to entice a married man from his wife.

I mean, what type of tramp puts on a full face of makeup to work the night shift when the only one awake to impress would be my husband? This heifer. Not only was her Dolce perfume being warn at a suffocating dosage, but I bet she'd strategically chosen the tightest floral printed scrubs she could find to accentuate her curvy hips and large breasts too. Chicks like her always did the most and her demeanor reminded me of my sister Debbie who I despised.

"Excuse me," Michael said when the coughing subsided. "Thank you for dinner baby. I really just wanted to introduce you two while I had the chance. I don't want you to use up too much gas with the car running idle like that and plus we gotta get back inside and set up the rooms. I love you. I'll call you on my break if I get a second," he said ushering me towards my car and squeezing my hand with feigned warmth. Before I could say or do anything else, he was headed back towards the double doors to the facility.

I felt the uneasiness then as I watched him speed walk away from me and toward her. It was the first time since Michael and I had been married... hell since we'd been together, that I genuinely felt threatened by another woman around him.

"Nice meeting you," Marlene threw over her shoulder sashaying behind him as he held a door politely open for her.

Two weeks later, it was the scent of her Dolce perfume on his clothes when I did laundry and on my bed sheets that instigated my suspicions. Michael's excuse was that they worked in close quarters and; therefore, he couldn't avoid her perfume occasionally rubbing off on him. Supposedly, her scent on our sheets came from him falling asleep in his scrubs after work. He had an answer for every question and the few inquiries I made were treated like the petty concerns of an insecure woman.

Like a good wife, I played along with his excuses on the surface and simply dropped the subject after my initial probing. It's easier to find out the truth when people think you've bought their lies and I didn't want him to be alerted to change his behaviors more than he already was. I came home early from work the next day and hacked into his phone while he slept with the passcode I'd always known, but never used.

I went directly to his Facebook app and searched her name on his friend list. Low and behold, the thirsty THOT already had a man and 2 kids to boot! According to her profile, she was 32 and had been with a guy named Randy Cambridge since 2009.

Both of her kids looked under the age of 5 so I assumed he was also the father of both of them. After I got my fill of looking at her pictures and reading the inbox messages between her and Michael, I went to review his text messages and call logs.

Their texts were few, but the conversations were too risqué to be innocent. Especially the ones that included close up shots of her clean-shaven vagina with her fingers demonstrating what she missed about his dick.

I was beyond livid and marched out of the bathroom with his phone in my hand ready to bludgeon him to death with it... until I thought better. I decided that I would get more proof of his acts and then divorce the pants off of him. I suppressed my urge to confront him and purchased an alarm clock with a surveillance camera in it on my way home from work the following day and replaced the old one on my bedside table with it. It had an option to record when there was motion or to watch it live stream and I initially set it for motion recording.

I stayed late to work that day and used another employee's computer to plug in her information on Spokeo and let Google searches act as my personal sleuth. That's when I discovered that Miss Homewrecker had an affinity for knives. She was apparently a Miami native before she brought her hot ass to Atlanta because she had 2 prior arrests in Dade County, both for stabbing offenses. According to court records, one was a domestic dispute with a boyfriend on South Beach over another woman in 2006 and the other was a knife wielding drunken altercation with her current man Randy, in 2011.

I couldn't imagine why the man was still with her if the details of the report were true; but if so, he'd hung onto her even after she scratched his car with the knife and then stabbed him in his hands and shoulder with it. I couldn't understand why Michael would sacrifice our marriage for this hoodrat, but he had.

To add insult to injury, two days later the clock recorded Michael and Marlene in my bed while I was visiting my dad that Saturday. Now, if I'm anything, it's methodical and patient thanks to the many years of practice I had keeping under my family's radar. Best believe, all sexual activity between us ceased from that day on though. I never saw him use a condom with her and I certainly didn't want sloppy dick sucking seconds. Honestly, it kind of pissed me off that his advances had become so infrequent by then that I'm not even sure he noticed I was holding out.

The disrespectful asshole repeatedly brought her to our home to fuck both while I was at work and while I visited my father. I assume it was because the family she had plastered all over her FB and IG might be home to catch them more than I was. Michael was probably too cheap to spring for a hotel room and doing it at work must've been too risky since there were surveillance cameras there. Unfortunately for him, there was surveillance at home too.

Each time I saw him sleeping peacefully when I got home from work, especially on days when the clock recorded him cheating, I wanted to hurt him. Make him pay for the irreparable pain I was feeling inside by his betrayal. The more I thought about it, the more I realized that I stood to lose more in a divorce than he did. I'd been on my job for 6 years, made more money, paid the majority of the down payment on our house and the lion's share of the bills.

Hell, for all I knew, the courts would make us sell the house or give it to him entirely and make me pay alimony to him. I'd be damned if he'd get our house to share with his whore! That's when I decided that divorcing him was no longer an option for me. The punishment wouldn't be enough for him. For them! It was my knowledge of his side-chick's past indiscretions that birthed my plan of execution and their ultimate demise.

The digital clock in the car read 10:09 a.m. and I was making good time. Eight minutes later I drove the Camry in back of the garage where it had been stored for the last couple of months and locked up before going to get my car. Once Debbie became my dad's designated driver to his appointments, the decision was made to park Stephanie's car in back of the garage to free up the spot for hers.

The land back there was essentially an extension of their backyard, but it was on the far end where nobody really went. Everything back there was obscured from view from the front yard unless you went around the L shaped bend to see it.

My baby blue Corolla was parked beside my dad's cherry red, Buick Roadmaster inside the garage today though, so I tossed my now empty backpack in the passenger's seat and grabbed my cell from the cup holder. I was happy to see that I hadn't missed any text messages or phone calls that might make my lack of response seem suspicious. The last incoming text was from Michael during our morning convo at 6:19 a.m.

Me: Hey baby. Good morning. Is there anything in particular you want me to add to the grocery list today?

Michael: Good morning. Just bread and Taquitos.

Me: I think you're part Mexican eating Taquitos all the time. LOL

Michael: LOL. Whatever. You love me.

Me: I do. You love me too.

He responded back with a thumbs up emoji making me squint with resentment. I'd only texted him to ensure there'd be proof of my location but the fact that there wouldn't even be a last "I love you" exchange between us distressed me some. Was he so smitten with Marlene that he didn't even want to fake it anymore? I would've asked him more questions if it hadn't been necessary to slit his vocal cords... but it was.

Anyway, I left my phone at Daddy's to prevent cell towers from tracking my service anywhere but at Charles Foster's residence while I was tying up loose ends. Since I was where I was supposed to be now, I called my best friend Shantel as I headed through the garage door into the house and scanned the kitchen for signs of life.

"Hey girl," she answered on the second ring sounding horse.

"Hey. Did I wake you up?" I asked heading down to my dad's room and cracked the door open to peep in on him.

He was laying on his side snoring lightly with his back towards me. Perfect.

"Yeah," she said yawning. "But it's cool, I was already awake before. I just fell back to sleep. I needed to get up anyway. What's up with you?"

I never had a lot of friends, but Shantel has been the most loyal and consistent one I've ever had. I've only unequivocally trusted 3 people since my mom died. One is my father, one is Shantel, and the other was on the floor of my bedroom as rigamortis set in.

Shan and I met our Freshman year at Spelman when the sassy, coffee brown, short girl from Queens came busting in my dorm room demanding she get the bed on the right and talking a mile a minute. I'd applied to the all-female African American liberal arts college with the hopes of better connecting with other black women since I hadn't been too successful doing it growing up.

I was originally put off by Shantel's bossy and bubbly personality though. It was hard enough for me trying to open up on campus when most of my peers were once again questioning my lineage, without the aggressive and talkative chick dictating our every freshman move.

You have to remember that I was coming from a household where the women were bitchy, vindictive and cynical most days. I was new to dealing with the warmth and positivity she projected.

Eventually, like most people, I came to adore and envy Shan's charismatic personality; even accompanied by her northern pushiness and sarcasm.

She had a good heart, made friends almost as easily as I breathed air and quickly became one of the popular girls around campus. Becoming her roommate and launching a friendship with her turned out to be one of the best things that ever happened to my social life.

Being Shantel Lewis' sidekick got me into a lot of parties and noticed by elitist circles of people I know would've ignored me otherwise. Beautiful, smart, funny, ambitious and charismatic, her middle-class background didn't hold her back from anything.

She'd been married to Jahari a year longer than Michael and I were married, and she had a 4-year-old son named Shamari. Jahari loved Shantel like I'd never seen a man express love for his wife before, and I envied the bond the 2 of them seemed to have with one another.

She was a prized catch in school, but Jahari was the one she ultimately had eyes for. It was obvious in the way she lit up when his name was mentioned and in the gleam in her eyes whenever he entered a room.

Jahari was just as doe eyed when Shan was around, and I never trusted that the 2 of them hadn't snuck off to screw in some obscure spot at parties whenever at least one of them wasn't in sight. I wished Michael and I had had that.

"Just washing breakfast dishes," I told her turning on the water at the kitchen sink.

"Oh okay. You still over at your dad's?"

"You know he's still got a few more weeks of treatment before we'll know how well it worked. I don't mind though. I like spending time with my daddy. I think he likes the company," I answered truthfully.

"I can tell. Not to be mean it's probably easier without Stephanie lurking around. You've been a lot happier and livelier since you started seeing him regularly."

"Have I?"

"Umm hmm. No disrespect, but you're usually one tone. Everything is everything. Lately, you've been more animated when we talk, and I can tell you're enjoying getting closer with your dad. I think the time you're spending with him is good for you instead of sitting in that house alone all of the time while Michael's at work watching NETFLIX and the ID Network," she said shuffling on the other end.

"Are you calling me boring?" I chuckled. "Because I am definitely *not* boring. Plus, if my bestie hadn't moved back to New York on me, maybe I'd have more to do than just go to work and watch T.V. all of the time."

That was the utter truth, but I had been hanging with my co-worker Angie a lot since Shan moved away but I downplayed it since she could be just as territorial about our friendship as I could. Shan had 2 girl-friends she hung out with a lot when she was here in Atlanta, Bri and Casey, that I wasn't particularly fond of, and I know her recaps of their outings used to annoy me, even though I never said so.

Shan giggled.

"I'm not saying you're boring. You know I don't think you're boring. Anyway, believe me, if I could move back to the A tomorrow I would. I'm still feeling my way around my job and the hustle and bustle of NYC isn't as fascinating to me as it was when I was a teenager.

I know I told Jahari I'd give it 2 years but, that was before I realized we didn't secure that loft in Manhattan and we were gonna be living 3 blocks from his momma's house in the Bronx instead.

I've never had a problem with his mom in small doses. You know, holidays, birthdays, brief summer visits... but this is too much. I swear this woman is gonna drive me to drink with the way she tries to control every move we make. I thought I married a man's man. Jahari is always a take charge kind of guy around me, but around his momma? He's like a little boy again.

Don't get me wrong. I like Evelyn and I'm glad Shamari is getting to spend so much time with his grandma and that she watches him for free while we work, but still. She's always got 2 cents to add to whatever I wanna do with raising him or running my own house, and some task for Jahari to complete at *her* house. He's almost over there more than he is over here.

I love her but, she acts like she doesn't even know how to change a light bulb without calling Jahari to do it. It's driving me crazy Greer. He's over there right now doing God only knows what for her and it's not even 11 o'clock yet."

"Aww, he just loves his mommy," I teased adding dishes from the right side of the sink into the newly formed soapy water.

"Girl shut up," she sniggered. "We all love our mommy's, but this is ridiculous. She needs a man of her own so she can stop using mine up. Son or no son. At least Michael's only gone a lot because he's working and not because his mother is monopolizing his time like a side-chick."

"True, but she still meddles. If Ms. Nina suggests it, Michael's probably going to do it whether I'm for it or not. No matter what it is," I complained honestly.

"But we can't even get in a quickie when Shamari is asleep without her ringing the phone about something. I swear I think she has a cock-blocking-camera in our bedroom. It's uncanny how often she interrupts whenever we're about to do it.

Then she has the nerve to keep asking me when I'm gonna give her another grand baby. Like, when are we supposed to make this baby when you keep occupying all my man's time ma'am?

Seriously. This morning, I was about to get some, so I turned the ringer off on his phone so she couldn't interrupt us. It was early too. Like 6 something.

So I wake him up with some head. I get on top and get ready to ride the pony before Shamari gets up to watch cartoons. I'm all hot and bothered and he literally had just put it inside me when guess who comes knocking at the front door?"

"Oooohhh!" I roared laughing. "What the hell for?"

"She said a pipe in her shower bust and water was spraying all over the place in her bathroom. Now correct me if I'm wrong, but that's why you call a plumber.

Jahari is a marketing executive. He doesn't know *thing one*, about fixing a busted pipe. Tell me why she came rushing over here with no regards to my sex life, because he wasn't answering his phone. Really? He's not answering his phone on purpose!

I'm telling you Greer, she got cameras in here. I'm about to start checking all the clocks, smoke detectors and teddy bears in the house," she joked.

I found the thought of her placing hidden cameras in the house hysterical.

3

Greer

"She didn't plan that out at all," I tell my dad popping a few Cheetos in my mouth as we watch an episode of SNAPPED in his bedroom.

"Yeah. I guess that's how she got on the show. If she'd gotten away wit' it, we wouldn't know nothin' 'bout her," he said putting a fork full of baked Tilapia into his mouth.

"True," I nodded with an inside joke I told myself knowing that my face will never grace an episode of that show.

The women that ended up on SNAPPED were the ones that either didn't plan their murders well, or didn't plan for them at all. My steps had already been numbered since I got up this morning and were mentally choreographed for everything that would follow.

I only had a couple of hours left to spend with my father before it would be time for me to go to the grocery store before heading home. I would text Michael's cell while in the store to ask whether he wanted beef or chicken Taquitos, to which he wouldn't respond of course. I'd send him a confused emoji when he didn't respond and text him minutes later that I was going to get chicken since he must be asleep.

When I arrived home with a car full of groceries, I'd leave the trunk up and the front door open while bringing one bag inside to the kitchen for good measure. I'd then go upstairs, later claiming to the police that I went to investigate why he didn't answer or come down when I called up for his help with the rest of the bags.

At the threshold of our bedroom door, I'll stick 2 fingers down my throat to bring the contents of my last meal back up as evidence of my shocked reaction to discovering the macabre scene. Screaming and crying, I'll barrel down the steps and out the door to retrieve my cell from my purse, which I'll strategically leave in the car.

Hysterically and loudly, I'll have a total meltdown in my driveway as I call 911 and recap what I found in clear sight of anyone in ear or eye shot to witness it. Easy peasy.

Smiling at my own level of cunning, I brushed orange crumbs from my pink SPELMAN COLLEGE T-shirt and blue jeans while sitting cross legged on the bed beside Daddy holding a bowl of Cheetos.

"Sides, it's mostly white ladies that do stuff like that. No offense. Black women just shoot or stab ya right then and there and worry 'bout consequences later," Daddy chuckled.

"No offense? No offense to who? Me? I'm not white daddy. And you got some nerve talking because I got these green eyes from you and you're almost as light as I am," I shot back playfully.

My father looked a lot like a younger version of the singer Smokey Robinson with light skin, curly hair and green eyes. My mother was also green-eyed, but the tint of mine was an emerald shade like my daddy's.

"Anyway, that is not true. There's been plenty of black chicks on this show," I protested with a smirk shoveling more Cheetos into my mouth before he could get a word in edgewise.

"I know you not white Babygirl. I meant, no offense to white people in general. But I bet mo' Becky Sue's and Megan's is on there than Keisha and Tawana's," he continued smiling jokingly while herding the green beans in his plate together to scoop onto his fork. "I don't know which is worse though. The one that stabs ya in the middle of the argument or the one that waits until ya go to sleep."

I was enjoying the energy he had today. It was good to see him in good spirits and eating so heartily. The days he's like this are few and far between since he's been on radiation treatments for the last 6 weeks.

My dad was diagnosed with Stage 2 prostate cancer 2 months ago, and his best option to force it into remission was External Beam Radiation Therapy or EBRT, 5 days a week for 9 weeks.

As you can imagine, radiation would take a lot out of anybody; but at 64 years old, it's really been taking its toll on him. Even on the days he doesn't have therapy he's usually extremely fatigued and his appetite is low if not nonexistent.

He insists that if Stephanie was still alive, he wouldn't be sick at all; and he could be correct. She was big on homeopathic treatments, herbs and elixirs and their house was full of both homegrown and purchased forms of the stuff.

The circumference of the backyard was surrounded with manicured Oleander bushes that Stephanie and my dad planted both to beautify the yard and to deter the Bobcats and other animals from lingering on their property.

In 2000, Stephanie and my dad opened a nursery where she could generate profit from her green thumbs and occupy her time while my dad was on the road. FLOWER ME WITH LOVE is in a plaza on Cumberland Drive and each of us had to work there after school whether we wanted to or not.

Stephanie's love and knowledge of flowers, plant life and herbs was extensive and she was the most at ease on her knees in the backyard garden when we were kids. As crazy as I used to think her insistence that we drink her elixirs when we were healthy or ingest her natural remedies instead of going to the doctor were, our health was always above average.

My dad was convinced that had she been around to take care of him, his cancer would've been eradicated without the radiation treatments he was enduring weekly. But Stephanie wasn't here to do that, so listening to medical professionals was his only option.

My half-sister Debbie takes him to his appointments Monday through Friday since she only lives 4 streets over and is a stay-at-home mom. Let her tell it, she deserves the Mother Teresa award for chauffeuring her own father to doctor appointments even though she wasn't doing shit else while her 6-year-old was in school all day until 2 weeks ago.

Granted, she had been managing the nursery since Stephanie died and my dad was ill, but there were 3 other employees that she delegated responsibilities to, and I doubted she was doing much above delegating.

Since I work full time and live about an hour away, I started coming over Friday's after work, and staying overnight at my dad's to help him out and spend some time with him. My stepmother passed away 5-months ago so my siblings and I are the only ones left to look after him. My older brother Shawn lives in California and my baby sister Donna is always more involved in her personal life than she is with the family so that left me and Debbie to do most of the heavy lifting.

My daddy, Charles "Chuck" Foster was a truck driver for 30 years before he finally retired 6 years ago at Stephanie's prompting and started a mobile locksmith business so he could stay local. When he got sick, he couldn't answer customer calls like he used to, so he closed FOSTER MOBILE LOCKS and sold his van to Will to use as a loaner vehicle at his shop.

I hate to sound callous, but her death was the best thing that ever happened for my relationship with my father. I'd never spent this much quality time with him ever before and as one of the few people I felt truly loved me, it did my heart good to share these fleeting moments with him.

All growing up he was on the road more than he was home, and when he was home, he was either sleeping or consumed with whatever drama he and Stephanie had going on. I never felt at ease talking to him in her presence because she was always trying to intimidate me into keeping quiet about her treatment of me when he was out of town.

My biological mother died in an apartment fire when I was 5, and since she was the only one in her family that moved to the states from Romania, there was no one but my dad who could take me. Besides my mother, my father was the only other relative I knew.

At that time, Stephanie and my dad had been married for 14 years and had 3 kids; so yeah, you do the math. Stephanie was none too thrilled to have to raise a child her husband fathered during their marriage. With a white woman none the less who was as far away from Stephanie's dark Mahogany complexion as could be.

I remember the hatred in her eyes and the way she protested the day he brought me home to stay. She must've seen him pull up in front of the house because she was already waiting for us when he opened the door.

"Now Chuck..." she started with one palm open in the air like she was about to praise Jesus while shaking her head from side to side. "Don't make me lose my Christianity on you tonight. The kids are sleep and I've had a long day already. Lord knows—"

"Cut out the foolishness woman. I'm just gonna sat her down here while I unload my pickup," he said aggravated pushing me in front of him with his hand on the small of my back as I stutter stepped forward timidly.

"I don't know where you're gonna take this little bastard, but you damn sure ain't gonna bring her up in here with my kids!" she shrieked blocking our path in her thick Alabama accent pointing her index finger at me while I cowered up against my daddy's pant leg. "You must be out your cotton-picking mind if you think this is gonna fly with me! You think I'm gonna raise the proof that you couldn't keep your dick out of another woman while you're married to me? The hell I am! I told you last week, I told you last night, and I'm telling you now... I'm not raising that child!"

"Steph, don't you call my Babygirl a bastard again. I done tol' you 'bout your mouth befo' now. Look here, if you mean no when you say no, then you must mean to raise all of these kids without me around then, 'cause I'm not givin' my baby to the state. If I have to move out and get my own place so she has a place to rest her head, then I will. I'll call my sister to come stay with me for a while when I'm on the road until I find anotha' way to take care of my daughter. Whateva' I gotta do, she's stayin' with me," he growled lowly with one hand on my back and the other shaking in her face while I peeked at her around his pants leg.

Stephanie was 5'4" with big breasts, round hips and a flabby mid-section courtesy of childbearing weight she never fully lost. Her eyes might have been a pretty brown once but whenever she looked at me, they were always narrowed into a muddy glare. Her hair was wild and frizzy around her head and she was wearing a flowery housecoat tied in the front with dingy slippers. She glowered at me with her face contorted and then cut her eyes back at him with a look that said she would kill him before she allowed that.

"You say what now? Oh no the hell you did not say you would leave your wife and 3 children for this bastard child? You're the one who cheated! 15 years I gave my life to you. Fourteen of them married, and this is how you treat me? You got some damn nerve coming up in here threatening me like I'm the one who should be bending!

You're always on the road any God damn way so it's not gonna be nobody but me wiping her ass and feeding her! You just gonna make me play momma to the child when every time I look in her face, I see the white bitch you stepped out on me for?" she complained pacing the warn carpet in their quaint living room by the door where we stood.

"Why you so stuck on Irina being white?"

"Because she ain't nothing like me! If you like white women so much, why'd you marry me then?" she yelled into his face.

He turned his head away from her and sucked his lips under in a way that I knew he was trying to maintain his composure.

"You worry 'bout the wrong things. Stuff that didn't have anything to do with why it happened. Anyway, this ain't the time or place to talk 'bout it around my Babygirl. Now if you can't accept her, then I'll walk out that door right now and you won't see me again until I come to visit my kids," he told her as a matter of fact while rubbing his hand lovingly against my back to sooth my trembling little body.

I was dressed in a pink frilly sundress with white patent leather shoes on and my hair was in a single poofy ponytail. Frankly, I was afraid. I didn't want to live with that mean lady at all. I really just wanted my mommy! But my daddy said she had gone to live with the angels, and she couldn't come back so I was going to have to live with him now. I looked up at him still wearing his big rig uniform and a head full of curls sticking out beneath his cap. His clean-shaven face was stern and when I looked at her, a river of tears was streaming down her angry face.

I squeezed my eyes shut and silently prayed she was about to send us to live by ourselves just as she spoke.

"Chuck... you can't... leave me," she said through sobs.

I opened my eyes to see her looking upwards with both hands on her head.

"You can't leave me and the kids. How you expect me to love this little girl like you want me to when I hate everything that created her? Don't you care nothin' about my feelings? About how much this would hurt me?" she began pleading while beating her chest passionately with one hand and turning her gaze to him. "Don't you even care about what your own kids are gonna think? How you expecting us to love that woman's baby when she tried to destroy our family?"

My dad sighed deeply and wiped his hand across his forehead. "Steph, I love you. But I love my kids too. *All* of my kids. I know I'm to blame for all of this, but we can get through this if we try. The kids are gonna love her just fine. If you give it a chance, I'm sure you'll love her too. Irina is gone now and I'm all she has. Don't punish Greer for what we did. She's innocent in this. She lost her moma Stephanie. I don't want to go. But I will if she can't stay."

She clasped one hand over her mouth stifling whatever cry almost escaped and looked away before turning back toward us with fresh tears brewing. Her eyes softened for once when her eyes fell on me and I stared hopefully back at her.

Nodding she said, "Okay. If this is what you want. I'll do my best to love her like my own. But you gotta do more than you do now."

My dad was elated and took her lovingly into his arms planting several kisses on her face and over her tear-stained cheeks. At first, I was smiling too, relieved that she'd changed her mind, until I looked into her face. As my father embraced her, Stephanie's eyes iced over like a skating rink and if looks could kill, I would've been decapitated.

That, was the first day of the rest of my life with my step monster.

"I know I can't wait till all this hospital stuff is over. I still got a lot of years ahead of me, and this cancer got me feeling like an ol' man," my daddy said snapping me back from my thoughts. "My grand baby wants to go fishin' and I'm ready to take her. Every time I see her, she asks me 'bout it. Damn cancer ain't gonna turn me into a slouch for my grand. Three more weeks of this mess and I'm gonna be back in business."

"I know Daddy," I agreed with a smile.

"You know Debbie's starting to show now. They plannin' to name him William Charles if it turns out a boy," he stated watching me curiously between chews.

I huffed and shifted on the bed picking up the remote from the nightstand and channel surfed while a commercial was on. Debbie and I share a mutual disdain for each other but that never stopped my daddy from trying to facilitate a kumbaya between us. Now that Stephanie was gone, he was ill and Debbie was 4-months pregnant with her second child, he was extra sentimental about our family's broken relationships.

"You girls need to be tryin' to get along betta' now with yo' stepmom dying, and me sick. Life's too short for blood to treat blood the way you girls do," he continued without waiting for my response.

"I know daddy," I replied sweetly flipping back to our show and looking back at him with a smile. "You know, I'm not the one who has a problem. You really should be talking to her about this. She's never liked me, and she probably never will. I'd love to play auntie to her kids. But she doesn't want me to, and she doesn't tell me anything, so what else can I do? She's done a lot of awful things to me that you probably don't even know about and now that we're grown... I'd just rather not have to deal with her until she's decided to stop mistreating me."

Simply put. I hate the bitch. She's done too much for me to ever change that. But for my daddy's sake, I usually pretended to be open to it. I loved hyping up how she's victimized me though. I mean, I really was a victim of Debbie's in the past, but I hadn't been taking too much of her shit since Stephanie's reign ended. It was almost like I shed my flying monkey suit like all of the dancers in The Wiz as soon as the wicked bitch was dead.

He sighed placing one hand over mine and squeezing affectionately.

"You know Babygirl, I'm not gonna live foreva'. You, yo' sisters and yo' brotha' need to make sure my grand babies are gonna have a family to call on when they need ya. You need to be able to have family to call on when *you* need them.

You so anti-social. You don't come to family reunions, barbeques, nothin'. Now I know some of how you feel is because of how you been handled with the family and all, but you my daughter. I claim you. I've *never* been ashamed of you. You keep your head up and don't let nobody make you feel less than them fo' any reason."

"Isn't that sweet. You in here stroking Greer's ego again daddy?" Debbie said sardonically standing in the doorway grimacing with her arms folded over the top of her protruding belly.

She was carrying pretty big for a chick who was only 3 months along if you asked me. I cut my eyes at her wishing I had knives to assist. Lucky for her, I've had years of practice masking my desire to rip her eyes out and shove them down her throat, so I just reverted to protocol. I digressed.

"Your belly's getting big already," I commented amiably with a doe-eyed expression, knowing it would get under her skin.

Debbie hadn't quite snapped back to her pre-baby figure since she had Tamia so she was already self-conscious about her weight and I knew the mention of it from me of all people, would irritate her.

She snorted with one hand on her hip and her black curly wig dangling around her full face with a scowl.

"I'm pregnant. What did you expect?" she snorted.

"Alright now Debbie. Don't come in here startin' no mess with all of that attitude," my father told her sternly moving his plate from his lap to the small portable table beside his bed.

She sucked her teeth like a juvenile and rolled her eyes filling the doorway with her fat ass dressed in black leggings and a long yellow V-neck blouse.

"Whatever daddy. Where are the keys to your car? Will is outside and he was gonna check out the oil leak you were complaining about, but the keys aren't in the bowl," she asked him glowering at me.

Alright, so maybe I missed one note in my plan. I forgot to put the freaking keys back in the bowl when I came in. Damn it!

Debbie's husband Will is not only a sweet, friendly, 6'2", teddy bear of a man with the build of Lennie from OF MICE AND MEN, but he's also a mechanic. I haven't figured out why he ever wanted any parts of the evil witch before me, but he married her 10 years ago and appeared to have every intention on staying with her forever.

In typical form, I allowed her snide remarks to go without response while my expression remained unchanged and I seethed inside. Silently, I was kicking myself for forgetting to put the keys back in the dish, but it was a minor glitch with an easy fix. It was just my luck that she'd choose today of all days to come by for his keys.

"I have them. I was looking for something in the storage shed out back and daddy has the key to it on his key chain. I'll go get it," I answered before he could respond to her and moved toward the doorway.

She eyed me suspiciously twisting her mouth and asking snidely, "Looking for what? You ain't got nothin' in there."

I tilted my head matching her stare with a grin and waited for her to move. At 5'6" I stood at least 3 inches taller than her, but I usually didn't challenge her. I was still on a high from murdering Michael though so lil' Debbie needed to tread lightly.

The passive Greer that she was used to antagonizing was slowly leaving the building. I didn't owe this heifer any explanations and she wasn't getting one from me without good reason.

Debbie looked me up and down and sucked her teeth. "Did you hear what I asked you? And why are you all up in my face?"

My grin widened as our eyes remained locked; but I still said nothing. If I didn't know any better, I'd think I saw a flicker of fear in her eyes.

"Debbie!" my daddy's voice boomed. "Cut it out and move out the damn way," he demanded as she looked around me to him and then side stepped with a screw face.

"I'm just asking her why she's in the storage shed daddy. She ain't had nothing in there since she got married so what's she in there for? And what's with the deaf-mute act while I'm talking to her? Don't you wanna know what she was doing in there?"

"No, I don't. And why you back here today anyway? This is Saturday, ain't it? This ain't yo' day. Saturday is yo' day off over here. Who's running the shop if'in you over here? And where is my grand baby anyway?" my daddy rattled off exasperatedly sipping his OJ.

"Well damn daddy. I know it's not my day. I was trying to get your car fixed so it'll pass inspection to renew your registration before your birthday. Were you planning to do it yourself? 'Cause I'm the only one who keeps track of everything you've got to do since mommy died and if it wasn't for me, half this stuff probably wouldn't even get done.

Louis is managing the shop and Tamia is at Will's mother's house. *Excuuuuse* me for interrupting your time with your favorite if I'm only welcomed over when it's my day or when I'm with Tamia. Was Greer gonna get your car fixed for you or nah?" she whined loudly as I trotted down the hall and upstairs to my old room, now a spare bedroom, and retrieved the keys.

I brought them back with a smug smirk and politely placed the keys in her open palm while she shot daggers back at me.

"Here you go," I said jovially passing her and climbing back onto the bed in the spot I previously occupied.

"Pshhh," she hissed at me with squinted eyes and a curled lip.

"Debbie, just go'head now if you gonna do it. You got the keys, and tell Will I said thank ya," Daddy said shooing her with a wave of his hand.

Her mouth hung open in disbelief and she motioned like she was going to say more, but changed her mind. Squinting at me disgustedly, she turned on her heels in a huff and left.

"I'm sorry Daddy. I forgot to put the keys back when I took them this afternoon. I've been dreaming about my mother a lot lately and I was kind of hoping some of my mother's stuff would be in there," I told him meekly.

"Babygirl you don't have to explain nothin' to me. I loved Stephanie, but I swear sometimes Debbie's the reincarnation of everything that got on my nerves 'bout the woman. Always got her nose buried in other people's business like she don't have enough of her own," he complained.

"I know Daddy, but I still wanted to tell you why. Since Stephanie died, my mom's been on my mind a lot and I haven't seen any of those pictures you used to show me of her when I was little in years. It was a stretch, I know. I was just kind of hoping Stephanie didn't throw them away like she used to threaten."

My mother had indeed been on my mind more lately, and I did think that Stephanie might have stashed her memorabilia in the shed, if she hadn't trashed it. I never bothered to rummage through the place where the Foster family's old furniture, clothes and items that lost their usefulness went to die. It was just a convenient lie I concocted should my having the keys ever come up in conversation with the police. My half-sister was prone to say anything.

Daddy placed a comforting hand on my knee and our green eyes peered into each other.

"Whateva' you did, I know you had good reason to do it Babygirl," he said earnestly.

My heart skipped a beat as I searched his face for the deeper meaning in his statement. His weary eyes appeared to be analyzing my reaction just as much as I was studying his. Were we still talking about the shed or something else?

Regardless, I smiled warmly at the first man that ever loved me and wondered if another man would ever love me that way again. Clearly, Michael had not.

4

Greer

June 2015

Al Green sang about love and happiness through the speakers as sunlight soaked everyone in the backyard who was willing to battle the sweltering heat for daddy's birthday. The smell of barbequing meat and corn on the cob wafted through the air while people I didn't know, and ones I hadn't seen in ages talked, laughed and mingled both in and outside of the house.

Daddy made a point of having me here since I hadn't been showing up to anything with more than immediate family in the past. He even made me help with the decorations and had me pick up the cake from Publix. I actually didn't mind since Debbie claimed she was too busy to do it and I knew I wouldn't have to tip toe around her miserable behind.

The awning over the backdoor entrance provided little shade from the blazing sun as I stepped off the porch in a spaghetti strapped handkerchief dress, shielding my eyes with one hand. I headed towards the food filled table with Daddy's birthday cake in the center of it and admired my work. Multicolored helium balloons were weighted down so that they hovered over the middle of each square table scattered across the yard, blue and pink streamers were hung around the food table in front of the oleander bushes with a big 65 dangling in the middle. Blue was Daddy's favorite color and although pink was mine, the pink symbolized his cancer survival.

"Greer! Girl I need you to do me a favor. Can a brother get a beer while I'm slaving over this grill in 100 degrees please?" Will begged comically with beads of perspiration congregating on his forehead and the sweat in the pits of his Cowboys T-shirt spreading.

"Where's your wife? You know how she is and I don't want no trouble with her today. But I'll get you one on my way back... if you don't spontaneously combust first," I quipped, turning slightly to look at him as I continued walking.

"Aww, that's cold blooded!" he whined chuckling while painting the searing chicken on the grill with barbecue sauce as his creepy friend Rodger drank me in with his eyes. "I'm sure she wouldn't mind you saving my life! Let me get a Heiny."

Rodger's gaze made my skin crawl and I quickly turned my attention back to my destination, still feeling the tall, burly, light skin man with coke bottle glasses and too much acne for a man in his 30's eyes on my back. Something about him just screamed "I'm a kidnapping rapist!" to me.

He and Will had been friends for years and they also worked together at Will's shop, but he was weird. Only a psycho would be out in this heat wearing gray mechanics overalls, even if it was unzipped passed his naval revealing the dingy wife-beater beneath it.

Tamia and my brother Shawn's daughter Crystal raced past me in their sundresses giggling with their hair swishing every which way in pigtails and braids. I was glad my brother and his wife came down from Cali with their kids because Tamia had someone her own age here to play with.

She spent way more time at my dad's house than I realized before I began spending more time over here myself. Consequently, I started getting to know my niece better too, whenever Debbie wasn't around blocking that is. She was cute, sweet and imaginative. Daddy and Will doted on her like she was the center of their universes and it was evident that Debbie was just as jealous of her daughter as she had been of me when we were kids. Pathetic wench.

We would always be oil and water. The more time that passed, the harder it was becoming for me to digest her catty remarks and foul behavior while suppressing the urge to stab her into the silence I fantasized about. Motherhood hadn't softened her maliciousness at all after Tamia, but I'd hoped she'd become a little more relaxed after her second child. For her own sake really. Hoping is apparently for suckers, because juggling a 7-month-old and a rambunctious, soon to be, 7-year-old daughter, had only made Debbie nastier.

I was still stuck playing the grieving, passive aggressive, people-pleasing, pitiful wife I'd always been for a little while longer. Michael's case was finally going to trial next week, and I anxiously awaited it coming to an end so I could shed my old skin and embrace the new me I found the day he died. Oh yeah. A lot of things have changed in the year I had to find myself and contemplate my future without my husband.

Daddy guzzled down the remainder of his beer while seated at a card table he'd pulled out to play spades with 3 other men that I didn't know from a can of paint.

"Set!" an older bald-headed man sitting across from my dad hollered, slamming an ace of spades down on a pile of hearts in the middle of the table.

"Aww y'all cheating!" one of his gray-haired opponents protested throwing up his hands and tossing his remaining cards down on the table. "Dave, man... I saw you giving Chuck the signal."

"What signal?" Baldy, who I assume was Dave retorted with a snicker. "Unless he signaled that ace of spades to magically pop into my hand, we ain't cheating 'bout a damn thing. What we're doing here is called WINNING. Something you and Renaldo obviously know nothing about. All the rest of my cards are spades suckas!" Dave, rubbed it in as my father laughed heartily in agreement and the other man, whose name I didn't get, continued to bicker about his defeat.

I was ecstatic to see Daddy looking so happy for a change. Luckily, his cancer was in remission and sands looking a little older than he had previously, he was in a much better place both mentally and health wise. The vibrancy that had always been in his eyes was back, and it was easy to see he enjoyed being in the company of so many friends and family.

"Babygirl, you see your old man whipping these old men in cards?" Daddy asked grinning wide as his opponents playfully protested loudly.

"Yes Daddy," I tittered smiling and kissing his forehead.

Regardless of my joyous mood, I still felt the daggers Aunt Gretta was shooting at me unprovoked from a lawn chair off to the side. She was holding Debbie's youngest Willa as the baby played with a balloon tied to the arm of the chair. The crow's feet around her eyes deepened as she continued glowering at me with no shame.

Now there was absolutely no reason for the fat cow to hate me other than the fact that her baby sister Stephanie had. Aunt Gretta adored Debbie, Donna and Shawn, but quickly gave me her ass to kiss when presented with the opportunity.

Everybody on Stephanie's side treated me like the family pariah since I was the only one of the kids my daddy claimed that wasn't actually birthed from her black hole, but whatever. Gretta was the only one of their clan at this barbeque and I wasn't planning on letting that gorilla-faced, pot-bellied old biddy kill my joy. The more I smiled, the more she scowled, and the more that made me smile.

My joy quickly wilted though when Tamia's squealing grabbed my attention. Debbie's right hand was clamped down on Tamia's arm like a vice grip, and all color had been snatched from the child's angelic face. The veins in Debbie's neck were visible even at a distance as she shook the girl and spoke harshly to her.

"Didn't I tell you to quit running back here with all these people? Huh? Y'all falling all into Grandma's bushes and pushing people. This is my third time telling your little hardheaded butt to stop. Stop. Running," Debbie barked into Tamia's grimacing face as the child's eyes filled with fear and tears, roiling anger in the pit of my stomach.

"Yes Mommy, but-" the child whined.

"But nothing! When I tell you not to do something, don't do it! Stop making me repeat myself like you're too retarded to understand what I'm telling you."

My thoughts instantly morphed back to childhood. Stephanie was notorious for yanking the soul out of me whenever I did anything she remotely found disturbing, and Debbie was emulating her perfectly. Obviously, like mother, like daughter. Though I knew Stephanie was far worse than her mini-bitch, Debbie was still a tyrant, and Tamia didn't deserve her wrath any more than I had.

I watched Tamia flinch with each venomous word her mother spat, and I couldn't believe nobody was doing or saying anything about it. I know a lot of guests were preoccupied in conversations and probably didn't see or hear the scene playing out because of the music; but there's no way that mine were the only eyes watching.

In a heartbeat I was wrenching Debbie's hand off the child and glaring heatedly down at her. Another second of her bullying Tamia would've been a second too long.

"She understands," I said standing between them. "Calm down. You're embarrassing her and yourself."

"What?" Debbie bucked flaring her nostrils like a bull ready to charge. "Since when do you tell me how to discipline my child? I don't give a damn about embarrassing her or *you*, because I'm damn sure not embarrassing myself. I'll talk to her however I see fit. When you get some kids of your own, then maybe we can talk. Until then, you keep your opinions and your mouth shut about mines. This is *my* child."

"I know she's *your* child. But she's also *my* niece, and I don't have to have kids to see that you're overreacting. It's a party. She's having fun with her cousin. Grabbing all on the child's arm like that is too much Debbie," I challenged with one hand symbolically shielding Tamia from her mom while she stood behind me sniffling.

"Is that right?" she asked sarcastically folding her arms and looking like an angry sweet potato in that ill-fitting orange shorts jumper with her curly wig matted down on her head. "So now all of the sudden you're soooo concerned about your niece who you never even took the time to know for most of her life? Girl pl—"

"Is everything okay?" Aunt Carrie interrupted appearing with raised brows concernedly beside us.

My dad's baby sister was in her late 50's, but managed to look 10 years younger with a shape better than Debbie's. Her honey blonde and brown hair was cut simply above her shoulders with bangs hovering just above her warm brown eyes as they darted between me and the dragon.

"Hell no," Debbie answered with her signature eye roll. "Greer feels like she knows more about how I should raise my child than I do."

"I'm sorry Mommy. Me and Crystal was just playing tag. I forgot not to run," Tamia squeaked with her bottom lip quivering, ready to ball.

Carrie and I looked kindly at her and then back to Debbie, whose expression remained unchanged. I sympathized with the little girl because I knew all too well what it was like to be on the receiving end of Debbie's venom. I didn't give a damn if Tamia was my daughter, Debbie's daughter or the daughter of Satan himself. I just wanted to protect my niece the way nobody ever bothered to protect me when I needed it.

"She's just a kid Debbie. She probably just got caught up in the excitement," I defended. "I'm not trying to tell you how to raise her. I just think that maybe you don't realize how hard you were grabbing her. I'm just trying to keep everything festive and light for Daddy's birthday. The last thing he's gonna wanna see is Tamia crying—"

"Bitch I don't need your lecture. I know why we're here," she lashed out snaking her neck as she stepped closer to my face.

"Whoa. Whoa," Aunt Carrie refereed placing both hands between us.

"I don't know what's going on right'chea, but what I *do* know, is it better stop RIGHT now," Daddy's stern voice ordered as he hoisted a sobbing Tamia into his arms.

She strangled his neck and buried her face on his shoulder fearfully.

"I'm sorry Granddaddy. I was just playing."

"Daddy! Put that girl down before you have a heart attack out here in this heat," Debbie insisted frowning with her hands akimbo.

"Child if anybody's gonna give me a heart attack it's YOU! Out'chea fussin' and arguin' over nonsense."

"Me? I'm not the one minding other people's business. You told me not to start nothing with her bougie ass today and I didn't! She came over here to me and my child, minding *MY* business with a knife in her hand like she's about to cut somebody," she ranted gesturing towards the knife I'd completely forgotten I was carrying.

Blowing out a frustrated breath, I waved my free hand dismissively.

"C'mon Debbie. Don't even try it. I have this knife to cut the cake and I never even lifted it. Why would you even say something like that? Are you trying to imply... you know what?" I paused conjuring up the tears I needed to support the act I was about to put on. "I know you what you're trying to do. For you to even insinuate for one minute that I was going to stab you. Knowing that Michael's trial is coming up..." I spoke sobbed in broken sentences as my ducts turned on the faucet full blast.

All eyes were definitely on us now and Aunt Carrie instantly pulled me in by the shoulders for a hug.

"Awww, noooo baby. Don't cry," she comforted as I looked pitifully between the faces of my father, Aunt Carrie, and the stone-faced shrew. "That's not what she meant at all."

Inside I was dancing a jig because Debbie's bullying had backfired for once. I was hamming it up for the crowd like an Academy Award winning actress. Since I became a widow, the pity party was always full of attendees, and I was certainly not above enlisting everyone present at Debbie's expense. She was way too comfortable victimizing anyone she chose to, but today, that wouldn't work.

When we were younger, she'd torment me until my hysterical cries fed that evil beast inside her. Typically, it ended with me in a wailing ball on the floor of my bedroom. Even when I kept my distance and stayed to myself, she seemed to seek me out specifically to tease, like a weak seeking bomb.

Of course, being the outside child, I always yearned for the acceptance and love of my stepmother and half-siblings; but they, especially Stephanie and Debbie, were less than willing to give it. The obvious disdain and constant ridicule from the family as a whole, transformed me into a timid and mousy girl. I was nothing like the happy and exuberant child I remembered being when I was with my mom.

Even though, the older I got, the less I actually recalled about who I was under my mom's wing. Regardless, I knew I hadn't felt useless and unwanted living with her. These Foster women had broken me down to the lowest factor from the day my little feet permanently entered their home. I was almost like Cinderella, except Stephanie wholly preferred me to be out of her sight more than in use as the family maid.

All of us kids had chores, and honestly, they were doled out to us reasonably. Punishments weren't though. I'd be locked in the hall closet for hours; stripped naked and whipped with the belt; made to stand squatted with my back to the wall until my legs locked up... whatever Stephanie decided to do.

The other kids got punished for their wrong doings too, but never to the extent that I was or with as much malice and satisfaction as she delivered my fate to me. She reveled in bringing me misery in ways that wouldn't be evident to my father when he was home. I was warned not to tattle, or I'd receive worse. I believed her.

Whenever he came back off the road, I'd bask in his love and attention for as long as I could until his next trip. I rarely dared to stand up for myself when he wasn't home to save me from the backlash. The summer I turned 13 however; my resentment of their treatment started to supersede my fear of their consequences. I was sick of Debbie's belligerent bravado, and having my father home gave me the courage to concoct an appropriate payback.

"Light, bright, almost white," Debbie sang from my bedroom doorway, flanked by 3 of her hood-rat friends. "What you in here doing? Practicing how to talk like a white girl?" she teased flipping her freshly curled locks and looking to her sidekicks to cosign with a sinister grin.

Seemingly on cue, her cronies chuckled watching my discomfort and playfully nudging each other. I maybe weighed 85 lbs soaking wet at the time, and I was still built like an ironing board since most of puberty's amenities hadn't hit me yet. Debbie outweighed me by at least 40 lbs at 18. She was taller, thicker, slicker and meaner than I ever even thought about being to anyone.

"I'm practicing my lines to try out for Desdemona in Othello," I stupidly defended as if she actually cared what I was really doing.

Smirking she snatched the paper from my hand and gave it a brief once over before balling it up and dropping it to the floor.

"I knew it would be a white girl. Why you trying to play a white girl?" she asked scrunching her nose up in objection.

"Doooon't!" I begged picking up the paper and smoothing it out. "It's the lead female in the play. I don't care what color she is. Everybody else that's trying out is black too," I reasoned.

"Too?" Debbie's friend with her hair cornrowed to the back aped as the other 2 snickered. "You ain't black."

"I'm not white either," I replied getting sassy and rolling my neck causing my long ponytail to sway. "But since y'all keep calling me white, why wouldn't I try out for a white girl part? Y'all are so racist. Anyway, this is my room. Can you please leave?" I rebutted boldly.

"Who's this youngin' talking to?" Cornrows asked Debbie with a snarl. "Deb, you better get her."

"Ooohhh... she ain't scared of you Danita," the other brown girl with braces and micro-braids mocked with a giggle leaning against the door frame.

"She's trying to play you," Reva, Debbie's short-haired, fat best friend chimed in stuffing a Snickers bite in her mouth and eyeing me from head to toe.

Out of nowhere, Debbie shoved me hard in the chest down to the carpet and towered over me as I gazed helplessly up at her trying to hold back the tears I felt forming.

"Don't get smart with my friends you little half-breed. You're lucky you even have a room, you freeloading bastard. My momma should've put her foot down and kicked you outta here a long time ago. Just because you're Daddy's favorite, that don't mean I won't beat your ass up in here. You know I'll do it too," she challenged.

I stared back at her in defiant silence but didn't make a move because I knew she meant every word. I couldn't fight my way out of a paper bag at the time which was evident the prior week when she slapped me hard enough to make my teeth rattle in my head and I did nothing. Of course, I went crying to Stephanie about it and was simply told to grow a backbone and to stop being a crybaby.

I wasn't close with my other siblings but neither of them treated me like the scum of the earth the way my step-monster and her vindictive clone did. I sucked up most rounds of humiliation like a sponge and simply retreated to the room I shared with Donna to submerge myself in books. Still, it was becoming increasingly harder to take the punishment without retaliation. By the time Debbie and her hench-women left the house, I'd already developed the plot for my revenge and made a B-line to the bathroom.

I took Debbie's rainbow-colored toothbrush from the holder, dropped my pants and sat on the toilet with a grin. Making sure the bristles were directly under the stream, I drenched it in my piss, then shook it off and dried the handle with toilet tissue. Satisfied, I placed it back in its slot, washed and dried my hands, then sought out the brand-new bottle of thick white hair conditioner from under the sink.

Debbie was obsessed with her hair. She was so proud of how healthy, shiny and thick it was; especially since it almost reached her elbows in length. It rivaled my own long curly mane, and it was the one area I believe she thought she had a leg up on me. She washed and conditioned her hair weekly like clockwork with the best affordable products from the beauty supply store down the street.

I opened the conditioner smelling the sweet coconut scent, then emptied two thirds of it into the toilet. Snatching the nearly full bottle of NAIR from the medicine cabinet, I emptied almost all of it into the gap in the conditioner bottle, put the cap back on and shook it up. Satisfied that it was mixed well, I placed the conditioner back under the sink and stuck the NAIR in the waist of my jeans.

My dad was doing yard work, Shawn moved out months earlier, Stephanie wasn't paying me any attention, and Donna was outside playing. Debbie and her friends said they were going to the mall so there was no time like the present for me to grab the Christmas money from my doll head and scurry from the house without notice.

I hurried down to the beauty supply store, tossed the NAIR bottle in the trash can and purchased a new one along with a duplicate of Debbie's new conditioner. I rushed home, put the NAIR in the medicine cabinet and hid the conditioner under my bed.

That evening, I lingered in the bathroom door watching Debbie brush her teeth before bed as she glared confusedly at my reflection in the mirror and turned around scowling at me.

"What do you want freak?" she asked snidely with the toothbrush hanging inside her mouth.

I guessed she either hadn't smelled the urine on her toothbrush or she thought it was coming from the commode, but I was more than elated to see it was being used on her dirty mouth. Her remarks went in one ear and out the other that night. I was winning.

"Nothing. I just have to use the bathroom," I told her with a devious smile.

"Don't you see me in here? You—are—so—weird. Wait your turn," she said rolling her eyes and shoving me from the threshold before slamming the door in my face.

I snickered and walked back to my room, pleased with myself and patiently awaiting the next night when I knew she'd wash her hair and I'd get my final revenge. My dad was home that night too, so I had a reason to hang in my brother Shawn's room with him, close to the bathroom. Since Shawn moved to California, my dad had taken to watching television in his room where he could control the remote instead of battling with my stepmother for it.

Somehow, I managed to keep a straight face through my excitement while Debbie walked around with the conditioner on her freshly shampooed mane for the 10 minutes the bottle directed. I sauntered in and sat on the edge of the bed making idle conversation with my daddy to make sure I'd have a front row seat when the NAIR kicked in.

Out of nowhere, Debbie darted passed the doorway into the bathroom and I heard the water running instantly on full blast.

"Mom! Mom! My head is burning! Mooooom!" Debbie screeched minutes later as Stephanie barreled up the stairs, damn near breaking her neck rushing to her daughter's aide.

"What! What!" I heard Stephanie exclaiming in a panic as Debbie babbled crying hysterically.

"It hurts! It burns!"

"Okay, Okay. Let me help. Move your hands," Stephanie told her. "What did you put in it?"

"Nothing! I was just conditioning it," she whined through sobs.

My dad and I looked at each other and I let him lead the way as we headed to view the circus in the bathroom. I wore a genuinely shocked expression when I peeped inside and saw Debbie's head all sudsied up with reddened patches on her scalp where hair used to be.

"It's all coming out Ma! Oh my God it's coming oooouuuut!" Debbie shrieked.

"I... I'm trying to help baby... I don't know," Stephanie replied dumbstruck while helping to rinse Debbie's head.

"Mooooom!" Debbie yelped with her head still in the sink, stomping in frustration. "It buuuurrrns! Wh... what's happening," she continued weeping while Stephanie picked through her scalp delicately with her fingers.

"Come with me downstairs and let's use the sprayer at the kitchen sink baby," Stephanie ordered guiding Debbie's head from under the faucet and turning it off while handing her a towel.

"Your momma's got this," My father assured me with a pat on my shoulder as he went back into Shawn's room when the announcer screamed that the Falcon's scored a touchdown.

I nodded innocently and leaned against the door frame peering at Debbie and Stephanie with my fingers entwined behind my back.

"Can I help you with anything? Do you want me to hold—" I began to offer sweetly.

"No!" Debbie screamed cutting me off with a hateful glare in her tear-filled eyes while wrapping the towel loosely around her head and racing passed me downstairs.

"Chile'… just go. Go mind your business," Stephanie commanded pushing past me, quickly following Debbie's lead downstairs.

I shrugged and strode slowly to my bedroom, delighting in the shrilled sounds of misery resonating upstairs from the kitchen. Donna was in our room watching FAIRLY ODD PARENTS on Nickelodeon, so she paid me no mind when I reached under my bed and put the conditioner into the rim of my jeans.

With Debbie and Stephanie downstairs, that was my chance to remove the evidence. I hurried back down the hall and into the bathroom, shutting the door and locking it behind me. I pulled the bottle from my waistband and emptied the same amount it appeared Debbie used into the toilet. I took the tainted bottle and hid it under my clothes to smuggle out and dispose of it later.

Flushing, I then pretended to wash my hands, and strolled calmly from the bathroom, downstairs and outside to discard it in a neighbor's trash can. Debbie cried for days and stayed locked up in her room for weeks afterwards since the damage left her with bald and breaking patches between her long locks.

Stephanie's beautician suggested Debbie shave it all off so her hair could grow back evenly, and told her to wear wigs and weaves in the interim if she needed to. From what I heard, her scalp was burned, and her hair never fully recovered from the damage, though it did grow back. All I knew was that I hadn't seen her without a weave or a wig in ages.

With the way I'd been feeling since putting Michael down though… baldy locks better watch herself with me. I was long sick of being her whipping board, and knowing that she was inflicting the same cruelty on her own child was just as infuriating. Tamia reminded me of myself as a little girl and seeing Debbie victimize her brought me right back to that place mentally. Why Will wanted to raise kids with her evil ass totally boggled my mind. I wouldn't put her in charge of a puppy, let alone a child.

Not that I'm the most kid friendly person you'd ever meet, but I usually got along with them well. Unfortunately, I never developed a relationship with Tamia at all before this summer. Not that Debbie would've allowed it even if I had wanted to. After Michael and I got married, I tried to spend as little time as possible in Stephanie and Debbie's presence since I always felt stunted around them and they despised me anyway.

Because Debbie lived so close to the house, she'd always spent a lot of time over here with Stephanie, cackling and doing whatever mean girls do. Once she became a mother though, from what I know, Tamia was left to the attentions of Stephanie and my dad while Debbie did God only knows what with her free time and Will was working. She's the "stay at home mom" who rarely stays at home. At least not with the kids.

Before she had Willa 7 months ago, Tamia was usually scooted off to her paternal or maternal grandparents when she wasn't in school. This time around, since Willa had some respiratory issues and other baby illnesses in succession, Debbie was forced to care for her own child most of the time. Anybody with eyes could tell she'd rather be doing anything but mothering though!

If you ask me, she fakes almost everything good about herself because she's really a self-absorbed, reformed drug addicted tyrant. Oh yeah! In her early 20's she was wild as hell. Stephanie was always on her back about staying out until the wee hours in the morning, stealing money from her purse and coming home drunk or high a lot. Oh yeah. And when I say high, I'm not just including weed either.

The last straw for my dad and Stephanie was the night they were called to the hospital because she overdosed on cocaine. I was only about 16 then so I wasn't given all of the details, but I know she was facing criminal charges and it caused the miscarriage of a child she didn't even know she was carrying. Whatever they worked out, she never did any time but they did pay for her to stay in rehab for 3 months.

When Debbie got out, Stephanie was on her ass about attending church every Sunday more than ever before. As long as we lived under Stephanie's roof, everybody but my dad had to attend services, but Debbie had been dodging that mandate previously. Not long after, she met Will on a church sponsored trip to Florida and obviously tricked him into believing she was a good God-fearing woman for the year they dated before he proposed. She's been faking it, very poorly I might add, ever since.

I'm sure that on some level Will sees that she's not at all the woman he thought he was marrying, but I don't think he believes in divorce and he seems to genuinely love her dirty draws. When she says jump. He gets a trampoline and tests the wind factor. Since Mommy Dearest finally started dropping them children he was begging for, he was happier than a midget with a growth spirt. Even worse, there's been talk that she might be preggo again.

The mere thought of Debbie possibly raising a clan of mean girls' like her and Stephanie made my stomach hurt.

"I'm sorry. I'm sorry. I know this is Daddy's birthday and I promised myself that I wouldn't cry for once since Michael… I just wanted everybody to have a good time. She's just a little girl. I didn't mean for it to get to this," I whimpered unleashing my tears. "I'm sorry Daddy. Just give me a minute," I said breaking free of Aunt Shelia's grasp to wipe my eyes as his softened ones harden toward Debbie.

"Are you serious right now? Grow up. Now you wanna be the victim when you're the one who—" Debbie started after me as I looked on glumly.

"Just shut up Deborah!" Daddy yelled as Luther Vandross' old school hit "Stop To Love" began playing. "Are you too fool to see when you're talkin' too damn much? You got my grandbaby and Greer cryin' over the nasty, nasty things that come out of yo' mouth and you *still* talkin'. Be quiet!"

It took everything in my power to suppress my smile and refrain from blurting out, "*Oooooh*! You in trouble!" like the little sister Dee from that old sitcom WHAT'S HAPPENING. The faces in the peanut gallery looked both bewildered and concerned, but the most gratifying expression of all was Debbie's. She was on the verge of crying too.

"It's okay Daddy. She doesn't care. She never cared about me," I muttered dejectedly palming my mouth and trotting into the house dramatically.

Sometimes playing the victim was fun.

5

Debbie

"Im sick of that gal," Aunt Gretta, who I called A.G., told me between puffs of her cigarette in her raspy Alabama slow drawl. "Greer ain't nothin' but the same little piss ant she was as a little girl, all grow'd up. I'm surprised she even came since she always thanks she's too good to hang with us. I guess since she ain't got no husband no mo' she's wantin' to be around family."

"I know right? She ain't no family of mine. Nobody needs her ass comin' around now," I agreed securing the bottle in Willa's suckling mouth as she dozed off in my arms.

I was still pissed that Will refused to give me the keys to the car after Daddy chastised me in front of everybody like a damn child. I had a good mind to walk home and leave him and these damn kids here to fend for themselves, but I changed my mind since Greer's wimpy ass left right after we cut the cake. The day I let that pale-faced, stuck up attention whore run me out of my mother's house, will be the day they find my dead body on the steps. She's lucky my momma wasn't alive to set her straight.

"You hear me child?" A.G. asked tapping the chair I sat in beside her.

"No. I'm sorry. What you say?"

"I said, your husband is trying to get your attention. But he's on his way over here now so..."

Just like she said, Will was approaching with a slice of red velvet birthday cake on a plate and a big goofy grin.

"Here baby. Since you're out here being all anti-social while everybody's inside watching Pop open his gifts, I thought you might at least want some ca—"

I swatted the plate on the floor as soon as he tried handing it to me and stared at him defiantly. Did I want a piece of cake? Nah Nigga I wanted you to come up off that grill and defend your wife! The mother of your children who is raising your kids that you wanted! Is what I was thinking, but didn't say.

"C'mon now Deb," he whined throwing his hands up before scooping the broken cake from the grass back on the plate and throwing it away.

You're damn right I was being anti-social. Why would I go in there and fake like I wasn't mad when I was while he shucked and jived with my father? Not today when I was already sleep deprived from being up at all hours of the night because Willa had a terrible diaper rash. I held my tongue when Daddy ripped me a new one earlier; but I wasn't gonna stand for any more of anybody else's BS today.

A.G. chose to sit out here with me like the loyal G she is since she likes to chain smoke and gossip about folks anyways. With my mom gone, A.G. was the closest thing I had left to a mother and she'd always had my back since I could remember, so this time was no different. She helped me to put some things into perspective and if it wasn't for her talking me down, I absolutely would've snatched Daddy's car keys and drove myself home after Will declined.

"Just go on back in the house before I snap out. I don't even wanna look at your face right now."

We stared at each other in a stalemate with only silence and Willa's sucking sounds between us before he started glancing around like a dog hearing a whistle.

"Awww Baby do you hear that? That's our song. How can you be mad while our song is on?" he asked two-stepping in front of my chair with that goofy smile again.

"He makes me happy, so veeeery happpyyyyy

I don't know how to beeee!

It's been a long tiiiiime since I had someone who loves me
I owe my thanks to Thee
I knooow it could not happen wiiith-out your love
Oo Oo Oo. Wiiithout your looove..."

He sang along with Alicia Myers as her voice came through the speaker singing her old school song "I Want To Thank You". The volume was turned down when everyone went inside, but you could still hear it if you listened close. My eyelids hovered low and I pursed my lips as A.G. smacked her lips and shook her head at his foolishness.

"You really is clueless ain't ya," she stated more than asked Will before blowing smoke out the side of her mouth. "You best leave this chile' 'lone til she calls if you know what's good for ya."

I smirked. A.G.'s tongue, much like my mother's and my own, was as sharp as always and she would cut you long and deep. Granted, she was nothing to look at, but I loved her to death. My brother said she looked like Ceasar from Planet Of The Apes when he saw her today and nearly made me choke on my juice laughing. She wore her hair in a short natural, had deeply etched age lines in her dark brown face and flat, yet wide features surrounded her sunken eyes.

Luckily, my mother shared very few physical traits with her besides their complexions and; therefore, my mother's good looks mixed with my father's, blessed all of us Foster children with mirror worthy faces. In spite of her 275 lb frame and unappealing facial features, A.G. was never lonely unless she wanted to be. In fact, she was on her fourth husband, Ernest, right now.

If he wasn't on the road driving trucks like my dad used to do, he probably would've been right here rubbing her calloused feet and stealing kisses from her hairy lipped mouth like she was Angela Bassett, per his usual M.O. I didn't envy her looks, but I definitely envied her ability to trade up each time she married to a man that wanted to give her the world.

"Now Gretta, you stay out of this," Will addressed her with one hand.

"Don't tell my aunt what to do. You were quiet as a mouse when you should've been defending me earlier, so don't get a backbone now," I spat re-positioning Willa's now sleeping body so that her head was now snuggled between the crook of my neck as I put her bottle on the table beside me.

"I was on the grill Deb. I didn't even know what was going on till after he'd already said his peace. Plus, this is his house. I wasn't gonna push up on your father at his house, on his birthday, talking crazy when I didn't even know what happened. One minute I'm cooking, the next minute you were in my face demanding the keys and trying to leave me and the kids stranded over here out the blue."

"Yeah whatever. You always claim you didn't know what was happening when it comes time for you to stick up for me, but you're always on the ready for everybody else. I told you Greer was trying to tell me how to discipline Tamia and Daddy took her side.

God damn it. What else did you need to know? I'm your wife. I'm the one who suffered through labor, and the one raising these kids while you're working. You should've automatically had my back," I said hostilely.

A.G. nodded, "Umm hmmm. She's right."

Will looked like he wanted to cuss both of us out, but I knew he wouldn't. Nah, my bible toting hubby didn't cuss at all and he hated when I did; which is why I always did it just to get under his skin when we argued. He may have been in control of providing financially for me and the kids, but he wasn't in control of me or my mouth. Never that. My mother made the mistake of marrying a man who was constantly telling her how to talk, act and dress and he still brought home a baby with another woman. Not this gal.

"Alright Debbie. I'm sorry I didn't see what happened and come over there to stop it, okay? Now can you stop being, petty and childish, and stop cussing around my daughter? You're blowing this whole thing out of proportion. She just wanted you to stop grabbing on Tamia like that in front of everybody."

I shot up from my chair causing him to take a few steps back. Surprisingly, Willa didn't even stir.

"Are you fucking serious? Are you standing here taking her side after you just said you didn't know what happened? Your daughter was running around here like a chicken with her head cut off and I put a stop to it after I already told her to stop it before. Would you rather I let you discipline the kids from now on? Or better yet, maybe you want Greer to throw some more suggestions in on how I need to raise my own child. Is that what you want?"

"No. Babe, that's not what I'm saying. I'm sure she didn't mean any harm. She was probably just trying to keep everything upbeat for your father's birthday. Last year this time you were just getting over the loss of your mother, Pop had cancer and Greer's husband was brutally murdered. Now, we've got a new baby girl, Pop's cancer is in remission and Greer's getting back with the family—."

"She's not back with the family. She was never a real part of our family and nobody cares if she's here or not but Daddy. Greer's just one of my father's mistakes that the rest of us had to accept because her mother died," I disputed while A.G. nodded and grunted her agreeance, further charging the battery in my back.

"She don't care about me, you, Tamia, Willa or anybody else but Daddy. She was just fine acting like she was too good for us before her cheating husband got killed and left her all by her stuck-up self. Now you think I'm gonna let her tell me how to raise my own child when she ain't raised nair a baby and don't barely even know Tamia?" I shrieked.

"Look honey, calm down. All I'm saying is that you should count your blessings and thank God for having this opportunity to be with family instead of letting little disagreements like this throw you off keel. Now you know what Pastor Henly said; you gotta stop flying off the handle like this. Your blood pressure has been way too high and you're stressing yourself out way too much. Now God brought Greer back into your life for a reason and your father's happy.

Y'all are adults now Debbie. It's time to stop blaming the child for the sins of the parents. I've never seen her say or do anything disrespectful to you. I think you just dislike her so much that you can't see the forest for the trees. With all the losses and near losses this family has gone through, I think this should be a lesson in humility, and this is just as good a time as any for family to come together.

You're so angry right now I can literally see it coming off you. You gotta let this stuff go Baby. It's unhealthy and Un-Christian," he cautioned like some kind of Sunday school teacher reaching for my hand as I snatched away.

I bit my bottom lip and shook my head in frustration trying to keep myself from telling him that both he and Pastor Henly could kiss the inside of my Un-Christian ass. When we first got together, I was happy to have found a God-fearing man that made me want to live my life right. Over the last few years though, both he and his holier than thou ways were getting on my nerves. Marriage counseling at our church with Pastor Henly wasn't doing a damn thing for us. All the Thursday night sessions we spent pouring our feelings out were starting to become little more than Will's way to tattle on everything I said and did.

Things were already pretty crappy with us before my mother died and if not for the night, I let him get some on our anniversary, the only way Willa would've been created would've been via Immaculate Conception. I was sick of being the only one in the house doing for the kids and his bible thumping at me anytime I wanted or did something he disagreed with.

I thought he might lighten up once the baby was born but he just got more fanatical about what I was teaching the kids and following the way of the word like some kind of Jesus freak. And umm... meanwhile he wants to talk about my Un-Christian like behavior, he needed to be confessing to Pastor how he's been beating off to porn in the middle of the night when he thinks I'm asleep instead of coveting his wife.

I hadn't felt the urge to do more than drink in years, but lately, I found myself wondering whether a taste of some white might make life a little more bearable. I'm not a drug addict or anything, but I definitely used to party hard back in my younger days. Who could blame me? My brother took the first thing smoking to Cali when he graduated and went to work for his friend's father building movie sets and left me alone to deal with the family bullshit.

My mother was working me like a slave in her stupid flower shop and whenever Daddy wasn't on the road, he was here on my back about everything I did while praising the air Greer breathed. I got tired of vying for his attention and trying to get out from under my mother's thumb, so one day I just said, "Fuck it" and decided to do what I wanted to do.

Reva's brother Revar was in love with me and he was heavy into dealing everything from weed to heroine back then, so he didn't mind letting us get a hit of coke or a few tokes of whatever he had in his personal stash.

Unfortunately, I partied a little too hard a couple of times and ended up in rehab the last time when the police got called. I actually scared myself when I OD'd and woke up in the hospital with IV's in my arm, police charges pending and my parents making threats. I ain't cut out for jail, and the fact that I almost met my maker at 21-years old made me wanna straighten up my act.

Of course, to my mother, that meant I needed to spend more time in church, and after rehab, I had no choice but to attend regularly if I wanted to continue to live under her roof. Being that I didn't have any skills to do anything but work in her flower shop and I didn't have anywhere else to go, I did as I was told and decided I'd marry the first Nigga that could take care of me.

A couple of years later, I found Will, Greer got into that bougie black bitch college in the AUC and started creating a life totally separate from the rest of the family's. Since her husband got killed, Will was under the impression that she was some kind of damsel in distress, and that we all needed to embrace her back into the fold.

Puuuuleeeaaase! Nobody needs her input in our family business, and I don't need her lurking around my husband. My man is real Christian, but all men can be tempted, and I always suspected she had the same whore gene her mother used to lure my father between her legs. My mother taught me to never leave a woman who isn't 20-years older than you are or in a wheelchair around your man alone unless you wanna risk being replaced... and I don't. I don't put anything passed her fake acting ass. She can pretend to be sweet as pie all she wants to, but I ain't buying it and I don't feed into it either.

From the day Daddy brought the little half-breed home we were expected to accept her lovingly just because she was our sister by way of a technicality and her mom was dead. Pshh! So what! My brother and I listened with our backs pressed to the wall from upstairs the night Daddy gave my mother the ultimatum. Either accept the little girl clinging to his leg or he was gonna leave all of us.

We couldn't believe what we were hearing. My baby sister Donna wasn't even 1 yet, Shawn was 14 and I was only 10-years old. How was he gonna choose Greer over all of us? His own flesh and blood! I decided right then that I was never going to accept her no matter where she rested her head. She wasn't no better than me and I was gonna let her know it every chance I got.

The next morning my parents introduced her to us with fake smiles and my dad holding Greer in his arms like a trophy. My mother looked broken, Greer looked nervous, my brother looked pissed and I was looking like, 'That bitch is too big to be picked up!' Instantly, I was demoted from being Daddy's little princess to playing second fiddle to the weird little mute who didn't speak to anybody but my father for the first week she lived with us.

They bought an extra bed and rearranged Donna's room so that they could share while Shawn and I kept our own separate ones. The first day my dad left to go back on the road it was obvious my mother was pained to have to take care of the other woman's child. In the beginning she was depressed, kept going into her bedroom and crying with the door closed. Her moods swung every which way at the drop of a hat. A.G. looked out for us many a day when Mommy was too distraught to do it herself. The strong black mother I knew my mother to be had transformed into the weakest family link.

Over the years, she exchanged depression for the traits of an angry, dejected and insecure woman. She questioned and nagged my father about everything, and it always seemed like they were arguing about something. I never blamed her for being suspicious though because he'd already proven he couldn't be trusted when he brought the evidence of his dick slip home. Hell, she just didn't want another one.

Even when Daddy was home, he spent most of his time doting on his pale-faced favorite or entertaining Donna while the rest of us got whatever attention scraps were left. Shawn didn't care as much, while I cared a lot. I was a Daddy's girl before Greer came along and turned me into the invisible daughter who only got attention when I was teasing Greer.

I started hating her more and more as time went by and I noticed people constantly complimenting her green eyes or long curly hair. I can admit that I was jealous. I already felt like I was in constant competition with her for my father's affections, and people wanting to know more about the little girl I felt was taking my place conjured an instant bitterness in the pit of my stomach.

I started satisfying the kids in the neighborhood and the one's at school's curiosities by making up stories about her sadity, narcissistic and crazy behaviors. Because she was so quiet, it was easy to keep the fibs and assumptions about her thriving. She was already an outcast, so she typically kept to herself and consequently, nobody ever bothered to ask her. She was the perfect victim for my lies, and I lied a lot!

Once Greer married Michael's job-hopping ass, she was virtually a ghost around here. I figured her eggs were probably defective since she never bore any grandkids for my father to spoil locally. Knowing how much he always talked about it, I know she definitely would've given my Daddy one if she could've.

I thought once I gave him a grand baby, he'd finally start giving me the adoration I craved since his precious white meat hadn't done it and Shawn's kids were too far for him to see them regularly. That didn't work. Daddy adores Tamia, and now Willa too; but he still acts like I'm a pesky gnat who hasn't lived up to his expectations. He praises Greer's every accomplishment like she's working at the White House or something.

See, this is the BS that gets under my skin about him. I practically waited on my daddy hand and foot while he was going through his cancer treatments, while taking care of my own child and being pregnant. You'd think that would earn me some loyalty from him right? But noooo, not when it comes to his precious Greer.

He'd chew me out for her as soon as look at me. Then! Then! My husband didn't even bother to come to my rescue when the mother of his children was being attacked! Like what type of sucka shit is that?

Being a stay-at-home mother is no cake walk either, especially since Mommy passed away and I have to drive all the way to Douglasville to drop the kids off at Will's parents when they're not with Daddy. Damn, I never even wanted any kids but I do a hell of a job dealing with Tamia's whiny, hardheaded ass if you ask me.

Then with Willa and all the ailments I've had to put up with from her... she's had everything from Colic to constipation to ear infections. I'm exhausted most of the time to the point where I need a drink just to get myself through the day. Where's the sympathy for what I go through? Huh? The only reason Will cares about my stress level is because it might get me to the point where I won't be around to take care of his rug rats.

After Michael was killed and his sidepiece got arrested for it, Will was quick to hop on his soap box alongside my father talking about all the support we needed to be showing Greer and how we needed to come together. In their dreams. It was too bad Michael was dead but it's not my fault she married a cheater. I knew for a fact that if I ever found out that my Will was cheating, he'd be laying in a plot right beside him.

Funny thing is... I never did find out what Greer was doing in the shed that morning, and I wasn't even sure that was actually why she had Daddy's keys. I know how serious murder cases are, so I kept my mouth shut about that little incident when the police came around verifying her whereabouts at the time. Still, she'd definitely been a lot different since that day.

I'm not stupid, I realize seeing your husband's murdered body might change a person; but still. She was suspiciously different to me. I just couldn't put my finger on it. I'm not saying the police were wrong about what happened to Michael, but Greer had this underlying sneakiness about her that made me think she knew more than she was letting on.

Besides, whenever we clashed now, she wasn't backing down as much as she used to. Even when she did, she kept this weird expression on her face like she really wanted to scratch my eyes out.

You know what? Fuck her and fuck my daddy! If she's so great, let her take care of everything for him. If she's sooo much better than me, let's see how much better than me she is at making sure everything is running smoothly with my mother gone. I'm not kidding either. I'm not gonna handle the flower shop, Daddy's finances, picking up his medications, or any of that crap. Hell, I may not even let him see Tamia if I don't feel like it.

"Take your daughter," I told Will interrupting whatever lecture he was still giving me and handing him his sleeping daughter.

He reluctantly took her as I slid my hands into his pants pockets and retrieved the car keys.

"I'll call you later A.G." I told her storming off through the yard towards the front of the house.

I was more than a baby making wayward daughter and these Negroes were gonna learn today!

6

Greer

Kendrick sucked ravenously on my neck while drilling all 10 inches of his manhood inside my quivering walls. My lids fluttered and an orgasm built as I whimpered long overdue pleasures to the gods. Gripping the edge of the ottoman I was sprawled over, I concentrated on the heat between us, tuning out the thumping on the ceiling from the tenant above.

I'd had a brief meeting with Kita in 2B when I arrived. She was headed from her second-floor apartment down to the basement laundry room just beside Kendrick's unit with a green basket full of clothes and a scowl.

I greeted her politely, but aside from sizing me up and chewing her gum extra hard, she didn't open her mouth to speak. She was an unimpressive looking light skin woman with micro-braids that robbed her of her edges and brought attention to the gold bull ring in her nose. Her beady gray contact wearing eyes glared at me as the thin slits she used for lips remained closed. I wondered if she was also the product of an interracial couple, but assumed I'd never find out since she was too rude to even speak.

"*Heeeey* Ken," she'd said flirtatiously finding her voice and increasing the sway in her hips when he opened the door for me as she passed.

I don't know what it was about me that made some women feel like they could blatantly disrespect me with no regard, but it was something I'd long tired of and wasn't planning on putting up with for much longer.

"Hey Kita," he answered curtly hugging me at the door.

"What's up with you not answering your phone anymore?" she asked pausing at the top of the stairs to the laundry room and resting all of her weight on one leg. "Your phone working for that bitch though huh?"

"We've already been down this road Kita. This is *exactly* the type of mess I was talking to you about. Just go'head about your business and stop embarrassing yourself," he answered ushering me into his place.

I pretended to be unaffected by her name calling though I didn't appreciate her unprovoked hostility at all. I'd come to see Kendrick on a special mission, and no disgruntled THOT was going to deter me from it.

"Embarrass me?" I heard her reply with much attitude as I stood beside him with a hand on my hip. "Look Ken, don't get cute in front of your company before I blo—" she continued as he shut the door on her conversation, leaving her dejectedly on the other side.

"Sorry about that," he apologized eyeing my outfit. "Damn. You look sexy."

I'd strategically adjusted the straps on my dress to hike my breasts up and reveal more cleavage than I had at Daddy's barbecue. I also primped my hair to give my curls more volume and reapplied my make-up in the car to make me look more seductive. Judging from the grin on his face and the visible bulge, I did good.

He was wearing nothing but flimsy boxers, allowing his chiseled chest to get the recognition from my eyes it deserved. A game he must've been playing on X-Box was paused on the 55" that hung over the fireplace in his living room.

"Hmph. Thank you," I huffed feigning an attitude. "Maybe this was a bad time to drop by. I don't wanna cause any issues with you and your girlfriend."

"Baby, I'm single as a dollar bill. I took her out a few times and laid the pipe down on her, but that, does not a girlfriend make. Enough about her childish ass. I want to focus on *your* ass," he said licking his lips. "And it's looking nice in that dress."

I already planned to give up the cookies to Kendrick before I arrived, but thanks to Kita's brazen mouth, I made sure she got a play by play of it. After nearly an hour of him screwing my brains out, she'd begun banging on her floor, which only gave me added incentive.

"Ooooh! Oh yes. Make me cum," I coached bucking my ass into his thrusting hips.

He grasped my curly locks and jerked my head back aggressively, growling his demands. "Tell me how much you want this dick."

"I... I want it bad. I want it soooo bad," I answered with bated breaths.

"Say it. Say you want this fucking dick," he ordered.

"I want that fucking dick!" I cried out kegeling his manhood.

I frequently had vulgar thoughts, but I rarely voiced them. Cuss words like "shit", "bitch", and "fuck" were reserved for my mental vocabulary, but in conversation, I refrained from using them. I was finding it liberating to speak them aloud this time though. Especially in the midst of steamy sex.

Kendrick was riding me like a wave as I glanced back at his coffee brown body and licked my lips lustfully. Sweat glistened from the ripples in his abs while his muscular arms controlled my movements like he owned the remote. Releasing my mane, he turned my face and took my mouth into his, still driving himself into my gyrating hips and cupping one of my exposed breasts.

I was in a state of euphoria, and when his lips traveled to my neck again, suctioning my flesh between them, my wanton mouth hung open like a guppy. Lord knows my mind, body and soul needed this, and baby boy was giving me more than I expected. More than Michael or anyone before him had ever given me.

"Ummmm... that's right baby. Give it to Daddy," he goaded while my punani responded with multiple tremors and the sound of him pumping in and out of my wetness echoed. "Ummmmm... you hear that pretty pussy sucking on my dick? I gotta taste it one more time."

Abruptly, he pulled out of me and hunched down, planting his face between my ass cheeks and his tongue inside my soaked box. I squirmed and moaned while he worked it and 2 fingers in and out of my walls, making lapping sounds and reveling in my responses.

Michael wasn't much of a talker during sex. Even when he was with his sidepiece, so Kendrick's vulgar confessions of lust both surprised and turned me on. It made me feel desired in a way I hadn't experienced before and that, made me want to reciprocate his fervor.

"You taste so sweet," he affirmed sucking my bud from behind before French kissing the slit of my opening ferociously.

"Kendrick... please... I... I can't take it. I'm about to cum... Ken... Kendrick... I'm about to *cuuuuuum...*" I shrieked at the top of my lungs, digging my nails into the ottoman's cushion just as my orgasm peaked and I let out a vulgar squeal of approval. "*Fuuuuuuck!*" I bellowed as my essence flowed into his mouth.

The banging on the ceiling increased and the smile on my face followed suit. This man had me shaking and purring like a virgin again, and the pent-up energy I'd tried to release with kickboxing lessons was finally being exorcised through my vagina. Weeks of secretly flirting during and after work had finally amounted to this; and I was not disappointed.

Without warning, he stood and plummeted his erection back inside my awaiting cave, causing me to howl out another plea for more, "*What are you trying to do to me... Yes... take it.*"

"See what you've been missing? This is mine now," he declared in my ear while the hater upstairs pounded her floor the way he was pounding my pussy.

My sex creamed all over his manhood again, just as a few small chips of paint from the ceiling rained down on us. Kendrick paused briefly and we both glanced up.

"What the fuck?" he uttered perplexed as we chuckled in unison. "That chick is crazy."

I stifled another giggle with my hand and the faint sound of her yelling for us to 'Shut the fuck up already' penetrated the walls.

"She's gonna put a hole in the floor," I told him.

He shook his head with doubt and a smirk, slapping my ass, clenching my throat, and yanking me in for another kiss. The taste of my own juices on his tongue increased my arousal, causing me to let out a low moan. He entwined his fingers in my hair, forcing my back to arch further as he plunged deeper between my folds.

Several thrusts later, Kendrick finally exploded inside the condom with a loud grunt. My entire body shuddered with gratification and I slumped forward, resting my face on the plush cushion with my arms outstretched and my body exhausted. I pulled my mussed hair to one side and smiled at the thought of doing this with him again.

His kisses on my shoulder blades and back sent another wave of tremors through me as he slowly withdrew himself. His handsome face was damp with perspiration and he fell to the carpet with a sigh, rolling over onto his back. I missed this feeling of bliss after sharing myself with a man; but it was devoid of the love I missed more.

My vagina hadn't been stimulated by anything other than a battery-operated boyfriend for more than 14 months so this, was like heaven on earth for my body. Despite the prior location of Kendrick's dick, shamefully, he wasn't even in the running as a replacement husband.

At 5'6" and 22-years old, the Usher Raymond look alike who worked in medical records at Franklin Family Practice, was too short, too young and too financially unstable to fill that role. The dilapidated apartment we were currently screwing in was evidence of his short pockets, and I didn't want to become a sugar momma to the office eye candy. This past year hadn't been a cake walk for me and I wasn't about to kick up dust in any aspect of my life when it was just beginning to settle.

Kendrick's winning smile and penchant for licking his lips had a way of turning on the faucet between women's legs. The young single girls in the front office flirted with him non-stop, and a few married trollops on staff shamelessly threw themselves at him too.

I never indulged in their gossip and I kept every interaction within eyesight of another person, professional. I did the same with Kendrick until a few weeks ago when curiosity and loneliness superseded my moral compass. His work was mediocre, and he was consistently tardy, so that gave me cause to have him in my office for warnings and reprimands often.

Behind closed doors, I wasn't quite so professional. Michael had been dead long enough for me to be able to date whomever I wanted, if I wanted to. But I didn't want to. I wasn't ready to invest in any other man just yet and I didn't want any fresh rumors floating around at work since my private life had already been subjected to public scrutiny for over a year.

My intentions with Kendrick were only going to be of a carnal nature, so there was no need for anyone but the 2 of us to know about it. Those prudish ways Stephanie's sex shaming had nurtured all of these years were about to be dashed out permanently. All her teachings had gotten me was a husband whose sex life was more entertaining with his side chick than with his wife. I'd had nothing but time to replay the lurid scenes I witnessed on the clock's recordings in my mind over... and over... and over... again.

My ego was crushed watching the 2 of them going at it like wild rabbits in the same bed he basically snooze-stroked me in when we made love. The joke was really on me when I discovered that my sexy lingerie, reverse cowgirl positions and occasional head weren't keeping Michael from straying. Marlene talked, fucked and sucked like a porn star from what I had seen, and I was going to too before I found my next husband.

No one but my B.O.B. was privy to the many nights I'd fantasized about Kendrick's lips all over my body while I worked my clit in the privacy of my bedroom. My friend Angie, a Nurse Practitioner at FFP had her little suspicions, but I played ignorant to her accusations since technically, nothing had been going on with me and Kendrick other than talking.

I hadn't even mentioned his name to Shan and if I was going to tell anybody, it would've been her. We still spoke periodically, but our conversations were shorter and less detailed than they had been.

She still wasn't acclimated to the move, and her time was often compressed into a window of schedules. Her job as an Actuary at an insurance firm paid more than her job in Atlanta had, but she hated the atmosphere.

Of course, she wasn't the only one to blame for our downgraded communication. I hadn't exactly been reaching out as often either. Playing the grief-stricken widow was an exhausting role and it drove me to become even more introverted than I already was.

The fear of slipping up and incriminating myself somehow plagued me, so I used much of my alone time to soul search and plan my future. My routine had intentionally become predictable; in case I was being monitored by anyone who still remained suspicious of me.

I was either at work or at home when I wasn't at my father's, and on those rare occasions that I went out with friends, I came in early. Especially since my mother in-law was still keeping tabs on my whereabouts.

There were still times when I missed my husband and genuinely wept because he was no longer on this earth. But the truth was, the man Michael was on the day he died, wasn't the same man he was when I married him. I didn't actually regret losing *him*. I regretted losing the man I thought I married.

I never imagined it would take this long for the wheels of justice to turn; however, so the 6 or 7 months I thought would be necessary to invest 100% in my role as the mourning wife had runneth over way longer. Who could blame me for finally seeking a little satisfaction of the flesh after so long?

Yawning, I glanced around at Kendrick's apartment and wondered how much of his check went toward paying to occupy it. It was a drab studio style floor plan where you could see into every room from the living room. It reminded me of my sister Donna's first apartment. Small, quaint and damn near empty. Kendrick lived in a decent enough area for somebody making under 30-thousand dollars a year, so I guess it served its purpose for a bachelor with no kids.

That flat screen was probably the most expensive thing in the apartment. Fruit crates took the place of end tables beside his couch and a large floor lamp stood in the corner. A few cheap print pictures hung on the walls leading down a short hallway to a single bathroom and bedroom where I'd spied an unmade bed, beer bottles and a pile of clothes on the floor earlier. Ugh. If I haven't mentioned it previously, I'm a bit of a germaphobe. Thank God he hadn't tried to take me back there to have sex.

I was simply torturing myself by analyzing the small kitchen adjacent the living room where I could easily see the sink stacked with dirty dishes at the moment. Bread and other sandwich stuff rested on the counter by a microwave, and beer bottle necks protruded from the overflowing kitchen garbage can by the front door, making me wonder if he'd had a party or just drank a lot.

He'd mentioned that he was some sort of party promoter on the side before, so I guessed he socialized too much to take time to clean up his mess. The other time I came by, he knew I was on my way hours in advance. This time, he'd only had 30-minutes notice. My skin was beginning to itch just thinking about what might be crawling among the mess in his kitchen or even worse, in his living room. I shook it from my thoughts and refocused.

"I know Keisha hates us," I stated. Intentionally mispronouncing the chick in 2B's name.

He smiled. "Kita. She'll be alright. That girl is obsessed. Sitting up there listening to us like a perv," he said coolly brushing his hand against my nude thigh. "I know the landlord better not be trying to charge me for no ceiling damage or I'm gonna report her ass," he laughed.

"If I was in her position, I'd probably be jealous too," I said sheepishly. "Had I known you were gonna put it down like *this*... I would've given in sooner."

Seductively he retorted, "I wish you would've. I understand that it's complicated, with you being my boss and just getting over losing your husband, but I'm here for you," he said gazing into my eyes.

"Thank you," I said gently touching his arm, hoping he was ending conversation on that topic there.

"I know you must be happy they're finally about to put that bitch away so you can put it all behind you," he said like he pitied me. I pitied his ignorance.

If he was trying to dry up my snatch like the Mojave Desert, he was doing an excellent job of it. The last thing I wanted to think about after my first dick induced orgasm in over a year was the embarrassing coverage of my life in the news and the woman my husband was cheating with.

Since when was he interested in talking to me about anything other than himself, sex, or himself again? Now that the well was dry, I glanced at my wristwatch and noticed the time.

"I gotta go," I said jerking up like I'd been tased, instantly grabbing my dress from the floor.

I know Kendrick had me ready to pledge allegiance to his dick earlier, but I hadn't seen my friend since Michael's funeral, and I was excited to see her.

"Damn, what did I say? I'm sorry I--" he apologized propping himself back on his elbows.

"No. No. I just. I just realized what time it was. I gotta go pick up my friend from the airport."

"For real or are you just trying to get away from me? You mad?"

I shook my head as I slid my dress over it and my naked vagina reminded me that my panties were still at large.

"I'm not mad. I really *do* have to pick up my friend from the airport in about 2 hours. I have some errands to run first too. I'm not mad. How could I be mad after how good you just made me feel? You're lucky I'm leaving at all. You have no idea how much I *reeeeally* needed that," I crooned sweetly, not wanting to seem as agitated as I actually was by his banter.

"Actually, I *reeeeally* think I do have an idea," he mocked me smiling, standing to his feet. "You be at work looking all uptight with your butt cheeks clinched together like you been holding in your farts all day. Or at least you were before you started talking to *me*."

I burst out laughing and reached for a pillow from his couch, bouncing it off his head.

"I do *not*," I protested.

"You do. It's cute though. Sexy even. I love a woman in charge. You walk around all... official. Talkin' bout, 'Kendrick, did you file those charts yet? Kendrick what time did you clock in? Kendrick, I'm going to need to see you in my office.' That's my favorite one by the way.

"You calling me in your office, with those sexy legs crossed, giving me just enough of a view up your skirt to make me wanna eat that pretty pumpum under the desk while you give me orders," he said stepping into my face, gazing mischievously at me. "Now that I've actually had a taste, next time you're gonna have to let me do that for real."

I blushed and bowed my head in embarrassment. Happily drinking in his raunchy compliments and leaking out their effect between my legs.

"You're sooo nasty," I chuckled cupping my mouth.

"I *am*. Are you blushing?" he peeked underneath me, lifting my chin with his finger. "You know what? In getting to know you this past few weeks, you're nothing like I pictured you to be. Especially in bed. You're not half as controlling as most older women are. Even at work you're more into following the rules than you are about controlling how we do it.

You're a bedroom submissive."

"A submissive?" I balked still searching for the underwear he charmed me out of. "Do you see my panties?"

"Yeah. You're all about doing what you're told to do. Submissive. You like to be guided. Controlled," he replied bending down and coming up twirling my lace thongs around his index finger.

"You're psychoanalyzing me now?" I questioned snatching them mid-twirl from his digit.

"No. Just making an observation. I guess having to manage everything and everybody at work all the time can get exhausting, so when you're fucking, you don't want to have to be in control too. 'Cause, you are a little uptight about that time clock. I mean, what's a few minutes?"

I pursed my lips and cocked my head.

"A few minutes over a long time adds up. Plus, I manage the office. I don't own the practice. You know the doctors notice who is and isn't on time *too*. If you know you're supposed to be at work every day by 8:00am, and you live 30-minutes away, you should know, after a year and a half, what time you need to leave to accomplish that.

You and Nicky seem to be the only ones that can't get that concept right. Like, what's the problem? Do you need me to show you how to use an alarm clock?"

He threw his head back in laughter as I slid my sandals back on.

"Nah. C'mon. I'm not late that much," he quipped slapping me on my butt before rolling the condom from his penis and tossing it in a small trashcan beside the door. "I can't speak for her, but I do try. I just don't make it sometimes."

My eyes followed the rubber's demise into the basket and noticed another condom already at the otherwise bare bottom. My antennas and my eyebrows went up at the same time wondering when and *who* the last dick rider was. I hoped it wasn't that troll Kita, or maybe it was Nicky.

The attitudinal medical assistant whose work was good, but whose disposition with me always seemed unnecessarily rude, irritated me. Nicky kept it professionally curt, never crossing the line enough to earn her a reprimand or a pink slip; but it was obvious she didn't care for me.

I don't know why she didn't like me, and I never cared enough to find out as long as she did what she was supposed to do and didn't make my job any harder than it had to be. Unfortunately, she was a favorite of a few doctors at the practice, so firing her on an irritated whim would've raised questions.

"You okay?" he asked searching my face.

"I'm fine. I'm just gonna use your bathroom real quick before I go if that's okay with you," I told him heading down the hall to it.

"I guess it is since you're already going," he teased.

I took a washcloth from a shelf above the toilet and took a bird bath in the sink. In the process, I reminded myself that who he was screwing before me didn't really matter. If he wasn't in the running to be my husband, then who he was dealing with in addition to me was insignificant as long as she didn't interfere with me.

I'd intentionally kept our conversations shallow and sexually guided outside of typical work conversations because I didn't want to find myself falling for this young pretty boy accidentally. Knowing how long it had been since I'd been in the romantic company of a man, and understanding that my heart was still vulnerable, I wasn't going to take any chances.

Luckily, he was already predisposed to talking about himself, his looks, his muscular body, his dreams of being a big-time party promoter and desire to show me the tool God blessed him with. He showed little interest in who I was outside of work other than trying to stimulate my libido with dirty talk, hence why his earlier mention and probing into my situation with Michael ruffled my feathers.

Primping my hair and straightening my clothes, I exited the bathroom and strutted passed him standing in the kitchen. He was drinking some green concoction from a jug as I arbitrarily picked up my pocketbook from the couch, causing the contents to spill out onto the carpet.

"Crap!" I fussed bending down to shove everything, including my handgun, back in before Kendrick rounded from the kitchen counter to help. It was a small black Ruger LCP .380 that I was licensed to carry, but didn't need him to know I had. After Michael's murder, my daddy felt uneasy about me being all alone in the house with no protection, so he suggested I arm myself.

I wasn't afraid in the least to be alone in the house, but I did like the idea of learning how to shoot. I purchased it 7-months earlier and hit the gun range whenever I could.

"Damn girl. You got everything but the kitchen sink in there don't you? You got more candy than my kid brother," he joked as I shoved 4 chocolate bars, a container of gum and a bag of Twizzlers inside along with my make-up, mirror, Visine, wallet and keys.

I shrugged.

"That way I'll never not have what I need, and the candy helps me calm my nerves. I just make sure to work out and keep my dental appointments," I told him smiling as he handed me a few other items strewn on the floor.

"Candy, helps calm your nerves?" he chuckled. "I think that's the opposite of what candy is supposed to do."

"You want one?" I offered a Hershey Almond bar.

He frowned up and pushed the candy away. "Poison."

"Poison? Don't tell me you're some kind of freak who doesn't like candy?" I joked.

"That chocolate has almonds in it right?"

"Yes. You don't like almonds?"

"Naw. I'm allergic. Like deathly allergic to them. I can't have anything with almonds in it or my throat will close up like a nun's pussy. I almost died when I was 8 after eating my aunt's almond chicken. I don't touch the stuff," he said going back in the kitchen and drinking more of that slushy substance.

"Ewww... what is that anyway?" I asked scrunching my nose.

Whatever it was looked disgusting, and the fact that he was drinking it straight from the jug instead of pouring it in a cup bothered me too.

"Kale, raspberries, spinach, bananas, a dash of fish oil, cinnamon, grapefruit juice, and yogurt. It's good for you. Wanna try?" he asked offering it to me while wiping his mouth with the back of his hand.

"Hell no. Sounds and looks disgusting. Yuck."

"It replenishes the nutrients in your body and helps me keep this sexy physique," he said smacking his abs with one hand and flexing the muscles on his arms.

"I'll take your word for it. It looks like puke."

"Aww c'mon now. It doesn't look that bad."

"You're allergic to almonds. Do you carry an Epi-pen? Seems like something we should know at work in case you ever have a reaction."

He shook his head nonchalantly.

"Nah, I don't need one. I haven't had a reaction since I was 12 when I didn't know they put almonds in a dessert I ate. Now, I always ask first and I don't eat anything with nuts in it. Peanuts, cashews, almonds... nothing. It's safer like that. The only nuts I fuck with... are attached to my dick," he chuckled.

"Ooop! Oh no you didn't. You're silly," I said putting the candy back in my bag and emptying 2 cube shaped pieces of *Ice Breakers* gum from the container into my palm. "Do you eat gum?"

"Yeah, but I don't want any. Thanks."

I was starting to feel awkward. It had been a long time since I'd slept with anyone other than Michael, and even longer since I'd been on a date in any capacity. Was I supposed to kiss him goodbye? Give him a hug? Wait for him to make the first move? Tell him I was going to call him? Or wait for him to say he was going to call me?

"Soooo... I'll... text you..." I said tentatively.

"Okay," he replied putting the jug back in the refrigerator and coming to wrap his hands around my waist. "You do that. I really did enjoy you. I'd like to enjoy you again sometime soon. You're gonna be out all next week right?"

"Yeah. Court," I said casting my gaze down.

He lifted my chin and placed his lips on mine. I stumbled back against the door as his tongue probed my mouth and his hands gripped my ass. I lost myself in his kiss, grabbing his neck and pushing my body up against his. When our lips parted, I let out a longing sigh and folded my lips under bashfully.

"Drive safely Sexy," he said softly.

"I will," I replied with a smile.

Walking to my car, I hurried my pace to escape the Georgia heat as I fished through my purse for my keys.

"Yeah. Take your cracker ass home," a snarky voice mumbled behind me just as I passed the stairwell.

I turned to see Kita emerging from it with a smug expression. Her shape reminded me of Sheri Shephard's oddy body from The View, and at close range, she was barely even as mediocre as I'd given her prior credit for. Her denim shorts were too tight for the roll of fat in her stomach that showed under her purple tank top, and too short for the amount of cellulite on her thighs.

She looked like a busted can of biscuits from the waist down, though her rotund breasts attempted to divert attention away from it.

"I beg your pardon?" I replied politely perplexed.

She paused, eyeing me slowly from head to toe.

"Why are you talking to me?" she asked nastily.

"Oh. I'm sorry. I thought you said something to me," I retorted still smiling. "Kita. Right?"

She looked aggravated by my mention of her name. Which was funny considering the effort she put into making herself seen earlier.

"Girl, you don't know me. Keep my name out your mouth and just get in your little Corolla and drive away. This ain't what you want," she threatened continuing to walk, switching her lumpy ass and snickering.

She looked even younger than Kendrick and outweighed me by at least 20 lbs. Her rough demeanor and the scratch on the bridge of her nose which looked like a war wound, gave me the impression that she'd had more fights than I'd had birthdays. Even with my kickboxing classes, I might have had to shoot her if it got ugly; and I couldn't afford any new blood on my hands with the trial coming up.

I turned back towards my car, disinterested in giving her ratchet ass anymore of my attention, just as her flip flops clapped against the steps leading to her second floor apartment. My temper was easily incited since I'd killed Michael, which was one of the reasons I'd stayed to myself and avoided too much contact with people outside of work.

Ignoring the urge to obtain the exhilarating feeling I got from slitting Michael's throat haunted me now when people provoked me. Just that little taste of vengeance at such a heightened level had me fiending for it like a crackhead. Sometimes the slightest infractions provoked a need to right their wrongs to me and Kita's insolence, though small, made my nerves twitch. Especially after the earlier incident with Debbie.

I pulled my keys out and reached for the door handle as my eyes fell upon a deep, thick, haphazard scratch that lead from the driver's side door to the back passenger's side of my car. I stepped back in disbelief with my jaw on the ground. What the hell! I was parked within the lines and there was plenty of space between my car and the ones on both sides, so why would someone do this?

I circled my car and saw a similar scratch on the passenger's side except the word "SLUT" was also carved underneath it. My shoulders tensed and anger quickly swooned inside me as I clenched the keys tightly in my fist. Kita's words replayed in my mind again.

'Just get in your little Corolla and drive away,' she'd said.

She knew my car. That vindictive twat. Feeling watched, I glanced back at the building and spied Kita's grinning face turning away as she lackadaisically unlocked the door to her unit and vanished inside. Just imagining her satisfaction at my dismay fueled my ire.

I blanked my face and took 2 deep breaths before rounding back to the driver's side. Everything in me said I should march up to her door and pistol whip her on sight; but I valued my freedom. I had too much to lose to do anything so drastic in broad day light.

I calmly got into my car, tossed my bag in the passenger's seat, and leaned into the rush of air blasting from the AC with the start of the ignition. I swept my tongue across my bottom lip as I contemplated my next move. My car wasn't anything to write home to mother about, but it was *mine*. Kita didn't even know me, and I was sick of women disrespecting me for sport. Kendrick was a single man. Her issues should've been with him. Not me.

Now she'd gone and let her jealousy write a check her ass was gonna have to cash. I had somewhere to be and something to do, but I'd be damned if I was going to leave without retaliation. No matter how minor it was going to have to be.

I saw the petty tramp peering at me from the window of her unit with a smirk before she drew the blinds. I took another deep breath and wrung my hands, gripping the steering wheel like the Jaws of Life and backing out of the spot. I drove passed the 2 story apartment buildings lining the streets on both sides of his complex under the speed limit and in deep thought towards the exit.

Thinking better, I detoured down a street that lead me to another area of his complex and made a U-turn. I pulled into a parking space in front of the building next door to Kendrick's and cut the engine. I dug through my purse for the plastic jar of ICE BREAKERS and opened it. I'd only bought it the day before, so there were still 36 of the 40 cube shaped pieces of gum it came with left. I took a handful of quarters from my purse, shoved my bag under the passenger's seat and took the keys from the ignition.

Locking the doors with the remote on the key chain, I scuttled down the sidewalk until I was again in front of Building C. With deliberation, I hurried down the stairs to the laundry room and surveyed the row of 6 washing machines and 6 dryers until I spotted 2 dryers in motion with Kita's green baskets waiting on the counter near them.

Two washing machines were also in motion, but I wasn't concerned with those. I could see that both dryers with Kita's clothes had a little over a half hour to go on their timers. I paused one and scrutinized the garbs inside. It included jeans, shirts, a few maxi dresses, blouses and underwear. Some were name brand, but most weren't.

I laughed to myself before emptying half of the ICE BREAKERS into my hand and sprinkling them inside the dryer, making sure to mix the cubes in well between her clothes. Adding 2 quarters to the load, I increased the heat to the highest temperature and started the dryer back up.

Moving on to the second dryer, which contained her whites, I repeated the same process over again with the ICE BREAKERS. My lips curled into a wicked grin as I stood watching the clothes rotating in the receptacles for a few moments with my arms folded across my chest.

"This ain't what you want," I mocked Kita's previous words as I headed back to my car.

7

Greer

"Ugh!" I yelled feeling for my phone between the seat and the armrest while keeping my eyes on the cars in front of me. I looped the airport slowly for the second time while searching for Shan curbside and hoping she'd exited by baggage claim on the South Terminal even though she'd only had a carry-on.

I went home and switched to Michael's black Yukon after the incident with my Corolla for obvious embarrassing reasons. That cut into my time to grocery shop and delayed me enough so that I couldn't meet her inside.

I stopped at the crosswalk as people talking and handling their phones moseyed to and fro with suitcases in tow. I spotted Shan with her head down, keyboard hustling something herself.

Her expression was intense and her posture exuded aggravation. My text message notification went off just as I'd placed my foot on the gas. Oh boy. Miss impatient must've been texting me.

Her red halter draped slightly over the top of her fitted jeans as she waited impatiently, glancing right passed me in the Yukon, I'm sure looking for me in my Corolla. Her huge black shoulder bag rested on top of her small roller suitcase as she hovered over it impatiently in multicolored heels.

"Damn girl! That booty's so big I can see it from the front!" I cat called in a husky voice rolling down the tinted passenger's side window of the Yukon.

She rolled her eyes and cut them in my direction, ready to check my ego and read me my rights, until she saw my smiling face.

"Girrrrrl," she laughed brushing the long bangs from her forehead as I threw the car in park and got out. "Honey. I was like, 'Who is this clown using that tired ass line?' What you doing in that big truck wit' your late ass? You finally traded in Rolly?"

Rolly was what she called my Corolla. I'd had it since my senior year in college and we'd had many spring break, road trip, and girl's night out adventures in it. Bri, one of Shan's friend's, was flashing an expensive Rolex watch when we all hung out one night and Bri quipped that it probably cost more than my car. Shan joked that my Rolly had wheels, and so the nickname was born.

"No, this was Michael's truck," I answered hugging her tightly. "I am not that late either. You know I'm usually on time and your flight came in early. I didn't even have time to park."

"Umm hmm," she murmured playfully chastising me. "It was only 15-minutes early. You were supposed to be here already by then. You know I sent you a text."

"I know. I was pulling up when it came through. I dropped my phone right before you sent it."

"When did he get the Yukon? He had a Cherokee before, didn't he?"

"The engine blew on it, and it was gonna cost more to fix it than to just get a new truck; so, he did. This is only like my third time driving it too. I'm debating on keeping it or trading it in."

She nodded giving the Yukon an approving glance as I dropped her carry-on in the trunk and got in the car.

"It is pretty nice. It has a lot of room in it too," she said scanning the inside once she got in. "You should keep it if the note isn't too high."

"It's not the note that's too much. It's the gas that costs an arm and a leg. I like driving it, but I hate filling it up," I told her retrieving my phone before pulling off into stop and go airport traffic.

"At least the price of gas is lower here than it is in New York. I think I've driven my car 7 or 8 times max all year because of it. Wherever you go, parking costs so much it's cheaper to just hit the subway or call an

Uber and get dropped off. That's the plus about moving back to N.Y. I love the easy access to transportation. You traded Rolly in?"

"No. It's just parked back at the house. So how was your flight? You hungry?" I asked directing the conversation away from my car.

I was already pissed about Kita defacing my vehicle and I didn't want to talk about it unless I wasn't going to have another choice. I didn't have the luxury of a garage to conceal the damage, and the thought of someone from the media spotting it during trial coverage had my stomach doing flip flops.

Getting it fixed before Monday was going to be a task, and desperate situations called for desperate measures. I sent a text to my brother in-law before I left my house pleading for discrete assistance; to which he responded that he would call me later. Now all I could do was hope and wait that he could fix it tonight or tomorrow.

The last thing I needed was to be caught driving a car with the word "slut" keyed into it right before I was thrust into the eye of the storm of what was coined the "Sleeping with the enemy murder trial" by the media.

Not to mention that Shan was bound to see it once we got to my house if Will couldn't come through for me before then.

"Sadly, that's probably the most sleep I've gotten all week. You know Shamari was sick for 3 days until yesterday morning," Shan was saying as I returned from my thoughts.

"Oh no, you didn't tell me he was sick. Is he okay now?" I said sympathetically.

"Yeah. It was some kind of stomach flu. You know how it is with kids and daycare. If one gets sick, they all pick up the bug eventually," she advised flicking her wrist.

Even though I didn't have any children myself, I knew that to be a true statement with the rush of kids we had coming in for appointments to the office lately. We had to be careful to sanitize and disinfect everything in general working with patients, but I took special care to sterilize anything I touched near the pediatrics offices. Snot nosed kiddy fingers loved to touch things, and I didn't want to be infected.

"You hungry?" I repeated.

She stared at me with a sarcastic smirk, making me laugh out loud.

"What?" I asked.

"You know my greedy tail is always hungry. Stop playing. I've been craving some gator bites and blackened catfish from SIX FEET UN-DER all week. Isn't that where we're going?"

I laughed. That was indeed where I was headed. I knew that was her favorite place to eat in town, and since I wasn't cooking, I figured she would opt to eat there.

"And we've gotta sit at the rooftop bar and have some Lemon Drops like old times too," she said bouncing giddily in her seat like a child while typing on her phone.

"Who's gonna drive us home while I'm getting drunk off Lemon Drops with you?"

"You don't have to get drunk Greer; but you can get tipsy. Hell, we can call an Uber if you have too many. I know you can probably use a drink right now, and I know I can use some alcohol salvation with the mess I'm dealing with back home."

"What mess are you dealing with at home?" I questioned glancing between her and the road.

She sat back in her seat, exhaling loudly.

"Chile', what mess isn't going on at home? I hate my job, I hate living back in New York, and I hate being away from my own family. It's like we moved to New York, just when they were moving to Atlanta. Even Shelita moved out of Queens to Philly with her boyfriend.

I've got some girlfriend's up here to hang out with, but you, my family, everybody I have to rely on is somewhere else. Meanwhile I'm around Evelyn 23/6. I'm on edge and we've been at each other's throats almost every day."

"About what? It's not like y'all to be arguing like that."

"I know," she said throwing her hands up. "But for the last few months, it's like that's all we do. Then of course, he runs over to his mother's house, which just makes me angrier. I feel like I'm turning into a whole 'nother person since we've moved. I'm stressing all the time, my tolerance levels are lower and I'm just not happy.

I don't even know what to do about it. He loves his new job. He loves being back around his mother and his family. He's totally back in his element, but it's not mine. Not anymore. I don't want to raise Shamari in New York where life is faster and harder than here in Atlanta. I feel like if we don't move back now, he's never going to do it."

Her face was balled into a frown as she leaned an elbow on the door and rested her head on her wrist. I felt guilty for not knowing how bad things had gotten between her and Jahari. She usually joked off whatever she was complaining about whenever we discussed any issues she was having, but now I could see that they were deeper than she'd led on.

"You know I'm rooting for you to move back to Atlanta. I haven't seen my godson in over a year, and I miss my bestie; but if Jahari's dead set against it, then you've got to try other options. Maybe you can find another place to rent in Queens. When's your lease up?"

She sucked her teeth shaking her head with doubt.

"That man is not unlatching from his mother's teat. I already suggested that we move. I told him that I might not be so pressed to move back to Atlanta if we at least got more than a hop skip and a jump away from his mother. Nope. He's totally against it. He doesn't want Shamari to be cared for by strangers when his mother can do it for free. I mean, believe me, I get that. I love that Shamari is bonding with his grandma and it saves us money, but she can still do that with us living further away.

He's over there so much that some days I feel like I'm single again. Jahari and Shamari are over at Evelyn's and I'm in the house cleaning, working or watching movies all by myself. It's ridiculous. Like I'm competing with his mother for my own husband's attention. Don't get me wrong. I love her. You know I love her, and we get along fine, but they got me feeling like an outsider in my own family. Jahari wants to go over there every day and Shamari is right on his heels."

I knew all too well what it was like to feel like an outsider in your own family, but I was sure that a little more time and communication would improve her situation, whereas mine was never so easy. Shantel and Jahari had been together longer than Michael and I and I had faith that their bond was stronger than this rough patch.

"Anyway," she continued turning her frown upside down. "I'm supposed to be here to visit you and to support you through this trial. Not for you to help me fix my life Iyanla," she laughed. "Turn up! Let's just get some good food and some strong drinks!"

Shan danced around in her seat, turning up the rap song playing on the radio and waving her arms over her head as I took the exit. Hey, if she didn't want to talk about it anymore, then we wouldn't. The thought of having dinner and drinks with my friend brought an easy smile to my face anyway.

It only took a few minutes for us to be seated at the rustic seafood restaurant where rooftop seating provided a view of the historic Oakland Cemetery. Our waitress was a petite goth looking redhead with piercing blue eyes to match the ones in her ears, eyebrow and cheeks. After ordering our favorite appetizers, we settled in with our drinks and gazed out at the scenery.

"So how was your dad's barbecue?" Shan asked taking a sip of her Lemon Drop.

"Just peachy," I answered satirically.

"Oh boy. Don't tell me Debbie acted an ass at the party."

"She flipped out on me in front of everybody."

"For what?" she asked as I rested my arms on the table.

"Because she's crazy. Tamia was running around playing with Shawn's daughter and she grabbed the girl up like she just robbed a bank. The vice grip she had on her arm, shaking her around in front of everybody, it was too much. So, I stepped in between them and I just kind of told her to let it go. It wasn't that serious for her to be reacting like that."

Shan's eyebrow went up, but she kept quiet.

"I know the kids didn't need to be getting too close to those oleander bushes since they can be poisonous; but they weren't even close," I said raising and dropping my shoulders. "They were playing like normal kids until Cruella Deville stepped in to squash it all, yelling and humiliating the child in front of everybody."

"Umph," she murmured still sipping her drink and averting her eyes from mine.

I didn't like her response. Shan was rarely at a loss for words, so her silence spoke volumes.

"What's that mean? You think she was right?"

Her eyes softened as she sat her glass on the table.

"I'm not saying that I agree with her, but I can understand why she might be upset. Moms can be really defensive when somebody starts telling them how to discipline their child. Right or wrong, it's kind of not anybody's place sometimes. Again, I'm not saying that how Debbie handled the situation was correct. I'm just saying I get where she's coming from. Evelyn likes to add her 2 cents to how I raise Shamari way more than I feel is necessary too. It's a touchy subject for some parents."

I swallowed hard, incredulously sipping on my own drink. Was she serious? So because Tamia wasn't my child, I wasn't supposed to say anything when I saw her own mother treating her like a rag doll? Or was Shan's comment an even deeper dig at my not having children at all? She knew Debbie's history of tormenting me as a child. That alone should've been enough to warrant her support of my actions.

"You were probably totally right. I'm just saying that--"

"Yeah, I understand what you're 'just saying'," I interrupted indignantly. "I don't have to be a mother to know when someone's behavior is inappropriate towards their child. I've been the little girl Debbie has treated like that before, so I know what kind of person she is. I wasn't gonna just stand by and watch her manhandle a little girl for simply doing little girl things. Especially when that child is my niece."

"Okay," she conceded. "You're right. You know better than anybody how she is. What happened?"

I debated with myself whether I was even going to continue the story or not since Shan had already taken Debbie's side. Whatever I said afterwards would probably be taken with a grain of salt in her mind anyway if she thought there was even a sliver of merit in the way Debbie reacted.

"C'mon. Don't be like that," she goaded playfully slapping my palm when I still didn't resume. "What else happened?"

A slight breeze helped to cool my ire as I glanced out at the cemetery, watching 2 middle aged white women standing over a tombstone. One knelt and put a bouquet of what looked like white lilies and white alstroemerias on the grass in front of it. I was keen on flowers from working at FLOWER ME WITH LOVE, and I thought the women had made a good choice.

I wondered if anyone ever visited my mother's grave. I hadn't been to it since the day she was put into the ground when I was 5. Consequently, as an adult, I didn't even know where she was buried if I'd ever wanted to. I made a mental note to ask my father about that and a few other questions that had been plaguing my thoughts lately. I wanted to know more about the white side of my DNA and he was the only one I knew to ask.

Our waitress brought out appetizers, took our drink orders for a second round, and disappeared back towards the bar.

"Greer, I--" Shan began before she was cut off by the sound of an oh too familiar female voice.

"Shantel!" Bri screeched walking pompously up to our table with her arms outstretched.

I recognized her side kick Leslie and another girl I didn't know following closely behind. They all squealed with joy and Shan popped up to hug them in kind. I painted a smile on my face, watching them resentfully. This couldn't be a coincidence.

"I texted Bri to tell her I was in Atlanta, and that we were heading to SIX FEET UNDER. She didn't tell me her and the girls were gonna swing by," Shan stated jovially like she was reading my mind.

Bri grabbed a passing waiter by the arm and stopped him as Shan took her seat gesturing towards me like I should be glad. These were her friends. Not mine. I felt a way about seeing them, but happy didn't describe it.

"Hi. Can we get 1 more chair for this table right here please?" she asked the slender blonde guy.

"Sure," he answered sliding a chair from a vacant table to the head of ours.

Our table was capable of seating 6, but was only set for 4 initially like most tables on the rooftop. Of course, Bri sat in it like the head bitch she always portrayed herself to be, putting Shan and I on either side of her.

Spelman was saturated with women from all walks of life, many of which I was privileged to be associated with. Still, there was a hierarchy of the student body that few who didn't derive from similar backgrounds were favored to breach. Bri and Leslie were from wealthy families with rich histories and braggadocious lifestyles. Even with Shan being from a basic middle class, single parent home, they'd welcomed her into their cliquish fold and allowed me to tag along as a courtesy.

In various not so subtle ways, Bri, Leslie and a few others in their clique reminded me that I was an interloper. My involvement with most of the women in their circle had been minimal after graduation, and usually only occurred during parties for Shan or college driven events. I hadn't seen either of them since Shamari's first birthday party and I wasn't thrilled to be seeing them now.

"Greeer. How have you been?" Bri sang between MAC nude color covered lips, swinging her nutmeg tinted Brazilian weave over her shoulder.

True to her usual form, she was severely overdressed for what the establishment required. Her all-white shift dress with pink stilettos was accentuated by pink diamond earrings and a rose pink Cartier watch. I don't know who designed her clothes, but there was no question that they were just as expensive as her jewelry.

"Yeah. Long time no see. It's good to see you," Leslie chimed in sitting on my right with sunglasses hiding her eyes and loose curls framing her tiny face.

Tall, plain and curve less in a simple yellow shirt dress and sandals, her shades prevented me from confirming the insincerity I suspected was there in her eyes. Their third leg sat beside Shan and nudged her good-humoredly with her shoulder, and Shan wrapped an arm around her like they were old friends.

"I'm fine," I replied finishing off my drink and spying Shan over the rim of my glass while she deliberately avoided my gaze.

"Good. Good. That's my little sister Brenna. I don't think you've met before. She just graduated from the yard in May," she said proudly gesturing toward the unknown woman. "She's starting law school in the fall."

Brenna opened and closed her palm in a friendly hello, and I smiled back politely. Looking at her, I could see the resemblance between the two. They both had gingerbread complexions and large protruding eyes over upturned noses. Brenna was a much prettier version of her older sister in my opinion.

Bri always looked like a professional MAC makeup model, but Brenna only wore eyeliner and lipstick with a touch of blush. Her ebony hair was layered neatly down to her shoulders which were exposed by the boat-neck blouse she wore over cargo shorts.

"I can't believe little Brenna is so grown up now. I keep thinking you're still in high school," Shan beamed.

Brenna blushed and giggled. "High school? I've been grown girl. You're still looking young as ever though. I'm loving your hair."

Shan's hair was brown with light brown highlights, tapered at the neck, short on the sides and long in the front. Her hair was always tight, and I admired her ability to try new styles without a second thought. I'd never attempted any adventurous hairstyles or cuts myself, but as I looked at her glowing face, I thought maybe it was time that I did.

"Shan, why didn't you let me know you were coming to visit before today Soror? We could've made plans to do something. Or is Greer going to be monopolizing your time the whole time you're here?" Bri pouted impishly.

I guzzled down my drink and rolled my eyes behind my tipped-up glass. 'Why didn't you let me know you were coming to visit before today Soror?' I parodied her whiny voice in my head. I knew I had to be the only one at the table who hadn't pledged A.K.A. and Bri knowing this, liked to remind me of my exclusion. I knew with Bri being the former chapter V.P., there was no way her little sis had missed the opportunity to join.

College must've been some of the best years of Bri's life because she loved to harp on those days. Pledging is one of the few quintessential things that Shan did during those years that I didn't.

I was psyched when she introduced the idea our junior year, and I was prepared to do whatever was necessary both mentally and financially to cross over. I envied the bonds sororities nurtured. The potential for me to be a part of a greater sisterhood was exciting. Finally, I was going to get the acceptance I'd yearned for but never received from anyone. Or so I thought.

My outlook on a lot of things was forever changed one fateful night after a seemingly innocent date with Bri's brother Keith. I was invited to the apartment they shared to watch movies, drink wine and eat a parmesan chicken dinner he'd cooked himself.

My memory is fuzzy for everything that evening after my second glass of wine. The next thing I knew, I was stumbling confusedly from his room with a throbbing head, wrinkled clothes, a sore vagina and a broken spirit.

Instead of coming to my evident need for aide, Bri erred on her brother's side of the story, which was that I'd gotten drunk, slept with him that night, and woke up with buyer's remorse. The 2 convinced me that my word against theirs would only result in my own humiliation, and with Shan gone to Virginia that Labor Day weekend, I'd retreated to my room to cry and lick my wounds in silence.

When Shan returned from her trip, I'd already decided to take what troubling memories I had to the grave with me; and I hadn't told another soul about it. No one except Michael, years later. Needless to say, my desire to join any faction which allowed Bri or any of her minions to have control over me was squelched after that incident.

Shan was baffled by my sudden change of heart about pledging over the course of a weekend. We'd actually argued about it, in addition to what she perceived as my aloof and withdrawn behavior. She and I weren't on speaking terms when she started going through the pledging process. Though I'd pushed her away, I still resented and envied the bond she developed with her line sisters despite my declination to pledge.

That semester, I threw myself into my books and took an internship at Northlake Hospital shadowing a human resources executive. By New Year's, we had had a come to Jesus over a bottle of Moscato and cartons of Chinese food. Consequently, our friendship was salvaged, and my continual need to people please and gain acceptance led me to stupidly socialize with Bri for Shan's sake, regardless of my hatred of her.

Unexpectedly being thrust into her midst again dredged up the loathing feelings I reserved for her in my gut, and reminded me that neither she, nor her brother ever atoned for their actions.

"I told you I was coming last month to see Greer," Shan replied.

"Excuse me," our waitress said returning with our appetizers and placing them in the middle of the table. "I was going to ask if you were ready to order your entrees yet, but I see that some friends have joined you. Did you ladies want to order?"

"Yes. Bring us menus please, and I'll take a vodka cranberry," Bri commanded taking charge as she always did.

"I'll take one of those too," Leslie said raising a finger.

"I want what they're having," Brenna advised gesturing towards our drinks. "They look good. Margaritas?"

"No. Lemon Drop martinis," Shan confirmed.

"Okay. Can I see your ID's please?"

Bri huffed and reached in her clutch, producing her driver's license with a limp wrist as Leslie and Brenna showed her theirs. When our waitress noted them all, she excused herself to put their orders in and came back quickly with menus.

"So much fried food," Leslie complained with a frown as she probed the options.

"Les, I'm not worried about that, and you shouldn't be either with those washboard abs," Shan laughed making Leslie smile.

"That's how I keep them that way. Baked food, lots of vegetables, Zumba and I run 3 miles every morning," she said to resounding groans from all of us.

"I do yoga and that's it. My hair is not 3-mile every morning ready," Bri joked.

"Shoot, mine neither," Brenna cosigned.

"Maybe Greer could do it with that long-mixed hair. You're looking surprisingly good yourself Greer. What do you do to stay in shape? Are you jogging like Ms. Thang, here?" Bri questioned me with a smirk as she eyed me from head to toe.

She was unsurprisingly looking like the bitch I always thought she was and if she wasn't careful, I was going to demonstrate what I did to stay in shape instead of verbalizing it.

"There's nothing surprising about it," Shan said in my defense. "She's always been in good shape."

"Oh, don't be so literal Shantel. I didn't mean anything by it. It was a compliment," she said innocently. "It's not like she's had her stomach stretched out by 2, 8-pound big headed boys like I have. If she didn't have a tight body, I'd be questioning her self-worth. What are you waiting for?" she continued baiting me with a chuckle.

Her cronies laughed along like she was Kevin hart while Shan ogled me uncomfortably. I had no idea why my lack of children had become the topic of the day, but all of these bitches were getting on my nerves acting like motherhood gave them a license to judge women who didn't have any.

I pretended to find her remarks amusing too as I stuffed a catfish bite into my mouth while fuming inside.

"Bri. Come on," Shan scolded.

Bri twisted her mouth, rolling her eyes, and leaning back in her chair coolly. Then, just as quickly, she jut forward and grabbed my hand between hers.

"Oh my God. I'm so sorry Greer. Please forgive my insensitivity. I wasn't thinking."

I chewed my food slowly and cocked my brow in bewilderment. Although she certainly owed me an apology, for much more than anything she'd said at this table, I wasn't sure why or what she was apologizing for. I guess my expression showed it, because she immediately elaborated.

"I totally forgot. It just dawned on me that Shan is here because Michael's murder trial is coming up. Yes?" she stated glancing at Shan, then back at me. "Oh girl. Please forgive my jokes about you not having kids. I really hope that horrible bitch gets life in prison for snatching your future with Michael away.

You know he and Cam used to get in trouble in school a lot together," she snickered speaking on her husband and Michael's relationship. "He was a good guy though. He didn't deserve what happened to him and I can't imagine how you're dealing with the humiliation of the whole world knowing he cheated on you.

It's probably a good thing that you don't have kids to have to suffer through all of this too. I know we're not as close as Shan and I, but we are friends. I would never be so callous. I hope you know I didn't mean to be insulting to you with my little wisecracks. How are you holding up?"

All pity filled eyes were on me as I sat dumbfounded. She was full of horse shit. Neither she, nor Cameron reached out to me after Michael's death, or attended any of his funeral proceedings. She was such a phony, and her entire aura reeked of inauthenticity, from the time she referenced me as her friend.

I'd seen Bri verbally rip a female limb from limb without breaking a smile or getting a hair out of place while their egos disintegrated into ashes before my eyes. I wasn't stupid enough to think I was exempt from her fangs.

Our waitress came back with drinks for the table before I could respond, which was a blessing, because the PC reaction I needed to give was going to be a feat to execute. She's been getting away with crushing people like peons for as long as I've known her, and just once... I wanted her to be the one getting crushed.

"Are you ladies ready to order?" our waitress, whose name I remembered was Tracy as soon as Shan said it, asked.

"Yes," everyone said in Unison as my phone chimed inside my bag.

Retrieving it, I saw Will's number on the screen.

"I'll take the Blackened Shrimp n' Grits," I told Tracy and excused myself to take Will's call.

"Hey," I answered timidly striding towards the restrooms. "Thank you for calling me back."

"No need to thank me. You're family. Sorry for getting back to you so late. Your sister is still on a rampage and I didn't want to call you back while she was around. I've only got a few minutes to talk. What did you say happened to your car now? I'm looking at those pictures and that's crazy," Will asked speaking quickly and in whispered tones.

"I don't know. Some girl must've got my car mixed up with somebody else's and she keyed it. I came outside from my friend's place and that's what I saw. I can't be driving to work or court with that scratched in my door. Plus, I don't know if cameras are going to be following me around this week because of trial coverage. I went through enough public scrutiny last year and I don't want or need any extra attention on me.

I know this is short notice and it's late already, but is there any way that you can take it to your shop and buff it out or something?" I begged leaning against the wall outside of the bathrooms.

"You know; your car is pretty old. Matching that baby blue exactly is just not gonna happen, and it's too deep to just buff it. Your best bet is to get them buffed out and get the whole car repainted."

"Okay. Can you repaint it dark blue? I always wanted to change the color anyway. And if you can, can you do it tonight? Or tomorrow?"

"No. No. I can't do anything if you don't want Debbie to know about it. Not me personally I mean. The shop is already closed today, and we're closed on Sunday's too, so if I go in, she's gonna be suspicious."

My heart dropped to my feet, feeling the impact of my hopes dashed. The media had probed into every nook and cranny of my life during the first month that Michael's murder started running on the news, and I wanted to provide as little ammo as possible for them to shame me with this time. I could check with Donna to see if the auto shop she worked in would fix it discretely, but I didn't want to have to explain it to her or anyone else. She and Debbie were way closer than she and I were, and I know she'd spill it faster than I could say it.

Will was a different animal though. He had a soft spot for me in spite of Debbie's contempt, and he was a sucker for a damsel in distress. We'd had a few meaningful conversations over the years, and it was obvious to me that he didn't approve of the way Debbie or my stepmother behaved towards me, even when he kept silent about it.

"What I might can do for you is get Rodger to handle it. If you still got the key under the floor mat, I'll just give him directions to your house and tell him to have somebody drop him off so he can drive it to the shop. Now he can't paint it, but he can buff those scratches down as much as possible for ya. Then I can have my guy Terrell use a similar color to repaint your car first thing Monday morning.

You won't be able to pick it up till Tuesday if you wanna drive it, but it'll look good as new. Terrell's good at his job and the scratches don't look too deep to remove. Whatever she used, it wasn't a key though. No key would pull up the paint the way it is. I'll have him get any other random ones that might be on there from years of driving it too."

"Okay. That'll work. Can you make sure Rodger keeps this between us though please? It's gonna be hard enough sitting in court day after day hearing about what happened between Michael and his killer without something silly like this making news," I advised teetering between relief and dread.

On one hand, I was happy Will had come up with a way for me to get my car fixed quickly; but on the other hand, I didn't want creepy Rodger knowing where I lived, being in my car or my business.

"That goes without saying. He's not a gossiper, but I'll let him know to keep it between us if you want me to."

"Thank you. How much will all this run me?"

"Aww Greer. You get the family discount. I'm gonna say about... 300 dollars. Can you work with that?"

"Definitely. I really appreciate you helping me out Will. I didn't have anywhere else to turn. You know Michael always handled this kind of stuff. Car stuff," I answered pouring it on thick as I watched the girls eating, drinking and being merry at the table without me.

"That's what family is for. Now let me get off this phone before my lovely wife comes out to the garage looking for me," he snickered. "I'll call Rodger and have him get on his way to your place now. How are you gonna get around in the meanwhile?"

"I still have Michael's Yukon."

"Good. Alright then. Call the shop Monday and we'll take it from there. Everything's gonna be okay."

"Thank you."

"You're welcome. I'll talk to you Monday," he said hanging up.

I lingered against the wall, watching the crowd talking, laughing and drinking as the sun began descending below the horizon. At our table, Bri was in mid-laughter at something Leslie said while Shan shook her head in amusement and Brenna played on her phone.

I had to keep my emotions in check when it came to Bri and her antics. Notwithstanding her lame apology, I knew there would be more low blows to come if she was given enough room to slide one in.

It was pretty ironic that such a narcissistic, callous person was also a mental health professional. I can only imagine how many people needed to seek someone else in her profession due to something she'd done to them.

My fingers caressed my bottom lip as I observed the Barracuda savoring the attention from her underlings, and mused ways to knock her down a peg or two... or six feet.

8

Greer

"Come take a picture with us!" Shan coaxed with a wave in a loud drunken shrill as they all made their way to a prime spot for a photo on the rooftop.

Shan snagged a passing patron to take pictures of all of us together, but Bri suggested they also get one of just the 4 of them skee weeing and putting up their sorority signs. "No offense Greer," Bri declared.

I shook my head no and scooped up a spoon full of Blackened Shrimp and Grits.

"No. You guys go ahead. Take your sorority pics like Bri said. I don't need to be in them. I gotta eat to soak up some of this alcohol before I throw up. I can't drink like I used to anymore. We're definitely gonna have to call Uber," I returned with a phony smile.

"Aww GG. Come take one with the whole group though," Shan pled as Leslie turned back and took her by the arm.

"C'mon girl. She ain't got to be in it if she doesn't want to," Leslie said dragging Shan away.

"Just take one," Shan begged holding up her index finger.

I didn't care. They were leaving me at the table all alone, and that's what I wanted. Tracy had just delivered another round of drinks for Bri, Shan and Leslie, and I needed unwitnessed access.

We'd been there nearly 2 hours, eating and drinking, and they were all tipsy or close to drunk, but I wasn't. After my phone call, I cut Tracy off on her way to put our orders in and told her that I would like my future drinks to be virgin. Basically, I'd just be drinking lemonade with a sugared rim.

Brenna was Bri and Leslie's designated driver, so she'd quit drinking at 3 drinks, which wasn't soon enough if you asked me. She was definitely tipsy, while Bri, Shan and Leslie were only a drink or 2 away from being pissy.

I'd partied with these girls enough in school to know how they liked to drink, and though they were tamer than they had been in our college days, they still drank like fish. I pretended to keep up with them. Matching them drink for drink. Faking inebriation and giggling at whatever stupid remarks they made.

I gave in and ended up taking 2 pics with them, but I headed back to our table after that instead of offering to turn photographer. I needed alone time at the table, and this was as good a time as any. Shortly afterwards, I used the open Visine bottle hidden in my palm to drip as many drops as possible into Bri's drink without being seen.

Luckily, they were all so vain that even after the guy stopped taking pictures for them on each of their phones, they were still held up taking "ussies" of themselves. When they returned to the table, my near full 1-ounce bottle of Visine was empty and back in my bag.

"Okay, he was cute," Leslie said flopping down in her seat while exposing all 32 teeth with her sunglasses on her head.

"You can have him," Bri assured Leslie devilishly, immediately tasting her Vodka Cran when she got back to her seat. "That wedding ring is nothing but a piece of medal for dudes like him."

"I don't mess with married men," Leslie rebutted, saying the only thing I'd ever respected her for.

"Psshhhh. There's married men, and there's men that are just married. Married men, like *my* Cam, carry themselves like other women don't matter. They don't stare too long at randoms, waste their salaries on strippers, or flirt with every pretty girl they see. Marriage is more than just a word or a piece of paper to them.

Men that are just married, are different. They're *legally* committed to a wife, but they act like they're single whenever she's not around.

Hell, some of them act single even when she is around. Ol' boy that took our pictures, is just married. He wears his ring so you'll already know what you're getting yourself into," she said superciliously, holding her drink with a limp wrist. "Please, he was looking at all of us like edible arrangements. If I hadn't shooed him off, he would've still been taking pictures of us right now," she laughed.

"Hmph. That's gonna be any heterosexual man. Just because a man gets married, that doesn't mean he suddenly can't see a sexy woman in front of him. He doesn't have to be unfaithful because he's *looking*. You always think men are after you anyway. Shoot, how do you know Cam is so innocent?" Leslie challenged the queen bitch to my surprise.

I put a spoon full of food in my mouth to mask my smirk and watched the volley between them. Bri cocked her neck back indignantly and sat forward with her eyes stabbing Leslie in the face.

"First off, I said he was looking at *all of us* like edible arrangements. Not just me. Secondly, I know Cam is innocent because he *is*. I know my husband. Do you know something I don't know, Ms. Still Single With No Kids?"

Brenna snickered. I nearly choked on a shrimp and Shan gasped. I didn't miss Leslie's mortified expression either as she nervously wiped imaginary food from her mouth with a napkin.

"Look Bri, you're all the way wrong for that. I'm single by choice until the right man comes along, and I'm not having any kids until that happens. Why're you getting so upset? I didn't say Cam was cheating on you. I'm asking questions Ms. High And Mighty Know-It-All."

"See now. That right there is what's forcing me to put you in your place. I'm getting upset because I don't like your tone of voice. I was just making a little joke that you could sleep with him if you wanted to, since you were complaining about your *dry man spell* in the car. Of course, I wasn't serious about you doing it. I still know a man that's ripe to cheat when I see one though. I council them all the time.

I'm the *only* certified Psychologist at this table. You're a Travel Agent. You should know how to stay in your lane by now when discussing things I know about, and you don't. Now we've been girls a lot of years Les; but don't get out of line if you don't want to be put back in your place."

"Bri! C'mon," Shan admonished with a reddened alcohol induced stare.

Bri cut her eyes at Shan and glared back at Leslie while drinking her Lemon Drop laced with Visine. In a few more sips, her drink would be totally gone. There were a lot of myths about pranksters using Visine to cause severe bouts of diarrhea, but I knew from working at a medical practice that the results would be much more severe than that. Happy butterflies fluttered in my stomach as I waited patiently for the side effects to kick in.

"Well, Bri," Leslie said with drunken attitude as she swallowed the last of her own drink. "I didn't realize I had to be a certified psychologist to have an opinion. I know it's a crazy thought, but you don't know everything. Shit. I'm ready to go. Y'all ready to go?"

"No. I'm not ready to go," Bri answered arrogantly playing in her hair. "I'm finishing my drink, and I haven't had dessert yet. It won't kill you to wait a little while longer. Where's Tracy? As soon as our waitress comes back, I'll order some Key Lime Pie, and when I'm finished eating *that*, we can go. Or you can go now if you can't wait."

Leslie sucked her teeth and looked at Brenna, who was playing in her hair like her sister, and looked like she was siding with her too. I was enjoying the show, but Shan looked troubled by their bickering. Her mouth was usually running a mile a minute, but liquor mellowed her out.

Everyone else's plates were clean, and I only had a couple of bites left of mine, so I knew Tracy would be over soon to clear the table, take dessert orders, or bring the check. I ate the last of my food and drank my virgin Lemon Drop with the same silence that matched everyone else at the table, though the bar itself was alive with conversation and music.

Minutes passed and Tracy finally made an appearance. Bri placed her order, and clapped her hands together like a Catholic school teacher when she told Tracy she was going to need it quickly. The crazy look she gave Bri was hilarious, and I knew she couldn't wait for us to get the hell out of there.

No one else wanted anything, and though Shan initiated some small talk, Leslie's attention was now solely on her phone, and every glance in Bri's direction was laced in repugnance. I was shocked to see how things played out. I guess their friendship wasn't as strong as it had been. Or else alcohol made Leslie realize how sick she was of being treated like Bri's puppy.

"It's getting kind of cold out here," Bri said warming her arms.

"You think?" I asked, glad the Tetrahydrozoline in the Visine was starting to work.

"Yes," she confirmed with a lethargic expression.

Shan shrugged. "Not really."

After clearing her throat a couple of times, Bri drank the rest of her Lemon Drop, then sipped some water. Her eyes were beginning to glass over, and she began opening and closing her mouth like the intake of air through her nose wasn't enough.

"Are you alright?" I questioned placing a caring hand on her shoulder.

She blinked a few times and teetered in her seat a bit, then touched around her face with the back of her hand like she was checking her temperature.

"I think... maybe I had too much to drink."

"You look like you're gonna puke," Brenna told her. "C'mon, let's go to the bathroom," she said scooting her seat out and coming over to Bri's chair.

"Yeah. I think I may need to," Bri agreed pushing away from the table.

"I hope she's alright," Shan said as I looked on and Brenna took Bri by the elbow to lead her towards the restrooms.

When they got about 2 feet away, Bri's liquidized entree spewed from her mouth like pea soup in the movie *The Exorcist*. People parted like the Red Sea amidst murmurs of disgust and pity. Her expensive white dress and pink pumps were now splattered with vomit, and her mouth was an open spigot to the contents of her stomach.

Someone shoved a bucket beneath her since they didn't want her hurling a trail through their establishment. She kept retching and heaving into it until there was nothing left, and she was visibly exhausted. My face showed concern, but I was elated. More than I had been in months.

I enjoyed watching the conceited twat's public suffrage. It was about time that *she* was the one being embarrassed in front of a group of people for a change. Shan's half-drunk ass tried to assist Brenna with her sister, but they looked just as comical trying to help her and avoid contact with puke at the same time.

I don't know what Leslie was thinking, but she dropped her shades back over her eyes, even though it was almost 9:30 at night, and went back to her phone. It wasn't until it was evident that Bri was having additional trouble breathing that Leslie's lack of concern turned to fear.

Brenna left Shan and people from SIX FEET UNDER'S staff to tend to Bri while she rushed to Bri's clutch and retrieved an inhaler I never knew she needed. By that time, both Leslie and I were also offering what support we could around Bri and everyone was in a panic.

"Does she have asthma?" I asked Leslie.

"Yeah. Oh my God. I hope she's gonna be okay. I thought she just had too much to drink, but she looks really bad," she answered teary-eyed, now genuinely concerned.

I massaged her shoulder sympathetically and fabricated some tears of my own. I knew one of the possible effects of ingesting Tetrahydrozoline was causing shortness of breath, or even halting it in some cases. What I didn't know, was that Bri had asthma. Woot Woot!

It was a slim probability that the quantity I gave her would cause death after just one dosage. Mixed with the alcohol and her having asthma though, I might've gotten what I really wanted. My heart palpitated with glee and fear at the same time. I couldn't be sure that an investigation in this case wouldn't lead back to me.

Someone called 911 and an ambulance showed up in no time. Bri was led downstairs where they checked her vitals put an oxygen mask on her and started to administer and IV. Funny enough, after they were ready for transport, your stubborn highness was adamant that she didn't want to go to the hospital.

"You might have alcohol poisoning Bri!" Brenna exclaimed climbing in the back of the ambulance with her. "This isn't the time to be pig-headed."

Bri shook her head with what strength she had and removed the mask.

"No hospital. They can do everything that needs to be done right here. I'm a doctor. Cam's a doctor. I will not be brought into the hospital for alcohol poisoning and besmirch our reputations," she insisted through labored breaths. "I just need some fluids and some rest. I don't need a hospital."

I chuckled inside at her arrogance. She's a freaking psychologist for Christ's sake. Not a psychiatrist. She's a doctor by degree. Not a medical doctor. She can't even prescribe medication. I doubted anybody at any hospital would know her ass on sight except as Cameron's wife.

"Ma'am, I think it's in your best interest to be seen by a doctor. This could be more severe than alcohol poisoning. I wouldn't recommend you take that cha—," an attractive brunette paramedic attempted to advise.

"Listen. I'll sign the waiver and give you my insurance information. Money isn't the issue here. I just needed some fluids and you're already giving it to me. I don't need a hospital."

"Ma'am...," the brunette began to protest again."

"If I die, it will be my own fault. Brenna, bring me my purse please. You can bring me that waiver," Bri ordered putting the mask back on her face.

After a few more minutes of debate with the brunette paramedic and her partner who came to add his 2 cents, Bri got her wish. They left the IV in until it was used up, and left her in Brenna's care after they got their waivers and paperwork signed.

I was delighted that there'd be no documented evidence that she'd been poisoned, but disappointed that she'd escaped death when it was so close.

Bri laid across the backseat of Brenna's gold Mercedes Benz looking like death warmed over. With Brenna at the wheel and Leslie riding shotgun, we said our goodbyes and they headed towards Vinnings to bring the Queen Bee home to her hive.

Now, I was perfectly capable of driving us home, but since I was supposed to have drank as much as the girls had, I called an Uber. We got Shan's bag from the back of the Yukon and put it in the trunk of our Asian driver's Kia Sorento. Shan and I talked about the evening's events the entire drive home and she confided in me that she wasn't as close with Bri as she once was.

She said her text was only meant to be a courtesy notice so Bri wouldn't see it on social media and get upset. According to Shan, her sole purpose of coming back to Atlanta was to spend time with me and to be my support. It warmed my heart to hear her say that. To be acknowledged as a priority. My friend's priority.

I always felt like second fiddle to Bri, and today hadn't felt any different when I was blindsided by her arrival at our dinner. It must've been God's will for her to get payback today though, because I had no thought or intentions on punishing Bri before then. Okay, I take that back. I had *thought* about it over the years, but never seriously planned it.

In fact, I know I wouldn't have ever had the courage to execute any plan I could've come up with prior to Michael's death. Things were different now. I was different now. And I liked it.

Pulling up to my house, I saw that my car was no longer in the driveway, bringing a smile to my face. That meant that Rodger had come to get it earlier and thankfully, I wouldn't have to explain the scratches to Shan.

It was almost 11 pm when we got in the house, and I was as happy to see my couch as I was to lay down across it. Shan sat on the matching brown leather loveseat and threw her head back against the headrest.

"Woo! Girl!" Shan said loudly as she kicked off her heels. "Tomorrow has got to be a better day. I feel like I need a drink to recover from going out for drinks."

I grabbed the T.V. remote from the coffee table and surfed channels for something good to watch. Finding nothing, I settled on the ID Network, as usual.

"What is this?" Shan asked folding her legs under her butt and squinting at the show.

"*Homicide Hunter.* It chronicles murder cases solved by Detective Kenda."

She frowned. "Gruesome. How can you watch this kind of stuff? I'd have nightmares."

"Why?"

"Because the news is depressing enough without having to see an entire show dedicated to showing corpses and glorifying murderers. I would think it would be traumatizing for the victims of such violence. This doesn't bring back horrible memories of what you've experienced?" she asked softly.

I shrugged.

"I was watching these shows long before I found myself in the middle of a crime scene. It doesn't traumatize me. It actually makes me feel better to see police executing due diligence and getting these criminals convicted. It gives me hope that justice is going to be done for Michael just like it has been for the people on these shows.

I don't even understand why it took this long just to get someone everybody knows killed him, to be convicted of it. The wheels of justice haven't just been slow, they've been at a near standstill. Thanks to her, I'm just starting to try and put my life back together. This doesn't even feel like my real life."

I told her flipping over on my back, lying my head against the arm of the couch and sighed.

"I know honey, and I'm sorry about that."

"Even with the entire room redone, it's still hard for me to sleep in there. I sleep down here on the couch more than I sleep in my own bed," I lied throwing my arm across my face. "I feel like his soul is trapped in our bedroom. Sometimes, when the entire house is quiet, I think I hear his voice. I dream about him all the time. Then I wake up, and he's not there, and I go numb."

"Aww sweetie. Have you thought about seeing somebody to help you get through this? Like a psychologist?"

"Somebody like Bri?" I joked and Shan laughed.

"Yes. Somebody like Bri. But *not* Bri obviously."

When our laughter settled, I continued somberly.

"Seriously though, I have thought about it. There are mornings when I miss him so badly that I don't even want to get out of bed. I don't want to be weak though. I know I have to move on. So I changed the color of the paint in our room. I got new bedroom furniture, I had new carpet put down... but I would've had to do that anyway because of the soaked through blood," my voice cracked. "Nothing is helping. I'm thinking maybe I should move."

"Maybe you should. I know you've got good memories in this house with Michael, but I can totally understand how the horrific memories of that day would make you want to leave," she said matching my solemn tone. "I worry about you being here all alone. You said they finally paid out the insurance money, right? Use that to start over fresh."

Although I was nowhere near as sad or troubled by my living arrangements as I pretended to be for Shan, I had actually been considering moving very soon. Luckily, I hadn't acted like a wife who killed her husband for the insurance money by calling about the claim too quickly. In fact, I hadn't called Principal until a full 3 months later.

I remembered watching an episode of CSI where any circumstances involving foul play automatically warranted a separate investigation by the insurance company, so I knew to expect it. Since Michael was unmistakably the victim of a murder, they needed to make sure they weren't going to pay his killer for doing the deed and I wasn't going to peg myself as being guilty by being money hungry.

The fact that Marlene was charged and behind bars awaiting trial evidently wasn't enough for them to release the funds quickly. They still snooped around my family, my job and questioned me just like the police did to compile enough information on me to warrant cutting the check. I was already financially stable enough to sustain the lifestyle I was accustomed to even without Michael's paycheck. I had access to both our separate and joint checking accounts in addition to our joint savings. There was no rush.

The day they approved issuance of it to me, I took 2 days to call them back for good measure. I didn't want to give Marlene's defense lawyer any straws to grab at other than what they were already bringing to the table.

"Yeah. I think I will. You know, I'm not always alone here. Ms. Nina has been coming over at least once a month if not more to have dinner with me. You know he was her only child so, with him gone, she's the one who's all alone.

I can't say I was all that close to her when he was alive, but now that he's gone, it's like she's a different person. Almost like the mother I never had," I lamented.

"Embrace it. You can never have too much love in your life Greer, and if anybody deserves it, you do. Particularly that motherly love. I know you missed out on a lot of time with your biological mom, and Stephanie was--"

"A raging, bipolar bitch."

"Listen to your mouth! You cussing now?" she guffawed.

I smirked. Maybe those first 2 drinks had affected me after all. I didn't actually mean to say that out loud.

"Speaking of family, I need to call Jahari," she said taking her phone from her bag. "He called me while we were at SFU, but by the time I saw it, it was too crazy to call him back."

"I'll take your suitcase up to your room then," I told her getting up from the couch as she swiped the phone's screen.

"Thanks hun."

I put her stuff in the spare bedroom and went to my own to get more comfortable. Thankfully, the temperature had dropped to the low 70's from the scorching heat we'd had all day. I put my hair in a banana clip, and slipped on some boy shorts and my cotton tank that I usually slept in.

When I came back down, Shan was still on her cell, so I went into the kitchen and fixed myself a glass of juice. Thinking over the day's events, I found myself grinning like the cat who ate the canary.

My dad enjoyed his party, Debbie got checked in front of a crowd of people, I had the best orgasm of my life so far, my best friend was in town for a week, and I finally got revenge on Bri Stanford's self-important ass. Oh yeah, and I gave Kendrick's jealous neighbor a dose of her own medicine.

"Alright baby. Shelita's calling me on the other line so, kiss my baby for me and I'll talk to you tomorrow," Shan was saying in the receiver when I came back into the den.

I got cozy on the couch again and got ready to immerse myself in the *WIVES WITH KNIVES* episode already playing.

"Yes... I know. I gotta go babe. Okay... okay. I love you too. Mmmhmm... I gotta go babe. Shelita's on the other line... Good night," she said pressing her screen again with a huff.

"Hello? Hello? Shelita? Damn," she said defeated. "I told him I had to click over, but he just kept on talking," she fussed hanging up.

No sooner had she hit END, than the phone rang right back in her hand.

"Hello?" she answered cheerfully.

My eyes were on the television, but her silence after only saying hello got my attention. Her cheery expression sunk like the Titanic as she listened to whatever was being said on the other end intensely.

"What's wrong?" I inquired in a whispered voice.

Shan's eyes were pooling within seconds, and her chest rose up and down with the speed of someone who was about to burst into tears. My heart dropped, assuming that it was her sister Shelita calling back with bad news. I silently prayed that no one she was close to had passed away. I knew it would absolutely crush her if anything happened to her mom.

After a couple of minutes of the same, I got impatient and more worried.

"Shan. What's going on? Why are you crying?"

"Jahari. Jahari. Jahari!" Shan said through gritted teeth as tears drenched her face and she got increasingly louder.

I was utterly confused.

"Jahari you motherfucker! Pick up the phone!" she screamed. "Pick-up-the-fucking-phone-Jahari! I can hear you asshole! Pick up the God Damn phone!"

Then, either he hung up or she got tired of shouting his name, because she propelled her iPhone across the den like a seasoned pitcher. It crashed against the wall and fell to the carpet with a cracked screen.

Hate and despair radiated from her eyes as she turned to me yelling, "He's cheating on me! The bastard is cheating on me with that squeaky voiced bitch he used to fuck in high school!"

I was speechless. Wendy? That was the only one of his exes Shan had spoken of previously. She was Jahari's ex-love from high school, and his mother also watched her kids during the day.

Shan said she got a bad vibe from the woman the few times she saw her while picking up Shamari from daycare. She thought Wendy introducing herself as Jahari's "ex-first love" was divisive, and she didn't trust the other seemingly innocent pleasantries they exchanged either.

Jahari surmised that Shan was misreading Wendy's character without merit, and reassured her that even if she hadn't, it was trivial since he only had eyes for his wife. Now, it appeared that there was more to the story.

"Who? Wendy? I don't want to believe he'd do that. What did he say exactly?"

"Oh, he said a whole fucking lot is what he said! That asshole must not have disconnected when I clicked over, so it rang back. When I picked up, I heard him saying how sexy she looked in her thong and that she needed to take it off.

She kept giggling and said he had to wait until they finished dinner to eat his dessert. He told her he was too hungry to taste her to wait.

Then it got quiet. That's when I started yelling to him to pick up," she told me with a stare as cold as ice.

Had there been a fly in the room, it could've easily flown into my open mouth. There was no way she could've misheard that situation.

"He's supposed to be at home with our son, but I bet Shamari is at his mom's while he's fucking that ho! I know one thing though! I know he *better not be* in the bed where I lay my head with that bitch!" she ranted furiously pacing the floor.

"How could he do this? *Why* would he do this? I'm his *wife*! We have a son!" she exclaimed angrily stopping in the middle of the floor and wiping her tear-soaked cheeks.

"*Ohhhh,* honey," I cried out wrapping my arms around her and drawing her head into my chest. "I'm sorry. I'm so sorry."

"I hate him Greer. I hate him *sooo* much right now. I wish I could kill him and that bitch," she cried.

I bet she did.

9

Greer

POW! POW! POW! POW! POW!

"Two to the head, 2 to the heart and 1 to the crotch," I said turning to Shan with a grin.

POW! POW! Two more shots resonated with a boom.

"Correction. Two shots to the crotch and one in the stomach. They really need to increase the amount of points you get for the crotch," I chortled.

"I had no idea you were this good of a shot. Hell, I didn't even know you had a gun," she said amazed.

"Practice makes perfect."

"Oh. You're a good shot," she affirmed as I pressed the button to bring the bullet riddled, masked robber target up to the window while I changed the magazine.

The target had scores marking key areas to aim at. 25 points for the center of the face, 15 points for anywhere on the head, 20 points for the heart, 15 points for the chest, and 10 points for the shoulders or lower torso.

The higher the points, the more difficult the shot. I suggested we come to the gun range to let off some steam, but I didn't tell her that I frequented it more than I did church, and she didn't ask.

Sunday's between 9am and 12pm was the best day to come to WITHIN RANGE for semi-privacy, because it was one of the few ranges open before noon.

I said changing out the target paper to an identical one. "Since Daddy's cancer has been in remission, I've been coming out here with him a lot. Or by myself. You ready to try?"

Biting her bottom lip, she nodded and nervously adjusted the goggles and protective headset over her ears. She wiped her hands nervously against her black leggings as I sent the target back down the track and helped her with her pose.

"Focus right there," I said showing her the site with my index finger. "Line the site up with your target and aim for areas with the most points.

Lisa says you should always aim at the chest as a rule of thumb. That way you're more likely to hit something vital on the body even if your aim is off.

Let's be honest, if you're ever in a situation where you have to shoot somebody, you don't want to just wound them. If you didn't want to mortally injure your target, you wouldn't be using a gun on them."

"I guess that's true. Who is Lisa? Some new girl you're hanging with?" she questioned lining her gun's site up and side-eyeing me.

"I wouldn't say that. We've hung out a few times. She's the girl that waved at me when we were getting our gear at the counter."

Lisa co-owned the range and thus, she was frequently on the premises when I came to hone my skills. We'd chatted on several of those occasions and she'd given me shooting pointers often. Her upbeat personality reminded me of Shan's, only today wasn't the right day to make the comparison since upbeat didn't describe my bestie at all.

"Okay. Arms straight out in front. Aim. Focus your site on the target. Relax. Then shoot," I coached the way my dad had taught me.

"Do I brace myself for the kickback?"

"There's very little recoil. Just relax and hold the gun firmly. Remember that you're in control."

"Listen to you guiding me like a professional. *There's very little recoil.* Let me find out you're dangerous," she sniggered.

I smiled devilishly. Let her find out indeed. At least she'd loosened up enough to laugh a little. She had a total meltdown, blustering about

Jahari's betrayal, and beating herself up with hindsight memories of red flags she didn't take as clues to his infidelity before.

She was convinced the lulls in the conversation she eavesdropped on were because they were kissing, groping or both, and that sent her into a raging tailspin. I contemplated telling her how I reacted to witnessing Michael and Marlene going at it on video the first time; but I couldn't.

I never told the police or anyone that I'd actually seen footage of the 2 in action. Shan was my best friend, but even she couldn't be trusted with information that could lead to me switching places with Marlene in the Dekalb County Jail. I kept my mouth shut.

Shan's bare face and somber expression betrayed her misery as she emptied the clip and turned to me for more rounds. Her shots were all over the place, but they hit the robber inside the lines, and that was all that counted.

It was unconventional, but I found going to the gun range to be surprisingly cathartic when I was angry, upset, emotional, or just needed to think. Undoubtedly, Shan's threats to murder Jahari and Wendy were simply fueled by anger, and were emptier than Ryan Lochte's head.

Still, I hoped shooting off a few rounds might help her temporarily purge some of her injured feelings. Imagining my enemies replacing the target had certainly helped me on numerous occasions.

Luckily for Jahari, Shan's conscience would prevent her from seeking retribution the way I was now geared to deliver it. She's been known to let the Queens girl out to fight when pushed to the limit, but she wasn't homicidal by any means.

Like most cheaters, Jahari basically fed her the same BS Michael and a lot of others feed their wives to lull them into a false sense of security, while they play hide the sausage with the next woman.

I felt her pain. Not only because I was witnessing the obvious agony on her face, but because I knew what it was like to have your entire future with somebody flash before your eyes at the hands of another woman.

The betrayal hurts. The insult to your intelligence while they deceive you with lie after lie, hurts. The fact that their disgusting behavior causes you to be insecure about your own worth, hurts the most. It feels like a long cool knife being jammed into your heart... and I never planned to experience that feeling again.

About 45 minutes later, we'd shot off all the rounds I purchased, and Shan seemed a little less glum than she had been when we arrived. She still wasn't too talkative, but there were traces of amusement when she'd scored high.

"Feel any better?" I asked her, taking off my goggles and headset.

She shrugged. "Not really. I think I feel... empty. Everything I thought I knew about my marriage, about my husband, I don't."

I sucked in my lips and nodded before speaking. "Are you going to talk to him when he calls?"

She looked at me like I'd asked her if she was going to lick the floor, then up to the ceiling with a sigh.

"No. I don't have anything to say to him. He's just gonna lie through his teeth and make me want to bust his head open. Plus, I don't want to do this on the phone. I want to look him in the face when I confront him."

"You're just going to ignore his calls the entire week you're here?"

"Yep."

"What about Shamari? How are you going to talk to him without talking to Jahari?"

"Easy. I'll call while he's at Evelyn's. Jahari isn't off this week... that I know of," she replied with a roll of her eyes. "Not unless he took off to spend more time with that bitch."

"She's gonna want to know why you're not talking to her son."

"People in Hell want ice water. As long as she has *my* son over there, she's gonna let me speak to him when I want to. For all I know, she knows he's been creeping with Wendy," she grimaced rubbing the back of her neck.

"No, I can't believe she'd do that. She likes you, doesn't she?"

"That doesn't mean she won't cover for her son. Shit she likes Wendy too. She watches her kids. She's known her longer than she's known me, and they have that whole Bronx connection thing going on."

I gathered our stuff in silence and held the door for Shan, passing her her bag as we exited the target practice room.

"Did you enjoy yourself? Was this your first time at a shooting range?" Lisa asked Shan as I turned our goggles and headsets into her over the counter where guns and rifles were shown for sale.

"I liked it. Yes, it was my first time," she answered with a fo'smile adjusting the strap on her bag over her shoulder.

"Well Greer is a natural. She was shooting like a pro after only a few months training. We give shooting lessons Tuesday, Thursday and Saturday's," Lisa stated kindly while starting to clean one of the goggles.

Lisa was petite and pretty with big, beautiful, cognac-colored eyes, and an espresso complexion. Her onyx shaded hair was in shoulder length Bantu Knots and she was dressed simply in jeans and a black T-shirt with the range's logo on it.

"I don't live here," Shan answered dryly.

"Oh. Where are you visiting from?" Lisa continued politely.

"New York," she answered turning away from her and giving me a look that screamed for Lisa to shut up.

Probably picking up on Shan's obvious desire to be left alone, Lisa addressed me.

"Did you want to pick up anything else? We've just got in a new stock of mini stun guns. I've even got *pink*," she coaxed with a wink, knowing that pink was my favorite color.

"What's she need a stun gun for when she has a handgun?" Shan asked snidely.

Unfazed, Lisa answered cheerfully, "Because sometimes you can't get to your gun in time. This new mini we have in is small enough to fit in the palm of your hand," she said walking down to another case and coming back with it.

"Sounds tiny," I chimed in with interest.

"VIPERTEK VTS-880 - 35,000,000 Volt mini stun gun with a LED flashlight," Lisa read from a display card as she placed the small pink item in my hand.

"This is cute," I exclaimed with a grin as Shan glared disinterestedly at it and then me. "How much is it?"

"Girl it's super inexpensive. $12.00"

"What? I could shock the shit out of somebody with 35,000,000 volts for just $12?" I laughed glancing at Shan.

"Yep. Do you want to go ahead and get that? Maybe add some rounds too? It sounded like y'all unloaded most, if not all of the ones you came with."

"Yeah. I think I will. I'll get that and 4 boxes."

"Race! Grab 4 boxes of Winchester 95 grain FMJ's for me please!" she shouted at a handsome, milk chocolate, 6-foot drink of water who was sitting behind the ammunition counter on the other side of the store on his cell.

He nodded and held up his index to her for a moment while continuing his conversation. I'd never seen him before. With his looks, I absolutely would've remembered if I had. I wondered if he was a new hire.

"I've never seen him before. Did he just start working here?" I inquired casually.

"Who? Race? No. That's my partner. I'm surprised you've never met him before. But then again, he's usually not here this early. *Especially* not on Sunday's."

Shan and I watched him like hawks as he put the phone in his pocket and got the boxes of ammo.

"Fine isn't he," Lisa giggled.

"Hell yeah he is," Shan agreed shoving into me. "Is he married?"

"No, not married. But he's got a girlfriend. At least I think he does. They break up and get back together more than Transformers; but you ain't heard that from me."

We laughed, but Shan and I stopped abruptly as he started approaching. He looked at each of us suspiciously and put the boxes on the counter as he came behind it.

He was sexy without trying to be, and his lean and athletic body didn't hurt. Nor did the way the short sleeves of his Harley Davidson shirt hugged his muscles.

I'm sure I was blushing like a ripe tomato, and even Shan had perked up from her intolerant mood. Which made me side-eye her. Hell, she was still married.

I forced myself to look away so I wouldn't look as thirsty as he made me feel; but damn he was attractive! Knowing he was a business owner was even more appealing. With the upturn my finances took since I cashed in on that policy, I wasn't even considering anyone who didn't have their act together.

His dark, deep-set eyes were fixed on me when I glanced back at him leaning against a shelf, so I smiled.

"What are ya'll lovely ladies over here laughing about? What, is my shirt too small or something?" he asked wittily in a smooth baritone voice, placing one hand in his jeans pocket.

"Since you asked, it *does* look like you're wearing a smedium. Go up a size or something. We can tell you're in shape. You don't have to cut your circulation off to prove it," Lisa told him still laughing while ringing up my purchases. "It's none of your business what we're laughing at, nosy. Thank you for bringing these over here. You can go now."

"Please excuse her poor manners. She's not usually this rude. I'm Race. We own this together," he informed us, holding out his hand to shake Shan's first, then mine.

"You have *beautiful* eyes," he said letting our shake linger. "I'm sure you hear that a lot though, don't you?" he asked as Lisa bagged my purchase stealing glances between us.

"On occasion I do, but thank you," I replied evenly.

I hadn't forgotten that Lisa said he had a girlfriend. I know she said he and his girl were on and off, but if they were on, then his flirting with me was a turn off.

"That'll be $98.79 Greer," Lisa said taking my charge card from me as she and Race exchanged a look I couldn't quite read.

"Don't you have somewhere to be?" she asked him.

"Are you trying to get rid of me? Your boyfriend is supposed to be meeting me here, but he's late. You don't have him out there running errands for you, do you?"

"Man, don't even try it. He went to your grandmother's this morning and I haven't seen him since," she retorted with a hand on her hip.

His phone sang Kid Ink and Chris Brown's "Show Me" in his pocket, signaling that someone more important to talk to than us was calling.

I doubted it was Lisa's boyfriend, whomever he was, or else it seemed like he would've said so. He frowned and shot us a one hand goodbye as he took the call walking down the length of the long gun display counter toward an office door.

"*Now* you wanna call me back, huh? Where were you..." he was saying before he disappeared into the office.

"I guess they're back on," Lisa mumbled.

"You don't like her?" Shan pried.

Lisa frowned like the question insulted her, and looked back towards the office. Seeing that he wasn't in earshot, she spoke in a hushed tone, leaning over the counter.

"I like her. I just don't like her for him. Me, Race and his brother Geo been friends since the sixth grade. Me and Geo have been together almost 3 years, and Race is like a brother to me. I just wanna see him happy.

Song is good people, but I just don't think she's right for him. He met her through me, and sometimes I wish they never met. They fight, they make up, they fight, they make up. It's not healthy."

"Her name is Song? Like music?" I asked thinking the name was pretty and wondering if she was a reflection of it.

"Like music."

"Is she a singer? It seems like with a name like that, she should be a singer or doing something musical," Shan picked up.

Lisa chuckled. "No. If she did, she'd probably sound like Kim Kardashian on helium or Michele'."

"Who? That *R&B Divas* show lady that used to be married to Dre?" I questioned.

"Yeah her. Song has a deviated septum. It's some kind of thing with her nose that makes her voice sound nasally, and she can't smell anything either."

"She can't smell anything? So how does she taste her food? Know if she stinks? That's crazy," Shan commented.

Lisa shrugged. "I wondered the same thing girl. I have no idea, but apparently her taste buds work. I don't know about the rest. I think there's a surgery she can have to fix it, but I don't think she's pressed."

Personally, I couldn't imagine not being able to smell. I loved the aroma of flowers, baked goods, sweet perfumes and a plethora of other things.

"Wow. That's wild. Anyway girl, let us get out of here," I said starting to head towards the door with my stuff. "I'll see you next time."

"Alright then," she said with a quick wave as Shan trailed me.

As soon as we got in the car, Shan warned, "Don't ever tell that girl any of your business. She can't hold water. I know more about Race and his girl than I know about *her*."

"She talks a lot, but she's cool. I don't really have anything to tell her that she can't read online or see on the news anyway. She's harmless."

Shan rolled her eyes and looked out the window as I started the car. Funny how she expects me to be cool with her douchey acting girlfriends, but anytime she meets a friend of mine, she finds an issue.

I was still driving the Yukon, but I hooked up my phone to the Bluetooth in it. When my phone buzzed in the cup holder, I glanced down at the face on the screen and answered through the Bluetooth connection on the steering wheel.

"Hey Birthday boy," I answered on speakerphone seeing Daddy's picture on the screen.

Although his birthday party was the day before, his *actual* birthday was today.

"Babygirl. You still done went to the range? I thought you said Shantel was comin'," he questioned.

"She's right here. I took her with me," I told him backing out of my spot.

"Hey Mr. Chuck," Shan sang with a genuine smile. "How you been feeling?"

My dad loved Shan from the first day he met her, and the feeling was mutual. He relied on her to be my protector away from home, and she promised him she would be. I thought it was funny that he wanted Shan to look out for me, but Stephanie got to screw me over for decades.

"Hey there now my New York peach! I'm feeling good. Mighty good. How you likin' it in the big apple?"

She twisted her lips but still answered jovially.

"Umm... I'm not really. I might be moving back here sooner rather than later," she told him, which made my head snap in her direction.

"Is that so! That big city life ain't fo' you no'mo' huh? I'm sure Babygirl will be happy to have you back. What y'all doing for dinner?"

"I don't know," Shan answered looking at me.

"Nothing special Daddy. I was going to cook. Why?"

"Simone's cookin' a big family dinner fo' my birthday. They leave out in the mornin' back to California you know. We ain't had a family dinner with the *whole family* since befo' Steph passed. Carrie's gon' come. Even Donna claims she's brangin' her fast tail over," he jibed.

I looked to Shan mouthing, "Do you wanna go?" and she nodded, amused by his commentary.

"Is your *other* daughter gonna be there?" I asked unenthusiastically.

"*All* of my children and grandchildren will be there. Including you. Now I'm askin' ya to come, but I'm tellin' ya to be there.

I don't expect no foolishness out of you, her or anybody else whilst we're celebrating my birthday. I don't know how many more of these I'll have to come and neither do any of you.

Simone says dinner's gon' be ready 'round 6 or so. I expect you and Shantel to be there 'round about that time."

I groaned.

"Daddy, I don't really feel like going at it with that fool anymore. I've already go—"

"Babygirl, I expect you and Shan to be there 'round 6 I said. I don't want to hear nothin' mo' 'bout what happened yesterday, or the day befo' that, or the day befo' that. Act yo' ages damn it.

You ain't all right and she ain't all wrong. Stop this shit. Now don't make me raise my voice while you got Shan in the car wit' ya. You hear what I'm saying to ya Babygirl?"

The cautionary tone in his voice let me know that there was gonna be hell to pay if I defied his "request". 'You ain't all right and she ain't all wrong,' I satirized his voice in my head. Oh yes the hell I *was* all right!

I'd hoped I wouldn't have to see the untamed shrew anymore for a long while, but I would honor my father's wishes.

"Yes Daddy," I dragged looking at Shan to cosign my agitation, but she was preoccupied by the scenery.

"Alright then. I'll see y'all gals tonight. Drive safely," he retorted hanging up without waiting for my reply.

We drove for several minutes in a dead silence besides the music on the radio. She didn't seem to want to talk and I was okay with that until she was ready.

I stopped at the *Chic Fil A* drive through on the way home, and we ordered some food to tide us over until dinner. Shan's dismal demeanor was contagious, and I was beginning to feel melancholy too.

I wondered what Wendy had that was so great, that he'd jeopardized his family to be with her. If a woman as beautiful, smart, accomplished, charismatic and family oriented as Shan couldn't keep her man from cheating… who could?

"I thought you said Rolly was at the house last night?" she asked randomly as I parked. "You parked somewhere else?"

"Are you sure you're not a detective instead of an Actuary? I swear you don't miss anything. It's in the shop. I forgot," I said casually.

"Shit. Apparently, I've been missing a lot," she retorted unmistakably referring to her marriage.

I didn't respond as we went inside and dropped the bags of food on the island. I left my keys and bag on the table by the door as usual, while she hung her bag on the back of a kitchen chair.

"If Michael was still alive, knowing fully what he did? Do you think you would've staid married to him?" she asked catching me off guard.

I wanted to be honest, but I'd sold the police on my intentions to stay with Michael no matter what he was doing on the side. I know a lot of conversations were replayed during trials and I had to stick to what I'd said to them. Even if it was a bold-faced lie.

"Uh… you know… I wish I could say that I would've been strong enough to leave; but I wasn't. I married for better or for worse. I couldn't see myself without him until I didn't have him anymore. As hurt as I was by it, and still am, I would've wanted to work through it."

She sighed and looked around like she was taking in my words.

"I'm gonna tell you something that I haven't told *anybody else.* Other than the police," I disclosed taking our food from the bags.

"What?"

"I'm embarrassed to admit it, but I suspected he was cheating on me before it happened. I confronted him about it. Of course, he denied it. Said I was crazy, blah blah blah… but *we* know. Women feel it in here when something isn't right," I said patting the place over my heart.

"I didn't want it to be true. I didn't want to believe he'd do that to me when I was doing my best to keep him happy. I let it go. I figured if he *was* cheating on me, he'd stop knowing I was on to him. I thought fear of losing me would make him stop.

He started being a little more romantic. Calling me in the middle of the day when he should be sleeping, stuff like that. I stopped smelling her perfume on his stuff too. I thought it was over. I thought maybe it was just the 7-year itch, and since he'd gotten it scratched, he was done with her.

I just wanted to move on with our lives. He was going to be changing to day-shift soon and we'd be back on the same schedule again. I was foolish," I said regretfully swiping tears away. "I guess as long as she was still willing, so was he. But you know what? I still would've fought for my marriage," I added.

Though it was the furthest from the truth, I had honestly been rethinking how I handled things. Maybe men like Jahari, Michael, and even my father were worth giving a second chance. Maybe it was the women who were the real problem.

My father swore to my stepmother for years after his affair with my mother that he never cheated again. Marlene was the first and only woman Michael cheated with that I knew of; and Jahari... I doubt he would've cheated if not for the lure of that old flame, whatever it was.

These women knew the men they were sleeping with were married, but they pursued them anyway. They were trifling, immoral and disrespectful.

I loved my mother, and I only had fond memories of the short time I had with her, but I wouldn't have had the miserable childhood I experienced if she'd been virtuous.

The inner struggle to feel valuable in a house where I was the biracial, bastard, secret lovechild forced on the offended wife was great. I hated Stephanie growing up, and still did in adulthood, but I as a scorned wife, I understood her better now.

There was no way in hell I would've been able to raise a baby Michael would've had in an affair. It wasn't my fault that my parents wanted to sleep together more than they respected the sanctity of marriage, but I was the one being punished for it.

"See, but he kept doing it. That's just it Greer. How can I ever trust him again?" Shan said sorrowfully. "For all I know, he's been planning this since the day we moved back. Or even before. I feel stupid.

No matter what problems we've had, I *never* thought about cheating on him. Not enough to act on it. We promised each other that we'd never disrespect each other like this.

She's pretty but she's got a bunch of kids, works check out at Wal-mart and still lives with her mother. She's not even a fucking upgrade," she wept resting her elbows on the table and covering her face.

I watched her sympathetically as her ringing phone interjected. She didn't budge to retrieve it, but dropped her hands and looked at me with puffy eyes.

"You think that's him?" I asked.

"Yeah. I'm glad he has a custom ringtone. The screen is black for everything except text messages for some reason. You know, in addition to it being cracked," she smirked through her tears.

"How many times has he called today?"

"Just twice. He sent a text too talking about 'Call me when you get up. I miss you Bae.' Fuck him," she said drying her face with a napkin and plucking a waffle fry from the bag.

I took a bite of my chicken sandwich and mulled over her situation in my head. I was glad she was staying, but I think I would've left to confront him in her place. Unless I had a more diabolical reason not to that is.

"Bri texted me that she's doing better by the way," she stated changing the subject.

"Oh. That's good. I can't believe she refused to go to the hospital. She's something else."

"That's Bri for ya. Once she makes her mind up about something, that's it. She had the nerve to be talking about how mad she was that she never got her Key Lime Pie. Like really heifer?" Shan laughed.

"Umm Umm Umm. Who paid for that by the way? I know I never gave them my card for my stuff," I asked authentically.

"Uh... I think Bri did. I didn't pay for mine either. I don't even remember getting a check. Do you?"

"Nope."

"Aww hell. I think I remember Brenna giving Tracy a card to charge, and I'm sure it wasn't her own. You don't think they would've let us leave without paying do you?"

I shrugged. We ate and talked more about the night before, staying away from anything that would direct us back to Jahari. By 5 o'clock, we'd discussed everything from what I'd want in a new house, to drama at work, to updates on our siblings and her mother's new husband.

When we got to Daddy's house, the garage and driveway were filled with his Roadmaster, Shawn's rented Altima, Carrie's ILX and Will's Highlander. I parked on the street in front of the house and Shan and I walked up in conversation.

"Auntie Greer!" Tamia hollered bursting through the screen door and into my arms with Shawn and Simone's daughter Crystal hot on her heels.

I hadn't seen Crystal since she was an infant, so she didn't know me too well. Still, the little girl wrapped her arms around my waist just as Tamia had.

"Hey! Why're you so happy to see me?" I asked surprised.

I'd never been greeted this heartily by Tamia before, but I liked it.

"I'm always happy to see you!" she squealed with a cherubic smile. "Plus, Papa said we could eat when you got here."

"I see. You're not happy to see me. You're just hungry," I pouted playfully.

She jumped up and down shaking her head vigorously beside me as Shan and I continued into the house and Crystal darted off towards the dining room yelling that I had arrived.

"I'm happy to see you too Auntie Greer, but I'm hungry! Auntie Simone is making mac and cheese, meatloaf, cabbage, candy yams and cheese rolls!" she exclaimed excitedly. "Who're you?" she asked Shan skipping towards the door with my hand in hers.

"I'm Shan. You've grown into such a big girl. You're, Tamia? I haven't seen you since you were a little baby. How old are you now?"

Tamia nodded exposing her missing front teeth.

"I'm 6 and 3 quarters," she stated proudly.

"Three quarters huh?" Shan asked amused.

Tamia bobbed her head vigorously.

"My birthday is in 3 more months. September," she continued holding up 3 fingers.

In the kitchen, Aunt Carrie was the first to greet me with a warm hug, then repeating it with Shan. I could always count on her to be welcoming.

"I think the last time I saw you was at Greer's wedding. Sharnell?" Carrie asked Shan.

"Shantel," she corrected still smiling.

"I'm sorry honey. Blame it on my mind and not my heart."

"No problem. I remember you. Ms. Carrie. You still look great."

Carrie waved her off with a grin.

"Girl just call me Carrie. That Ms. and Mr. stuff before somebody's name is for old folks."

"I beg your pardon," my father said pretending offense as he kissed me on the cheek and hugged Shan right behind Carrie. "She calls *me* Mr. Chuck."

"Case and point then," Carrie teased sticking her hands in the back pockets of her distressed jeans.

I spotted Simone in the kitchen pulling a tray of cheese rolls from the oven, while Shawn, Will and Debbie sat at the dining room table.

Simone was Filipino and Black with Asian eyes and jet-black wavy hair down to her butt. She reminded me of Chilli from that 90's group TLC, and at maybe 5 feet, she was just as short.

Willa sat in a highchair beside Debbie's chair cooing while Colt, Shawn and Simone's 15-year-old showed my sister Donna something on his phone by the door to the living room.

Colt looked like a darker version of Kobe Bryant in his youth with a short curly fade, braces and the 5'11" height to match Shawn's.

Donna looked cute as a button with her hair piled into a curly bun atop her head. Loose baby hairs accentuated her heart shaped face and brought out her hazel eyes.

Her large hoop earrings touched her cheeks when she smiled and hugged me wearing a tight cut off shirt and tighter jeans. Donna had the natural curves I wished God had blessed me with and "bad bitches" paid for.

She had a degree in fashion marketing, but was working the front office at some former basketball player's auto-shop instead of using it.

When I asked her why, she said the work was easy, the money was good enough and that her "sponsor" took care of everything else she needed. She traveled more than a stewardess and partied like she was on spring break all year round, so I guess it was working for her.

I greeted everyone but Debbie with a hug and reintroduced Shan to everyone else. Debbie sneered at me and addressed Shan curtly. Shawn's return was stiff towards me, as usual, and he was back talking to Will before he was out of my grasp.

Shawn was emotionless when it came to me and had been since the day my little feet touched the Foster home doorsteps. I'd caught him looking at me with contempt many a time over the years. He simply loathed me in silence.

He was never mean to me, but he basically regarded me like a piece of furniture he could ignore. Growing up, when he wasn't writing in his journal or reading comic books, he was doing everything else *but* talking to me.

As adults, he spoke when necessary, occasionally contributed to conversations I was included in, and called to express his condolences when Michael was killed, but that was it.

Despite my reservations about attending dinner, it went off without a hitch. We ate heartily and the conversation flowed around the table boisterously. Shan even surprised me by being her typical vivacious self while I did more listening than I did talking, per my usual.

"I have an announcement to make," Debbie spoke up when most plates were bare.

All eyes were curiously on her, including Will's.

"What you announcing, Baby?" he asked her with furrowed brows.

She rolled her eyes at him resentfully and sat back in her chair with a sly grin as she tapped the table annoyingly with her press on nails.

"As of tomorrow, Greer is going to be handling all of Daddy's financial and personal needs. Whatever he doesn't want to handle himself that is. I'll still work at FLOWER ME WITH LOVE 3 days a week, 'cause that's my mother's shop and it's her legacy. Other than that, I'm not gonna be Daddy's errand girl anymore."

Everyone, especially me, was stunned into silence. What the hell was she talking about? Daddy hadn't discussed anything with *me* about taking over a damn thing.

"Deborah, what silliness you talkin' 'bout now? I ain't made Greer in control of nothin' different than she's always been," Daddy spoke up.

"I know you haven't. That's why I'm doing it *for* you. I've been the one doing everything for you since Momma died. Shit, since *before* Momma died. It's a thankless job.

Donna gets to live her life with no strings attached. Doing what she wants like she's still a teenager. Shawn gets to act like he doesn't even know us 12 months out of the year while he writes for the *Huffington Post* like he's Jonah Jamison on Spiderman or something.

You don't appreciate all the stuff I did when you were going through your cancer treatments, and you're even less grateful now that it's in remission. *I* was the one running around here cooking, cleaning, taking you to appointments, managing your banking online, keeping the lights and gas bills paid… that was *me*.

I took care of you and my own family at the same time; even while I was pregnant," she attested, becoming more animated with finger gestures. "Still, that wasn't enough. Greer's still your favorite no matter what she does or *doesn't* do.

I'ma let her earn all this praise you always have for her. Since she's so *awesome*. Since she's so *smart*. Since she's your *favorite*. Let her do it all. I quit. I'ma fall back from it all. You let her do it."

"C'mon Debbie. Not now," Donna appealed reaching across the table to touch one of Debbie's tapping hands. "Have you been drinking already?"

"No, I haven't been drinking," she spat snatching her hand away from Donna. "Why not now? This is the best time when everybody is here. That way nobody can say I said anything I didn't, or that I wasn't 100% clear about when I said it.

Since Momma died, I've been taking over her role for Daddy, while still filling my own. But he don't care," she said looking at my father whose light complexion was beet red with anger. "Soon as his *Babygirl* shows up, I'm gum under his shoe and she's the Princess Bride. Well not no more."

"You know what gal? You ain't got to raise another finger in yo' life to help me do *nothin'*. I didn't know you was only doing it so I'd tap dance fo' ya. I thought you was takin' care of me 'cause I'm yo' daddy. I ain't never let you go a day in yo' life without nothin' you ever needed, but you still whinin' 'bout not getting' enough attention."

"Probably because of Momma. After the great light bright got here, I was invisible," she shot back resentfully.

"Is that right? Whatsamatta? Everybody havin' too good a time fo' ya at this dinner? You so miserable you can't go a whole dinner wit'out startin' some mess? You just miserable," he spat harshly. "You ain't happy if she ain't unhappy. Somethin' is wrong wit' yo' soul!"

"Daddy," Donna interrupted while the rest of us sat mute.

"Okay Pop. Let's all just calm down," Will followed trying to make peace. "This is getting out of control. Now Debbie feels like—"

"Shut up Will," Daddy told him. "I don't need you to run my life Deborah. I been doing that befo' yo' spiteful ass was born, and I can do it now. I swear if it wasn't for my grands, I wouldn't fool wit' ya no mo' than I have to neither," he continued castigating Debbie.

"If I'm miserable it's because I was brought up by a lying, cheating, father who was out screwing white women and making bastards instead of being home with his family!" Debbie spat venomously as she shoved away from the table.

"Debbie!" Aunt Carrie called. "Chuck, now y'all stop this here. This was—"

"You so worried 'bout competin' with Greer all the time, you don't do nothin' with ya own wretched self. You just a hateful, jealous woman is what you are; and I hope you don't raise my grands to be that way just like ya!" Daddy yelled back.

Shawn looked on calmly, but with a frown like he was watching a movie he didn't like. He adjusted the thin rimmed glasses on his face and exchanged apologetic glances to Simone, who was staring down at her plate like it was going to beam her up.

"Fuck—you—Daddy!" she roared causing the baby to erupt into cries.

Everyone gasped. Will picked up Willa, while attempting to verbally calm Debbie down and Tamia started whimpering too.

It was taking everything in my power to remain calm as she disrespected my father like that, but I had to bide my time. I wanted to jump up and stab her with the knife stuck in the meatloaf in the middle of the table.

I wanted to watch blood gush from her foul mouth and watch her eyes roll up into her head in a final farewell, but all I could do was cry.

Rage filled tears poured from my eyes because I needed to end her, but couldn't. Because I'd dropped the idea of killing her before, and now she was here humiliating me again and disrespecting my father. Debbie's, ungrateful, insolent, waste of flesh didn't deserve to breathe the same air as my father.

The room erupted with banter and arguing between Daddy, Carrie, Donna, Debbie and Will as the rest of us looked on wide-eyed, including Shan. All were in defense of Debbie not speaking to my father that way, and Shan tried to console me.

I was gonna keep playing the elk now because I needed to, but I was done arguing with Debbie. The first opportunity I got, I was gonna stop her from breathing.

10

Greer

Court wasn't half as entertaining as *Law & Order* and *20/20* would have you believe it to be. After 3 days of listening to police, material witnesses and experts testifying ad nauseam for the prosecution, the real meat of the case was discussed during the defense's presentation on the last two. Regardless, I was thrilled that the entire trial was finally coming to a close.

It was a hot 87-degree day in Atlanta, so everyone had on airy summer wear, which was counterproductive since the temperature in the courtroom was set to iceberg.

My stomach was growling like a pack of Pitbull's in a dogfight, so I had a hard time focusing on what was being said between craving some fried green tomatoes and trying to warm the goose bumps on my arms. All attention was on the attorney for the defense team as he grandstanded in front of the jury box.

John Fullsome gave a lively delivery in a too tight charcoal suit, causing his graying comb-over to wisp about as he insisted that the prosecution hadn't sufficiently proven their case beyond the reason of a doubt.

I glanced at the elder Judge Ellis watching Fullsome over the rims of his glasses while he avowed his client's innocence in his closing arguments. Ellis reminded me of Mr. Drummond on that old T.V. show *Different Strokes*. He was a balding white man, probably in his late 60's, who was too stubborn to shave off the white tufts of hair surrounding his shiny noggin.

He clearly was not up for any shenanigans in his courtroom from the stern way he spoke and issued instructions. It was also easy to see that he didn't like long proceedings either. Adjournments ran for lunch like clockwork, and I caught him checking the time on his watch more than once during some of the testimonies.

The Prosecutor, Lisa Ramos, appeared to be unbothered by Fullsome's performance thus far. She sat stiffly with her hands clasped on the table and her ankles crossed in high heel black Manolo Blahnik's. An expensive looking pastel pants suit fit her petite form tastefully as her brunette hair cascaded sleekly down her back. Her dark eyes watched Fullsome with an unimpressed countenance as she periodically whispered something to her second chair.

She'd closed first. The body language and expressions of most of the jurors made me believe they were convinced. In this case though; most wouldn't be enough. If *all* of them didn't vote to convict, Marlene would be out and hoing again within 24 hours of the verdict.

Fueling my agitation was Fullsome's notable confidence in his delivery that he would persuade the jury to discount it all. His murder case acquittal track record was better than his cheap appearance would lead one to believe. I hadn't heard of him prior to my Google search, but I discovered that his name was attached to a lot of big cases in Georgia, and his winning streak made him more than a formidable opponent.

"You see ladies and gentlemen; the Prosecution has simply *failed* to prove their case against my client. It would be an atrocity to convict her of a crime that she did—not—commit. Especially with such flimsy evidence," he said sourly, tugging on his suit jacket and pacing.

Probably because the tight fit of his suit was stunting his circulation, I surmised humorously.

"The *only* thing that the prosecution *has* been able to prove is that my client had an affair with Michael Patterson, and that she was not initially forthcoming with that information. Now, did Marlene Braxton *have* an affair with the victim? Yes. Was it wrong? Yes.

Like Mr. Patterson, my client was also in a long-term relationship and she didn't want to admit her indiscretions for fear of losing her family. She sat right up there on the stand and told you that herself though, didn't she? *Of course,* she wasn't forthcoming in the beginning. How many people having an affair are?

She had no idea that she was a suspect when the police told her that Mr. Patterson was deceased. She didn't even know how he died at initiation. Had she been aware that they were investigating a murder *first,* and that *she* was a suspect, she would've told them the truth from the beginning. You saw the tapes. She was genuinely surprised and broken up when they told her what happened. *Genuinely,* surprised," he emphasized connecting his palms together.

I scoffed louder than I intended, grabbing the attention of a few people including, Judge Ellis and Attorney Fullsome. I maintained the blank expression I'd carried since he began his long as hell dissertation though.

It was ridiculous for anyone to believe that a woman, who lived in the projects of Miami (judging from her former address on court documents), didn't understand that homicide detectives coming to her door meant that they were investigating a murder. C'mon now.

Fullsome cleared his throat, tossing me a disapproving glare and continued on with his rant.

"Does the fact that she had an affair with him make her a bad person? Perhaps. But what it *doesn't do,* is make her a murderer. Marlene Braxton *is not* on trial here today for a lapse in moral judgement ladies and gentlemen of the jury. *That* is something for her to take up with her God when the time comes. Not for a court of law to decide.

All of the evidence presented to you here is circumstantial *at best.* She didn't even have a motive. Sure, they presented a couple of text messages between them. Messages from weeks earlier showing that Michael wanted to call off the affair.

But obviously he didn't. In fact, other text messages and my client's testimony showed that they'd had more than *6* additional rendezvous after that text conversation. *Six*," he told them holding up 6 digits.

"I realize that my client's history of violence has also been called into question; but like I said when the prosecution brought it up; they're reaching. They're attempting to villainize Marlene for defending herself against attacks by her children's father. Granted, they were young, and immature at the time, but she wasn't the aggressor. Even so, Michael Patterson was practically decapitated. Randy Cambridge's injuries were not life threatening.

You all saw him in court here just a day ago. Clearly, she didn't kill him, and he testified himself that he didn't believe her intention had been to do so at the time of their altercations. Hence, why they were back together and attempted to work their relationship out.

Now, the DNA evidence..." he mentioned with finger quotes. "Was also not conclusive. Ms. Braxton doesn't dispute that they had sex early that morning or that she took a shower at the victim's home before leaving. So yes, her DNA was found.

That doesn't exclude the possibility that another party took a shower behind her does it? Certainly not," he said shaking his head as my mother in-law, sitting to my left, reached over and took my hand in her own.

I began crying silent crocodile tears for the benefit of the jury and judge, but Ms. Nina's face was dry. She wasn't one to wear her emotions on her sleeve, and she'd been stoic all of the days of trial thus far. Masking her feelings during court, she kept her head held high and her lips tight as she spoke quietly to me. Her eyes glued on Fullsome.

"He's a despicable man to represent that woman after what she has done to our family."

"He is," I cosigned wiping tears from my eyes and sandwiching her hand between mine briefly, before releasing it to rub my chilling arms. "There's no defense for what she did?"

Ms. Nina nodded slowly, running her tongue across her teeth. Her typically youthful face looked ages older since the day she found out her only son was sent to hell earlier than expected. Make-up aided in concealing the dark circles plaguing her face, but her hair seemed grayer and her typically healthy frame had slimmed considerably.

Ms. Nina was decked out in her best church gear each day of trial, and this day was no different. She wore gold rose petal earrings and a necklace with a matching pendant that rested against the blue material of her well-tailored dress. Her hair was neatly curled and framed her face making her resemble a softer and shorter version of the former news anchor Monica Kaufman.

If I didn't already tell you, I wasn't much of a fan of my mother in-law. She was overbearing, controlling and boundary less when it came to her son. All traits that reminded me too much of Stephanie.

Ms. Nina had no qualms about imposing her beliefs and ideas on our life, and 9 times out of 10, her momma's boy son implemented whatever *she* wanted over what his wife needed.

Being the people pleaser that I always was, I never put up a noticeable fuss to her or Michael, so she had no idea how much she really got under my skin. Michael knew that I wasn't thrilled with her meddling in our business, but since I silenced my own voice so frequently and let mommy dearest have her way, it was never a topic we argued about.

Honestly, I didn't get any joy in her anguish. I mean, she loved him like nobody else did and so did I. Funny enough, losing Michael must've inspired her to develop motherly feelings towards me that she'd never expressed before. She was always cordial and friendly to me; but she was never maternal.

I always felt like she simply tolerated me being there because she knew he was going to have to marry *somebody* eventually, and if that somebody was me, so be it. Not knowing quite how to interact with her anyway, I kept them polite and short as much as possible.

When news broke of the murder, she was the first one to my aide other than my father. We cried together and tried to make sense of it all. Or at least I pretended to try along with her.

She offered comforting words and came to my house to shield me from the media through the humiliation of Michael's infidelity being exposed. She was the one who planned the funeral and arranged to have a crime scene clean-up crew come in to sanitize and dispose of everything the blood ruined.

Essentially, that meant carpet removal, disposal of the mattress, bed linen, and having them scrub the walls and other items they felt were salvageable. I don't know exactly how much it cost because she covered it all without even asking, but I heard that kind of work could cost in the low thousands to do.

Yes, Ms. Nina was treating me pretty good without knowing she was catering to the person who slit her son's throat. Even through her own tears, she would come by the house and cook and check in on me while I grieved quietly in my room with the door closed.

In her presence, and around anybody else, I had my role down pat. I took a leave of absence from work for a few months and used it to lounge around the house in my pajamas binge watching Netflix and keeping close to my room in case Ms. Nina or my dad popped in unannounced.

I was ready to cry on cue or to lay depressingly catatonic while they spoke to me as I stared into space or buried my face in a pillow. Ms. Nina, my dad and most recently Shan, all suggest at one time or another that I see a counselor to help me deal with my loss and the trauma of finding Michael's body. Of course, I declined.

I didn't want to risk some super psychologist figuring out that I wasn't as distraught as I'd pretended to be, nor did I feel like juggling my emotions to have to convince yet another person of my grief. Not having to be *on* 24/7 was one of the benefits of my living alone. Sure, I had a few genuine moments of grief for everything I'd lost; but not enough that I wasn't spending the majority of my alone time watching T.V., sleeping and snacking.

Hell, I actually gained an extra 10 lbs while his mother and the jail bird seemed to be losing weight from their depressed lethargy. Thank God I started back kickboxing and toned my newfound thickness. Nevertheless, Ms. Nina and I were now staunch allies in court as we sat shoulder to shoulder hoping for the same thing. Marlene Braxton's conviction.

Fullsome was trying to shift the blame to me. He frequently insinuated that I or *someone* else was the actual culprit the entire trial. I knew it was his job to insert doubt in the jury's mind, so I would be a fool to have thought he wouldn't. Still, I was too far ahead of him to worry about his groundless speculations. I was praying hardest that he would wrap up his presentation sooner rather than later so I could go eat.

"Here's another thing ladies and gentlemen. Now this... *this* is very important. My client's fingerprints were *not* on the murder weapon. It was a kitchen knife belonging to the Patterson's. Why would my client have had any reason to be in their kitchen while the victim slept? Don't you think it all seems a little nonsensical?" he expressed with raised open hands, looking from face to face.

"Take this pen for instance," he told them pulling a ballpoint from the breast pocket of his jacket and holding it before them.

Butterflies swarmed my empty stomach as some of the jurors faces contorted in thought. God damn. What was Matlock about to do now? Though the abundance of circumstantial evidence was damning, Marlene was far from endearing, and the media had eaten her alive right from the beginning.

I thought Lisa Ramos put on a hell of a case but what if this turd in a suit could persuade the jury differently? When the murder first broke, the local news was covering and reporting on it almost daily. Once they realized there was a mistress with an entire family of her own involved, that's when all of the names began.

They were calling it the "Sleeping with the enemy murder" and calling her the "Murderous Mistress." I was truly tickled at the media's creativity, and thrilled that they were already pegging her as the murderer in all of their assumptions. It was a real-life spinoff of a *LifeTime* movie.

They portrayed Michael and I both as a model, likeable, middle class couple whose lives were disrupted by a work affair. A couple of people at SLEEP ONE and even a few patients came forward to add their witness accounts of their inappropriate closeness to the already scathing information of Michael and Marlene's torrid affair.

Neighbors, close friends and family were also officially interviewed by police, and reporters *unofficially* searched for whatever dirty laundry they could air from whoever was talking. My nosy neighbor Karen ended up testifying for the prosecution. She and her Pomeranian Sheba were in her front yard when I got home from Daddy's, and she witnessed my actions from across the street. She was a chain-smoking brown skin woman in her 60's with short black hair, hard wrinkles etched into her face, and a gut a baby kangaroo could probably nap in comfortably.

Karen talked way too much for my taste, but Michael often chatted with her while I maintained cordial, but distant pleasantries with her and her shifty looking husband George. He made my skin crawl and reminded me of "Ned the Wino" from the T.V. show *Good Times.* You know how some people just *look* like they stink? He was super skinny, his dark skin always looked dry and ashy, and his hair was never properly groomed.

I hadn't seen him for months before the murder. Let the neighborhood gossips tell it, he ran off with a co-worker from the factory job he worked. Supposedly, her being left in that big house alone is what accounted for the inordinate amount of time Karen had been spending out with Sheba smoking Newports on her front porch. Karen's face was the first familiar one I saw on the 11 o'clock news recapping what she witnessed to the cameras.

Of course, Marlene's arrest record for her knife wielding domestic violence offense didn't fare well in the court of opinions either. The Huffington Post got wind of our story and did an entire cover story on it and her history of violence. That, her being the last known person to see Michael alive, and her bodily fluids still on his dick, added nails to her coffin.

Fortunately, Marlene's immediate appearance of guilt, the staged evidence corroborating it, my uncontested alibi and my woeful performances eventually convinced the detectives that I was also a victim. More importantly, it supported a case for *her* guilt. I'd done an excellent job of assuming the role of the grieving wife, and since I kept to myself even before the incident, it was easy to do so afterwards.

For a good while, I couldn't leave the house or have company without a reporter or detective documenting my every move or wanting a quote.

The sensationalism of the case made news again when the trial started and brought out a large audience to sit in on it. All eyes were on the "Murderess Mistress", the name a blogger penned when she was arrested, and on me.

Thank God I had Shan at the house keeping me company and helping me to maintain my sanity. My house phone rang unanswered each day and I only answered cellphone numbers I recognized. I learned how resourceful the media and trolls who enjoyed harassing people were the first time. This time, I wouldn't be fooled.

Now, I was just hoping the demonstration Fullsome was about to pull out of his ass would be quick and pointless so's not to give the jurors reason to question the guilt the prosecution already placed on Marlene's head. Too much had gone into ensuring she'd be punished, and it *needed* to happen.

Fullsome took a brief trip to the defense's table and retrieved a folded piece of paper. Returning to the box, he handed it to 1 juror, a leather-faced white woman; instructing her to stab a hole in it with the pen. She complied and attempted to pass the pen back to him as Prosecutor Ramos, crossed her legs with a loud sigh that drew a moderate amount of attention.

"If you'll be so kind as to pass this around to your fellow jurors," Fullsome asked leather-face after cutting his eyes at Ramos.

When it got into the hands of the 5th juror, Fullsome handed the paper to them and asked them to stab another hole in it, which they did. The pen was handed to every juror until it came back to him. He then wiped the pen down with a handkerchief and held it up for all of us to see.

"Now... if the police were investigating who stabbed that piece of paper, who would they find guilty? Juror number 1? Juror number 5? Or maybe one of the other jurors who handled the pen. We all touched it, but since the fingerprints were wiped from it, who's to say who really did it?

You know who would be the number 1 suspect? Me. Why? Because *I* am the last one seen holding the pen. Does that make it true? Not at all. A weapon with no fingerprints could've been wielded by *anyone.*

It belonged to the Patterson's. We know that they both had access to it don't we? Yet only one of them is still here to ask. So... can we conclusively say that it was *my* client who committed this heinous crime? Not at all.

The prosecution would have you believe that the miniscule traces of his wife, Greer Patterson's, DNA in that shower proves that she wasn't the killer. Does it though? I say it means the exact opposite. Why was there so little of his *own wife's* DNA in the shower of their master bathroom?

Was it because they hadn't in fact been sleeping together in the same quarters for so long that she wasn't using it? Was it because they were *indeed* estranged as my client says Michael Patterson told her?

I think it was. Marlene had no reason to kill him. She was already getting what she wanted out of the relationship. She didn't *want* him to leave his wife for her. She already had an entire family life of her own. They were simply... having sex; but his wife," he looked around dramatically. "*She* had a motive. Greer Patterson had a *big* motive. She, was a woman scorned."

He pointed an accusing finger at me with a glare as the jurors and spectators followed suit. I held an incredulous expression and shook my head sideways while streams of liquid anger fled from my eyes. Random gasps spread throughout the courtroom as Shan grasped my arm supportively and my daddy's buttons were immediately pushed.

"Now wait a minute now! My daughter has been through enough because of this woman without you accusing her of murdering her own husband! You know you're reachin'! Why don't you concentrate on yo' guilty client!" Daddy demanded.

"Mr. Foster! Mr. Foster!" the judge said banging his gavel harshly at the same time the prosecutor interjected.

"Your honor! Is there a point in Mr. Fullsome antagonizing the victim's wife during his closing arguments? Greer Patterson is *not* on trial here today. Marlene—" Ramos bellowed shooting to her feet.

"I digress. I digress," Fullsome said quickly cutting off Ramos and submissively smirking towards the jurors as the courtroom filled with murmurs.

Ramos leaned on her desk glowering at Fullsome like she had something scathing to say, but was debating on saying it. Her pink, slit like lips, curled in a snarl, she exhaled with aggravation and glanced between the judge and her husky opponent.

"I apologize your honor. I apologize Mrs. Patterson. I'm almost done," he advised with a phony apology and turning back to the jury.

"Order! Order!" Judge Ellis yelled banging his gavel as the voices settled into silence. "Mr. Foster. You will contain yourself for the remainder of this trial or you will be removed. Are we clear?"

Anger still blazed in Daddy's eyes as he draped his left arm across the back of the bench and nodded to the judge. Always my protector.

"Son of a bitch," he mumbled.

Ms. Nina's shoulder's rubbed mine, and she exhaled angrily, crossing her arms across her chest. Ramos slowly lowered herself back down to her chair as I tossed my hair back over my shoulders and sat up straight on the uncomfortable bench in my conservative green dress.

No matter how good Fullsome was, he wasn't good enough to prove I did it, or that his client *didn't* do it. He could take his Matlock tactics and shove them up his fat ass.

Ironically, my not taking showers in the master bedroom anymore wasn't even part of my plan. I simply didn't want to share my body wash with the ho my husband was screwing anymore. Marlene was bold.

I knew Michael wasn't using it because he never had before, and said it smelled too fruity for a man to wear. So, when my body wash started dwindling fast as hell, it was yet another sign of his infidelity. Not that I needed more than the videos to know what was happening, but one day I marked it at my last use before work anyway. Sure enough, when I got home, it was lower.

I moved all of my feminine products, body washes, shampoos and conditioners to the spare bedroom after that. I know black women don't wash their hair in the shower every day but so what. I didn't want to take any chances.

My usage of the guest bathroom was easily explained to the police. The shower head in there was more powerful than the one in our master bathroom, so I preferred to use it more often. Subject closed.

Fullsome continued trying to persecute me even though his fat ass had just supposedly digressed.

"The prosecution certainly didn't *prove* their case. It *is* their burden, you know? Isn't it just as possible that Greer Patterson came home earlier than expected, unseen, and found him passed out after his latest tryst and killed him? Of course, it is.

Greer testified that she suspected he was having an affair, yet she claims they only discussed it once. *Once?* I don't know about you but I don't believe for one—iota—of a second that she let it go that easily. I know *my* wife wouldn't have let it go at 1, and I doubt any of your significant others would have either," he said side-eyeing me as low chuckles resonated through the courtroom.

Inside my blood was boiling.

"Sleaze ball attorney," my daddy said as I eyed Marlene intensely.

I wondered what *she* was thinking. If she knew that I was actually the one who did it or if she was just willing to go with whatever might get her off. I wondered what it was like for her being in jail for a crime she didn't commit, and losing her family for the one she did.

She sat erect with cuffs on, watching Fullsome plead her case with a remorseful and hopeful gaze. Even as her pathetic life hung in the balance, the vision of her lovely face incited a pang of jealousy in my gut.

Her Chinese bob had grown out into a shoulder length stringy mess that was swept back behind her ears exposing her defined cheekbones.

The bare-faced chick sitting before me was a far cry from the stunner I'd met at SLEEP ONE the night Michael introduced us, but her beauty was undeniable. My green eyes envied the genetics that molded the woman who stole my husband from me as much as they despised looking at her.

The pastel dress she wore hung loosely from everywhere but her breasts and ass. Her slightly less voluptuous frame refrained from filling it out completely. I'm sure her attorney's advised her that wearing it any tighter would make her look like the slut she was.

Marlene kept a meek expression on her face at all times and totally avoided eye contact with me since the first day of trial; but I knew, *she knew,* I was staring. I bet she could *feel* me looking at her the way my eyes locked in on her flesh. I reveled in the torment masking her face each time her character was assassinated by the prosecution. A veil of guilt sheathed her adulterous reputation, and I hoped it would lead to her conviction.

I especially loved it when Ramos would refer to her as a "cold blooded murderer," because she really was. She may not have killed Michael physically, but she murdered my marriage the minute she enticed my husband to cheat on me. Same thing.

Memories of watching videos of her fucking my husband in *my* bed, in every position they could think of, tortured my mind. Yes, she was beautiful and obviously tempting, but I was his wife! Where were her morals? Her love for her kid's father must've been just as shallow as she was.

When her Baby's daddy came to court on the day he had to testify, it was clear that he'd written her trifling ass off. Her apologetic and pleading looks toward him did nothing to shave the ice from the stares he returned. And I almost creamed my pants when she teared up as he glowered at her leaving the stand.

Even better, she must not have had anyone to make the $200K bail for her because she remained locked up the entire time since her arrest. I guess that's the price you pay for being a trifling, sneaky, conniving, whore.

Michael apparently wasn't her first affair on her kid's father from what was revealed, and I doubted he would've been the last. The judge disallowed any mention of it from being used as evidence. I knew it was just another brick of information to bury her character. The jury was supposed to discount it, but they couldn't un-hear it, and neither could I.

"There are a number of *other* scenarios that are just as plausible, if not *more* plausible than *my client* being the cold-blooded murderer she's been labeled as. It's unfortunate that Atlanta P.D. didn't do a better job at investigating this case, because if they had, I suspect Greer Patterson *or* someone else would be sitting here," he said making brief eye contact with me, then back to the jury.

"Ladies and gentlemen of the jury, it would be a *grave* injustice if you were to punish my client for having an affair... by convicting her of murder. Especially when *she* is not only innocent, but the prosecution hasn't proven their case. They simply haven't proved it.

I leave the fate of Marlene Braxton, mother of 3, in your very capable hands. I hope that you will return with the only *just* verdict that there is so that she won't have to spend any more time away from her children than she already has. Not guilty. Thank you," he told them casually walking to the defense table, placing a reassuring hand on Marlene's as he sat.

I was sure at least 4 of the 7 women on the jury were "team guilty bitch" before Fullsome's closing argument, and their faces didn't show a change of heart afterwards.

They were black women who watched Marlene with poorly disguised looks of disdain, and I made a concerted effort to garner their sympathy with my own solemn gazes. I couldn't read the other women's faces and the men... well who knew how they'd vote since most of them were probably cheaters anyway.

Judge Ellis looked sternly to the jury as he gave them final instructions before deliberation. Shortly afterwards, a couple of pushy reporters and news cameras flanked me, Ms. Nina, Shan and Daddy, looking for comments as we exited the courthouse at adjournment.

Finally, I just stopped to give them the soundbite they wanted so they'd leave us alone. Sweeping my hair from my face, I entertained a gangly looking white woman with over processed blonde hair in a coral suit as she immediately shoved a mic in my face.

"Mrs. Patterson. I'm sorry for your loss. What do you think the verdict will be?"

"I don't know what they're going to do. I'm just hoping that the jury makes the right decision so that we can try to move on with our lives knowing that Michael got justice.

Marlene didn't just take away a son and a husband... but she took away any hopes I had of having children with him; or that his mother had of grandchildren. He didn't deserve to die that way. *Nobody does.* I hope she gets life since she took away his," I said into the camera with glassy eyes.

Now all we had to do was wait for the verdict.

11

Greer

Me, Shan, Daddy and Ms. Nina went to a southern cuisine restaurant a mile from the courthouse to eat and awaited the jury's decision. I knew it could take minutes, hours or even days for them to agree on a verdict, but I was hoping it would be speedy. Lisa Ramos was kind enough to ensure that someone would call or text me when the verdict was in.

I scarfed down the fried green tomatoes and collard greens I ordered while Daddy and Ms. Nina small talked like old friends about some jazz musician who'd recently passed away. Shan picked over her food and typed on the new phone she exchanged her old one for at Sprint the day before.

My eyes darted between them while I sipped my sweet tea, taking in their body language. Shan and I exchanged glances too. This was probably the most conversation they'd ever had with each other given how my stepmother patrolled Daddy in the midst of other women.

Stephanie squelched her insecurities by making sure my daddy barely traded more than a hello with anyone possessing a vagina. Ms. Nina was an attractive woman for her age, and that presented a threat for Stephanie.

"Greer, you probably don't even know who Harold Battiste is do you?" Ms. Nina asked me skeptically.

Before I could finish my last gulp to answer her, she turned to Daddy. "These kids now a days don't have any real appreciation for what *good* music is. You know, when musicians played their own instruments instead of relying on a bunch of keyboards to make a song sound good.

He nodded in agreement glancing at me and Shan with a mouthful of rice pilaf. One thing about Chuck Foster, he loves to eat. He's always had a hearty appetite, and once the cancer went into remission, my daddy's hunger went into overdrive. His gut was becoming more noticeable too.

"They shol' don't," he cosigned.

"That's why I made sure that my Michael appreciated the classics. Chuck, did you know he could play 4 instruments?" she asked Daddy with her fork positioned above her plate of barely touched fried chicken. "Yes, he could. The violin, the saxophone, the flute *and* the piano. Just like his daddy. Michael Sr. was playing in a band when I met him. He was *very* musically inclined and so was my boy."

I refrained from rolling my eyes and smiled pleasantly at her while dabbing the corners of my mouth with a napkin. Ms. Nina knew she was exaggerating about Michael's mediocre playing talents, but I was gonna let her have that since she was taking so much pride in it.

I was surprised to hear her say anything kind about Michael Sr. after all of the horrible things she'd said about him in the past. I'd only met him 3 times and 2 of them ended with Ms. Nina and Mike in an ugly argument.

Michael was far from a musical prodigy, especially since his father was rarely around to help him hone his skills. You couldn't tell Ms. Nina Michael didn't walk on water and write the 10 commandments though. Not then, and not now.

"You know; I've been meaning to ask you if it would be alright if I took some of his things home with me. Things that probably wouldn't have any sentimental value to *you*, but would mean a lot to *me*. Like his flute... stuff like that," Ms. Nina asked, finally taking a bite of her food.

I wanted to say, "Yes bitch! Please do! I was just waiting for this trial to be over before I got rid of all his shit anyway!" Instead, I gazed somberly down at my purse while retrieving my wet wipes and then back at her.

"Yeah. Sure, you can Ms. Nina. I guess it's about time I start to let some of his stuff go now, huh? Actually, I've been thinking about moving."

"Moving? Moving where?" Daddy questioned.

She paused, put her fork down and placed a caring hand on my wrist as I cleaned my hands.

"aby I didn't mean to upset you," she said tilting her head trying to meet my downcast gaze. "You never said you were moving. I just thought..."

"No. No. I'm not upset at all. He was your son. It's only right that you should have some of his things. I haven't even started looking for a place to move yet or put the house on the market."

"You're gonna sell the house? So soon?" she asked troubled.

I could see her already gearing up to tell me what I should and shouldn't do, and I wasn't about to go for it.

"Soon? It's been over a year of me sleeping in the same house, the same *room* where he was murdered. I think I've given it more than enough time. Don't you?"

Daddy cleared his throat and spoke.

"Yep. I do think it's been long enough. Time for you to move away from those bad memories and move on with yo' life. Start all over again."

Ms. Nina looked astonished, and said so.

"Move on? Start all over? Okay, we don't have to rush the girl into just forgetting all about my son. We're just now about to find out if he's gonna get proper justice for Pete's sake. I *definitely* think it's too soon to move on."

"I'm sure he didn't mean it that way Ms. Nina," Shan backed Daddy.

"Let's talk about this later. I think I've cried enough in public this week to last me a lifetime," I replied replenishing the moisture in my eyes with an eye dropper.

When you have to cry as much as I've had to in previous months, I discovered that Visine was a necessity to ensuring my orbs didn't end up dry as desert sand afterwards.

My phone buzzed with a text message interrupting whatever remark Ms. Nina was going to make next. Thank God. It was from someone at Lisa Ramos' office letting me know that the verdict was back in.

Wow! It hadn't even been 2 hours yet. I'd heard that a quick verdict usually meant guilty. I didn't want to jump the gun, but I was inclined to believe it.

I let them know what the text said, and Ms. Nina summoned our waitress immediately with a snap of her fingers. I hated when people did stuff like that. It was so pretentious. Ms. Nina and Bri were a lot alike.

My eyes bore down on Marlene, already seated at the defense table when we entered the courtroom. She whispered something to her attorney and shifted nervously beside him. I wondered how she was able to afford Fullsome at his advertised rate and was told by Ramos that he took her case pro bono. More than likely for the high level of publicity.

Within minutes, we were rising for the jury, and then again for the judge's entry. Fear riddled Marlene's face as her eyes darted worriedly between Judge Ellis and the jurors. You could hear a pin drop in the courtroom as the foreman, a slender black man in his 40's, handed a bunch of paperwork to the bailiff to give to the judge.

After looking it over, Judge Ellis glanced at Marlene, at me and then back to the jury with the same blank expression he'd worn the entire trial. Confirming the documents were in order, he passed a single paper back through the bailiff to the foreman and instructed him to stand to read the verdict.

Marlene and her attorney also stood.

"In the case of the state of Georgia vs. Marlene Braxton, as to the count of malice murder, we the jury find the defendant, guilty."

The courtroom erupted into excited murmurs as tears streamed down Ms. Nina's face and Marlene instantly began wailing, almost crumbling to her knees. Fullsome held her up as officers rushed over to ensure she stayed on her feet.

"I didn't do this! No! I'm not guilty!" she cried as Fullsome spoke encouraging words to her about filing for appeal and what not.

Then and only then did she tearfully, look directly at me. Hate and fear seemed to occupy the same space in her face as I leered at her through narrowed eyes. I briefly allowed the corners of my mouth to curl into a sly smile and winked at her. Bye bitch! I screamed internally at her.

Instantly, my face contorted back to grief, and I turned to Daddy, weeping into his chest. I thanked and praised God aloud for the justice he bestowed upon us. As expected, Judge Ellis demanded order in the court, and we all sat back in our respective seats.

He additionally ordered Fullsome to control his client, who was still crying hysterically and muttering, "*Nooooo*" repeatedly. Once calm was restored, each jury member was polled to ensure they all voted guilty, and then Ellis gave a speech which I ignored in lieu of basking in my own mind at Marlene's misery.

I watched as she cried quietly with her head down on the table and Fullsome sat uncomfortably beside her tight lipped. Ramos wasn't smiling, but satisfaction was written all over her face at the prosecutions table like it was inked in neon Sharpie.

Judge Ellis allowed family who wanted to give statements to speak before the court since he was prepared to issue sentencing. Ms. Nina went up, newly composed and standing strong while glaring directly into Marlene's face for the first few minutes of her scathing rant.

Her statement was angry, pain filled and passionate. In closing, she pled with Judge Ellis to give Marlene life with no possibility of parole. You know I had my beige ass right up there pouring it on thick with tears and a runny nose next.

"I... I've been waiting for this moment for so long that... that I can barely speak. It has been more than a year of torture. It's bittersweet because I'm happy that she's being punished for what she did but... but I still don't have my husband back.

I know he wasn't perfect, but I loved my husband with everything that I am; and she took him from me. From the world. I don't even know *why*. Can you make her say why?

I have nightmares about finding his body. I think about how painful his death must've been. That's all because of her. She's forever torn my life apart and she's never even told us *why*," I sobbed profusely.

"She and her attorney have accused me of something they both know *she did.* Like she hasn't hurt me enough. They spent this entire trial bashing me and making her look like a woman who just made a *mistake.*

She's obviously violent. She's even been violent with the father of her children. She'll be a danger to society if she's let out *ever* again. She's a black widow. A murderer. I can't even bring myself to speak her name. And I pray I won't have to.

I ask that you never let her out to do this to someone else again. Thank you," I ended clearing my tear-filled throat and walking briskly from the podium dabbing my face with tissue.

Marlene's mother, Justine Nalley was the last to speak. She looked maybe 20 years older than Marlene, and she wore her hair in a short blonde fade. She wore minimal make-up and had a banging body that proved where Marlene inherited her large breasts and ass. She was wearing a casual yellow and white flower-patterned sundress that stopped below her knees and yellow heels.

Her eyes were red from crying and she coughed using her balled up hand to cover her mouth before excusing herself and speaking.

"Your honor. I know my daughter has made her share of mistakes; but she's a good woman. I know with everything in my heart that she didn't do this. She's a good, hardworking and loving mother to my grandchildren, who *need* her. I realize that she's already been convicted; and I am really sorry for the Patterson family's loss," she said glancing at me sandwiched between Shan and Daddy. Then to my mother in-law.

"I just hope you will give my daughter a chance to see her children grow up. Thank you for your time," she said sniffling and walking away as my eyes went to Marlene.

She was sitting up straight in her seat with her face drenched and puffy from crying, watching her mother walk solemnly back to her seat in the galley. Then she looked at me.

Once again, Judge Ellis was talking, but I tuned him out since I now had Marlene's undivided attention. Her jaws tightened, and I could see that the newly emerged blank stare I was giving her was ruffling her feathers.

Oh yeah. I think she knew the truth. She just couldn't prove it. Her biggest problem, was that neither could anybody else. Still, the way she ogled me made me feel insecure and threatened. I knew she didn't have anything to hold over me, but it felt like she did. It felt like she was challenging me somehow.

I closed my eyes and recollected the look of terror in Michael's eyes the day he paid the consequences for his indiscretions. Oddly, or morbidly enough, depending on how you look at it, it soothed my anxiety.

It brought back the memory of how powerful I felt snatching his life from him, and knowing that he was as confused about why, as I was about why he cheated. Even Steven.

"Greer, are you okay?" Daddy asked shaking my shoulder with the arm he now had wrapped around me.

I must've zoned out. I nodded to him but noticed people in the courtroom leaving.

"Why are they leaving?" I asked perplexed.

"It's over now Babygirl," he replied hugging me closer. "He sentenced her to life imprisonment with the chance of parole in 30 years."

My mouth unhinged. I couldn't believe I'd missed his entire sentencing. Marlene and all of the attorneys had already vacated their seats along with the judge and nearly everyone else in the courtroom.

I couldn't believe it was over. That home-wrecking bitch was going to serve out the rest of her days regretting her slutty ways and I could finally... *finally* be myself.

The media swarmed us again leaving the courthouse, and this time I gave them a statement without resistance. Ms. Nina also shared her feelings to the screaming reporters with microphones.

Court T.V., local news channels and those types of shows were all jockeying to get quotes. We stood there answering questions for no less than a half hour.

Eventually, Daddy and Shan ushered us away to the parking deck and we left in separate cars. Ms. Nina in her Ford Fiesta, and the rest of us in Daddy's Buick Roadmaster.

Daddy didn't come to trial the first 3 days, but he was there for the last 2. Shan and I stayed the night at his house Thursday night so that we could all ride together and save on parking.

I stepped out of my shoes and started undressing as Shan entered the spare bedroom we shared, drinking something from a glass.

"Girl, your father is hilarious. He's down there on the phone talking to one of his boys about a 'Honey dip he's gonna scoop up' tomorrow night for dinner," she giggled.

"What?" I asked with my eyes bulging. "Who's he taking out to dinner? My Daddy's dating?"

"Evidently he is. When he called her a "Honey Dip", I almost spit out my drink laughing. He's been a widower long enough now and he's not getting any younger. You ready for a new stepmomma?"

"Shut up girl. It's just a date," I said good-humoredly. "Just because you have a new stepdaddy, don't try to marry my daddy off."

"Speaking of him, he just bought a motorcycle. Can you believe that? What the hell does a 69-year-old man need with a motorcycle? If he falls off that thing, instead of getting road rash, he's just gonna turn to dust."

I was stepping my second leg into my jeans as she said it and I almost stumbled to the floor with laughter. She made a few more cracks about him being a "ghost rider", needing a hearing aid and her mother riding in a side car attached to it, and that was all she wrote.

We roared like teenage girls at a slumber party with me lying on the floor clutching my stomach, and her lying across the bed. Us laughing together in that room, my old room that held so many unhappy moments, made me warm and fuzzy inside.

I'd always thirsted for a sisterly bond when I lived here but never quite got it. Donna and I shared a few fun moments, but most were in secret to avoid Debbie from barging in and destroying it.

I was never allowed to even attend a slumber party, let alone have one with any of the few girlfriends I managed to make during my adolescence. This room was filled with memories of unfulfilled dreams, isolation and gloom for me. Until this very moment.

Our merriment was cut short by the sound of Jahari's familiar chime on Shan's phone. She still hadn't spoken to him directly, and he'd only gotten more persistent.

True to her word, she ignored every call and text message he sent, and she'd refused to tell Evelyn anything when she called to speak to Shamari either.

On Wednesday, Jahari got clever and answered Evelyn's phone when she called, but all that got him was dead silence and a dial tone. He tried to put me in the middle of it on Thursday, but I was already on alert to ignore his number and any unknown callers.

She looked apathetically at her phone as she finished changing into shorts and a tank, then laid down across the bed again.

"What are you planning to do right now? I'm kind of tired," she said with her eyes already closed.

"Uh… nothing really," I replied brushing lint from my scoop neck shirt as I slid into my NIKE's. "Go ahead and lay down. I'm just gonna go kick it with Daddy for a while then, and maybe go through some stuff in the shed."

She nodded without opening her eyes and balled up in a fetal position. I'm sure the stress of avoiding Jahari was weighing on her just as much as his cheating was. There was no escaping the inevitable, and I understood how the eminence of it could be exhausting.

Daddy was watching *Sports Center* in the living room, reclined in his favorite chair with a beer when I entered. He'd changed into blue and white basketball shorts and a white T himself.

I used a scrunchy to tie my hair back as I plopped down on the couch adjacent his chair and exhaled loudly.

"I can't believe it's finally over. I still don't like that she could be out in 30 years. She'll be younger than you are now if she makes parole."

He took a swig of his Heineken and eyed me impassively. Why was he looking at me like that?

"Thirty years," he stated leaning back in his recliner, looking at the T.V. again. "That's a lot of years to be punished. I drove trucks fo' 30 years. Almost half of my life."

I was probably just being paranoid, but I felt like he was judging me. Like he knew something he wasn't saying and wanted me to own up to it. I shook the thought and surmised that now was as good a time as any to ask the questions that had been heavy on my mind.

"Daddy, was my mother the first woman you cheated on Stephanie with?"

Surprise registered in his green eyes as he rubbed his stubbly chin with unease while contemplating his answer.

"No. I cheated a time or 2 befo' Irina. You know, I was only 22 when I married Steph. I didn't know nothin' much 'bout bein' a man, a husband, let alone a daddy. I ain't even know my *own* daddy, so he ain't showed me how to treat a woman.

Of course, I had common sense. I know a man s'posed to be there fo' his family. My momma struggled a lot bringing up me and Carrie wit' no man in the house. When Steph come at me wit' bein' pregnant, I did what a man s'posed to do. I married her.

I wasn't ready to be faithful to her yet though. She was a good woman, but she wasn't enough to make me neva' want anotha' one," he stated earnestly.

"You cheated because she wasn't enough woman for you?"

He mulled over my question while drinking from his beer and came to a conclusion that seemed to trouble him to deliver.

"At first I s'pose she wasn't. She was unwilling to do some things and too stubborn to stop doin' others. Sex wise," he paused uncomfortably. "Other women was thrillin'. Sometimes a man just wants the thrill. It ain't till ya realize it's 'bout more than that that ya stop chasin' it. I ain't 'bout to go into details. You *still* my daughter, and some stuff I just ain't gonna say," he grinned.

"Did you still cheat on Stephanie after my momma died? I know you said before that you didn't but… did you really?" I asked leaning forward with my hands clasped.

It was the $64,000 question I'd wanted to know the answer to for ages. Stephanie's insecurities about his fidelity had plagued me as much as it had her, if for no other reason than I didn't know if men were capable of being faithful.

He nodded and rubbed his chin again.

"I ain't neva' wanna hurt her like that again. Wasn't no sex worth the pain she suffered fo' me. She was raising my daughter the best she could, and I loved her for that. It wasn't easy bein' gone like that like I was and not havin' no warm body to cozy up to some nights; but I did it.

She ain't neva' let it go though. That jealousy made her mean as a rattlesnake sometimes. I guess I deserved it. She knew it was mo' women befo' Irina, but somethin' 'bout her bein' white got to her pride. Plus, she was the only one who had my baby too."

"Did you love my mother Daddy?"

He gazed wearily into my eyes, ran a hand across his forehead and exhaled.

"I did sometimes. We was just havin' fun when it started. She was workin' off the books at a rest stop on one of my usual routes. Irina was *beautiful*. She had a smile that opened up heaven's gates and a sparkle in her eyes for anything new.

She listened to me talk 'bout my day and my travels like I was talkin' bout Spain or Paris. She was one of them… daredevil types. There was an old T.V. show called *That's Incredible*, where they showed people doin' crazy stuff. Skydiving, tightrope walkin', eatin' fire… she loved that show.

She was funny too. Her English was still kinda broken up, so she would mix up her words sometimes and we'd laugh. She was takin' some classes tryin' to get better. She was smart. Just like you," he smiled reminiscing.

I was completely enthralled with in the conversation. He'd never spoken so freely about my mother before. Stephanie flipped her wig every time my mother was even referenced, so *speaking her name...* that was like a death wish.

"Did she know you were married?" I asked evenly.

I had to know whether my mother was just like these other ho's out here with no morals or respect for marriage, or if it just appeared that way. I needed to know if I was being cursed because of the sins of my parents, or if it was just the way of the world.

He hung his head. Looked at me under his lids and gulped down more beer. He didn't answer me for a few more moments, and I was about to repeat myself when he finally spoke.

"I told her. After the first few whiles we got together. I ain't proud of it. I didn't used to wear my ring too much back then," he said looking at the shiny gold band on his ring finger I never remember seeing him without. "She was a good girl. I didn't tell her about Steph and the kids till she told me 'bout you."

"Daddy! How long were y'all together before she got pregnant?" I asked aghast. "Like what was she supposed to do then? She didn't have any family here, did she? You told me she was here all by herself. Why would you do that to her?"

He ran his hands through what curls he still possessed and surfed his tongue guiltily over his gums.

"Greer, Babygirl I love you, but... you weren't s'posed to happen. I wasn't s'posed to stay wit' her. I had a wife and kids."

"So, I was a mistake. Did you want her to abort me Daddy? You said you loved her *sometimes*. Sometimes before or after she had me?" I asked aching inside that my precious father who loved me so much, might never have wanted me.

"Babygirl, none of my babies were planned; but none of y'all were mistakes. You grown now, so I ain't gonna hide the truth from ya'. I didn't want Steph to find out 'bout you; but I wasn't gonna abandon no child of mine neither.

"I started helpin' yo' momma out wit' ya. Comin' to visit when I could. Bein' a daddy to ya when I had the means to."

I cut my eyes at him. "That didn't answer my question. Did you love her before or after I was born?"

"I loved her fo' bein' the mother of my daughter."

"Ok. What then? You were just gonna keep me a secret forever before she died? How exactly did she die anyway? I know it was in a fire, but how'd it start?"

Now it was Daddy's turn to cut his eyes at me.

"What you sayin' child? You askin' me if I killed yo' momma?"

"I'm asking you what happened to her. All I know is that she died in an apartment fire. I don't know any details. I don't even know where she's buried."

"She ain't," he retorted gruffly, finishing off his Heineken.

"She ain't what?"

"Ain't buried. She got cremated by the state."

"By the state? Why?"

Daddy sighed and scratched the back of his head before forming his words.

"Listen Babygirl. Like I told ya befo', yo' momma didn't have no kin out'chea. She was already burnt too bad for an open casket and she wouldn't have had nobody much at a funeral anyhow."

"She would've had you. She would've had me," I said insolently. "How did the fire start?"

"The police say it was fireworks. It was the Fourth of July and people was shootin' 'em off all ova' the place. A roman candle got shot through her window. Maybe some kids shootin' 'em off too close to her window or somethin', I guess.

It was a hot day and she always had her windows open instead of runnin' the AC. Them fireworks caught on her curtains while she was sleep on the couch. Set erry'thang on fire and her too."

"That doesn't even make any sense. How old were the people who did it? How much time did they get for starting the fire?" I asked lividly.

"They neva' found out who did it. Lots of people was shootin' off fireworks in there that day. Ain't nobody claim to see who did it though. They neva' charged anybody."

I shook my head and rubbed my hands up and down my face.

"So nobody paid for her death and you couldn't even pay for her burial? Wow," I said in disgust.

"Yo' stepmother would've bit my head off. Now I did wrong, and I admit that. Wasn't no sense in makin' Steph suffer any mo' than she already had to. It wasn't easy tellin' her I had a daughter wit' somebody else, and now my daughter was gonna come live wit' us."

"Wait. If my mother was cremated, then whose funeral did I go to? I distinctly remember going to her funeral. I had a pink sundress on and my white patent leather shoes got scuffed up when I tripped going to throw the white rose in her casket," I disputed.

I remembered her funeral vividly. It was the same day he brought me home to meet my step-monster.

"That wasn't her funeral. You kept askin' fo' yo' momma and I felt bad you didn't have no way to say goodbye to her. So I took ya out one day to the cemetery, and we drove 'round till I found some people havin' a funeral.

I took you ova' there and pretended like it was *yo'* momma in that casket. I let you throw a rose in there wit' the otha' people, since they ain't know we didn't belong. Then I brought you home wit' me."

I didn't know why I was tearing up, but I felt an enormous amount of grief. Sadness for the loss of my mother who was deceived in life and discarded like nothing in death.

"Where was I when the fire happened? With you?"

"You were in the house 'sleep. Yo' room was in the back, away from the fire, so a neighbor got ya out through a window befo' the fire department even got there. Report said she was passed out drunk on the couch in front of the T.V. Them curtains used to hang right behind it."

"Drunk? She was passed out drunk with me in the house?" I rationalized in my head.

That didn't seem like the most responsible thing to do with a 5-year-old in the house but… maybe she had been celebrating the 4th.

"It's crazy that I don't remember anything about the day of the fire or even being in it at all. Damn. I wish I at least had pictures of her to remember her by. I wish Stephanie hadn't destroyed what I did have," I said quietly.

Daddy swallowed hard and looked shamefully into my eyes. Getting up slowly, he grabbed his keys from the bowl, put on his flip flops by the door and stood beside the couch.

"C'mon out'chea wit' me Babygirl," he said seriously.

I used my forearm as tissue for my tears and followed behind him outside to the shed. The keyring was full of keys, but he knew which one to choose without a glance.

I was surprised to see how neat it looked inside. The last time I'd been inside of it, it was overflowing with junk, boxes and cobwebs.

Now the walls were lined with shelves and neatly stacked boxes on each. All of the furniture was gone except a small desk against the back wall with a chair pushed up to it.

A key hook board was nailed to the wall above it with 7 rows of various sized key blanks hung against it. A green glass shade banker's lamp sat on the edge of the desk and a small key cutting machine sat next to it.

With both doors to the shed open, there was already a lot of light coming in, but he turned on the overhead light anyway. I'm glad he was proud of the way he straightened up the shed but, I really didn't care.

"Why are we out here?" I asked folding my arms across my chest.

"Tuesday, I gave myself a project. Bein' retired can get borin' and this shed been needin' some organization for a long while," he told me walking over to a back shelf and shifting a few boxes while peeking inside. "I been thinkin' 'bout maybe startin' back my locksmith business too. So I came out'chea to fix it up."

I rolled my eyes, unenthused by his timing and stared. Here we were for the first time *ever*, having a heart to heart about my mother, and he wants to show me his *project*? Deflecting much?

He pulled out a small box that sat on top of a big one, and put it on the desk. Reaching towards the back, he retrieved another 5x5 sized box from the shelf and placed it next to the other one.

Turning towards me, he waved me over and stood aside.

"Alright Babygirl. I didn't want to spring this stuff on ya while you was goin' through this whole trial thing and while ya friend was stayin' wit' ya. But here it is. I found where Steph put Irina's pictures and such."

"What?" I asked perking up and rushing over to the box. "Oh my God, these are the pictures! These are the ones Daddy!"

There were 2 photos, a gold bracelet in the shape of a coiled snake with ruby eyes, a partially singed green card, and a baby's hospital bracelet with my full name, Greer Talia Foster on it.

I squealed with joy and smiled from ear to ear, picking up each photo and examining it like the most precious of metals.

"Irina Amanar," I read off her name from her license. "She was only 32 years old when she died. November 30th, 1959."

Daddy watched me with satisfaction as I inspected each item in awe. Placing the bracelet on my wrist, I stared at the picture of her holding me as a baby with glee.

My mother's broad smile was contagious and anybody looking at it could tell that she loved me. The other photo had my father holding me while she fixed the pacifier in my mouth. I couldn't have been more than 2 in it.

"Greer. I want you to know that I did the best I could to make sure ya came up right. I know Steph wasn't always kind to ya, but I couldn't have ya go to foster care and I didn't want to lose my family.

I'm sorry I was out on the road so much when ya was comin' up, and I ain't tell you enough 'bout yo' real momma. If you got mo' questions to ask me, I'm here to answer them. I love ya Babygirl. Nobody'll eva' love ya mo' than me."

I threw my arms around my father and hugged him tight. It felt good to know he loved me, but I hoped he was wrong.

12

Greer

September 2015

"Greer, can you come out here please and talk to this patient? She's on the schedule for the 16th, but she's here for her appointment today. I tried to tell her that she's a week early, but she says she needs to be seen right now.

Dr. Shewmer only has 1 more patient today but he's leaving to do rounds at Dekalb Medical after that. We don't even have a NP to see her. Fatima and Jeanine are already gone, and Angie is already with her last one too. The lady says she's not leaving until she's seen. And looks old enough to die in the lobby while she's waiting. What do you want me to do?" Quincy asked sarcastically while leaning in my office doorway with her lips pressed together in annoyance.

"Okay. I'll be out there in a minute," I told her laughing at her old lady crack as I finished ordering supplies online for the nurse's station.

I liked the pretty little Latina with purple highlights in her long chocolate tresses and a thick Spanish accent. She was feisty, but friendly, and pretty good at her job.

It was 4:00pm and I knew at 6 months pregnant, Quincy was not in the mood for going back and forth with some old lady close to her 4:30pm clock out time. She'd already been snippy and emotional all day, so I was glad she came to me instead of my having to come out there later after she cussed the patient out.

Quincy huffed and waddled her way back down the hall. I took the necessary time to close out my order and print the receipt before straightening my mauve, Chelsea collared sheath dress and strutting towards the drama.

As I approached the appointment window, I saw a short elderly woman in a gray church hat and sweater, reaming out Nicky. Nicky was only semi-paying attention to her as she greeted another patient and handed him the clipboard to sign in.

"Yes ma'am. I understand what you're saying, and the Office Manager is on her way up to see you," Nicky said through a gritted smile as the old lady tossed her bag on the ledge.

"Now I have diabetes. I don't know what kinda schedulin' you all are doin' here, but I know I put today's date right there on the calendar on my refrigerator. Soon as I got home from my last 'pointment, I put it right on the calendar," she insisted pointing one wrinkled and shaking finger at Nicky.

"I have arthritis, high blood pressure, and sciatica. I need to be seen *to—day*, 'cause, I need to refill my medication and I don't drive. I had my grandbaby drive me up here—"

"Hi. Ms… Walker," I began as I glanced her name on Nicky's screen and stepped up to the check-in window.

"Well now who you?" she asked giving me a once over like I was a child who'd just gotten out of place.

"I'm Greer. I'm the Office Manager here. I understand there's been some mix up with your appointment dates and I'd like to see if I can help you," I advised with a smile, swiping my curly bangs from my face.

She frowned like I'd spoken in Chinese and looked around the waiting room before turning back to me.

"The onliest' way you can help me is to get me in to my 'pointment lil girl. Now like I was telling these here young ladies, *somebody* done put me in the system wrong, 'cause my calendar got today's date on it," she protested.

"Ms. Walker. I'm so sorry for any confusion here, but Dr. Shewmer has to leave to go to the hospital when he finishes up with his next patient, and we don't have anyone else that can see you today.

I can check the schedule to see if we can get you in sooner than next Wednesday though. What's another good day for you?" I asked reviewing the computer screen.

"*Ohhh* no. I need to be seen *to—day* I told ya," Ms. Walker demanded banging her handbag on the ledge repeatedly as a sight for sore eyes entered into the waiting room and stood behind her.

"What's goin' on Granny?" Race's sexy lips spoke as he placed a hand on her slight shoulder and our eyes met.

My heart thumped beyond my control with excitement as his smile greeted me and his grandma squawked. I hadn't seen his handsome face since the day Shan came with me to the range.

"Hey Greer. I didn't know you worked here," he spoke with a grin.

His chest was well defined in the charcoal Henley shirt he sported with jeans, and the single dimple in his left cheek peeked at me when he smiled.

"You know this woman Horace? Tell her to get me my 'pointment then, 'cause I ain't leavin' till I get seen and get my new *prescription.*"

"Horace?" I smirked leaning on the counter behind the window as he rubbed his nose awkwardly; his smile grown broader.

"Umm umm umm. Sexy," I heard Nicky say to Quincy in a not so hushed tone.

I turned to them, still donning my smile, but urging them to knock it off and get back to work with my eyes.

"Nicky, can you see if we have any earlier appointments to accommodate Ms. Walker please?" I asked as she grabbed the tablet from the counter and walked away from me.

"Sorry. I can't. I have to bring Dr. Shewmer's last patient back," she said smugly, sauntering to the waiting room door and calling for the next patient.

She got on my nerves. Sure, I could look the information up myself, but she was the medical assistant. Her ass wasn't in a hurry to take the patient back before.

"Quincy, can you please look up the next opening for Ms. Walker?" Quincy smacked her lips as she sat at the check-out desk, but scrolled the schedule on her computer.

"Friday at 3:00pm with a Nurse Practitioner," she replied.

Turning back to the window, Ms. Walker waited impatiently with her lips pursed and her head tilted.

"Ms. Walker, again, I'm sorry for the scheduling mix up, but we do have an opening this Friday at 3:00pm if you want to take that one. Do you want me to schedule that for you right now?" I asked sweeping my newly cropped shoulder length locks behind my ear.

"Can she hear? Didn't I just tell miss thang here that we ain't comin' back on no day? My 'pointment is right *now*," granny persisted to Race, then turned to me while straightening her silver-tinged wig under her hat.

I heard Quincy and Nicky snicker in back of me and I felt their eyes on my back before Nicky took the patient down the hall to one of the rooms.

"Granny, I can bring you back Friday. It's no problem," Race told her glancing from her to me.

"I don't care if you can bring me every day Horace. I'm gon' be seen right now because that's when I was s'posed to be seen."

Angie walked her patient to the check-out desk and gave Quincy instructions on making his next appointment before heading back towards the patient rooms.

"Hold on a minute," I told Ms. Walker. "Angie," I summoned her, leaving Race and his grandma at the window. "I know that was your last appointment, but we have a patient here who got her days mixed up and she's anxious to be seen. I think she mostly just needs her prescriptions refilled. Can you see her please?"

She cocked her brow and looked around me to the check-in window, up at the wall clock, then back to me.

"Who? That fine ass Mandingo?" she whispered with a mischievous grin, smoothing the hairs in her ponytail down and licking her lips.

"No," I grinned back feeling the same tingling in my loins she probably was. "The lady next to him. His grandma."

Her smile waned, and her mouth twisted.

"Seriously? I think Fatima had her before. She's a pain in the ass. I thought we were going for drinks after this?"

"We *are*. C'mon. Can you see her? She's refusing to leave until she sees someone, and I think all she really needs is her scripts refilled. Happy hour will still be going on when we leave," my green eyes pled to her.

Angie rolled her eyes and grunted.

"First round's on you," she affirmed.

"Okay. I'll have Quincy bring her back. What room?"

"Room 5."

"Take her back to room 5 please," I said tapping Quincy on the shoulder as I passed her to deliver the good news. "Ms. Walker, you're in luck. Angie's gonna be able to see you right now. Quincy will be right out to take you back to a room."

Ms. Walker perked up and transformed her scowl to a smile.

"Well now that's what I wanted to hear. Thank you baby. What's your name again? You say you the manager of this here office right?"

"Yes ma'am. My name is Greer. I'm the Office Manager."

"Good. Good. Is you black?"

"Granny," Race reproached her.

"Oh hush boy. Don't "Granny" me. She looks like one of us but I can't tell with them green eyes. I was gonna say thank you sista, but I wanted to be sure she was a sista before I called her one."

He licked his lips and shook his head, revealing his dimple to me again as Quincy headed to the waiting room door to bring her back.

"Yes ma'am. I'm black."

"You is mixed though right? Like President Obama," she continued, as my plastered smile was becoming more difficult to sustain.

"Yes ma'am. I think Quincy is ready for you now."

"I knew you was. I was just testin' ya to see if you was one of those Tiger Woods, 'I ain't black' type blacks; or if you was one of us," she smirked positioning the cane she'd had against the wall so she could walk with it.

Race ran a hand across his face as Quincy opened the door and he helped escort his grandma through it.

"You wait out here boy. You can't come in my 'pointment with me and see me naked," Ms. Walker told him as she scuttled beside Quincy with Race holding her arm.

"You won't be getting naked," Quincy told her sounding tickled.

"He don't need to hear about all my lady problems either. Just wait for me out there boy," Ms. Walker told Race swatting at his hands. "This young gal can take me the rest of the way. You ain't about to pop, is you?" she asked Quincy.

"No ma'am," Quincy replied with a full-on giggle.

Race released her and Ms. Walker chuckled a little too, probably amused by her own antics.

"Your grandmother is funny. I could tell she was dead serious about posting up at this office until we saw her today," I said playing with ringlets of my hair.

As hard as it was, I couldn't stop blushing and cheesing like I'd just won the Miss America pageant.

"I like your hair," he said taking me in from head to toe and back again.

"Thank you, *Horace*."

"*Yeeeahhhh*. About that. I hate that name," he smirked raising a fist. "My Granny's the only one who still calls me that. Even my mother calls me Race."

"Race fits you better."

"Your new haircut fits *you* better. It reminds me of the way Beyonce' looked in that *"Work it Out"* video from *Austin Powers*. Kind of like a curly lioness," he complimented.

"*Oookay.*"

"So how long have you worked here?" he asked looking around the office.

"About 6 years."

"I see," he nodded.

"Alright, it was nice seeing you again. You can wait for your grandma in the waiting room. It didn't sound like it would be a long appointment. Let me get back to work," I said turning to go back to my office.

He gently grabbed my wrist and turned me back towards him.

"Would it be possible for you to keep me company while I wait? I know you have work to do and everything, but I'd love to get to know you a little bit better."

"Why? Don't you have a girlfriend?" I asked unabashedly.

His pearly whites made a brief appearance as he shook his head no while gazing into my eyes.

"No, I do *not* have a girlfriend. Not anymore. We've been split up a couple months."

"Really," I stated with skepticism. "A little birdie told me that's just a little game the 2 of you play though. On and off again."

"A little birdie huh? Sounds more like a big-mouthed birdie named Lisa," he jested. "But seriously. I don't have a girlfriend. We're broken up permanently. So can I get to know you better now that you know I'm not out here creeping on my girl?" he asked stepping closer to me.

His cologne was intoxicating, and his smile made my insides melt. I loved his confidence, and his striking looks were certainly not working against him.

"Maybe another time. I have work to do," I said nearly stumbling back from him.

"Would it be possible for me to... I don't know. Sit in your office with you while you work for a little while? You could always say I was discussing my granny's bill if it came up. I'm the one who pays them all anyway."

I craned my neck back. "Is that so?"

I hadn't realized that he was still holding my wrist until I felt his thumb trace across it.

"I'm not a subtle kind of guy Greer. When I see a beautiful and ambitious woman that I'd like to get to know, I speak up. I wasn't in a position to do it when we met at the range, but I am now.

I hope I'm not being too forward for you, but I missed an opportunity once, and I don't want to have to wait for a third. Unless you're already taken," he asked tentatively.

"I don't think you'll be able to get to know me too well at the same time you're being quiet so I can work," I said making us laugh.

Behind me, I heard an exam room door close, and I knew it had to be Nicky on her way back to her station. I instinctually stood up straight and cleared my throat while nervously touching the nape of my neck.

"Can I take you out sometime then? Maybe you can give me your number and we can talk more about it when you get off work?" he asked as I tried, probably without success, to stifle my delight at his request.

Nicky arrived at her desk and started packing up her things while eying Race and I in her peripheral.

"I have plans after work but, sure. We can talk sometime. Maybe go out," I replied coyly.

"Hey, Nicky do you have Morrison's lab results? The system says he had his testing, but I never got them to scan in," Kendrick called out as he approached from a back office.

We were all looking at him, but Kendrick's eyes were darting between Race and I like he'd just caught one of us with our hand in the cookie jar.

"Fatima put them in your inbox before she left," Nicky said smirking impishly as she watched Kendrick's reaction.

"I have plans tonight, so not after work tonight," I answered focusing back on my new potential beau.

He took his phone from his jeans pocket, unlocked it and handed it to me.

"Put your number in it."

I took it from him and did as he asked, then handed it back; all the while noticing Kendrick pointlessly lingering around the check-out desk.

Even though we were sexing 2 or 3 times a week now and occasionally caught a movie or dinner together, Kendrick wasn't my man. I was just as free to do what I wanted, with *who* I wanted, as he was.

For all I knew, he was still screwing that nut job Kita from 2A. Speaking of which, that clown tried to confront me about the gum in her laundry when she saw me a week or so later.

Of course, I played stupid and vehemently denied any involvement in it, but it was clear she didn't believe me. So much so that the heifer rushed from her apartment on another occasion and got in my face making threats as I exited my car.

She wasn't ready for the .380 I brandished after she slapped me. The apologies flowed from her mouth like a heavy period as she backed away teary-eyed and frightened, back up the stairs to her unit.

I never mentioned it to Kendrick, and I don't think she did either; but she hadn't made an appearance while I was visiting since. The coward.

Regardless, Kendrick was not going to be the last man standing, so his feelings weren't primary or warranted from the cheap seats. He'd get over it. It's not like he had a choice.

"*Sooo...* my number is locked into your phone. I've gotta go back to work, and you need to have a seat in the waiting room. Don't be afraid to use my number now," I said seductively.

At least I hoped that's how it came out. That's what I intended anyway.

"I wouldn't ask for it if I was afraid to use it," he said watching me sashay off to my office.

I made sure to add an extra sway in my hips too as my heels click clacked down the hallway. Less than 15 minutes later, Kendrick entered my office and closed the door behind him wearing a snarl.

"What was that all about?" he asked leaning his back against the closed door with his arms folded.

"What was what?" I asked coquettishly without looking up from my computer.

He sucked his teeth and stared at me until I looked at him. "You gave that dude your number?"

"Yes. Is that a problem for you?" I questioned leaning back in my chair with my hands clasped in my lap.

He glanced around my office like it was a chore for him to express his thoughts, then back at me with an intensity I hadn't seen before.

"I don't know. When I saw you giving him your number and looking at him all googly eyed, I didn't like that shit. I know we're not together, but..."

"But what? You're bothered by me giving out my number? Don't you screw whomever you want without my interference?" I challenged. "We have an arrangement of convenience Kendrick. When it stops being convenient or necessary for either of us, we can end it. This has been fun, but it can stop."

His face screwed up and he locked my door before stalking over to my desk to give me a piece of his mind. Or so I thought. He cleared an area on my desk, sending my calculator, and some papers crashing to the floor.

Swiftly, he rounded it and got in my face as I opened my mouth to protest.

"Shut up," he commanded, grabbing me by my arm and pulling me into his. One hand gripped my ass forcefully, while the other took hold of my hair and held my head in position for his succulent lips to attack.

The urgency and ferocity of his touch had my juices flowing like Niagara Falls. Our tongues danced as he hiked my dress up above my hips and grinded the erection fighting for release from his scrubs into me.

"Wait," I whispered between kisses. "People are still... here."

"Be quiet then," he ordered into my neck as his tongue found its way to my lobe and traced it until I shivered under his touch.

"Aaahhh," I cooed as he hoisted me up on the long end of my desk and ripped my panties down my thighs.

Following his lead, I untied his scrub bottoms and shimmied them over his hips, wanting him inside me just as much as he wanted to be there.

I was still drunk off of seeing Race and I wasn't going to have any problems imagining that Kendrick was him while he laid his pipe.

My hands clamped Kendrick's back as he entered my sopping box, causing me to bite down on his shoulder to muffle my cries. My legs wrapped tightly around his back as I pulled him deeper inside of me and one of his hands cupped my breast through my dress.

"Oh, fuck baby. I don't want nobody else to have my pussy," Kendrick groaned into my ear as he pounded my sex and my walls spasmed with pleasure.

I ignored his crazy talk about it being "his pussy" because that was definitely crazy talk. He no more owned my vagina than I owned his loose dick.

Speaking of which, I knew having unprotected sex with him was foolish; but it was just once. Besides, I still had several boxes of the Plan B One-Step pill in my medicine cabinet to prevent any accidents from occurring.

We knew this had to be a quickie, and he knew my body well enough by that point to know how to get me off swiftly. My body was convulsing just as he began erupting inside me, and my muscles clenched him firmly within.

A thin coat of sweat glistened from his forehead as he leaned back and looked me in the eyes.

"Don't give him my pussy Greer," he demanded.

My forehead creased and I looked at him like he was crazy, because he most certainly was if he thought he was going to dictate my life.

"Get off of me Kendrick," I said pushing him further away as I scooted towards the edge of my desk and began pulling my dress back down.

He frowned and moved out of my way after pulling his scrubs back up.

"I'm serious Greer."

"You're crazy Kendrick," I brushed him off as I bent down and began picking up the things he'd knocked off of my desk.

He slapped my ass and I flinched, turning to him with a scowl. He was gazing at me seductively as I straightened the things on my desk again, but I was ready for him to leave my office.

Dr. Shewmer was probably gone to the hospital by then, Nicky and Quincy would definitely have left as soon as the last patient was done; but Angie would still be here unless she thought I left already, which was highly unlikely.

I unlocked the office door and opened it, only to be startled by Angie standing on the other side.

"I was just getting ready to knock," she said looking past me to Kendrick, then back at me suspiciously.

"Oh," I said self-consciously touching my hair. "I had to discuss something with Kendrick before he left."

"I'll see y'all tomorrow," he said with an attitude bustling passed both of us and out of my office.

I wasn't sure whether it was contrived for the sake of supporting my bogus story, or whether it was genuine. Either way, I hoped Angie didn't smell our sex in the air and hadn't heard our earlier moans.

"You wanna follow me to my house so I can change and then I'll drive?" she offered, still following Kendrick's departure with her eyes.

"Yeah. That's fine."

We were both silent for a moment before she left to gather her things from her office. I shut my computer down and got my own things, heading to the front of the office to lock up all the entrances into the practice.

Kendrick left the breakroom drinking another concoction from a water bottle and stopped when he saw me. Winking, he mouthed, 'Call me later' and downed more of his drink.

I shook my head in amused disgust as I cut the light off on the wall of the breakroom and Kendrick followed behind me.

"You must be headed to the gym since you're drinking that crap," I jibed.

"Yep. Every day now after work. The gym in my apartment complex is being renovated so I've been using the free membership we get at STRONG LIFE."

As a perk, Franklin Family Practice provided all employees with a free one-year membership to the gym across from the office park our building was in.

One of the practice partners thought it was a good incentive to promote good health, and the others agreed, so I guess it was a good thing Kendrick was taking advantage of it.

"Y'all walking out with me?" Angie asked standing by one of the employee-exits leading to the elevators and stairwells.

Franklin Family Practice was large, so we reserved the entire 4th floor. One you got off the elevators or stepped from the stairwell, you were immediately at the entrance to our glass double doors.

"I am," I replied.

"I take the stairs, and you should too," Kendrick responded walking out behind us with his satchel diagonally across his chest.

"Not," Angie said with a laugh and I waved him off too.

"You have a good night," I said pressing the elevator button.

"Alright y'all. Be safe," he told us going through the stairwell doors.

Angie's face was twisted up as she watched him leave and I was curious about the reason behind it.

"Why're you looking like that?" I inquired.

"Like what?"

"Like something is wrong. You having a problem with Kendrick?"

"No," she said unconvincingly as the elevator dinged and we entered.

I didn't bother to query further. Angie liked to run her mouth, so I knew whatever was going on, she'd spill it sooner rather than later.

Later came before we even descended the full 4 floors to the parking lot. She straightened the strap of her pocketbook over her shoulder nervously and cleared her throat.

"Are you seeing Kendrick too?"

I feigned surprise and clutched my throat like her accusation was ridiculous.

"Uh… no. Why would you think that?"

She shrugged and stared at the elevator doors while fidgeting with her pocketbook strap.

"I don't know. He has a weird energy around you. Plus, you're always calling him into your office with the door closed."

"First of all, I close my door every time I'm discussing something of a personal matter with an employee. Secondly, I'm always calling him in my office because he's *always* late or doing something to get himself in trouble. What, are you seeing him?" I questioned as we stepped off the elevators and headed to our respective cars which were only a few spots apart.

"Sort of," she said surreptitiously eyeing me.

I felt an involuntary pang of jealousy at the news as I searched my purse for my keys. Kendrick had a lot of nerve trying to cock-block Race when he was bedding one of the few people at FFP that he knew I was friends with.

"Sort of, as in you're sleeping with him? Or sort of, as in you're a couple?"

"We're definitely *not* a couple. Yet. It's only been going on a few weeks. He's really cool though. I'm just taking it slow. We'll see where it goes. Nobody's claiming anybody just yet," she tittered coyly.

"So, you *are* sleeping with him then?" I pried.

She shrugged and headed towards her Quattro.

"I have. And it was *gooood* too!" she teased shaking her rump.

"Well alright Miss Thang. Just make sure it doesn't interfere with work, and you won't hear a peep about it from me," I replied with a grin as fake as Nicki Minaj's butt.

"I promise we won't get caught screwing in my office," she kidded.

"Please don't get *caught*," I retorted with a wider smile than hers.

13

Greer

"I can't believe he thought we were just gonna welcome him with open arms. He might as well have just said, 'Hey kids. You know my best friend that you've been calling Uncle Jimmy for the last 20 years? He's actually my lover and I'm divorcing your mother to be butt buddies with him from here on out!' I'm just at a loss for words.

Like what the hell is happening? What about my mother?" Angie rambled drunkenly over her 5th Mai Tai of the night as I nursed my Appletini and ate my last fry.

For someone who claimed to be at a loss for words, she'd been babbling nonstop from the time the first drink hit her lips. Angie and I had become friendly enough that I didn't mind being a sounding board for her momentary misery though. I was actually kind of flattered that she would share such personal news with me at all.

I was glad I'd thought better when Angie initially volunteered to drive from her house, and convinced her to ride with me instead. Given her current state of inebriation, I would've had to confiscate her keys anyway. Angie was barely in good enough condition to *walk* to the car, let alone drive it.

Truth be told, I didn't want to come to THE HEN'S DEN anyway, but Angie was familiar with the hole in the wall bar and grill, and it was her choice. Personally, I had no interest in entertaining the local hooligans and wanna-be pimps that frequented it, but this was her go to spot.

She'd taken an hour to change into some tight jeans, a low-cut blouse and heels, all to entice these no-goodnicks with her ample bosom and flawless skin. I thought she was too pretty and too smart to keep going for these types of guys if you asked me; but nobody asked.

The music was decent and karaoke nights were fun to watch, but the crowd was typically money-grubbing locals who worried more about legalized weed than they did about kids they left at home.

The lighting was dim and 20 or so 4-person wide booths surrounded the circumference of the dancefloor and stage where occasional professional and amateur talents performed.

"Are you ready to go?" I asked picking up my purse from the seat and readying the keys in my hand.

"Go? Awww Greer. *No,* I'm not ready to go. We're girls. We're hanging out. We're chillin'. We're bondin'. We're relaxin'," she slurred with a big, inebriated grin. "Don't be such a prude."

"Girl we have been hanging, chillin', bondin' and relaxin' for hours. It's after 10pm already. I'm not being a prude, and *you* better not be late to work tomorrow either," I chastised lightly.

The waiter had already left the tab on the table and the bill came to just over $80 for the 2 of us. I went ahead and paid it since Angie hardly seemed coherent enough to calculate 20% of *anything* at the moment. She could pay me back later.

She wobbled to her feet and picked up her purse while downing the last remains of her drink. After burping loudly and looking around with a giggle, she determined, "I think you should drive."

"Yeah. I do too," I replied guiding her towards the door with my arm roped in hers as I held her up from the floor.

She tripped over her own feet and fell face first into the top of the passenger's side door of my Corolla, just as I'd opened it to help her in.

"Fuck!" she hollered out holding her nose as it began to leak into her hand.

"Girl," I sighed grabbing some tissue from my purse and handing a wad to her.

When she was secured in her seat, I got in on the driver's side and put my purse in the backseat.

"Damn, this hurts. You think it's broken?" she asked pulling down the visor and looking teary eyed at her swollen nose in the mirror.

"I doubt it. Just put your seat back and keep it elevated," I advised starting the car.

"I don't know why I'm asking you anyway. I'm the one who's the NP. Shouldn't I be able to tell if my own nose is broken?" she cackled, her nasally voice sounding even more so as she winced in pain.

Cupping the tissue in place as she reclined her seat, Angie asked, "You remember where I live right?"

"I think so. I don't know why your ass moved out to Texas Chainsaw-ville anyway. How the hell did you find a place that country, so close to the city?" I joked driving out of the lot.

"*Craig's List.* My rent is only $850 a month for a 3- bedroom, 3 and ½ bath with a 2-car garage. I'll take the drive to the woods for all that," she answered. "Plus, it's still only 15-minutes from work in good traffic."

"What do you need a 3-bedroom house for when it's just you?" I asked. "You got all that house to roam around in and you're just renting. Now if you owned it, I could understand. Because who knows what might happen in the future where you'd need all that space, but..." I stopped talking when Angie's loud snores perforated my ears. I couldn't believe she passed out that quickly.

Once I turned off of Turner Hill Rd, the remaining stretch to Angie's place was only going to be illuminated by my headlights and those of other cars I passed, with a hiccup of streetlights along the way. I had my brights on for fear that a deer or something else would dart out in the middle of the road and cause us to wreck. The roadside was already riddled with beaver, dear, raccoon and dog corpses almost every 2 or 3 miles.

Halfway to my destination, some douchebag driving behind me also thought it was a good idea to use their brights, which is hazardous and unnecessary when there's a car in front of you.

It was almost blinding to look in my rearview mirror, but looking in the side, I occasionally saw them swerving in and out of the single lane we drove in.

"Stupid ass is probably on the phone or texting," I said aloud as I drove the speed limit trying to ensure I didn't get in an accident or miss the next side street I needed to turn on to get to Angie's house.

After them trailing me for about 2 miles, I guess they determined that I was driving too slowly, so they started honking and riding up close to my bumper.

"Go to hell," I said smartly in my car after checking my speedometer and seeing that I was doing 49 in a 45.

I wasn't about to get a ticket or wreck, just because some inconsiderate jerk wanted me to go faster. I bet their impatient ass was probably from New York or somewhere and they'd be the first one with a deer through their windshield.

Just as I saw them in my side mirror attempting to pass me in the opposite lane, a raccoon dashed out from the trees lining the road. The driver's wheels screeched as they veered towards our car, and our wheels squealed too as I jerked to the right trying to avoid being hit.

The car lurched into the center of the lane as I hooked the wheel back to the left to prevent going into a ditch or hitting a tree, and the other car passed me.

My heart was beating out of my chest, and my hands were trembling at the near miss collision I thankfully evaded. I couldn't believe Angie had only shifted in her sleep and wasn't jarred awake.

"Assholes!" I screamed at the Ford Taurus, only yards ahead of me after almost running me off the road.

Pissed was an understatement for how I felt. I glimpsed the phone glued to the young driver's ear when our cars were beside each other for that split second. They could've killed us!

My foot had a mind of its own, mashing on the gas trying to catch up to the taillights ahead. For a split second they disappeared, and I thought I'd somehow lost them down another rural road before I spotted the car driving a short path down a gravel driveway as I passed it.

Slamming on the breaks, I backed up to the entrance and turned to go down it with every intention of cussing the driver out like Chris Rock on steroids. I was seeing red, so when the petite blonde exited her car in the dimly lit driveway, still yapping on the phone, totally oblivious to the 2-ton vehicle barreling towards her, I cut my headlights off.

I plowed into her with deliberation, and slammed on the breaks just as her body collided with my bumper and folded onto the hood before careening backwards into the siding of the house with a deafening thud.

Excitement pulsed through my veins as her body flailed in midair, only to bounce off the paneling and land on the ground, bloody and motionless.

I stared at the barely identifiable heap through my windshield, then at splatter on the side of the house that was evident even in the reduced light.

Throwing the car into reverse, I raced back up the path and sped out onto the road like a stunt driver in the *FAST AND THE FURIOUS*.

I nervously glanced over at a comatose Angie, as I flipped my headlights back on and drove pointedly towards my destination. I was both amazed and thankful that her drunk ass hadn't stirred awake, or I would've had a lot of explaining to do.

Minutes later, I found myself laughing hysterically as I thought about that reckless driver's body flying through the air. It reminded me of the way those life-sized dummy's looked on television sitcoms. I always roared when they tossed them around on Kevin Hart's *Real Husbands of Hollywood* and on reruns of *Martin* and *Married with Children*.

Too bad I couldn't share my amusement with anyone unless I wanted a felony hit and run charge under my belt. I didn't have an ounce of remorse for that lady's demise as I turned onto the last stretch of mile before Angie's house would come up. She had been a hazard on the road, and now she wasn't.

I had to shout Angie's name and shake her repeatedly to get her out of my car, but she came to and stumbled out eventually, holding her aching head and saying she felt like she'd been hit by a truck.

"My head hurts, my nose hurts… fuck it. My whole face hurts!" she complained while staggering from my car into her house.

"I guess it's safe to say you'll be calling in tomorrow huh?" I said following behind her into her bedroom where she sat on the edge of the bed and kicked off her shoes.

She nodded, then held her head with a groan while squeezing her eyes shut.

"Yeah. I feel like shit," she confirmed.

"Alright. Drink some water or take some aspirin. I'll see you on Friday," I replied softly. "I'll lock the bottom lock on my way out too."

"Thank you," she muttered, flopping backwards onto her queen-sized bed as I let myself out.

When I got in the car, it was no coincidence that Pharell's song "Happy" was playing on 107.5. That had to be fate. I sang along at the top of my lungs, confident that the reckless pile of shit lying on that gravel driveway couldn't identify my car if it was stapled to her. That is, if she lived.

I made it home in record time and parked facing the house beside the Yukon. When I got out, I walked around the front of the car to see if there was any noticeable evidence of what transpired earlier.

There was a slight dent on the hood and an indentation on the bumper, but there was no drastic damage to my car at all. I didn't see any blood, hair or anything of that nature on it, but to be on the safe side, I'd be taking ol' Rolly to the car wash at lunch.

As expected, Angie called out for work on Thursday. Though I was swamped with work all day, I was consumed with thoughts of the reckless driver's demise and oddly enough, Race.

I wondered when he was going to call me and what we'd talk about. I wondered what else he did besides owning the gun range and whether he was bedding other women while he waited for Mrs. Right to show herself.

Before I knew it, Saturday had rolled around again, and I was outside setting up tables for my garage sale. Even though I hadn't found a new home to move to yet, I was ready to get rid of the old and make room for the new.

What a difference a year made. I doubt I would've had as many people willing to help me when I was married to Michael as I had coming to help me now.

My dad could always be counted on to support, but Ms. Nina was coming, and Angie promised to drag herself out of bed to man a table for me. Even Lisa offered a helping hand when I told her about the garage sale at the range on Sunday.

It was a sunny day, forecasted to be in the low 80's with a chance of rain in the evening. The garage sale was only scheduled to last from 11am to 3pm and I hoped to get rid of everything within that time. I advertised it on Craig's List, in our HOA newsletter and I posted the sale on Facebook and Twitter.

Daddy was the first to arrive wearing his *Falcons* baseball cap, a *Falcons* T-shirt and shorts at 9am to help me set up. Of course, no matter how I'd arranged the tables in the driveway, he found a way to rearrange them better.

Ms. Nina was next at a quarter after, and she helped organize and label prices on stuff for me. Since I knew she was about her money as a former accountant, I let her determine the prices on everything.

Frankly, with the money I received from Michael's policy and my bi-weekly salary combined, I wasn't hurting for money by any stretch of the imagination. Sale price was the least of my concerns as Ms. Nina and Daddy pulled out items and set them out on the table.

Donna showed up at 20 minutes to 11 like a special invited guest, taking her sweet time to help out and complaining about the heat off rip. Her butt cheeks peeked from the bottom of her Daisy Duke's and her green halter top exposed her pierced navel and washboard abs.

Corkscrew curls hung down her back with green tinted highlights that matched her cream and green Converse sneakers. I don't know how much she spent on those weaves, but if I didn't know for a fact they didn't grow out of her head, I'd think they did.

People were already trickling onto the yard at 5-minutes to. Lisa and Angie were walking up the driveway at the same time, so when they reached me, I just introduced them.

Angie wore thick black shades and the swelling on her nose had gone down completely. Turns out it wasn't broken at all, so the shades were probably more of a fashion fixture than anything else. Her hair was in a messy bun and she donned a camouflage shorts jumper with matching Airforce Ones.

Lisa looked sprite and refreshed like she'd slept 20 hours and had the best orgasm of her life in the same day. Her hair was pulled up on the sides into a fo-hawk and her make-up was as flawless as a super model's. We were both wearing a tank and jeans, but her body filled her clothes out far better than I filled out mine.

I found out early on that people like to browse more than they like to buy. There was a whole lot of conversation, but minimal selling going on.

"Greer? Is this Mommy's phone?" Donna asked holding the cellphone I hadn't seen since I tossed it in the junk box the day of Michael's murder.

Her forehead creased with confusion. Ms. Nina, Lisa and Angie were preoccupied with the yard sale, but Daddy's eyes were fixed on me, as were Donna's.

"Is it?" is all I could think of before turning to a middle-aged white man who was interested in Michael's Mongoose bike. "Seventy-five dollars and it's yours."

"Seventy-five dollars is good but, how old is it? It has a few scratches on the frame and I'll probably have to change out those brake cables too," he said touching and investigating the bike even closer.

"Alright. I'll go down to $65 for you. Now I'm the one who bought this for him. I know that's a great price for this bike when he barely used it," I replied while racking my brain for an excuse to have Stephanie's phone.

Mister middle age mulled over the price for a minute, then pulled out a wad of 5's and counted out $65.

"I'll take it," he said handing me the money and grabbing the handle-bars instantly.

"Thank you. Enjoy," I told him with a smile as I started over to help Lisa, but Donna pulled my arm before I could.

"Why do you have Momma's phone?" she asked seriously. "And why was it in with all of your stuff to sell?"

I sighed and fingered my ponytail.

"You're gonna think I'm weird. Weirder than you already think I am."

"Whatever. Just answer my question. I know Daddy was trying to find it for months after she died and here you've had it all along. Why?" she asked impatiently displaying it in the palm of her hand.

"I needed something of hers for a psychic to channel her from," I said straight-faced as I made up a story off the top of my head. "I had some unanswered questions she never answered in life. So... so I was hoping she'd answer them in death," I said ashamedly.

Donna stared at me bewildered and Daddy simply walked away to talk to a lady holding a baby who was looking at the chase I'd sat out.

"I didn't know you believed in that kind of stuff," she said with a skeptical squint. "Did you get the answers you were looking for?"

I shook my head no. "Not really. Not from her, not from Michael, and not from my mother either. It was stupid. I know. Do we have to talk about this?" I asked looking around uncomfortably.

She stared at me a while longer before I could tell she'd let it go.

"No. I was just curious. It caught me by surprise when I saw it. That's all. You don't mind if I keep it do you?" she asked putting it in her back pocket like she already knew the answer.

I tried to remember if I'd ever saved anything other than the soft-ware on her phone. I didn't think I had, and I hoped for my sake that I hadn't, but there was a possibility that I'd downloaded the first record-ing of Michael and Marlene on that phone when I was learning the ap.

Daddy watched us curiously from the table he was selling stuff at and a guilty chill ran up my spine. He'd asked me more than once if I'd seen Stephanie's phone, and I had told him I hadn't. Now he knew I was lying.

The rest of the day was uneventful, and almost everything for sale was sold except a few little trinkets and that shady hairdryer. Angie had somewhere else to be, but me, Daddy, Ms. Nina, Donna and Lisa sat in my living room in ample air-conditioning, drinking cool glasses of lemonade and eating slices of pizza.

"Maybe you can come look at the books then," Daddy was saying to Ms. Nina as they discussed FLOWER ME WITH LOVE and Debbie's lack of help with it. "Cause Greer already got a fulltime job and that Debbie..." he shook his head in disgust.

"Well sure I will, if you need it. I don't know much about flowers, but I know a lot about finances. How's business been doing anyway?" Ms. Nina asked him while sipping her soda.

"It's good. I'm there a lot mo' now since Debbie only wanna come in when *she* wanna come in. I know how to run the store easy. I'm just not good with computers and keepin' paperwork right.

Steph did all of that when she was alive. She was good wit' business like that. Balanced my locksmith company books too. Debbie was doin' it befo', but she actin' like a..." he paused with a scowl, self-editing what he'd planned to say. "Greer been helping me, but I know she ain't really got time fo' it."

"Daddy, you back in the locksmith business?" Donna asked shoveling a third of the pizza she was eating into her mouth.

"I'm thankin' 'bout maybe just puttin' the machine at the flower shop. Lettin' people come in there like they do at Walmart. All that money I spent on them tools, they should be gettin' used somewhere," he declared.

"Sounds like a good idea to me Mr. Chuck," Lisa offered as she gathered her paper plate and cup, ready to throw them out.

"Let me get that," I told her, taking the trash from her.

"Thanks," she smiled flopping back down on the couch beside Donna.

Walking to the kitchen to throw the trash out, my cell rang from a number that wasn't saved in my phone.

"Hello?" I answered after I'd thrown the garbage away.

"Good afternoon beautiful," a man said on the other end.

"Good afternoon. Who is this?" I asked.

"This is Race. Did I catch you at a bad time?" he asked cautiously.

"No. Not really," I responded controlling my excitement to hear his voice.

"I'm sorry it's taken me so long to call. I had some family issues to handle and time got away from me."

"No problem," I said sitting in a chair at the kitchen table with the phone to my ear.

"How've you been?"

"I'm fine. I just had a garage sale today that went okay. Lisa was here helping me too."

"Oh really? I'm glad it went well. I'm too impatient to do stuff like that. I'd either take it somewhere to pawn it or donate it to GOOD WILL. Plus, I don't like sales. That's one reason why I rarely work the range."

"Why not? You seem like you'd be a good salesman. Just flash those pearly whites and the women would buy whatever you were selling," I complimented.

"If only it were that easy."

"It can be."

"Look. I'm not big on the telephone unless I don't have another choice. Do you have plans this evening?"

Talk about straight forward. He did not beat around the bush.

"I thought you said you were gonna call me so we could get to know each other better? You're going from zero to a hundred *real* quick right now. Slow down. I'm not that kind of girl," I flirted.

He chuckled. "I do want to get to know you better. But I figured we could get to know each other better on a date. Nothing fancy. I'm thinking something like, roller skating."

"*Roller skating? Are you serious?*"

"Dead serious. What, you don't roller skate?"

I thought about it amusedly. I hadn't been roller skating in ages, but I was actually pretty good when I did. I was in the mood to do something fun for a change, and who better to do it with than a fine man.

"I mean, I haven't since I was a teenager, but I can skate. Probably better than you at least," I teased cockily.

"I hope you're not a sore loser, because I'm surely gonna hurt your little feelings when I roll bounce all over your pretty little ego."

We laughed as I scrutinized my hands, seeing that a manicure was overdue.

"The only problem is, I didn't say I was going. How're you gonna call me up 3 days after you were all froggy about getting my number, ask me to go out within 60 seconds, and expect me to jump? Do I really seem that hard up for a date?"

"No. Not at all. If anybody's hard up for a date, I guess it's me. I've been thinking about you nonstop since Wednesday. If I'm being honest, I've thought about you a lot since the first day we met.

I knew you had a lot going on around then, plus I was also tying up loose ends of my own; but I don't see a reason to waste time if we have it. Life's too short to let opportunities pass you by if you don't have to."

"And you say you're not a salesman huh?" I asked hoping I sounded as sultry as I was trying to.

I knew he had to have known about the murder case. Hell, unless you were under a rock somewhere, everybody knew about it. I'd been recognized by several people before because of media coverage.

Even if he hadn't known, I'm sure Lisa would've brought it up at some point. She was talkative and he seemed inquisitive. They were the perfect match for gossip.

He made a playful clicking sound with his mouth.

"I can be persuasive when I need to be. If you don't want to go skating, we can do something else. I just want to see you. Talk to you."

I blushed as the butterflies in my stomach fluttered around like they were trapped under glass. I hadn't felt this giddy about a man since I dated Michael. Kendrick awoke more carnal desires in me than emotional. Race had aroused both, and he'd done it with barely a Coke and a smile.

"I've still got company, including Lisa. It's almost 4pm now. How late, or how early did you want to meet up?"

"You tell me. I'm free the rest of the evening, so it's your world right now."

"What skating rink did you want to meet at?"

"I was going to come pick you up."

"Uh… no you weren't. I don't know you yet to have you coming to my house."

"But you know Lisa. She'd never let you go out with some psycho weirdo."

"Yeah, but she doesn't know I'm about to go out with you yet. Maybe when she finds out, she'll warn me then," I giggled.

"She better not," he played along. "But if you'd rather meet up, we can do that too. It's SKATE PLACE off Pleasant Hill Rd. on I85 North. Are you familiar with the area?"

"I know the area, but I was gonna GPS it anyway. What time?"

"Is 8:00pm good? They start playing club music after 8, and if you're up for it, we can bowl and play laser tag too."

"Alright," I answered enthusiastically.

"Alright then. See you at 8. Bye beautiful," he said ending the call.

I practically floated back into the living room where Donna and Lisa were having a heated debate over the T.V. show *SCANDAL* and whether Olivia Pope was a sell-out ho or not. My father and Ms. Nina retired to the den where I assumed they were, discussing the financials she'd be helping him with.

I joined in on the debate with the ladies and we ended up cackling about that show and a bunch of others until close to 6pm when every-body left.

The skating rink was about a 35-minute drive per my GPS, so I rushed to the bathroom and spruced up my make-up just enough to highlight my attributes without making it obvious that I was trying to.

Race texted me that he arrived as I was parking in the lot of SKATE PLACE. There were a lot of cars and a ton of teens and adults heading inside as I got out. He met me at the door with a hug and a kiss on the cheek and my knees got weak as I inhaled the smell of his cologne and felt his ripped body.

He'd already been in and got our tickets for skates, he was just waiting for me to tell him my size. Once we were skated up, he led me to the rink with a sly grin as Beyonce's song "Blow" blared through the speakers.

I hadn't skated in maybe 10 years, so I was a little shaky starting off, but like riding a bike, you don't really forget. Race led me by the hand a few times as I sang the words to Queen Bey's song and beamed at the sexy man leading me.

It was obvious he was a skilled skater by the smoothness of his moves, many of which I'm sure were being done to impress me.

My balance was perfectly fine, but I enjoyed his hand on my waist, guiding me right where he wanted me, which was everywhere near him.

From the corner of my eye, I saw a tall dark skin girl checking out Race as she circled the rink doing her sexiest skater moves. She had thick orange coated lips, curves for days and what looked like naturally healthy hair in a long ponytail. She was dressed in circulation cutting black shorts and a flimsy off the shoulder orange top that showcased her flawless complexion.

Even with the strobe lights going, there was no question she was a stunner, and all the men... hell, some of the women too, were checking her out.

I was jealous as shit.

To make it worse, her and her cronies kept finding ways to skate near us. Or should I say, *near Race.* They flashed coquettish grins and orange lips bat her eyelashes and shook her hips at him even when I was looking.

By the 4th song in, I wasn't just jealous, I was angry.

"Hey, do you wanna sit down a minute?" I leaned in to ask as they started playing Silento's "Whip Nae Nae."

He nodded, grabbing my hand and leading me to the side after we rounded the top of the rink. Little did he know, I was seething inside at the impertinence those tramps showed and the inferiority complex the girl in orange gave me.

We found a space on a bench by the wall where we could both sit and did.

"Are you having fun?" he asked with his hand on my knee.

"I am. Thank you for inviting me out."

"Thank you for accepting."

"Ms. Patterson. What do you like to do when you're not working or at the shooting range?" he asked leaning back against the wall.

His eyes on me had me blushing again so I looked down at my hands as I spoke.

"Nothing really. I'm not the partying type. I read, watch television… sleep. What do you do Mr… is it Walker?" I asked realizing I didn't even know his last name.

"No. It's Banks."

"Alright. So what do you do other than own the range?"

"I—"

"Excuse me. You're Race right?" Orange lipstick interrupted us as she grinned in his face and put her ass in mine.

Race grimaced as he replied, which surprised me since she was so attractive. I expected him to be cheesing all in her face the way she obviously wanted him to be.

"I am. Do we know each other?"

"We don't yet, but I know *you*. I'm Hannah, but my friends call me NahNah. Your brother Geo gave me this tattoo right here," she said raising her shirt to show him a tatted mermaid on her hip. "But I was hoping to come back in to get you to put 2 big lion paws on my chest," she continued, pulling down the front of her shirt to expose her cleavage.

I folded my lips under and blew out a frustrated breath as she postured and blatantly disregarded me. I sensed that familiar feeling of inadequacy threatening my newfound confidence, and I had to do something to quash it.

"Hi, I'm Greer," I said reaching out my hand toward her.

She looked at it like I was trying to hand her a sack of shit and spoke, but didn't shake. I took my hand back and adjusted my crossbody Coach bag over my chest.

"So, Race. Do you think you'll be able to do me?" she asked trying to sound sultry over the loud music.

"Call the shop and see if they can fit you in NoNo," he told her grabbing my hand and giving her the cold shoulder.

I didn't even try to stifle my laugh at his flub of her name, and I was sure it was intentional too. Hannah's face was definitely cracked, and my laughing added to her embarrassment.

Rather than humiliate herself further, she fingered her hair looking back at her friends and strode off without response. I had a response for her though… but that would wait for later.

"I'm sorry about that baby. Some of these women act like they don't have any home training," he said looking into my soul with his dark eyes.

My insides pureed as he caressed my hand in his and shifted his gaze from my eyes to my lips. Without warning, his mouth was on mine, and my intuition told me he would be mine soon too.

Breaking from me, our eyes locked again.

"I've been wanting to do that since you got here. I told you, I seize the opportunity when one presents itself," he said baring that dimple I was growing to love already.

I smiled and changed the subject.

"You're a tattoo artist?"

He beamed. "I am."

"I would never have guessed. Don't all tattoo artists have 'em all over themselves?" I asked scanning him.

I didn't see one tattoo on him, but then he was fully covered in a rail notch neck thermal T-shirt and jeans.

"I have them. They just aren't always exposed. Tattoos are very personal to me. I don't share mine with everyone, but I can tattoo anyone."

I cocked my head. I don't know why, but he just got sexier.

"Is that so? Where's your shop?"

"In Little Five Points. It's called TAT LIFE," he said drawing back and clasping his hands together in his lap. "Do you have any tattoos?"

I shook my head that I didn't.

"Too scared, haven't thought about it, or don't know what you want?"

I thought for a second. "Probably all of those."

We shared a laugh.

"Maybe you'll let me give you your first one."

"Maybe," I answered feeling my bladder urging me to the restroom. "Do you know where the bathroom is?"

"It's over there," he gestured with his head to my right.

"I'll be right back," I told him rolling carefully on the carpet to it.

I did my business and looked in the mirror as I washed my hands in the sink. He felt so right. My nerves were on edge. I wanted this date to go well. I could feel my future in the balance.

The bathroom door opened and in walked Hannah and her 2 friends. She sneered at me and the other 2 made affronting sounds as one of them went into a stall.

Hannah and I made eye contact via my reflection in the mirror, and that was all she needed to engage.

"Is that your man?" she asked resting her weight on one leg.

"Yes," I answered without hesitation.

He wasn't now, but he would be soon.

"You move fast huh? I just heard he broke up with Song and he's already got a replacement. You must've been on the sidelines waiting," she said rolling over to the sink next to mine and looking me in the face. "There's always somebody waiting on the sideline."

I stared her down and ran my tongue across my bottom lip. How did this ho know who he was dating before? Did she know her? Or was she just in his business that deep?

I decided not to bother verbally sparring with her. What was the point when I already knew I was going to emerge the victor at the end of this anyway?

I smiled, dried my hands and withdrew what I needed from my bag as I rolled back out to Race. Concealing it in my palm, I reached out to him with my free hand and pulled him off the wall he was leaning on while scrolling his phone.

"You ready to get back out there?"

"Yeah," he beamed as I lead him back to the rink.

We skated, laughed and mimicked skate tricks when I noticed Hannah and her crew getting back on the floor as "Bitch Better Have My Money" by Rihanna began playing.

They skated passed us doing their typical sex infused moves, and Hannah wasn't shy about wanting Race's attention. The floor was crowded with teens and adults, both amped by the song, racing around the rink and doing tricks that startled less skilled skaters and sent them off to the sides.

Opportunity presented itself as Hannah approached us skating backwards, intentionally making a gap between Race and I. I was ready for her. Just as her hips brushed against me, I pressed the button on my stun gun, sending volts into her curvaceous body as the strobe lights masked any visible signs of the stream.

She instantly stiffened and timbered over onto 2 skaters in front of her before slamming face down on the floor as I veered right to avoid the collision. The pile up caused a chain reaction as other skaters leapt, swerved and fell trying to avoid the mound of people.

Quickly placing my taser back into the open flap of my bag, I found my way back to Race and covered my mouth in shock.

"Oh my God did you see that?" I quizzed. "What happened? Did she trip?"

He looked just as baffled as most of the people in the pile up and the rest of us that were now clearing the floor.

"*Yooo*, I don't know. I looked over and she was squeezing between us. Next thing I knew, she was on the floor."

We watched as people scrambled from the floor while others attempted to help an unconscious Hannah up and revive her. Her face was a bloodied mess as they rolled her limp body from the floor.

"So what do you say we get out of here?" I asked Race with a smile.

14

Greer

Race towered over me with his arms around my waist and our faces looking at each other.

"Do you want to grab something to eat? It's still early and we still haven't really talked much," he stated checking his watch briefly.

"Uh… I guess. Where do you want to go eat?"

"Since we're dressed casually, nothing too fancy. There's an Applebee's right there," he said pointing to the restaurant just across the lot in the same plaza where we were.

"Cool," I said wrapping my arm around his.

That brought a smile to his face and we strode over there together. I felt revitalized after witnessing Hannah's pretty face in a mangled mess. Served her right for disregarding my position and I didn't feel an ounce of guilt.

We were seated quickly at Applebee's and both of us drew the menus from the holder as our waiter introduced himself and took our drink orders.

By the time he brought my strawberry lemonade and Race's Sprite, we'd already discussed what we wanted and decided on appetizers and entrees. Race placed both of our orders and our waiter was off to make it happen.

"That was crazy with that girl collapsing like that, huh? I hope she's okay. Maybe she had a seizure or something," he expressed.

"Who knows. She sure knew a lot about you though."

He looked contritely back at me. "Hey, I'm *really* sorry about that. I'm not gonna lie like she didn't look a little bit familiar to me, but I don't know her. A lot of chicks know me and my brother because of our shop.

You wouldn't believe it, but there are tattoo shop groupies. We have 8 other tattoo artists at our spot, and let me tell you… the amount of women that are in and out of there sometimes who aren't getting a damn thing done is crazy."

"Sounds like a brothel," I teased. "If I come to get a tattoo myself, am I gonna have to battle my way through the THOTs?"

He shook his head. "Not for me. Maybe for them. I don't entertain that kind of mess. I'm not into women who only like me for what I can do for them. I like women who can do for themselves. Women who make me *want* to do for them."

"I see. Tell me about yourself," I said changing the subject.

His elbows resting on the table, he contemplated his answer for a second.

"I'm not sure what you want to know, but let me see if I can summarize. I'm 32. I'm the oldest of 3 boys. I own TAT LIFE with my middle brother George. We call him Geo. That's Lisa's man. My baby brother Ron is a Pastor, believe it or not. So we're pretty different from him."

"Are you named after your father?" I asked with a smirk.

He returned the gesture and sat back in his chair.

"Yeah. I'm Horace James Banks the second. My father passed when I was 13, so it's just been me, my brothers, my mom and my granny since."

I nodded and sipped my lemonade from a straw.

"Actually, more my brother's and my granny. My mother has a substance abuse problem. She's been in and out of rehab ever since I can remember."

"Oh. Is she… still alive?"

"Yeah. She's like a roach. Resilient. She's OD'd twice that I know of, but she's still here. My dad died from OD'ing on cocaine they were sniffing *together*; but that didn't stop her either. She left us for about 3 years while she was out in them streets.

Back when my brother Geo was gettin' fast money, she actually came to him for a hit. Fucked him up. *Bad.* Made him wanna do somethin' else. I was into petty crimes, car thefts, B an E's, but I was never a D-boy. Believe it or not, I'm a college grad. I was just lucky I was never arrested. I was just a lost dude trying to find my way."

"B and E's is what? Breaking and Enterings?" I asked jogging my *Law & Order* television show memory jargon.

"Yeah," he smirked. "I'm not proud of it, but I did it."

"Your mom and grandma didn't know you guys were doing all of that?"

"Umm… they knew. My grandma didn't like it. She's kicked us out before, but she'd eventually let us back in. She would never admit it, but she needed some of the money we gave her from the dirt we did.

Carmen, my mom, she had her own demons to battle, so she didn't say too much. She's clean now, but only God knows how long that's gonna last. I still kick her down some paper every now and then, but I mostly just take care of my granny."

"How did you end up getting into tattooing?" I asked sincerely.

He sat back like he was visualizing his answer. Gazing behind me into the past.

"Me and Geo could always draw. We're only 2 years apart, so we're a lot alike. Sometimes even I can't tell I'm the oldest," he snickered.

"One of my homeboys, Pharaoh, was dabbling in tattooing. He learned in jail, and he was giving the neighborhood dudes their tats. Once he showed me how to work those needles… I fell in love.

It's a way for me to express myself. My creativity, and literally, have it advertised on a walking canvas for eternity. That's a serious thing for somebody to trust you enough to let you place something eternal on them. You know?

Then I pulled Geo in. Eventually, he gave up that life; and me, Geo and my boy Pharaoh opened up TAT LIFE. Then Pharaoh got killed by his little sister's boyfriend in 2012. So now it's just me and Geo running the business."

"Wow," I replied as a lull fell over our conversation for a few seconds. "When are you gonna let me see *your* tattoos?" I prodded.

"In due time little momma. In due time."

I simpered. "Hmph. Okay. How'd you end up owning a gun range *and* a tattoo shop?"

"Believe it or not, the gun range was my uncle's. He had some health problems a few years ago and couldn't maintain it, so he offered me and my brother's the first shot at buying. Geo didn't want any part of it since we already owned the tat shop. That's all he cares about, and he didn't want to branch out.

Lisa got laid off from her company, got a nice severance package and was willing to cash in her 401K if I let her partner with me. Geo didn't mind, so we made it happen.

We've known Lisa since we were little. She's a little dingy with a big mouth sometimes, but she's got a good business sense and she's trustworthy.

You guys been hanging out a lot lately? She's mentioned you a few times and you said she was helping you with your garage sale."

"Uh… yeah. I guess we're getting to be good friends. She's got a good personality," I replied as he nodded. "So how do you know you're broken up with your ex for good this time?"

"Lisa and her big mouth," he grinned. "Yes, my ex and I did used to go back and forth a lot, but that's in the past. This time it's definitely for good. We were both trying to force something to work that just wasn't. I think we just didn't want to throw away all of those years and have to start fresh."

"How long?"

"We've known each other since Junior High, but we dated on and off for about 5 years. More on than off."

"What makes this breakup different than the other times?" I asked skeptically; probing his eyes for the truth to reveal itself.

"*This* time, she slept with another man while we were still together," he said tonguing the inside of his cheek. "I think she made it pretty clear right there that she wanted to see other people," he chuckled uncomfortably.

"I don't understand why people can't just be honest. If you don't want to be with somebody anymore, don't be. Especially if you're not married. You don't have to cheat," I said sweeping strands from my face repulsed.

"Hey... it's better to know before I put that ring on her finger and planted my seeds with her right?"

"True."

He stared at me strangely and I shifted under his gaze.

"Has it been hard for you dating after so many years of marriage?"

"Honestly, you're my first date since..." I trailed off and looked around uncomfortably. I'm not even sure I'm ready to risk my heart with anybody again. Once somebody you trusted so implicitly, betrays you on that level..." I sighed

"I hear you. My ex, travels for work, so it was already hard to set aside any insecurities about that. Then she turned around and cheated on me right here in the A, with somebody close to home."

"What does she do? To have to travel so much I mean."

"She's a flight attendant. The crazy thing is that she didn't just betray me. She slept with her best friend's man. If I didn't know it was true, I would never have believed it. Did you suspect your husband was cheating on you?"

"You must not have watched the trial," I stated sarcastically taking another sip of my lemonade.

I had met few people who, after knowing my name, didn't already know the run down on the "Sleeping with the enemy" case. Was Race toying with me?

"Actually, I didn't. I don't watch much television at all. I know the basics, like anybody else, but not the details. Ol' girl that stabbed him is in jail, isn't she?"

"Yeah," I said meekly, feeling ashamed of how harsh I was being on him. "I'm sorry. Excuse me if I come off as being a little defensive. It's just that… I feel like my whole life has been under a microscope since it happened.

Besides, it's not the most pleasant of conversations I like to have. One minute I was married to the love of my life. The next minute, he was gone."

We sat in silence for a moment as he sipped some of his own drink and I stared down at the table. Crap. I might've killed the whole vibe.

"To answer your question, yes I suspected. I confronted him about it, but he denied it. It's been really hard for me to even open myself up to the *thought* of dating again."

"I'm glad you opened yourself up to going out on a date with me, and I'm hoping there will be many more. Without people busting their faces on the floor," he snickered.

"I know right! How crazy was that. At least it wasn't either of us," I added.

Holding up my lemonade, he instinctually held up his Sprite.

"Here's to future dates that end with both of us in one piece," I said smiling slyly.

"Cheers!" we said clinking our glasses in unison.

When our orders came, we ate and talked with a fluidity that I hadn't experienced in years. He was a little blunter with his thoughts than I was used to, but it made me less apprehensive about speaking my own mind.

"So, do you like kids?" he asked studying my face.

"Uh, yeah. Some," I smirked. "Why? Do you have kids?"

"No, but I do want kids eventually. I just gotta find a wife first. I don't want to have a bunch of angry baby momma's dragging my seeds into my shop complaining about my late child support payments," he laughed.

"Well now that is good to know. We were waiting until we were more financially stable to try to raise a baby. Michael switched jobs a few times. There didn't seem to be any reason to rush. I guess we waited too long," I lied woefully through my teeth.

I was even beginning to impress myself with the ease with which each fib rolled off of my tongue. I'd never lied so much in all of my life as I had in the last year. They were all with good cause though.

"You've still got plenty of time," he urged patting my hand. "You're still young."

"Am I? I'm gonna be 30 in November."

"I'm no expert on the subject, but I heard 35 was the age where your biological clock could be an issue. You got a ways to go."

I self-consciously played in my hair and gazed out of the window in our booth. "I guess so."

"Tell me about you. About Greer. And I don't mean whatever media garbage has been put out either. I don't care about any of that. I want to know about you."

"What do you want to know?"

"Like, how many brothers and sisters do you have? Are you from Atlanta originally? The basics. I can see you're not really that talkative unless you're interrogating me. I'm gonna have to brow beat it out of you, huh?"

I rolled my eyes playfully and looked back at him.

"Ugh, I hate this. Let's see… Well… I'm the product of an interracial affair. My father is black. My mother is Romanian. I have 2 half-sisters and one half-brother from my father's marriage to their mother. My mother died in a fire when I was 5," I looked around exasperatedly because I hated being on the spot.

"I'm a Sagittarius. My favorite color is pink. I despise liars and cheaters… ummm… my dad had cancer last year around the same time all of that other stuff was going on, so I go see him a lot now. Time is short," I finished up.

"It is. Where does your dad live?"

"In Marietta."

"Oh really? Wherebout? I used to spend a lot of time up that way."

"Off Fountain Ridge Rd. Over by Perry Mill High school. That's where I grew up."

"Yeah. Yeah. I know where that is. My cousin's ex-girlfriend Mia Carter used to live over there."

My mouth gaped open. "Mia Carter. I think I know her. Did she have twin brothers named Dan and Dean?"

He brought his fist to his mouth and laughed into it.

"*Yoooo.* She did. Them boys were wild. My cousin broke Dean's nose in a fight in high school."

"That's crazy. They lived 2 houses down from where my dad lives."

"We used to be over that way all the time. I can't believe I don't remember you."

"I didn't get out much."

"What's your sibling's names? I probably know them too."

"Half-siblings. Shawn is the oldest, then there's Debbie and my baby sister Donna. Me and Donna get along pretty well, but the 2 older ones have *never* accepted me. Debbie lives here with her husband and my 2 nieces, and Shawn lives in Cali with his 2 kids and his wife.

Debbie likes to make my life a living hell when she can, and I'm more like the family ghost to Shawn. He only acknowledges me when he has to."

"Wow. That's messed up. What's their problem with you? Did your dad leave their mom for your mom or something?"

"No. I was a secret baby until my mother died. Then my dad had to take me in or let the state have me since there wasn't any other family here on my mother's side.

My stepmother wasn't a fan of the idea, and she let me every day of my life," I shared sipping from my glass of water.

"What kinda woman takes out her problems on a child? She wasn't abusive to you, was she?" he asked putting a fork full of cheddar jalapeno-topped mashed potatoes in his mouth.

"Whenever my father wasn't around, she was. She hated how I looked, how I acted, how I *breathed*. I couldn't do anything right, if you let her tell it.

All of her side of the family hates me, and my older half-siblings do too. Mainly because I was born bastardly and because I look too white. Both things I had and have no control over."

"That's fucked up. Excuse my language," he said instantly holding up a hand apologetically for the offense.

"No. It is *fucked* up. I'm not looking for a pity party, but it wasn't easy being hated in and outside of my house. All I had was my daddy, and he was a truck driver. He was out of town a lot.

That was perfect for Stephanie, my stepmonster, and my older sister Debbie to teach me what hell on earth was."

"Why didn't your father step in and protect you? I can't imagine letting my little girl go through all of that. Shit, I wouldn't even want to be with a woman who would mistreat my seed.

And somebody should've beat Debbie's little ass. Wouldn't be no kids of mine torturing their brother or sister. I'm not that tight with my little brother Ron, and truth be told, me, Geo and Granny think he's by somebody else.

You know my mom was out in them streets a lot like I said. Ron don't look nothin'... I mean *nothin'*, like me or Geo. But hell, he's still my brother. At the end of the day, you're still their blood."

I shook my head slowly and pursed my lips shamefully.

"I know for a fact Debbie doesn't see it that way. As for my father, I think he was in denial. Stephanie masked a lot of her behavior when he was home and threatened me when he wasn't. She died early last year before everything with my husband happened."

He looked commiseratively at me and pulled at his bottom lip in thought.

"You know what beautiful? Regardless of what we've been through, we've both found a way to come out of it winners. None of that broke us. Even the situation with your husband, as bad as it was, look who's still standing."

He had no idea just how prolific his words were.

15

Greer

"And you believe him?" I asked Shan while boxing on my Wii Fit and talking to her on my Bluetooth.

She sighed heavily and I could hear her switching phone positions.

"Yeah. I want to. He's doing everything he can to make it up to me Greer. He rented an apartment in Manhattan, his mom stopped watching that bitch's kids, he changed his cellphone number, and he's willing to move back to Atlanta if he can find a good job.

He even set up a counseling appointment for us yesterday. It was eye opening. It made me look at a lot of things differently."

"Umm hmm," I replied unenthusiastically.

"Look, he made a mistake. He regrets it and he wants me back. I've been punishing him for months now and he hasn't given up once. I'm miserable without him Greer."

I'd never heard my girl sound so weak before, but I guess love will do that to a person. When she'd gotten back home, she immediately laid into him about the affair.

Surprise, surprise. He denied it. Even when she told him what she'd heard, he kept trying to convince her that she was mistaken. It wasn't until she started throwing heavy objects like the toaster and the cookie jar at him that he fessed up.

She left him and took Shamari with her to one of her New York friend's houses for a week before she let Shamari go to Evelyn's again.

She hadn't given Jahari any leeway that I knew of in the past months though.

I'd been seeing Race frequently for 2 weeks now and apparently, Jahari had finally warn down her defenses.

"I had to do some soul searching of my own too. It took 2 of us to mess up this marriage, even though he was the one that violated it. I had to give myself some time away from him and spiritually prepare myself to hear what he had to say. I've been fasting, and I think that really helped us a lot."

"Fasting?" I questioned with a screw face as I threw blow after blow playing the game. "How is starving yourself helping y'all? What's it making you too weak to argue because you're hungry?" I sniggered.

"Shut up G. That is *not* what it does, and I'm *not* starving myself, I'm fasting. Didn't you grow up in the church you heathen?" she teased laughing too.

"Yes, I did, but there was too many big women and cheating men in there for fasting to have been the solution," I continued being silly. "But hey, if you think it's working, I'm not gonna knock it. I just hope you're right. I want this to work out for y'all if you want it to. Especially for Shamari's sake."

And I did. I wanted Shan to be happy, and if she could be happy with Jahari again, I really did want that for her. Maybe if I had given Michael a chance to make it right, he would've. Maybe my ridding myself of him for betraying me was more about my fear that he wouldn't choose me, over her, than the fact that I couldn't forgive him.

However, I was becoming a different woman now. I felt sure that Race was going to be my new chance and love, and *nothing* and *no one* was going to get in the way of that. Not if I could help it.

"I feel like you're judging me though for wanting to work things out with him," she said with the irritation in her voice evident.

"Judging you how? I'm just asking questions. I'm not in any position to judge *anybody* with the way my life is. I'm living in the house my husband was murdered in by his mistress and everybody knows it. What I look like judging you? Don't deflect Shantel," I defended myself.

"I'm not deflecting. Every time I talk to you now, I feel like you're being condescending, or you're questioning my decisions. We don't even talk on the phone like we used to."

"And that's *my* fault? We don't talk like we used to because of me? Because if my memory serves me correctly, we stopped talking like we "used to" when you moved to New York.

I went through an entire terrifying and humiliating ordeal with you making phone calls to check on me at your convenience. Why? Because I understood that you were trying to get your life together too.

Well now you're going through something with Jahari. I've been calling. I've been here for you as much as possible while trying to get my own life straight. What more do you want me to do?"

"At my convenience? Is that what you think of how I supported you?" she gasped.

I blew out a heavy breath and stopped working out. Shan was my best friend, and I didn't want us to be at odds, but I was starting to feel like we were growing apart. Maybe she didn't understand me anymore and I didn't understand her.

"That's not… look… Shantel I'm just trying to figure out my life after Michael. I'm sorry if I have been neglecting you," I conceded just as my doorbell rang.

"Was that your door?" Shan asked with attitude as I made my way from the den to answer it.

"Yeah. Lisa's coming ov—"

"Oh. I should've known," she cut me off just as I opened it.

"Hey girl," I greeted Lisa who walked in with a duffle bag that she sat on the floor as soon as she came in.

"Hey," she said back hugging me.

"Well let me let you go then since your new BFF is there," Shan stated spitefully.

"What? What is wrong with you?"

"Nothing. You go ahead and tend to your company. I'll talk to you later," she told me hanging up abruptly.

I looked at the phone incredulously and slid the one bud I had in my ear from the Bluetooth around my neck out. I was shocked that she was jealous enough of Lisa to hang up on me. It delighted me a little bit that she cared this much though.

"That's everything I've got," Lisa said flopping down on the couch in the living room.

"I appreciate it," I replied peeking in the bag to see 5lb weights, an exercise mat, rubber workout bands and a kettlebell.

Since I started dating Race, I felt like I needed to be the best me I could be. Lisa let me see Song's picture on FB one day and she was stunning. I didn't think I was insecure about Race's attraction to me, but it couldn't hurt to up it.

Even though I was already taking kickboxing regularly, I wanted the washboard abs my sister Donna, and apparently Song, possessed too.

"Were you working out?" she asked observing me in my pink sports bra, cotton shorts and sneakers.

"Yeah. On the Wii Fit."

"I swear you're obsessed with pink. I'm surprised this whole house isn't pink."

"When I move, maybe it will be," I answered sarcastically with my hands on my hips.

She waved me off and crossed her black legging clad legs at the ankle.

"What's going on Chica? What you cooking for Race tonight?" she asked watching me with a smirk. "I hope it's something good. Granny is making Lasagna and if he's passing that up to come see you, it better be good. 'Cause *baby*, I know I'm gonna be at her table," she joked.

Race had been over to my home once so far and I'd been to his place twice. Tonight, was the night I was going to serve him some home cooking and solidify my position in his life.

"I'm making braised short ribs and sweet potato soufflé with garlic asparagus," I said haughtily.

"Ummm. Sounds good. Song didn't cook anything that didn't come in a box or heat up in the microwave, so you've already got a leg up on her anyway."

"Seriously?" I asked taking a seat in the armchair.

Lisa and Song were evidently still decent friends, even though she'd screwed Race over royally. So, Lisa hadn't been as loose lipped about her previously as I'd hoped.

This was however, beginning to look like an opportunity to, now that she'd opened the door.

"Seriously. She's just not the Holly homemaker type, even though she claims she's ready to change and settle down."

"Lisa, I know that Song is your friend and everything, and you don't have to answer if you don't want to, but do you think Race would get back with her if she wanted to?"

"Nope," she answered without hesitation. "I'm not gonna lie. She had him wrapped around her finger when they were together, and I think he was even thinking about marrying her at one point, but what she did was the last straw.

You know how us women are. We can find a way to forgive a man for cheating because we don't want to lose all the time we put into that relationship. Most of us are just wired like that.

But men?" she shook her head slowly from side to side. "Once you cheat on them, they're done. Most of them anyway. Plus, the way she did it was downright trifling."

"How so?"

"Chelsea was supposed to be her best friend. Actually, I think they're related somehow too. Like Chelsea's mom is Song's mom's, cousin in-law or something crazy like that.

Anyway, Chelsea's boyfriend Tony used to crash over their apartment a lot. Song's a Stewardess, so she's out of town a lot and Chelsea needed a roommate because she's also a Stewardess but she's new, so her schedule is sporadic. Plus, she's trying to be a model too, so you know her money is up and down.

I thought it was the perfect arrangement. Hell, if I wasn't waiting for Geo to propose so I can move in with him, I would've tried to make it a threesome," she kidded.

I feigned laughter too, only because I wanted her to keep spilling the tea. I needed to know if this woman still posed a threat to my future with Race or not.

"So why do you think she slept with Tony?"

She threw her hands up. "Damned if I know. She told me that she was drunk, and it only happened once. Her and Race had an argument that night. She got drunk in the apartment alone. Tony came over to wait for Chelsea to get home from a video shoot, and supposedly, one thing led to another, which led to his thing in her thing," Lisa ribbed.

"How did they find out what happened?"

"Chelsea snooped through his phone one night and found a conversation he had with Song about what happened.

Lucky for song she was working because Chelsea wanted to whip her ass. The first thing she did after getting in Tony's ass was tell Race what she found.

Me and Chelsea are cool, but I don't hang with her like I have with Song. I don't know what *exactly* she saw, and Song being Song, she downplayed it.

I think she regrets it now. I know she didn't intend for Race to ever find out. She actually begged him not to break up with her this time and went to Granny's for help. She left out of there with no dice though.

Race washed his hands of her. Granny told her to take her hot ass home. Geo never really liked Song anyway, so I'm really the only one from the crew who still speaks to her."

"What about their mother? Did she like Song?"

"Lisa shrugged. Carmen is wishy washy. She don't care who they date, as long as it doesn't cut into the money they give her. Did Race tell you about her history?"

"He touched on her drug past some. I know they're not close with her."

"No. Not at all."

I just nodded and leaned on the arm of the chair listening to her continue to ramble. Lisa really did have a big mouth.

She stayed over for about another hour before she had to go and I needed to start getting ready for dinner. I showered and looked for something sexy that could hide the imprint of the granny panties I had to wear since I was menstruating.

I chose a simple denim, strapless dress and didn't worry about the shoes since we weren't leaving the house. I cooked and prepared everything from scratch, but I made a special red sauce to spread over Race's short ribs.

Since Michael's death, I've been reading a lot of books about love and how to keep it. I came across a book by Vance Randolph called *Ozark, Magic & Folklore.* In it, he said one old school method of guaranteeing love is to add your menses to a man's food or drink.

It being my first day on my cycle, my flow was heavy, which made it a perfect night to make dinner for Race. So it was easy to dangle my tampon over a bowl right after removing it, and let some clumps of blood drip into it.

As repugnant as the idea was to me, especially as a recognized germaphobe, I wanted to literally, pull out all the stops in my relationship this time around. Race was going to be my husband, and I didn't want to risk him falling victim to a whore's advances like Michael had.

"You look lovely," Race said when I answered the door with my hair freshly washed, curled and shiny.

"Why thank you. You look good too. But then you always do," I said kittenish.

"I'm impressed," he said when I led him into the dining room where he surveyed the table I'd set up with my best china, a flower arrangement, cloth napkins and wine glasses. "I haven't had anyone but my granny cook for me in years."

"We've got to change that. I'm not going to insult your granny's cooking by saying mine is better, but I'm a big believer in taking care of my man. Nurturing him inside and out."

"So, am I your man now?" he asked pulling me into him by the waist and looking down into my eyes.

I blushed and looked away, slightly pulling back from him with my head hung. "I don't know. You tell me."

He lifted my chin so that my eyes were gazing back into his. "Is that what you want? Are you ready for that?"

"Are *you* ready for that? We've only been dating a couple of weeks. I really like you, but I'm afraid I might be getting wrapped up too soon.

I've been saying I want to take it slow, but I don't know how to date "slow" after being married 7 years and with the same person for 9. I don't want to scare you away either."

The corners of his mouth turned up and he kissed my lips softly. "Whatever pace this is that we're going, I like it. I like *you*."

I smiled broadly and broke our embrace. "Have a seat so I can go make your plate."

He obliged and I went into the kitchen, spooning the sweet potato soufflé, asparagus and braised short ribs onto the plate. I dipped a basting brush into the bowl I'd mixed my menses and braising sauce in, and used it to paint his portion of ribs.

Grabbing the bottle of red wine, I had chilling in the refrigerator, I made my way back to the table with a huge smile. Dinner went well and he ate every morsel on his plate. I even served him a second helping of short ribs basted in my "special" sauce.

We tried to watch *Annabelle*, some stupid horror movie that wouldn't scare a kitten; but ended up talking, laughing, flirting, kissing and groping each other all through it. If it hadn't been for my cycle being on, I'm sure it would've ended with us sexing for the first time.

The next day I was walking on air at work and breezing through the hallway like wings were on my back. Race was definitely somebody I could see myself with for the rest of my life.

A light rap on my open office door got my attention, and I looked up to see one of the medical billers holding a bouquet of pink orchids. I beamed.

"Somebody thinks you're special. It's not your birthday is it?" Tisha asked placing it on the desk in front of me.

The way she was grinning, I would've thought they came for her. "They're beautiful. Who're they from?"

"Thank you for bringing them back," I answered bemused; intentionally ignoring her question.

She turned her nose up and sucked her teeth, mumbling something under her breath as she exited my office. Tisha was new, so she didn't know that I didn't share my personal business at work with random staff.

Lovely flowers for a lovely woman. Thank you for
dinner last night baby. I'm looking forward to feasting
on you soon. ~Race

My heart fluttered with joy as I sniffed the beautiful arrangement. Seeing that they were ordered from FLOWER ME WITH LOVE was a simple testament to the fact that he was a good listener too.

"*Ooo*! Look who's got a boyfriend," Angie teased appearing in my doorway in her lab coat, holding a tablet and her prescription pad.

I returned her smile and sat daintily back down in my chair. "I guess I do. I cooked him dinner at my house last night."

"Y'all have been hanging tough since he came in here with his cranky ass grandma," she said resting her tablet on my desk and sitting in the chair in front of it. "Now you're cooking dinner for him; you got a brother sending you flowers. So have you done the..." she asked making a circle with her index and thumb on one hand and pumping her index on the other in and out of it.

I gasped dramatically. "No."

She side eyed me. "Why not? You one of those 90 day waiting period types?"

"No. We just haven't done it yet. We've been getting to know each other personally first. We can have sex anytime."

"Hmph," she looked at me dubiously.

"Plus, I've been on my cycle," I added before we both burst into laughter.

"Girl! 'Cause, I was gonna say… you better get you some of that tall sexy chocolate."

"How're things going with your dad? I know we haven't had much time to talk one on one lately."

Angie sighed and rubbed her forehead. "Girl, it's going. It is what it is. The craziest thing that's come out so far is that my mother knew he liked men all of these years."

"Whaaaat?"

"Yup. She said, 'He dabbled a little bit in college, but I thought that was a phase.' A gay phase. Have you heard of that?"

I cupped my mouth and inhaled in shock.

"Chile' I can't with them. I just decided not to even worry about it. It's too much to put on my plate right now while I'm trying to find a man in Atlanta that isn't going through a phase too."

We chuckled.

"What's going on with you and Kendrick?" I followed, leaning back into my chair.

I'd been standoffish with Kendrick since I started seeing Race and I had no intentions on changing that. I cut the few phone calls I bothered to answer short, and I declined every solicitation he made to rendezvous.

Truth be told, I was kind of hoping things with Angie and Kendrick were going well. I never wanted him for myself anyway. I just needed him for sexual maintenance and practice enhancements. Now that his purpose was served, she could have him.

"We uh… we're good. We're cool," she said swirling her mouth around like there was more to the story. "He plays too many games."

"Why you say that?"

"Because he does. I don't have a problem keeping our thing secret at work. You know, fraternization issues and all of that. Especially with these grimy bitches around here throwing the pussy at him like a fast ball.

The problem is, I think he's fucking Nicky. I think he's playing the both of us."

My eyebrows went up. I couldn't stand that smug bitch, and I had my own suspicions that he was doing Nicky myself.

"Nicky," I said in a hushed tone in case anyone were to pass by my office. "Why her? Not that it couldn't be her, but I'm just saying. You've got another selection of hoes to choose from."

Angie threw back her head and laughed. "You're right. His little Usher Raymond look alike ass is probably screwing half the women in here. Hell, I thought you were sleeping with him too."

I swiveled my chair from her direction towards my computer and began logging on without response. She that protests too much looks guilty. So, I said nothing.

"How'd you come to the conclusion that he was seeing Nicky?" I asked again.

"They talk on the phone. They flirt around the office all the time, and he admitted that he's also been seeing someone else here. He wouldn't say who, but he was trying to "keep it real" I guess," she said using finger quotes and rolling her eyes.

"I wouldn't put it passed her."

"She's always up in his face kekeing and hanging around his desk in medical records. She's—"

"Did you need something Kendrick?" I said cutting Angie off as I noticed Kendrick loitering just outside of my door.

Angie turned toward him with her mouth agape.

Kendrick's eyes turned to slits as he stared at the bouquet of flowers on my desk.

"Nice flowers," he said through gritted teeth.

Angie squinted in confusion and looked back at me.

"Thank you. Did you need something?"

"I was gonna tell you that the MEDSTAT system keeps shutting down every time I scan in a record over 3 pages," he said casually sticking his hands in his scrub pockets.

"Okay. I'll call IT. Just process the ones with less than 3 for now," I advised looking back to my computer.

"Alright, I've got patients to see," Angie said standing and pursing her lips at Kendrick who watched her walk out but didn't leave himself.

In her rush, she'd left her prescription pad on my desk. Ceasing the moment, I shifted a stack of papers from one spot on my desk onto the pad.

"Did you need something else?" I questioned Kendrick wishing he'd get lost.

Boldly, he closed my office door and walked to my desk.

"You getting serious with this guy now?"

I frowned and sighed loudly. "Why?"

"Why? Because you've been brushing me the fuck off is why," he chastised. "Answer my question."

"Stop being so loud," I hushed him quickly.

His jaws clenched as he calmed himself down and I stared at him scoldingly. He was really overreacting, and if he wasn't careful, he was gonna expose us to the rest of the office.

"Are these flowers from the guy you met in the office? Or from somebody else."

"They're from him. Why're you acting so crazy about it? Aren't you seeing Angie now?"

He licked his lips and ran a hand over his face. "We're not *seeing* each other. We're fucking."

"Were we," I attested crudely.

"No, we weren't!" he yelled swiping my stapler off my desk and sending it to the floor with a crash.

I glared at him and tried to keep up a tough exterior, but his anger surprised and even scared me a little. Since when did he become this invested in me?

This fool was going to get us both fired with his antics. Only one of us could afford to be unemployed, and he's not the one with 500,000 other ways to chill.

Still, I liked my job, and I wasn't planning on losing it anytime soon.

"Kendrick. Please calm down," I said coolly, hoping he'd follow my lead as I stood trying to appeal to his sensitivities face to face.

Suddenly, both of his hands were around my throat and his breath was hot on my face like a dragon. I immediately started clawing at his hands and gasping for air as he stared angrily into my eyes, squeezing.

I would've predicted an easy break from his grip. Digging his eyes out with my fingers. Breaking his hold by putting my arms between his. But in the moment, I couldn't do any of that. The lack of air drained my energy instantaneously and the panic had me writhing around like a fish out of water.

"You trying to just throw me to the side like trash? I cared about you girl. If you was over your husband, you should've been trying to make it work with me," he growled almost raising me up from the floor.

He was way stronger than I ever would've thought for a 5'6" man. The anger in his eyes must've fueled his strength because it felt like the Hulk had me in a chokehold, and I was only getting weaker.

"Ken… stop," I managed, finally trying to get my hands passed his arms to his face as my own changed shades from lack of oxygen.

His tight-lipped stare poured fear into my heart as the pressure on my neck increased.

"Stop," I squeaked, trying to bring my knee up under my tight pencil skirt to knee him.

The material had little give, but he must've seen it coming anyway, because he dodged it. Still, he released me fully and stepped back from me. I clutched my hands to my throat, wheezing and coughing as he backed away from me guiltily.

"Greer. I… I'm sorry. I didn't mean…"

"Get out," I fought to say. "Before I… call… the police."

His formally menacing eyes pled for forgiveness as he motioned towards me warily. I snatched away and put one hand up to stop him as I regained my composure.

"Get out!" I yelled louder, but not loud enough to reach the hallway through my closed door.

He stared at me motionlessly, looking back and forth between me and the door like he had a decision to make and couldn't decide.

"Is everything okay in here?" Dr. Preston, our OBGYN asked rapping on the door and opening it at the same time.

I attempted to straighten up and recompose myself and Kendrick's eyes grew to the size of bottle caps.

Dr. Preston was an old gray haired white man with a handsome face like Tom Selleck on the T.V. show *Blue Bloods.* He observed Kendrick suspiciously, and then me.

"Everything is fine," I told him holding my throat. "Stupid me. I was drinking my soda and talking to Kendrick about his work at the same time, and it went down the wrong tube. I started choking, and he came over to help me."

Dr. Preston looked from me to Kendrick, then on my desk, I'm sure looking for the soda I was drinking. Luckily, I really did have a Styrofoam cup from lunch still visible by my computer.

"I'm fine now," I assured him with a weak smile.

"Alright," Dr. Preston said as Kendrick excused himself and exited my office hastily.

Dr. Preston watched him leave, then observed me skeptically again.

"You sure you're okay," he asked focusing on my neck.

"Yes. I'm fine. Thank you for checking on me. I'm fine," I verified self-consciously covering whatever he seemed to be looking at on my neck with my hand.

He nodded, looked around my office and then at my door.

"Did you want me to close this, or leave it open?"

"Closed please. Thank you," I replied happily sitting back down at my desk.

He returned my smile and shut the door softly.

And I started to cry.

16

Greer

Kendrick called in sick for a few days after the choking incident, and frankly, I was happy not to see him. Thankfully, there was only minor bruising on my neck. I was able to hide them easily since the change in weather made my sudden penchant for scarves seem like a seasonal fashion choice.

When he came back to work, he was punctual and diligent at his job every day, avoiding me at all costs. Eye contact was only brief, but my general behavior remained the same.

Still, I felt demeaned by the way he manhandled me, and I'd even had a few nightmares about it. He'd never shown the slightest violent tendencies before, and definitely none were displayed towards me.

Angie interrogated me about what happened after she left my office that day, but I gave her the same BS story that I gave Dr. Preston. She kept probing to see if there was more to my relationship with Kendrick than I was saying, but I gave her nothing.

As long as he knew how to keep his bipolar acting mouth shut, so would I. Silence is always golden. Especially when you don't want to be named as a future suspect.

On a better note, Race and I continued to build our circle of trust and were only a couple of days' shy of dating a month. Not by design, we hadn't had sex yet, but that was all about to change.

"Hey Daddy," I said kissing my father on the cheek as I entered his bedroom where he sat on the bed watching television.

"Hey Babygirl," he replied with his eyes glued to the T.V. "Damn shame 'bout that girl."

"What girl?" I asked playing with the ring of keys in my hand.

"That one that got run ova' out in Loganville. She died today. Somebody just ran smack into her in her own front yard and took off. She was a young gal too. Just home from college visiting."

"That's terrible. Did they catch whoever did it?"

"Nope," he said taking a swig of a beer he had on his nightstand. "They lookin' at her ex-boyfriend but they ain't got nothin' solid. It's crazy how people don't have no respect for life no mo'. I feel for her momma that came runnin' out to find her baby like that. Too bad nobody seen the car," he said sympathetically.

For a split second, I almost felt remorse for taking that little speed demon's life; but as quickly as remorse came, it left. Moving right along.

"That *is* sad. How's your leg doing?" I asked since he'd twisted his ankle pruning the bushes in the backyard and pulled some muscles in his leg at the same time.

He waved me off and rubbed his right calve. "It ain't that bad. Doc said to stay off it, but I can't get around if I don't walk. I'm gonna stay out that shop for a while though till I can stand a long time again."

"You need me to bring a wheelchair from work for you?" I kidded and he laughed.

"Hush yo' mouth girl. I ain't gonna need no wheelchair less my leg gets amputated. Your old man is as strong as a horse."

"Okay, Daddy. If you say so. I picked up a few groceries for you since I saw how bare your fridge was. Milk, bread, eggs and juice. I also left you a Tupperware bowl of some leftover chicken and rice I made last night. I'm about to go get the key machine from the shed. Do you need anything before I leave?"

"Your too good to me Babygirl. I don't need nothin' else. Thank ya. You want me to help ya move it to the car?" he asked preparing to stand.

I put my hand on his shoulder so that he wouldn't. "Daddy that thing is only 16lbs. I'm sure I got it."

"Okay then. Where you plannin' to put it? In the back?"

"No. Right on that back counter near where the plant food racks are. I think once people know they can get their keys cut in there, it'll increase the foot traffic. Does it have to be plugged in all the time?"

"No, it's portable, but ya gotta keep it plugged in to charge. It's been sittin' plugged in in the shed, so you should be alright to do it right off. You remember how I showed you to make the keys? 'Cause that Louis seems kinda slow to teach," he said jadedly.

"He's not slow Daddy. He's just one of those people that likes you to repeat stuff so he can make sure he understands. Anyway, I'm gonna go put it in the car and then I'll be gone," I said kissing his forehead.

"Okay. Drive safe then Babygirl. Call me when you get home."

"I'm not going home Daddy, but I will drive safely."

"You say you not goin' home? Where you goin' then," he pried.

I shied away from the question, hurriedly walking from his room, but he called out to me. "Use condoms!"

I laughed all the way to the car where I put my bag and the previously opened bag of fine ground almonds I found in his cabinets. I knew I'd seen it at their house once before. Stephanie probably used it for her elixirs just as much as she used it to cook.

Inside, I clicked on the overhead lights and strode to the back. As I was about to retrieve the mini key cutter and depart, I remembered that we'd also need blank keys if we were going to be duplicating them.

That meant I was going to need all, or at least *some* of the most common blank keys people used too. Looking around for an empty box to put the cutting machine and the blank keys in, I saw none. Scanning the shelves briefly, I presumed he probably had some things in separate boxes that I could combine into one.

Peering into various boxes I found a midsized one that was only half filled with some of Stephanie's sewing supplies, and one smaller box marked "Shawn's stuff".

I knew I could easily combine the contents into Stephanie's box, and use the emptied one to carry the machine and keys easily. As I was dumping Shawn's stuff into Stephanie's box, I came across a thick, blue, 500-page spiral book marked, "Shawn's Journal" in chicken scratch.

I recognized it as the book he was always writing in when we were kids. Curiosity got the best of me, and I skimmed a few pages of it before deciding to take it with me. I figured it would be an interesting way for me to get some insight on my brother who'd always been aloof.

I removed the key rack from the wall and placed it into the box vertically so the blanks would stay on their hooks. Adding the key cutting machine and Shawn's journal, I shut the lights out, locked the shed and proceeded to my car with the box.

Will pulled up beside me in the driveway as I was putting the box in my backseat.

"Hey there," he greeted me with a hug.

"Hey Will. Long time no see," I said for lack of something better to say.

"Yep," he replied standing awkwardly beside me and my car door.

"What you doing here?"

"I just came to hang out with Pop for a while. Debbie is driving me to drink and I don't want to overindulge," he answered walking by the hood of my car and running his hand across it. "What happened here? I thought we fixed up all the dents?"

Damn. I knew I should've just kept driving the Yukon and left Rolly parked.

"Hmph. Some fools were fighting in the parking lot at my job and ended up rolling around on my hood," I pulled out of my ass.

"Say what? Adults did this with their bodies?" he asked crossing his stocky arms.

"Yeah. Slamming each other around and stuff. It was crazy, but I didn't even care. Rolly being so old, I don't even care about fixing it. You just repainted for Christ's sake. It wasn't even worth it."

"That don't mean nothin'. They damaged your property."

I shrugged and opened the driver's side door of my car to get in.

"Alright Will, give the kids my love. I gotta go. Can you put Daddy's keys back in the bowl for me please?" I asked tossing him the keys, which he caught easily.

"Yeah. Sure."

I closed the door and cranked my car up, anxious to start on my way to my man and away from Will and his nosy observations.

I got out of the car straightening the material on my knee length knit dress and strutted up to the double oak French doors at the entrance.

Race's house was *a-maz-ing* to say the least. No matter how many times I'd been to it already, I still marveled at it's fabulous contemporary design. With wide overhangs and well shaded bands of glass it gave the illusion of being exposed to the outdoors when the curtains were open.

I loved the "C – shaped" floor plan with 2 bedrooms upstairs and a huge loft area in the center of the 2nd floor overlooking the downstairs great room. The ceilings were sky high with a long metallic light fixture hanging down between the floors.

The other 2 bedrooms were imbedded in the back of the house on the 1st floor, just passed a huge kitchen and glass French doors that led to an angular outdoor pool. The entire thing was furnished with strategically placed artwork and minimal furniture that covered large areas of the floor plan.

I was in awe of the décor and shocked to hear that Race was the primary decorator. To my surprise, he revealed that he'd gone to Georgia Tech and graduated with a degree in Architecture. He simply hadn't pursued it since he enjoyed tattooing more, and business was good.

Race opened the door within seconds of my ringing the bell and startled me with a passionate kiss I gladly accepted. Lifting me above his waist, he closed the door with one hand, then used it to toss my bag from my hands and carry me into his bedroom.

Oh Lord this man was sexy! I had already intended to make tonight the night we were going to be intimate, but evidently, he'd decided it would be too.

Lying me down on the bed, our lips and tongues still cavorting, his hands caressed my body with equal ferocity.

"I've been craving you," he moaned moving from my lips to my neck while cupping both breasts through my clothes.

He damned near made me orgasm right there. I had no idea I was in for this lustful introduction when he asked me if I wanted to come over his place after work. I couldn't have thought of a better way to greet me though.

"Oh my God," I muttered as he pulled the top of my dress down over my breasts and unleashed my nipples from my bra; only to suckle them one by one with his warm mouth.

With his hard member pressed against my thigh, there was no question he planned to impale me on it by nights' end. I reached down to caress it through his jeans, and he let out a gruff groan as he eyed me while flicking a nipple with his tongue.

In one motion, he lifted up, yanked my dress up over my body and head, then tossed it to the floor, leaving me shivering in my bra and thong on his plush California king. My tremors weren't from fear or chill, but from anticipation, as I voluntarily unlatched my bra while watching him discard his sweater, jeans and underwear seemingly all at once.

Finally, I saw the huge tattoo that covered the entire center of his chest, and part of his torso. It was a lifelike rendition of a black panther roaring. The monster that awaited me between his legs was erect and ready for action, and my mouth watered at the thought of it touching my tongue.

I was ready to exercise some of those pornographic moves I learned watching videos and practicing on Kendrick, on Race. I learned a lot of jaw relaxing techniques and gag reflex prevention moves from Google too. Like I've said before, if you can't Google it, it doesn't exist.

Judging from the size of his huge member, I was definitely going to be putting what I learned to use if I was going to deep throat him. Surprising him, I shoved him backwards when he started to straddle me and sat up to taste him instead.

Letting him see my saliva drip onto his dick first, I licked him from the shaft up to the head with sucking motions as I circled its circumference. Plunging his engorged head down my throat until my lips touched his lap, I let out a moan and let my fingers find my wetness.

"Oh *ffffuck*," he stuttered watching all 12" of himself disappearing between my lips, over… and over… and over… again.

My saliva coated his shaft while my tongue twirled around his head and my jaws vacuumed every inch down my throat. He forcibly pushed me off of him with a grunt within minutes and ordered me to lay down.

"Oh, shit girl. You trying to make me cum before I even get to see how good you feel?" he asked rhetorically exposing his dimpled smile.

Licking my lips lasciviously, I replied, "Then you just would've had to fuck me *after* I tasted you."

Lunging in for another passionate kiss, he sucked my bottom lip, then trailed kisses down to my breasts and my torso until he was between my thighs.

Licking, lapping and sucking my juice box with my legs straddling his shoulders, he devoured my pearl with delightful moans as I writhed in ecstasy.

The sound of his tongue sloshing inside my walls while his lips French kissed my clit, and his fingers massaged my chocolate star, aroused every nerve in my body.

"No! No Race! Don't make me cum! Don't make me cum!" I whimpered, wanting my first orgasm with him to be while he was buried inside of me.

Ignoring my pleas, he simply sped up everything he was doing at once, rushing me over the edge into a powerful orgasm that made my legs clench around his neck, and my nectar gush.

"Race!" I screamed; my body arching as every ounce of energy I had drained into his mouth.

Climbing up between my legs, he pushed my knees back to my shoulders and produced a condom from Lord only knows where. The anticipation of what was to come had my nipples hard as granite. He slid into me like the missing key to my lock as I cooed loudly with each stroke, salaciously gazing into his eyes.

I grasped the back of his head and crushed my lips into his while he gripped my thighs and thrust rhythmically in and out of me, slightly elevating me above the bed. Somehow, he'd driven me backwards into the leather wingbacked headboard, where he proceeded to bang *my* back out against it.

"Oh my God baby. You feel *sooo* fuckin' good," he uttered plummeting so deep into me that I thought I felt him in my spleen.

I grinded my pelvis into him as we synchronized our movements, our faces contorting in ways that only total ecstasy could command. I found myself wailing again as another orgasm escaped me, and his girth continued to drill deeper into my love. His mouth latched onto my collarbone as he stifled groans and pounded fast and deep.

"Arghhhhhh!" he roared, finally erupting like a volcano into my sex, and holding me still up against the headboard.

We stayed in that position for a couple of minutes. Breathing heavily in unison. Still connected by our flesh. Trapped in a moment neither of us wanted to end. I knew I loved him, and he had to love me too. He was mine.

His tan and white Tabby cat Juney jumped on the bed trying to join in on the love and I scowled internally. I'm not an animal lover. Pets are hairy, messy, germ carrying, freeloaders. I don't like dogs and I *really* hate cats. Not because I have any particular allergy to them, but because they're a sneaky, skittish breed.

Of course, the added element that Juney was a gift from Song to Race 8 years ago, made him especially repugnant.

"Hey boy," he said to the feline as Juney slinked his way to Race's outstretched hand. "That's a good boy," he doted as the thing purred loudly.

I smiled and pet him too, pretending to like the noisy fur ball as he purred and mewed, then flipped over on his back for a tummy rub.

Being that he was an indoor *and* outdoor cat, there was no telling what type of mites and germs he'd been smuggling in on his paws. The thought of what might have now been tracked onto the bed I was laying in ate at my cerebrum, but I kept quiet.

I'd already tried to poison the thing the last time I was over by "accidentally" dropping some chocolate I had in my bag for him as we watched a movie. He ate it, but the only thing I accomplished was gaining a new greedy friend who wanted me to feed him.

His 9 lives were numbered though, because I had something for him that would send him to the big litterbox in the sky sooner, rather than later.

Race flicked on the television just as his doorbell rang and his forehead creased in confusion. Looking back at me, he got up and slipped into some grey sweat shorts from a drawer.

"Let me go see who that is," he said rubbing the back of his head apprehensively.

As he turned, I glimpsed the words tattooed on his back. They were words written in Monotype Corsiva:

With Love Comes Pain.

With Pain Comes Sacrifice.

With Sacrifice Comes Love

How creative. I had to think up something just as deep for him to tattoo onto me. After all, he did say that tattoos were supposed to mean something. So mine had to have a significance that he'd appreciate.

I cursed the fact that my purse was on the floor in the foyer as Juney purred and approached me. I kicked the cat as hard as I could off the bed, and he yowled loudly before hitting the wall. Hard. As soon as his paws hit the floor, he took off from the room like the roadrunner.

I smirked. "Stupid cat," I said, rising from the bed and tiptoeing to the door when I heard voices.

"No. I don't care," I heard Race saying coldly.

"We can't even talk? I wouldn't be here if it wasn't worth at least a conversation Race. You know I still—" a whiny voice pled before he cut her off.

"Save the bullshit Song. We don't have anything else to say to each other. You made the decisions you wanted to make for you. So, I made the decisions I needed to make for me."

"But I didn't make a *decision*. I was drunk. I was vulnerable. He took advantage of me Race. Why are you punishing me for something I didn't have any control over?" she begged.

I stepped further out of his room so that I could get a better look at the woman he was speaking to, and I'll be damned if she wasn't even better looking in person than she was on social media.

If Meagan Good had a twin, I was sure as shit looking at her standing in Race's doorway. Her hair was loose, wavy and flowing to just above her shoulders, and my eyes were green with envy just looking at her.

She had to know it was too cold to wear that cut off sweater shirt with leggings. Even if the shirt was long sleeved. Like my sister, she had a belly ring, and praying hands were tattooed above it. Probably courtesy of the man standing in front of her.

I swear. Bitches with washboard abs can never pass up the opportunity to prove they've got them. I looked down at my own flat, but un-ripped stomach and hissed silently.

Race sighed. Unmoved by her pleas. "Listen, you gotta go. I don't have time for this and I have company."

She looked him up and down and then behind him.

"You have *company*? What company do you have dressed like that?" she asked with attitude. "Whoever it is, you know you're just dealing with them to get back at me baby. You know you're not happy without me. I'm not happy without you."

The entire time she was talking, he had a hand on the door and one on the frame keeping her outside, while looking down at the floor. He was definitely in thought about something, but I had no idea *what* he was thinking.

"Song. I don't want to slam the door in your face, so you should save yourself the humiliation now."

"You still love me Race. I know it and you know it. You haven't given me my apartment key back because you know you're gonna want to use it again. Just like you did a few weeks ago," she reminded him, placing a hand on his bare chest and gliding her fingers across his tattoo.

My blood pressure had to be near stroke level at that point. How dare that bitch touch my man? And what was she talking about a few weeks ago? Had he slipped and fell back into her pussy that recently?

"Don't move," he told her holding up an index finger as he left her at the door peering in.

Of course, she was looking towards his bedroom, where I was. But I'd scurried down the hallway to a spare bathroom for a better view at her, so she wasn't even looking my way.

Race returned to the door holding a keyring with several keys on it, as he removed one.

"I'm not taking the key back Race. This is just stupid. Can we just talk? I'm tired of standing at this door, and I don't believe for one minute that you have another woman in here with you."

"You can believe whatever the hell you want to. I don't have time to stand here and debate. You made your bed, and you fucked Tony in it. Here's your key. Goodbye, and good riddance," he told her with less feeling than an epidural, holding the key toward her for her to grasp.

She stared at it like it was a foreign object with her hands on her hips and audibly exhaled. I was glad that he was so matter of fact about where she stood with him.

My insecurity was beginning to simmer until she said, "That may be, but I didn't fuck him raw in it. You were the only one I slept with unprotected. You're the only one who could be the father of my baby. We, are having a baby."

He stood as stiff as a mannequin, and my heart fell out of my chest and into the pile of manure that was my life. Why couldn't this whore from before stay away from my man?

"That's convenient, isn't it? All these years we've been together, and you never got pregnant. You never missed a birth control pill. Now all of the sudden, since we broke up, you're mysteriously pregnant? Yeah right."

"When we broke up, I didn't have any reason to take them, since I wasn't having sex. I told you I wasn't cheating on you. That one time with Tony was a mistake. I'll keep apologizing for it for as long as you want me to. But whether you believe that or not, you need to believe this," she replied with that grating voice, grabbing his hand and placing it on her stomach.

He snatched his hand back and looked back towards the bedroom where I was supposed to still be. Running his hand through his low waves, he cracked his neck from side to side and addressed Song sternly.

"You gotta leave. I don't know if you're bullshitting or if this is real, but you gotta go. Either way, this isn't going to change anything between us today."

I could see the tears in her eyes and the evident hurt on her face.

"Race, you know I wouldn't play those kinds of games with you. I love you. I wouldn't say I was pregnant if I wasn't. I definitely wouldn't try to pin a baby on you if it wasn't yours."

"Here," he said handing her the key again.

She slapped it from his hand, and it fell on the floor just inside the door. Then she grabbed his face and tongued him down like a scene out of a romance film.

Watching them kiss was like looking at them through a fishbowl lens. It was as bold and, in my face, as it could get. I turned to go back to the room and get my things just as he jolted her off of him by the arms.

"Stop it Song. Now go home," he commanded, turning her around and pushing her out the door.

"Race! Wait! Don't do this," she cried with her hands inside the door frame while trying to wedge her body inside too.

"Damn it Song! Don't make me put my hands on you! Go home!" he ordered slamming the door in her face.

When he entered the bedroom, I was back in the bed, under the covers, still crying.

"Are you taking her back?" I asked.

He looked caught off guard by my question. Probably surprised that I'd been able to hear their conversation from his bedroom.

I needed to know what his intentions were before I made any other moves. One thing I was *not* going to do, was fight for a man who didn't want to be with me. Nor was I going to fight for a man whose feelings were torn between 2 women.

His bare feet padded against the hardwood floors as he got in the bed beside me. Taking my hands in his, he brought them to his lips, kissing them one by one and looking sincerely into my eyes.

"No Baby. I'm not taking her back."

"Is she having your baby?"

He sighed and dropped his gaze. "I don't know. She says she is. It's possible."

I wept openly as he used his thumbs to wipe my tears away, then kissed one eyelid at a time.

"I don't want to hurt you Greer. I didn't expect any of this, and I don't want to be with her. I want to be with *you.* But I'm gonna have to talk to her eventually," he confessed sounding a little choked up himself.

Her news clearly had him shook. We laid together in conversation for hours. Of course, top of mind was what he would do if she *was* actually carrying his baby.

As expected, he wanted to be an active parent in the child's life if she was, but he was adamant that he only wanted to co-parent with her. I should've been pleased that he wouldn't make the child suffer for the sins of its parents, but I was the furthest thing from it.

I didn't want to play stepmother to Race and Song's lovechild, any more than Stephanie had wanted to with me. The difference between us, was that I would never mistreat a child out of jealousy. I *would* however, eliminate it.

Race shared that Song's friend Chelsea told him she'd seen several text messages between her man and Song that proved they'd had more than one night of sex. Chelsea had even forwarded 2 naked pics of Song that she found in Tony's phone to Race as proof. My how familiar that was.

He didn't even bother to tell Song that he knew about them. According to him, there was no point in it. She had already proven that she was a liar, and he didn't think he needed to show her proof of something she already knew.

He seemed sincerely over her, and I was 100% certain that he only wanted to be with me now. Regardless, I couldn't let Song have his baby and remain a threat to our union for the rest of our lives. I didn't have to know her to know she wasn't lying. Or at least she believed what she was telling him was the truth.

We spent the rest of the evening talking, making love, eating, making love, and making love again. He was dead to the world by 1:00am, but I was wide awake with thoughts of how to secure the future with the man I loved.

I crept out of bed and into the great room where my purse had later been laid to rest. I picked through it for my keys and the plastic spray bottle I had tucked away inside.

Going into the kitchen, I located Juney's food bowl and coated the bottom of it with the solution.

"Meow," the cat mewed slinking between my legs and startling me.

Greedy little son of a bitch must've thought I had more candy for him. He sniffed around the bowl, smelling the sweet pancake like scent that rose from the anti-freeze I sprayed inside, and licked it up.

Supposedly, the taste of anti-freeze is equally as sweet as it smells, but the consequences of ingesting it are dire. Not having the time to waste on the cat, I headed to the front door, found the key on the floor, and went outside.

Barefoot and dressed in one of Race's T-shirts, I went to the backseat of my car and retrieved the key machine. Sitting it on the floor of my car, I looked for a blank key to match Song's house key, and set them in place to duplicate it.

I held both keys up to the light inside my car and they looked identical. Back inside, I placed one key back on the floor where she tossed it, and put the other in my purse.

Getting in the shower, I washed the grime from my feet and cleansed the rest of my body for good measure. I had to be as smart about what needed to be done, as I had been about everything else.

Slow and steady wins the Race.

17

Greer

November 2015

The day before a holiday we always had a skeleton crew, and this time was no different. The office was closing early so people could get an early start on their Thanksgiving celebrations, but we still had patients on schedule until 2:00pm.

Quincy was supposed to be working, but she'd gone into early labor on Sunday, so we weren't only a skeleton crew, we were short staffed. Tisha and Corrine were working the front office, and prepping patients in their rooms for appointments for the 2 doctors we had working.

Angie was the only NP on duty and Kendrick was in medical records since our other MR guy had seniority. Angie had been giving me the cold shoulder for a couple of days though, and I had no idea why.

"Hey Anj, you got a minute?" I bellowed from my office as she skirted passed it.

"Not really. I'm seeing patients," she replied snidely.

I was caught off guard by the venom in her tone and curious as to why it was directed at me.

"O-kay," I said slowly. "Can you make a couple of minutes free to talk to me please?"

She rolled her eyes in a huff and entered my office, standing in front of my desk glaring at me like I owed her money.

"Do we have a problem?" I asked evenly.

"Do we?" she mimicked.

"I don't know. You seem to be upset with me for some reason, and I don't know why."

"Like you care," she said sucking her teeth.

I cocked my head, genuinely perplexed.

"Why would you say that?"

"Cut the shit Greer. I know."

"You know what?" I asked trying to calculate which of the foul things I'd done she knew about, hoping like hell it wasn't the one she was present for.

She blew out an agitated breath and took one step closer.

"I *know* about you and Kendrick."

I stared at her blankly.

"Oh, the cats got your tongue now, huh? I asked you *specifically* if you'd slept with him and you told me no. You sat there and lied right to my face," she admonished me folding her arms huffily.

I ran my tongue across my teeth as I contemplated my rebuttal and wondered how she'd found out.

"We agreed not to say anything to anyone," I replied calmly.

"Really? That's your excuse? I thought we were friends. I told *you* that we were seeing each other even though that was supposed to be a secret too."

I just stared at her. I didn't know what she wanted me to say. Because she wasn't a woman of her word and I was, that was my fault? Whatever.

"You don't have nothin' to say for yourself?"

"What do you want me to say? It was just sex. We weren't dating and never planned to. There was no emotional attachment. Didn't he tell you that?" I baited her.

"He didn't tell me shit. Kita told me."

I blinked slowly at the mention of the bitch in 2A. Why was she still meddling in business that wasn't her own?

"Umph. Look at you. You didn't think I was gonna find out. I ran into her one day over at his place and she was saying how happy she was that he stopped seeing that crazy "half-white" bitch with the green eyes.

Oh yeah. According to Kita, you were hittin' Mariah Carey notes off the dick. You didn't think that as a friend, that was something you should've told me?"

"Angie, there was nothing to tell. Like I said, it was just sex. Did you ask him? I'm sure he'll tell you the same thing. You see I'm in a relationship with Race. We haven't b—"

"Save it," she cut me off and let me talk to the hand. "I asked him about it, and he said the same thing, but that's beside the point. I thought you and I were real friends. I shared personal information with you that I wouldn't have if I knew we were just *work* friends.

Look, I have a patient to see. So unlike you, I don't have time to play around in my office," she advised leaving my office brusquely without even giving me a moment more to plead my case.

I was slightly in my feelings about her ire towards me. I did consider her a friend, and I didn't want to be at odds with her, but who I was sexing wasn't really her business.

I brushed it off and hoped that her discovery wouldn't impede the ease with which my vengeance would be carried out against Kendrick. I'd been patiently waiting for the right opportunity to execute my plan against him and Song, and if Angie interfered, she might also find herself on the underside of a coffin.

Two o'clock came quicker than a teenage boy, and I was glad to see Angie hurrying out the door without stalling for Kendrick. Kendrick was usually the last one in, and the last one out next to me, since he routinely went to the gym after clock out.

I dawdled behind in the front office after everyone else on staff vacated the suite to ensure I'd catch Kendrick before he left. True to form, he was downing his health drink from the water bottle he had in the refrigerator as he came down the hallway.

I'd deliberately warn a button up shirt, now 3 buttons freed, with a skirt that revealed my thighs for the occasion of enticing him. Since it was a short day, it wasn't hard for me to sit at my desk the majority of it, so's not to draw attention to my risqué attire.

"Are you going home for Thanksgiving?" I asked him coyly as I leaned back on the check-out desk crossing my legs at the calves.

Kendrick stopped abruptly, observing my outfit and swallowed hard. "Why?"

I shrugged diffidently and sat on the edge of the desk instead. "I don't know. I'm just being friendly. I don't like that we aren't friends anymore. I miss you."

"Yeah, okay," he retorted tersely. "This what you wanted right?" he asked drinking more from his bottle, then briefly giving the bottle a strange look.

"Sort of. I didn't think you'd totally turn on me for seeing somebody else. You've been seeing "somebody else's" the whole time we were seeing each other, and I never complained.

I was really hurt when you lashed out at me the way you did," I continued in a meek tone while batting my freshly mascaraed eyelashes at him, and leaning forward so he could get a better view of my lace bra.

He licked his lips lustfully and advanced on me like I'd sent an S.O.S.

Clearing his throat a few times, he took another swig of his drink and said, "I'm sorry Bae. I was jealous. You know I would never put my hands on you like that if I wasn't. You forgive me?" he asked remorsefully touching my face.

I smiled and nodded. He used the opportunity to kiss me, allowing me to taste some of the raspberry, banana and almond flavors in his drink.

"*Ummmmm*," I said when the kiss broke, savoring the taste of revenge.

Like a fool, I'm sure he thought I was referencing his kiss, as I took him by the hand and led him to the stairs.

"Don't you have to go to the gym?" I quizzed.

He gazed at my propped-up breasts, my glossy lips, and then into my eyes. "Not if you still need me here."

I smiled deviously and took his hand in mind as I opened the door to the stairwell and gripped my keycard in hand. Confusedly, he followed behind me as the door closed behind us and I pressed his back against the wall above the stairwell.

"Why're you wearing gloves?" he questioned.

"I was wiping down my office for the Thanksgiving break with those Clorox wipes. You know how I hate germs and dust. I didn't want to get any of it on my hands though," I lied with a sly smile.

"Oh. So why you got me out here?" he asked beginning to massage his throat and clearing it a few more times.

"I don't know. It's always been a fantasy of mine to have sex in the stairwell. Now that everybody but us is gone, I just thought..." I trailed off, walking my fingers lazily up the buttons on his jacket.

He started to smile, but it was interrupted by a fit of coughs. I backed up a bit and watched him, as he pounded his chest and began wheezing.

"What's wrong baby?" I queried innocently. "Did something go down the wrong pipe?"

"I... I don't know. I think... I think... some... some nuts were... were in my... my drink," he muttered between hacks. "Fuck... I... I... can't..." he struggled to say as I frantically began patting his back in feigned concern.

"What? Nuts? You put nuts in your drink? I thought you said you were allergic?" I squealed.

Kendrick gazed at me with glassy and reddened eyes, his facial features already beginning to bloat. "I'm... I'm having a re—"

His blathering was cut short when I shoved him mercilessly down the flight of stairs. The startled look on his face as he reeled backwards was priceless. The missed steps on his way down set him up for a treacherous collision with several more near the bottom.

His water bottle slipped from his grasp and rolled down the steps before its owner followed. Kendrick landed with a thunderous thud as his head bounced off the wall at the bottom landing between the 3rd and 4th floor.

I used my keycard to enter back inside and briskly walked to my office to retrieve his cellphone from my desk drawer. I'd stolen it and turned it off just in case someone called for him while I had it and busted me with it.

I'm sure he thought it was in his satchel as usual, but I swiped it to ensure it wouldn't be involved in his "accident" in a way where he could call for help.

I powered the phone back on, and went back out into the stairwell. His phone immediately began chiming with missed messages and calls. Kendrick lay in a lethargic, moaning heap with his left leg in a disturbingly bowed position.

Going down 2 steps, I threw his phone against the wall at the bottom of the landing so that it would ricochet down to the 3rd level.

"Yes!" I exclaimed when it worked just as I'd anticipated.

Bringing my attention back to Kendrick, I smirked and offered him some departing words, "Happy Thanksgiving."

Going back into the office, I went back to my own and retrieved my bag and coat. I then proceeded to lock up the office as usual, making sure to turn off the lights, and headed towards the elevators. It would've been great if all my dastardly deeds were done for the day, but they weren't.

Race had only spoken to Song once that I was aware of since the day she popped up at his place, and that was to find out if she'd stolen Juney. The Tabby hadn't come back home at his usual feeding time the next day, nor had he shown his hairy face in the days that followed.

Race was convinced that Song took him or did something to him, because it was too coincidental that Juney disappeared after she showed up, in his opinion. Being the good girlfriend I am, I cosigned his suspicions wholeheartedly, so the wedge between them got wider.

Thanks to Lisa's big mouth, I knew that Song was working through the holiday. Apparently, she was already waiting on passengers on a flight to Brazil. Lucky her.

Fortunately, Song Harmon is about as common a name for a person as North West. So locating her address was a piece of cake with a cherry on top.

She lived in a gated apartment complex in Buckhead, but it was easier to drive in right behind another car with access than it was to duplicate her apartment key; and we all know how easy that was.

Per my usual M.O. when I want to be "incog-Negro", I parked further down than her actual apartment building. Exchanging my work heels for flats, I locked everything in my car except the items I needed and walked to her unit.

Letting myself in, I quickly shut the door behind me and surveyed her abode. Meh... it was nothing special. It was a nice floorplan with a bar counter between her kitchen and the living room. She had a balcony her own washroom and 3 bedrooms.

Her furniture looked very Ikea-ish and her artwork was blaze in my opinion. Snapping out of tourist mode, I went to the refrigerator and opened it.

This bitch's fridge was almost as bare as my father's had been. She had an open bottle of Sutter Homes white zinfandale, a half full jug of Sunny Delight, every condiment known to man, and a couple of left-over trays of take out.

Snatching the Sunny Delight from the top shelf, I opened the cap and put it on the counter. Taking out the baggie with the Cytotec pills I'd compressed into powder in the pill crusher Daddy had for his medications, I emptied the contents into the jug.

Unbeknownst to Angie, she'd written a prescription for my father to help with his joint pain and arthritis. I put the prescription in and picked it up at Walgreens with no problem since they'd become accustomed to seeing me when I was picking up Daddy's cancer meds.

Cytotec contains Misoprostol, and Misoprostol is the main medication in abortion pills. Since the only thing available to purchase over the counter was the morning after prevention, I had to be creative in this instance.

Putting the top back on the juice, I shook it up vigorously to ensure it mixed well. Since the pills weren't being taken as directed, I put way more than the prescribed amount to ensure it worked.

I put the juice back in the refrigerator and stuck the balled-up baggie in my shoe. As I started to exit, seeing the bleach on top of her washing machine impelled an additional idea.

Petty, though it was, I was determined to do it. I uncapped her nearly full bottle of bleach and looked for any and everything liquid to add it to in her apartment. Since the bitch can't smell anything, she wouldn't have any idea what products I put it in.

The fun I had! I put bleach in damn near *everything*! Mouthwash? Check. Shampoo? Check. Rubbing alcohol? Check. Makeup remover? Check! Check! Check!

I went into her kitchen, intending on dipping all of her silverware in the bleach too, but decided that would take too long. Moving too quickly, I accidentally knocked one of her glasses over, sending it crashing to the floor.

I didn't want to leave any evidence that would alert her beforehand that someone had been in her apartment, so I found the broom and dustpan in a closet and swept it up. Glancing down at the shards of glass, I got another idea that made me chuckle at the thought.

I remembered seeing a mallet in one of her kitchen drawers when I was trying to find the one with her silverware in it. Placing the dustpan with the shards of glass in it on the counter, I proceeded to bang them into even tinier bits.

I didn't succeed in breaking them all up into the fine pieces I wanted them to be, but there was enough to get the job done.

Going back into her bathroom, I located her bottle of lotion and brought it into the kitchen with me. Holding the dustpan steadily over the bottle, I used one of her knives to shave the teeny shards of glass into it.

When I was satisfied with the amount added, I put the rest of the broken glass into her kitchen garbage can. After screwing the top back onto her lotion, I shook it up to mix hazardous bits in thoroughly.

I made sure to put everything back where I got it before I left, and exited leisurely back to my car with a wicked grin that could only come from conquering your enemy.

Since I was going to be having Thanksgiving dinner with Race's family tomorrow, I decided to go by Daddy's before I went home. I hadn't been back by since the night I picked up the key machine, though we'd talked on the phone. Even better, I can't say I was too broken up to know I was going to be missing holiday dinner with the Shrew this year either.

I was surprised to see Ms. Nina's car in Daddy's driveway when I pulled up. I guessed they were going over some financials for the flower shop. I let myself in with the key Daddy gave me after Debbie showed her ass at dinner that time.

I put my purse down on the couch and strode towards Daddy's room while returning a text message from my baby.

"Hey, Daddy, I—" my sentence was caught in my throat as I witnessed not 1, but 2 wrinkled bodies having sex on the top sheet of my Daddy's bed.

They scrambled for cover as I squeezed my eyes shut, hoping they would burst in their sockets rather than open to see Daddy dicking down Ms. Nina again. F my life!

"Greer!" they both called out in embarrassed unison.

"Wow. I'm sorry," I apologized feeling like I was walking on Jello as I hurried back into the living room, ready to grab my bag and leave again.

"Daddy! Daddy!" Debbie's ratchet voice rang out as she marched through the house waving Stephanie's phone around in one hand.

She stopped in her tracks and leered at me.

"What the fuck *you* doing here?" she cussed at me.

"You didn't see my truck in the driveway?" I asked dryly, crossing my arms under my breasts.

"I forgot you don't drive the dumpy ass car no more bitch."

"What's all the name calling for? Who pissed in your Cheerios?"

Debbie smacked her lips and came closer to me, but didn't quite get in my face. It was a good thing she didn't too because my trusty pink stun gun was fully charged.

"Why was you using Mommy's phone to watch your bedroom?" she asked waving the phone in my face, alarming me a bit.

"What are you talking about?" I questioned her icily, hoping my voice wasn't trembling.

First of all, I gave that phone to Donna. What the hell was *she* doing with it? Secondly, how the H-E double hockey sticks did she know how I was using it?

I prayed silently, 'Please don't make there be a video on it. Please don't make there be a video on it.'

"Because, smart ass, I charged it and looked through her Apps. The most recent one used was a "Spy Alarm" App, so I turned it on to see what it was. Guess what I saw on it?" she quizzed coming even closer to my face. "I saw *your* bedroom. Can you explain why that is Ms. Sadity?"

We stared each other down as Daddy finally came out of his room with a robe wrapped around his waist with Ms. Nina trailing behind him in a robe too.

"Alright now. Everybody, calm down. I... we were plannin' on tellin' you all 'bout us but—"

"Uh... why does this old sow have on my mother's robe?" Debbie spat sizing Ms. Nina up as Michael's mother shrunk back behind Daddy.

"She ain't here to wear it now, is she Deborah? Now, what ya come up in my house hollerin' fo'?" Daddy spat back at her.

If my ass wasn't already 2 farts from the flame, I would've cracked up laughing; but not while Debbie was about to expose me.

"So you messin' with Michael's momma now Daddy? Were you messing with her when momma was still alive too?"

Debbie had no chill and the red hue of Daddy's face told me that his was also M.I.A.

"Look gal. If you came ova' here to act a fool, then you can take yo' narrow ass back on home to aggravate yo' husband."

"To aggravate my..." Debbie stopped and threw a hand up like she was stopping herself from going all the way off on Daddy. "You know what? I came over here to tell you that your daughter. Your *precious* Greer, was using Mommy's phone to spy on her husband.

Now I don't remember none of that comin' out during the trial. Did *you* know she was watching your son fucking his mistress Ms. Nina?" she addressed Michael's mother crassly.

Ms. Nina's eyes widened and immediately landed on me.

"No? No I bet you didn't know that," Debbie continued with her fuckery.

"You're crazy," is all I said, keeping my composure while the fear of what she might have discovered ate at me.

Yes Marlene was serving time for Michael's murder, but as was expected, attorney Fullsome filed for appeal. I didn't want or need anything surfacing that could help her case.

"No bitch. *You're* crazy if you think I'm buying that you took Momma's phone for some psychic to get in touch with her. Get the *total* fuck outta here!

You hated my momma in life and you damn sure wouldn't be trying to talk to her in death," she proclaimed.

"Shut up all that cussin' in my house gal!" Daddy yelled at her.

"That's all you heard Daddy? All you heard was my cussin' but not that this fraud of a daughter you're trusting with everything, lied? She knew he was cheating because she saw it happen!

I don't know where she's got the camera set up in that room of hers, but it's in there? Here! Look!" Debbie insisted, shoving Stephanie's phone toward him.

My father glanced at me, and then back at Ms. Nina who was frozen with her mouth open.

I sighed like I was exhausted by dealing with Debbie's antics. "*Sooo* what Debbie. What business is it of yours what I knew about my husband cheating on me?

All evidence is not admissible to be discussed during a trial. Or are you too stupid to know that? You didn't find anything out that the police don't already know. Just because it wasn't disclosed to the public, that doesn't mean shit.

Are you done trying to humiliate me now? Done disrespecting my husband's mother? Done making an ass out of yourself for the millionth time?" I chided her, hoping on my last prayer that they'd all bought my pretense that the cops already knew.

Debbie glared at each of us with scorn and shook her head in dismay.

Looking to the heavens, she let the phone drop to the floor and imparted, "I give up."

Eyeballing Daddy, she said flippantly, "We're not coming tomorrow for Thanksgiving dinner."

Then, as if she'd lost her ever lovin' mind… she shoved me on her way to the door. I don't know what made her think she could put her hands on me, and I would just take it like the little wuss I had been previously… maybe that was why.

Regardless, it was a bad move on her part. I smacked that heifer so hard she stumbled over her own feet into the wall by the door. Ms. Nina gasped when the sound of my hand across Debbie's face resounded through the house.

Debbie was so shocked that it took her a few seconds to react; but when she did… we ended up in a full-on brawl. We were flinging each other everywhere around that house between the foyer and the living room. Punching, pulling, scratching and even biting. She bit *me*, for the record.

When Daddy finally broke us up, some things that rested on tables, shelves and even the walls where we fought, lay in shambles on the carpet.

My dear old big sister didn't expect the super featherweight fight she got. I whipped her with all the frustration and anger I'd had bottled up for her since I was 5, and boy did it feel good.

Every ache I felt and drop of blood she drew from me, was worth seeing the damage I'd done to her now swollen face, blacked eye, busted lip, and best of all… broken nose. She wasn't dead, but killing her spirit was almost as good.

It was like Christmas came early!

18

Greer

The next day, my body ached like it had been used as a punching bag for Mayweather. It seemed like we'd banged up against every piece of furniture in reach during the fight. In addition to that, my right hand was sore from all the blows I landed on her hard ass face too. Moreover, my knuckles were all torn up and most of my nails were chipped or totally broken.

Other than a shiny left cheek, Debbie hadn't done any visible damage to my face thanks to her no aim windmilling. A heavy-handed stroke with my blush brush fixed that once I amped up my makeup to match it, so I was good.

Since I was spending the rest of the week at Race's, I had no choice but to explain what happened when I arrived at his house that night. I conveyed a half-truth version of events that made me look like the victim of Debbie's bullying yet again.

He was surprised, but sort of amused at the thought of petite little ol' me, opening up a can of whip ass on my sister. I'm sure I didn't look like a woman who could fight, hence all of the disrespect I got from other women.

Dinner at Granny's was great, and I enjoyed being in the midst of family minded people who included me in the mix. Granny's house was filled with Race's brother's, cousins, Lisa, and even his mom Carmen.

Granny was nowhere near as ornery as she seemed at the office that day. In fact, I found her to be generally sweet and funny, but stern.

After dessert, when most of us sat around Granny's living room, Geo surprised everyone by getting down on one knee in front of Lisa. She cried, accepted his proposal, and was a ball of joy the rest of the evening.

Friday, Race had to go into the shop to see appointments, so I spent ample time soaking in his Clawfoot tub, reading Shawn's childhood diary, and relaxing. I had to give it to Shawn, he was a good writer if nothing else.

It wasn't written so much like a diary, as it was like a first-person novel. It was interesting seeing things through the eyes of a 12-, 13-, and 14-year-old.

He didn't fill the entire 500-page journal, nor did he write in it every day, but what he did choose to chronicle was usually important. At least it was important to him.

Things like arguments he got into with his friends, the fist fight he won against a boy at school who stole his money, and the day he lost his virginity at 13.

I stopped reading in time to make dinner around 4:00pm for my man with a mixture of Thanksgiving Day leftovers and made from scratch rolls.

Things between Race and I were only getting better, and lying in bed beside him every night was just as blissful as I had hoped. Saturday morning, I received news from my real estate agent that we finally had a buyer for my home.

Believe me, selling a house where a highly publicized murder was committed isn't that easy. Race and I frolicked around the house until about noon, when he had to leave me for the shop again.

Not wanting to spend the time apart, I asked if I could tag along, and decided I wanted a tattoo too. Race wasn't exaggerating when he said the groupie life was thick at TAT LIFE.

Even with the frigid temperatures, these hos found a way to have their flesh exposed. I was watching them, just as hard as they were eye-balling me, when I went to my man's station and sat in the massage style chair.

"You ready?" Race asked me, sitting on the tattoo stool beside me as I fidgeted nervously in my seat.

"I guess so," I told him planting a sweet, longer than necessary peck on his lips.

Of course, that was mostly for THOT viewing purposes. Forty-five minutes later, I had a tattoo of a pink, crystalized heart over my chest with my initial G and his initial R in it.

"That's really pretty," a pretty mulatto girl with blue hair and tattoos from her collarbone on down complimented.

"Thank you," I beamed.

"What's it mean?"

"My heart has been crushed into tiny little pieces, but now I've found someone to put the pieces of my love back together again. That's why I put our initials in," I said gazing lovingly at Race who returned the smile. "And pink is my favorite color. So it had to be pink."

"That is so sweet," the girl said looking between us. "Race got a new boo."

A twinge of annoyance rose in my chest at the way she said that, but I didn't let it show on my face. This girl was apparently another tattoo artist at TAT LIFE, so I'm sure she knew, or at least knew *of* Song.

I couldn't tell if her compliment was just that, or whether it was shade.

"This is my baby," Race cosigned briefly grabbing my hand, then stood to his feet and stretched.

His phone rang, he looked down at it with a perplexed expression and answered.

"Hello… yeah this is Race. Who's this?" his expressions changed from confusion to shock as whoever was on the other end spoke their peace.

"I've got appointments spread out until 6 tonight, but yeah. I can answer whatever questions you have… is she okay?... Aww man," he sighed distraughtly looking at me and then Geo.

"What's wrong man?" Geo asked already mimicking his brother's expression.

Geo was shorter, lighter and not as good looking as Race in my opinion, but he was still attractive. He wore his hair faded around the hairline with long dreads hanging down his back and he had random tats all over his neck and arms.

The 2 of them looked like night and day, but you could tell they were brothers.

Race held up a finger to Geo as if to tell him to wait a minute while he continued on his call. I grabbed my cell from my purse and pretended to be doing something on it, but I was probably listening more intently than anyone.

"Alright then. It's gonna probably be about 8 o'clock or later though… okay… alright," Race said before ending his call.

He immediately cupped his mouth with a bewildered expression on his face, and turned to Geo. "*Yoooo* bro. Song is in the hospital."

"For what?" Geo asked going back to tattooing his client as though the news he got wasn't anywhere near as important as the news he was expecting.

"I don't know dude. They wouldn't be specific. They just said she was in the hospital and they wanted me to come down to the precinct and answer some questions."

"Shit. I wouldn't be goin' no damn where if they weren't gonna tell me why. They might be trying to pin whatever happened to her on you bruh," Geo said as nearby eavesdroppers cosigned.

"Yo. Call Lisa and see if she knows what happened," Race said a little jostled.

I'd be lying if I said I wasn't pissed that he cared this much about what was wrong with her. I was sure that whatever it was, it was probably a result of the mayhem I left awaiting her return.

I hadn't looked up from my phone during his conversation with Geo, but I wasn't feeling how freely he expressed his care for his ex in my presence either.

"I hope she's okay," I offered randomly.

Race looked at me like he just realized I was there and started reorganizing his tattooing supplies.

"Me too. I don't know why the police would want to talk to me about anything going on with Song. We haven't talked since she stole Juney."

I nodded, knowing that stupid cat probably crawled off into the woods somewhere to die. Geo placed a call to Lisa, and she was on the case like Olivia Pope by the time he hung up.

Race told me that I could take his Cadillac Escalade to grab something to eat or even go home if I wanted to. He was going to be in the shop for hours more with clients, and he didn't want me to sit around being bored.

I told him I would, and I was going to linger around for a while first to see if any additional news came in about Song through the grapevine. Not even 30 minutes later, the mouth of the south called Geo back with the total scoop.

"Bleach?" Race and Geo said in unison as Lisa spilled the tea on speakerphone.

"That's what Song's momma told India," Lisa confirmed.

I had no idea who India was, but she must've been close enough to Song's family for her mother to tell her the details, and close enough to Lisa for India to tell her.

"The police were taking a bunch of stuff from Song's place saying somebody tried to poison her. They know for sure they put bleach in her mouthwash and her contact lens case."

"Damn, who would do some shit like that?" a random in the shop said.

"I hope they don't think *I* did no psycho shit like that?" Race said insulted.

"Hell, they need to be looking at Chelsea. She's the one Song burned," Geo offered.

"The cops is already on to Chelsea. She's gonna be in for a rude awakening when she gets off shift today. Song's momma told India, Song couldn't breathe, she was throwing up all over the place and that her eye was burning. I guess she tried to put a lens in and it had bleach on it.

Supposedly, you could smell the bleach in the mouthwash and the contact lens case, but you know Song can't smell.," Lisa resumed.

"Can't smell? What's that mean? She can't smell?" A big dark skin guy with a Mohawk and tats everywhere my eyes landed. Including on his face.

"Nah bruh. She got a condition or something. She can't smell," Geo said as he injected more color into the mummy tattoo he was working on.

"Bae. Take me off speakerphone for a second," Lisa called out.

Geo did as he was asked and listened to what she was saying. Glancing back at Race who was setting up for his next client, he said, "Oh wow... Yeah that wasn't nothin' to say on speakerphone... Look, I'm in the middle of a tat so let me hit you back later... Thanks baby... I love you too."

When Geo hung up, he addressed Race. "Yo, let me holler at you a minute bruh."

Race stiffened and followed Geo to the back of the shop into what I assumed was their office. Several minutes passed before they came back out, and Race's face looked distressed.

I got up from the chair and placed a sympathetic hand on his shoulder. "What happened baby?"

"She lost the baby. I don't know if it was from the stress or what, 'cause I don't think bleach could make you miscarry. This is crazy. Man Greer. I know Chelsea was upset over what Song did but to poison her?"

"That's horrible," I said with my hand to my chest in feigned sympathy. "I understand wanting revenge against someone who slept with your man, but this is going too far."

I assumed Song had drank some Sunny Delight before using the mouthwash either before bed or first thing in the morning. I mentally pat myself on the back for such a devious idea.

That bleach probably had her throat burning like a prostitute's vagina, but I hated that there hadn't been news of her using the glass filled lotion. That might be the stealth surprise for her later after they rid all of the bleach filled items.

I couldn't believe how quickly it had all gone down. I was under the impression from what Lisa told me, that Song was going to be in Brazil for several days, but I guess she wasn't.

The news made me wonder how long it would take before Kendrick was discovered in the stairwell of the Franklin Family Practice building. I'd chosen the holiday weekend so that he'd die a slow death.

I knew just pushing him down a flight of stairs didn't usually kill a person like it did in the movies. If that person was severely injured in the fall while suffering from a deadly allergic reaction however, now that was a guaranteed win.

I decided to get something to eat for me and Race, and was nice enough to take orders from everyone in the shop as well. I spent the rest of the day chatting, laughing and debating with some of the staff and the clients in the tattoo shop.

It was an interesting environment to say the least, and the gossip that flowed through it was much like what went on in barber shops and hair salons.

Race dropped me off back at his house that evening and went down to the police station as promised. It hadn't actually occurred to me that he would be a suspect.

Considering the history between her and her ex-roommate, I just thought she'd be the automatic assumed culprit. Whether or not they could pin it on her, wasn't my concern, as long as neither Race or I were implicated.

By the time he got home, it was after midnight and I was coming up on the period in Shawn's journal when Daddy brought me home to the Foster family. I hated to put it down but, I had to help my baby unwind.

I listened closely without interruption as Race recounted the interrogation questions that were thrown at him. The similarities to my experience when the detectives grilled me about Michael's death were uncanny.

I was stymied to hear that he hadn't arrived home so late because of the time they kept him for questioning though. I couldn't even pretend I wasn't incensed that he'd stopped by Song's hospital room without telling me. Hell, that he stopped by Song's hospital room *at all*.

"You have to understand that we were friends before we were a couple Greer. I was hurt and pissed by how she treated our relationship, but I would never wish her harm.

She told me they had to put tubes up her nose to flush her stomach and everything. She's expected to make a full recovery, but they're keeping her over night for monitoring. She could've died," he explained undressing in the bathroom as I stood in the doorway already in my pajamas.

"I understand that you were friends first Race, but you could've at least told me you were stopping by to see her. I would've gone with you," I contested.

"Gone with me? Why? She's never even met you. That just would've created a hostile environment for no reason. Plus, I only stopped by for a short while to check up on her. That was my baby she miscarried Greer. I needed to say something."

"Oh. You're *claiming* the baby now?" I questioned with attitude.

He sighed annoyed and turned on the shower water.

"Are you trying to pick a fight? Because this isn't making any sense to me that you'd want to argue about this. Song said the doctors found large quantities of some drug that can cause an abortion in her system too.

That means Chelsea killed my seed on purpose. Even if it was Tony's and not mine Greer, that's still fucked up. I don't believe in abortions. Especially when somebody sneaks some shit in on you."

"Maybe she did it herself for attention," I suggested sourly. "I mean, you did say you've been ignoring her. Now she's got you running back to her bedside to check on her. How do you know she didn't take those drugs to abort the baby herself? Either because she knew it wasn't yours, or because you've been ignoring her?"

"Greer… just… just drop it. This ain't the time to have this conversation with me. You sound real bitter right now and I… just drop it," he told me angrily as he got in the shower and snatched the shower door shut roughly.

"What's the matter Race? I can't question the integrity of your little *Song?*" I asked spitefully. "She slept with her best friend's man right under your nose. Is it too much for me to speculate that she could be a lying, sneaky, cunt too?"

The shower door swung open with an unexpected force that made me jump back as Race emerged wet and slightly lathered.

"Shut the fuck up Greer! I said to drop it! Now you don't know her to talk about her like that. Song would never voluntarily have an abortion. She didn't believe in it and neither did I. Have some compassion for Christ's fuckin' sake woman!" he roared.

My feelings hurt, and at a loss for words, I spun on my heels and left the bathroom in a huff. From where I stood, it seemed like he still had feelings for that bitch. I was livid.

I gathered all of my things and shoved them back into the overnight bag I'd brought them over in, while grumbling to myself about how Race was acting. I was his woman now. How dare he defend his ex-bitch over me.

I didn't get home until nearly 2 in the morning, but it didn't matter. I was too angry to sleep anyway. I found a bottle of Vodka left over from a Christmas party more than 2 years ago and poured a tall glass of it for myself.

I loved Race. I'd never said it to him, because he hadn't said it to me yet but, I loved him. I was sure by the way he treated me and the way he made me feel that he loved me too, but I had to set the ground rules.

How would he have liked it if I left him to go visit Kendrick in the hospital while he was waiting at my house for me? I mean, he didn't know who Kendrick was, and Kendrick was too dead to be in the hospital but… that was beside the point!

Race needed to show me the love and respect I deserved. I would go to the ends of the earth for him if he needed me to.

He had no idea what I'd do for love.

19

Greer

Sunday was miserable. I woke up lying in the middle of my kitchen floor with an empty glass, an empty carton of fruit punch and an empty Vodka bottle beside me. My head felt like Justin Bieber was on drums in it, and I was cranky as hell.

At some point during the night, I had realized that drinking Vodka alone wasn't going to work for me. It was too strong and tasted nasty without something sweet in it, so I added fruit punch. I remembered talking aloud to myself and debating with the rebuttals that invisible Race would have for my arguments too.

I don't know why I didn't just continue to play my position instead of making waves. It wasn't the right time to discuss it and he told me so. He told me to drop it, but I didn't. Now I was paying the price for not being perfect. Just like I always had. I could never be perfect.

The entire day passed, and Race hadn't called or texted me once. I was surprised and hurt that he could let me go so easily. We hadn't said we were broken up or anything, but what if we were? Yes, I'd stormed out of his place without a word, but he was supposed to care. He was supposed to chase me. He was supposed to regret not making me feel more important.

By 11 o'clock that night, I had gone through 2 boxes of tissue crying over Race and I hated my phone for never having a message or text from him when I picked it up.

All this alone time gave me was room to think up random scenarios of betrayal in my head. What if what I'd done to Song actually ended up bringing them *closer* together rather than wedging them apart? She could play on his sympathies and get him back over to her place to console her. He was defensive of her already as it was.

"Song would never do that," I mocked him.

Maybe my mistake had been in not killing her.

I scheduled the entire week after Thanksgiving off because I had a ton of unused vacation time, but I expected to be spending it with Race. Now, it was looking like I was just going to spend it alone.

I was awakened Monday morning by the ringing of my phone, and I jumped to answer it laced with excitement.

"Hello?" I said predicting that it was Race finally calling to apologize.

"Hello, can I speak to Greer Patterson please," a man said on the other end.

"This is she," I said clearing my throat and feeling let down as I ran my fingers through my mussed hair and looked over at my new alarm clock.

Since Debbie's discovery of the video App, I had unplugged and trashed the old one. I cursed myself for not getting rid of that thing sooner, but it was serving its purpose as a timekeeper and woke me up on time.

It never occurred to me that anyone would ever discover it was anything other than a basic clock.

"Ms. Patterson, this is Detective Monroe at the Dekalb County PD. I'm sorry to call you while you're on vacation, but there's been an incident at Franklin Family Practice, and I was wondering if you had a moment to speak to me."

"Uh… yeah. Sure. What kind of incident?" I asked innocently.

"Are you familiar with Mr. Kendrick Spears?"

"Yes. He works in medical records for us. Is he in trouble?"

"No ma'am. I'm sorry to say, Mr. Spears is deceased."

I gasped. "How?"

"Well ma'am, that's what we're trying to find out. He was found in the stairwell of the building, and it seems as though he's been here since your office closed for the holiday."

"Oh my God! But he left before me."

"Did he? And what time was that ma'am."

"Umm… I think maybe 2:10pm or somewhere around there. I still had a little work to catch up on even though the office closed early at 2pm. So I stayed behind.

I'm almost certain I heard him go out the door to the stairs."

"Does he routinely take the stairs instead of the elevator?"

"Y… Yes. He's really into health and fitness. But how did he die in the stairwell?" I made sure to keep asking like any normal person who didn't already know how it happened would.

"It appears that he took a spill down the stairs and injured himself. It's possible that he wasn't able to get help for his injuries and expired sometime yesterday."

"Oh my God that's awful. He was so young," I exclaimed.

I guess it was gonna take some time for them to find out about the almond allergy and all of that. I'd been smart and planted the bag of ground almonds in the bottom draw of his desk where he kept all of his health stuff.

It was a risk that he wouldn't look in that drawer before leaving Wednesday, but it was one I'd taken, and it had paid off.

"Do you know if Mr. Spears had any issues with anyone at work that may have wanted to harm him?" Detective Monroe questioned me.

"No. Not that I know of."

"Did anyone else leave with him that you know of? Or was anyone else left in the office late with you?"

"I don't know. I was back in my office, so I didn't actually see him leave. I just heard the door close.

I was still working for about 20 or 30 more minutes, and then I left. I take the elevator though. Oh my God I feel so badly that I might have been able to save him if I'd just taken the stairs," I said somberly.

"Is there by chance a list of the badge access codes matched with employees somewhere we can get hold of?"

My breathing hitched as he asked the question. Why did he need that?

"Yes. I'm sure there is. Why?"

"We'd just like to be able to identify who came and went through the stairwell door that day is all."

"But his death was an accident, right?" I said attempting to keep my guilty voice from quivering.

I hadn't thought about the badge usage for the door. If they investigated it, they'd see that I was in and out of the stairwell multiple times within the window of his time of death. Fuck!

"Welp, we don't know yet ma'am. Let's hope so. When are you scheduled to return back to work Ms. Patterson?"

"N… next week," I stuttered. "It's not a bloody crime scene or anything is it?" I said trying to cover my guilty tone with naïve ignorance.

"No ma'am. I'd appreciate it if you'd take my number down and if you could please remit that badge information to me as soon as possible. If I just need to go through the building administration for that, I'd be happy to."

"Umm, no. No, I can get it for you," I said trying to think of how I was going to explain my in's and out's later on.

"I appreciate that. If you don't mind, I might be contacting you again in the future with more questions as the investigation takes shape," he advised before giving me his contact number.

For the first time since I'd begun taking matters of love and vengeance into my own hands, I was afraid of being caught. I thought I had been meticulous with the execution of my plans, but as it turned out, I'd made a few mistakes along the way. I swear if I ended up on *SNAPPED…*

Needing to get my mind off of all that wasn't going right in my world, I drove to the package store and re'd up on the Vodka. This time, I got Whipped Cream Vodka to help with the taste and coupled it with a 2 liter of Sprite.

Lying in my bed, drinking like a fish dressed in a jogging suit, I submerged myself in Shawn's diary. I was more than halfway through the thing, and save trying to decipher some of his chicken scratched words, it was a good read.

I was sure Shawn would just die, or would at least want to kill me, if he'd known I was reading it. I'd just taken a swig of my drink when I read the words that sent ice coursing through my veins.

July 4th 1991

Today he promised to take me and Debbie to the pool but he didn't. He never does what he says he's gonna do. Momma went to see Aunt Greta at the hospital so she took Donna and left us with Daddy. He don't never spend no time with us. He promised to let us shoot off some of them fireworks he brought back from Texas, but he kept stalling. It was already getting dark out.

He tried to leave me and Debbie alone at the house again while he ran out to whoever he's cheating on Momma with. I heard him on the phone with her saying he was on his way. I watched him out my window. When he got in his car, I waited till he was around the bend and followed. Bruce next door let me borrow his scooter while he was away in Tennessee for the 4th.

Daddy ain't even go far. She lives in the same apartment place as my friend Robin do. He ain't even have to take the highway. I watched him go to that lady's house and go inside. I dropped my scooter and ran across the street to look in the lady's window. Wasn't nothing but another building beside it, so I figured I could do it with nobody seeing me. She was a pretty white lady, but she was a white lady. He got to kissing and hugging her like he loves her. He ain't shit. I was thinking

he ain't shit and he better not leave my Momma for the white lady.

I almost knocked on the window, or even on the door to let him know I busted him. But I didn't. I just watched them. Everybody else seemed like, was popping fireworks but me. I was mad Daddy came over to see this white lady instead of hanging with us kids. They was talking for a long time. Laughing and touching and stuff. They turned on the radio and was dancing together. The lady was dancing with her back to Daddy, then he put his hand over her mouth with a rag. The lady started kicking and swinging, but Daddy held on till she stopped.

Daddy put the lady down on the couch and went to the back of the house for something. I couldn't see what. One time I thought he saw me in the window, but he was looking for matches. I got scared and ran back across the street to the scooter. I sat on the scooter watching the house. I ain't know why I was scared because I didn't see nothing happen. But I was scared.

Daddy came out the house looking real nervous. I ain't know why he was nervous. I wondered what was on that rag that made that lady go to sleep. He went and stood over by the window I was just spying on him from and opened it up. He lit a match and put his arm in the window for a while and then pulled it back out real fast like it got hot. Then he went over to his car parked in front and got out some fireworks.

I was pissed that he was gone shoot off them fireworks over here with everybody else while me and Debbie was supposed to be at home waiting for him to shoot them off with us. I watched him light them up and they started shooting up in the sky, but I saw a glow from the lady's window. Then Daddy aimed those fireworks at her window too and some of them shot inside. I thought he must be crazy. That lady gonna be mad as hell if he catch her house on fire.

Then just like I thought it, I started seeing fire coming out the window. Daddy stared at it, then he got in his car and left off. I didn't know what to do because that was crazy. It's like a lot of people was out, but wasn't nobody paying him no attention and he was acting weird in front of everybody.

I heard a crackling sound from the lady's house. I didn't know what it was, but then I seen some flames coming out that window and smoke too. Then I saw fire in a window in the front of her house. Daddy set that white lady's house on fire and I was just standing there watching him do it. I felt crazy. I got nervous.

One of that white lady's neighbor came out their house and asked me what I was looking at. I told him it looked like a fire in that lady's house. He looked at me like I was stupid and yelled to somebody in his house to call the fire department. Then I saw him running around the side of her apartment, and then he ran to the back of it. I jumped on my scooter and left off home.

When I got home, Daddy was in the backyard with Debbie shooting off fireworks with her. Told me I was late. I didn't say nothing to him. I didn't know what to say to him. He might've killed that lady. I might've witnessed a murder.

Rage filled tears streamed down my face.

Daddy killed my mother… and tried to kill me.

20

Greer

"I love ya Babygirl. Nobody'll eva' love ya mo' than me."

Daddy's words echoed in my mind as I stared at my mother's golden snake bracelet on my wrist. What a liar. He didn't love me. He never loved *me* or my mother either.

I know why I had no recollection of the fire. Because he'd knocked me out somehow. Probably with chloroform the same way he'd done my mother. He intended for both my mother and I to die in that apartment fire, but that neighbor had saved me.

All of these years, my father had pretended like I was the apple of his eye, when he'd tried to *murder* me.

I read those passages over and over again, just to make sure that I wasn't confused. That maybe all of this liquor I'd been drinking had had my mind playing tricks on me; but there it was in black and white.

Shawn had witnessed my father set my mother's apartment on fire, and unbeknownst to him, he'd seen him go in the back of the house to put me out just like he had my mother. I guess that sometimey love he said he had for her had worn off.

I walked over to the floor length mirror behind my bedroom door and stared at myself. Why did I have to be brought into this world this way? Why did I have to suffer for the mistakes my parents made?

Nobody loved me. My mother loved me. I knew she did. But my father had stripped her from me and tried to snuff me out. All because he wanted to keep his dirty little secret, a secret.

Because of him, I would never find a man to love me the way I wanted to be loved. No man would ever stay faithful to me. No man would ever choose me first. How could they when my own daddy hadn't?

I fell to my knees and wept like a newborn baby. Wishing I was a newborn baby again. A baby born to people who loved me. People who wanted me.

No matter what I did or how I acted, I was never going to get what I wanted. Race showed me that when he went running back to that lying, cheating, whore when he had me waiting at home for him.

I was never going to be enough, and now I was going to stop trying.

No longer giving a damn, I crawled on the carpet of my bedroom floor over to the nightstand where the bottle of Whipped Cream Vodka sat and took it by the neck.

"Cheers to love!" I slurred pouring as much of the liquor down my throat as I could until I spit some of it back up.

Lying on the carpet, ironically in the same spot where Michael lay bleeding out last year, I stared up at the ceiling with tears scurrying down the sides of my face. Nobody loved me.

"So, what! So, what!" I yelled to no one. "My momma loved me! Not that bitch Stephanie either! My *reeeeeeeal* momma loved me! My real momma loved me. My real momma loved me. My real momma loved me," I repeated like a scratched record.

That's when I realized that I was only screwed up because I didn't have my real momma. She was the only one who loved me, and my father took her away from me. He's why my life was in the shambles it's been in all my life.

Using the edge of my bed as leverage, I managed to stand to my feet, and grab my gun from the drawer by my nightstand. Stumbling downstairs; and I do mean literally, stumbling down the stairs, I got my purse and my car keys to go see Daddy.

I jumped in the Yukon and peeled out of the driveway blasting Rihanna's hit "Man Down" with all the windows down and the sunroof open.

"Rum, pum, pum, pum rum, pum,

pum, pum rum, pum, pum, pum

Man Down

Rum, pum, pum, pum rum, pum,

pum, pum rum, pum, pum, pum

Man Down"

I saw Race's face flashing across my phone's screen in my cup holder while I was doing my best car dances. I was excited to see him calling, even though I didn't want to be.

Turning the radio down, I answered on the speaker with attitude. "Yes?"

He was silent for a second before speaking, "Is this a good time to talk?"

"Not really."

"Not really. Hmph. Why's that?"

"Because I'm driving and because I don't want to talk to you," I said belligerently and probably louder than I intended.

"You sound drunk. You're not driving, are you?" he asked concerned. A hint of alarm in his tone.

"Like you care. Go tend to your pretty little *Song*. That's who you wanna be with isn't it?"

He sighed. "That's not who I want to be with. I *want* to be with you. I'm sorry for the other night. It was late. I was on edge. I didn't mean for you to leave out like that.

Then… well… this is something you're gonna learn about me. I'm stubborn. So even when I wanted to call you, and I did, I didn't. But see now too many days have gone by without me seeing you, or talking to you, and I don't wanna keep doing that. I miss you. I love you. I don't want to lose you. You didn't miss me?"

My heart nearly skipped a beat and I nearly hit the curb because I was looking down at my phone and getting sappy instead of watching the road.

"Yes! Yes, I did miss you! You love me? You love me?" I screamed both from excitement at his statement and fear of almost crashing.

He chuckled. "Yes, I love you."

"I love you too! I love you too!" I shrieked at the top of my lungs. "Look at God! Just when I thought things couldn't get any worse! They got better!" I testified.

"Alright. *You* are crazy," he laughed again. "Where are you headed right now? You haven't actually been drinking have you? I don't know if it's the connection or what, but your voice sounds slurred."

"I might have had a depressing bottle of Vodka," I said honestly.

Since we were in love now, we needed to start being honest with each other. Right?

"Oh shit girl. You can't be out there driving drunk. Where are you? Pull over and I'll come get you. Where the hell are you going anyway lushed out like that?" he asked dismayed.

"I'm going to see my Daddy. Yep. My dear old dad."

"Why you say it like that? Just pull over baby. Tell me where you are."

"I don't need to pull over. I'm already almost there. In 2 streetlights, then I make a left, then a right, then I go down a couple of streets, and walla! I'll be at my Daddy's," I said jokingly.

"Greer. You're gonna hurt yourself or somebody else driving like that. I'm getting in the car right now, and I'm on my way. What street are you on? Cumberland? Paces Ferry? Where? Pull over Greer!

You said your dad lived off of Fountain Ridge, yes? On Dan and Dean's old street. I'll be there in 15 minutes to get you then."

I just laughed. He was so sweet. My baby was all over the place with his questions. He cared so much about me. I put my hand over my heart tattoo and smiled as I turned down my Daddy's street.

"I'm already gonna be where I was going Baby. You don't need to come and get me."

"I'm on my way Greer. Are you driving the truck or your car?"

"I don't drive that damn car no more. It's bad luck. The cops'll probably pull me over and throw me in jail for hit and run the way my luck has been going."

"Hit and run? What are you talking about? Oh my God. Would you just pull over!" he shouted through the phone.

I blew Race a kiss into the phone. I'd explain everything to him later after I got answers from my Daddy. Then me and Race could live happily ever after.

"Okay baby. I'm at Daddy's now so I gotta go. I *loooove* you!" I sang before hitting disconnect.

When I hopped out of the car, I shivered at the cool breeze that whisked around my neck. I let myself into the house, not even bothering to close the door behind me, and immediately started calling for my father.

"Daddy! *Oooooh* Daddy!"

"Girl why you hollerin' out there? I'm in my room," he replied.

Smirking slyly, I swaggered into Daddy's room swinging my gun front to back. When I entered, he was standing by his dresser with his back to me, placing a new lamp on top of it.

"Babygirl, what brings ya by? Nina just brought me this here lamp and…" his voice trailed off as he turned to see me standing in the room. "Chile' what's wrong with you? You ain't drunk is ya? And what you got that gun out fo'?"

Well damn, did I *look* drunk too? The thought was so amusing that I laughed out loud at it. Daddy just stood there staring at me perplexed.

"So Daddy, why don't you tell me again how nobody's ever gonna love me like you do."

He frowned in confusion. "What? You drunk or high?"

"I'm drunk Daddy. But that's neither here nor there. I wanna know, did you ever really love me? Or have you just been pretending all these years?"

"Chile' what kinda foolery are you in here talkin' 'bout? You sound crazy. Of course, I love ya. Why ya in here askin' somethin' you already know the answer to wit' ya firearm out?" he inquired moving slowly away from the dresser and over to his bedside.

"Well Daddy, I don't believe you! You lied to me! You been lying to me my whoooole life Daddy. My whole life you were telling me how much you loved me, but that's just a big fat lie.

You know who really loved me? *My momma!* That's who really loved me. But you killed her," I said matter of factly and watched his face go from confused to shocked.

"You say what nah?"

"I *said...* you *killed* my momma. Oh yeah. The jig is up Chuck Foster. The jig is up," I told him waving my gun around in the air as I began pacing. "Shawn knows it too. I bet you didn't know that."

He stared at me speechlessly. I could almost see the wheels turning in his head as he tried to make heads or tails of what I was saying and tried to figure out how he was going to discount it.

"I didn't—"

"Don't you let another lie slip from your mouth old man," I cut him off pointing my gun at him in my best Charlie's Angel's pose.

He froze. Which was what I wanted. All of his moving around was making me dizzy. Or maybe I was the one moving around. I don't know. I felt dizzy.

"Do you think I'd be here right now if I didn't know for a *fact* that you killed my mother?"

"I... I didn't mean to do it. It was an accident. I was—"

I shot the floor by his foot and he jumped back almost tripping over the bed.

"It wasn't no fuckin' accident Daddy. Stop lying to me! I told you not to lie to me! Now you know I'm a good shot. The next one, if you make me shoot it, is going into *you. Shawn saw you do it!*" I screamed at the top of my lungs.

For the first time in my life, I saw fear in my father. He was shaking and his hands trembled as he touched the bottom of the bed frame.

"Why did you have to kill her Daddy?" I asked, an uncontrollable river of tears rushing down my face out of nowhere.

I was fine 2 seconds ago. Why the hell was I crying?

"I'm sorry Babygirl—"

"Don't call me that anymore!" I shouted at him.

"Okay. Okay," he glanced around his room like an animal trapped in a cage, and then back at me. "Irina was gonna tell Steph 'bout ya. She was gonna put me on child support too. She didn't feel like I was givin' her enough to take care of ya.

I told her I was doin' the best that I could. I was payin' her rent and comin' by when I could. Nothin' was good enough for her though. I was workin' myself like a Clydesdale and she ain't care nothin' 'bout it.

She wanted me to leave Steph and my kids to come live wit' her and you."

"You had to kill her for that? You tried to kill me too! Shawn saw you Daddy. He followed you over to her house that night because you left him and Debbie hanging at the house. He *saw* you do it."

Daddy put his head in his hands, and we stood silent for a few moments. Me glaring at him and him covering his face in shame. When he lifted up, his face was damp with tears. He had been crying.

"I'm not proud of what I did Babyg— Greer. I panicked. I didn't want to lose my family."

"I was part of your family too. You made me," I told him.

Both of us standing there looking like blubbering fools with wet faces.

"I know ya were. I just panicked. That night, she called me and said she was gon' bring ya by the house in the mornin' to meet Steph if I couldn't come by and see y'all. She said she was tired of missin' out on family barbecues and holidays. She said you deserved yo daddy to be there all the time.

I just couldn't do that Greer. I couldn't do that. Especially wit' no white woman. She was just s'posed to be sex and fun, but she went and got pregnant."

"Well, she didn't get pregnant by herself! If you weren't cheating on your wife, you wouldn't have had that problem! Why did you have to be such a cheater? You made me and then you wanted to get rid of me!

You were gonna let me burn up in there with her! Then you turned around all these years and tried to make yourself look like a saint for taking me in instead of giving me to the state!"

"I neva' said I was a saint. I felt bad 'bout what I tried to do. Once I saw yo little face after they told ya Irina wasn't comin' back… you was my daughter. Plus, the cat was already out the bag when that neighbor gave the police my company's name off ma' truck.

They tracked me down on the job. I had to take you."

I shook my head in disgust. "And you brought me home to a woman who hated the air I breathed. That bitch tortured me every chance she got, and you never stopped her! You let her make me feel like I was nothing! *Nothing*!

I've never felt like I've been good enough for anybody, and I never thought anybody would love me more than my daddy. Then I found out, my daddy, tried to kill me. You're a murderer!" I accused.

Daddy put a hand to his forehead and then dropped his arms, staring at me defiantly. "The apple don't fall far from the tree then now does it?"

Now it was my turn to be surprised. "What are you talking about?"

"I'm talkin' 'bout Michael. You think I ain't know you killed him?" he questioned me, eyebrows raised. "I knew it. I knew you changed my clock back too.

I got up like clockwork to go to the bathroom, and I knew I didn't sleep that late, so I flipped the cable box from the channel to the time. I ain't know why you did it, but I figured it would come to light later.

Then after I found out he was dead, I put 2 and 2 togetha'. You probably had them keys to use my car or Steph's, but you ain't use your own. I know 'cause, I looked out my window befo' I got back in the bed and yo car was still there."

My whole body felt hot. I couldn't believe he knew all along what I had done. I thought he maybe knew something, but I didn't know he knew it for sure. I still didn't take my gun off him though.

"So, what now? You standin' there wit' yo gun on me. You 'bout to kill me?"

"Probably. Like you said, it wouldn't be the first time I killed someone before," I answered smartly.

"Well, I ain't ready to die. I ain't fight this cancer fo' you to come in here and snuff my life out like a cigar 'cause of somethin' I did 30 years ago. Thirty years. Ain't that just ironic now?" he said breaking into laughter and confusing me.

"Ain't *what* ironic?"

"That's how many years that girl 'bout to serve for a murder *you* committed. You got some nerve comin' in here 'bout to wish harm on me fo' what I did. You ain't no better!" he spat lunging for the top drawer of his bedside table.

I knew what was in that drawer, and Daddy was a better shot than I was. Instinctually, I pulled the trigger, catching him in the side.

"Ahhhhhh!" Daddy screamed out, hitting the floor hard.

"Greer! What the fuck are you doing?" Race's voice rang out from behind me.

You could've bought me for a penny. How in the hell did he find me? I didn't even know how to answer.

"Help me! She's trying to kill me!" Daddy yelled out, betraying me like the dog he was.

Where was his loyalty? I was his own flesh and blood for Christ's sake!

"Greer, what is going on?" Race asked me again as I noticed that he also had his 9-millimeter drawn. He wasn't pointing it at me, but he had it on the ready.

If we were gonna have a chance at a future together, I guessed now was as good of a time as any to come clean. It's not like he didn't have a seedy past himself. Right?

"This man. My father, killed my mother."

"Baby. You're drunk. Put the gun down," Race coached me as he approached.

I wasn't trying to let him grab my gun. Not until he heard me out first and I knew what my next move should be at least.

"No. No I'm not drunk," I said putting my hand up for him to stop, and he did. "Okay I am drunk; but I'm telling the truth. You know that journal I've been reading, my brother Shawn's journal… I found out that he saw my father set my mother's apartment on fire. With *me* in it!

He didn't just try to kill my mother Race. He tried to kill me too. He tried to light my ass on fire! *His precious Babygirl*," I said sarcastically.

Race's eyes darted from me to Daddy as my father moaned on the floor.

"She talkin' like she's such a saint but she killed her husband," Daddy snitched.

I snapped my head to look at Race's reaction and his expression was blank. I debated with myself for a brief second on whether I should tell him the truth, or deny! Deny! Deny!

The truth is, the Vodka was starting to cloud my judgement. At least I think it was because I really had to pee, but I couldn't leave the situation as it was for a bathroom break. Choices. Choices. Choices.

"Just put the gun down Baby and let's talk about this. Your dad is bleeding pretty bad over there," Race said trying to sound all logical.

"Please Babygirl. I'm hurt real bad," Daddy pled from the floor.

"You just had to tell him didn't you Daddy. You just had to open your big fat, cheating, arsonistic mouth and tell my man didn't you!" I screeched, angry that I couldn't come up with a lie fast enough to explain away what he'd just said. "Shut up Daddy! Just shut up!"

I demanded waving my gun at him as he tried to pull himself up by the bed.

"You're crazy chile' and you're gonna be the death of me if I let ya be. If I'd have known then what I know now, I woulda left ya wit' the state," he mumbled.

"Oh is that how you feel Daddy? Is that how you feel?" I laughed shooting a slug into the side of the bed just to fuck with him.

"Don't Greer!" Race yelled, with his gun raised at me as I turned to him.

"Oh relax. I didn't even—" I started to say before 2 loud booms, followed by 2 piercing pains in my back knocked me forward into his arms, forcing me to drop my gun.

I was totally confused. He couldn't have shot me. He loved me. He wouldn't have shot me.

"No!" Race cried out holding me in his arms as his eyes instantly turned glassy. "Why did you do that?" he asked my father.

"I… she was gonna shoot me," I heard his shaky voice affirm as I started to find it hard to breathe.

I was still standing though. Drunk as a skunk as I may have been, I was still on my feet. Maybe I was being held up by Race, but technically, my feet were still on the floor.

I brought my hand up to my heart tattoo and it was bleeding. Was I hallucinating? How could that be?

"Baby. My heart is bleeding?" I told Race with a confused smirk. "Do you see that?"

"Yes Baby. I do see that. One of the bullets must've came through," he explained putting pressure on it with his hand.

I heard my father on the phone with the police, telling them that I came over his house trying to kill him and that he'd shot me.

It was almost laughable. Almost. If I could laugh through my pain when I could barely breathe.

"I really do love you Race. My… my heart bleeds for you," I kidded. "I really do love you."

"The ambulance is on the way Baby. You're gonna be alright," he promised. "You're gonna be alright."

I was already a little freaked out because I couldn't actually *feel* anything. My Daddy was a good shot. Did that son-of-a-bitch paralyze me?

"I can't… feel… anything," I said to Race as my breathing got harder and my vision began to blur with tears.

I had the urge to sing the words to The Weekend's song in that moment. "I can't feel my face when I'm with yooouuu… but I love it. But I love it. Oooo. I can't feel my face when I'm with yooouuu… but I love it. But I love it," I sang in my head because I didn't have the air or the strength to actually do it.

"I love you," Race said stroking my hair as I drifted off.

And that was all I wanted.

The End...or is it?

You decide:

Tweet #ComeBackGreer to @kfjohnsonbooks for more

Tweet #ByeByeGreer to @kfjohnsonbooks to kill her off

Enjoyed This Book?

Please leave a review on Amazon or Goodreads to share!

Other releases by K.F. Johnson:

BEHIND CLOSED DOORS: LOVE HURTS

LIAR'S BALL: BEHIND CLOSED DOORS 2

WHEN I'M BAD I'M BETTER

WHEN I'M BAD I'M BETTER 2

WHAT I'D DO FOR LOVE

WHAT I'D DO FOR LOVE 2

LOVE HURTS: SERIES COMPILATION

WHEN I'M BAD I'M BETTER FOREVER: SERIES COMPILATION

STABBED THIS CHRISTMAS: A NOVELLA

Join my mailing list and be the first to get sneak peeks, giveaways, contests, new release info, learn event appearances and more!

http://www.kfjohnsonbooks.com

"The Empress of romantic, murder, suspense", **K.F. Johnson** is a Queens, New York native residing in Atlanta, Georgia. As a child, habitually failing to make curfew before the streetlights lit, earned her numerous occasions on restriction where reading & writing became her main form of escape. Later, K.F continued to develop her talent while obtaining a B.A. in Psychology at Spelman College & acquiring an MBA. In 2012, she published her 1st book for her social media friends & family to see. To her delight, it went viral, repeatedly reaching #1 on Amazon's top 100 for its genre. Since then, K.F. has published multiple books, started One Ironwoman Publishing, been featured in magazines & nominated for numerous awards, both for her books & as an author. With her fan base cheering for more, this mother & wife has blossomed into a witty & cunning author, penning spicy, realistic & deadly tales of African American life to remember.